Also by Julia Brannan

HISTORICAL FICTION

The Jacobite Chronicles
Book One: Mask of Duplicity
Book Two: The Mask Revealed
Book Three: The Gathering Storm
Book Four: The Storm Breaks
Book Five: Pursuit of Princes

Jacobite Chronicles Stories
The Whore's Tale: Sarah (Autumn 2018)

CONTEMPORARY FICTION

A Seventy-Five Percent Solution

Tides of Fortune

The Jacobite Chronicles,
Book Six

Julia Brannan

DISCLAIMER

This novel is a work of fiction, and except in the case of historical fact,
any resemblance to actual persons, living or dead, is purely coincidental

Formatting by Polgarus Studio

Cover Model Photography by VJ Dunraven of www.PeriodImages.com

Cover models: Jason Tobias and Jax Turyna

Cover design by najlaqamberdesigns.com

In memory of Dennis Brady
A patient and easy-going man,
but very protective of those he held dear.
He was my inspiration for the
character of Duncan MacGregor.
May he rest in peace.

ACKNOWLEDGEMENTS

First of all, as ever, I'd like to thank Jason Gardiner and Alyson Cairns, my soulmates and best friends, who put up with me on a day-to-day basis, and who understand my need for solitude, but are always there for me. They've both supported me through every stage of my writing, and, indeed, in all my other endeavours, both sensible and madcap!

Thanks to the long-suffering Mary Brady, friend and first critic, who reads the chapters as I write them, critiques them for me and reassures me that I can actually write stuff people will want to read, and to my beta readers Angela and Claire for their valued opinions.

Thanks also go to Mandy Condon, who sends me useful articles, has already determined the cast list for the film of my books, and who has been a wonderful and supportive friend for over twenty years. Long may that continue!

I also need to thank some fellow authors. Firstly Kym Grosso and Victoria Danann, who have been extremely supportive and have generously given me the benefit of their experience in the minefield of indie publishing. They have both saved me a lot of time, money and tears, and I value their friendship and support enormously. Secondly Maggie Craig, historian and author, who has helped me hugely, both with her excellent books about the '45, and with further advice. It was wonderful to meet her at Culloden last year! Also to Helen Hollick, author not only of a host of excellent novels and willing imparter of useful advice, but also of the Discovering Diamonds blog, which helps to connect authors of quality historical fiction with new readers.

My gratitude goes to John Fitzhugh Millar of Newport House B&B, Williamsburg, Virginia, whose willingness to share his enthusiasm and expertise in all things nautical, and especially in the field of eighteenth century sailing ships was invaluable to me in the writing of this book.

Also a thank you goes to the National Trust for Scotland, who will now be stocking my books at the gift shop in Culloden Visitor Centre and to the lovely curator of the Clan Cameron Museum, who will also stock the Jacobite Chronicles. Both sites are well worth a visit, should you be in the area. Thanks also to the current Lochiel for the lovely postcard – it made my day!

And thanks as always go to Jason at Polgarus Studio for doing an excellent job of formatting my book, to the talented and very patient Najla Qamber, who does all my covers, puts up with my lack of artistic ability, and still manages to somehow understand exactly what I want my covers to look like! Thanks too to Jason Tobias and Jax Turyna, the cover models for Tides of Fortune.

To all my wonderful readers, who not only buy my books, but take the time and effort to give me feedback, and to review them on Amazon and Goodreads – thank you so much. You keep me going on those dark days when I'd rather do anything than stare at a blank screen for hours while my brain turns to mush…you are amazing! Without all of you I would be nothing, and I appreciate you more than you know.

And finally, to Bob and Dolores. You are wonderful people and I love you.

HISTORICAL BACKGROUND NOTE

Although this series starts in 1742 and deals with the Jacobite Rebellion of 1745, the events that culminated in this uprising started a long time before, in 1685, in fact. This was when King Charles II died without leaving an heir, and the throne passed to his Roman Catholic younger brother James, who then became James II of England and Wales, and VII of Scotland. His attempts to promote toleration of Roman Catholics and Presbyterians did not meet with approval from the Anglican establishment, but he was generally tolerated because he was in his fifties, and his daughters, who would succeed him, were committed Protestants. But in 1688 James' second wife gave birth to a son, also named James, who was christened Roman Catholic. It now seemed certain that Catholics would return to the throne long-term, which was anathema to Protestants.

Consequently James' daughter Mary and her husband William of Orange were invited to jointly rule in James' place, and James was deposed, finally leaving for France in 1689. However, many Catholics, Episcopalians and Tory royalists still considered James to be the legitimate monarch.

The first Jacobite rebellion, led by Viscount Dundee in April 1689, routed King William's force at the Battle of Killiecrankie, but unfortunately Dundee himself was killed, leaving the Jacobite forces leaderless, and in May 1690 they suffered a heavy defeat. King William offered all the Highland clans a pardon if they would take an oath of allegiance in front of a magistrate before 1st January 1692. Due to the weather and a general reluctance, some clans failed to make it to the places appointed for the oath to be taken, resulting in the infamous Glencoe Massacre of Clan MacDonald in February 1692. By spring all the clans had taken the oath, and it seemed that the Stuart cause was dead.

However, a series of economic and political disasters by William and his government left many people dissatisfied with his reign, and a number of these flocked to the Jacobite cause. In 1707, the Act of Union between Scotland and England, one of the intentions of which was to put an end to hopes of a Stuart restoration to the throne, was deeply unpopular with most Scots, as it delivered no benefits to the majority of the Scottish population.

Following the deaths of William and Mary, Mary's sister Anne became Queen, dying without leaving an heir in 1714, after which George, Elector of Hanover took the throne, as George I. This raised the question of the succession again, and in 1715 a number of Scottish nobles and Tories took up arms against the Hanoverian monarch.

The rebellion was led by the Earl of Mar, but he was not a great military leader and the Jacobite army suffered a series of defeats, finally disbanding completely when six thousand Dutch troops landed in support of Hanover. Following this, the Highlands of Scotland were garrisoned and hundreds of miles of new roads were built, in an attempt to thwart any further risings in favour of the Stuarts.

By the early 1740s, this operation was scaled back when it seemed unlikely that the aging James Stuart, 'the Old Pretender,' would spearhead another attempt to take the throne. However, the hopes of those who wanted to dissolve the Union and return the Stuarts to their rightful place were centring not on James, but on his young, handsome and charismatic son Charles Edward Stuart, as yet something of an unknown quantity.

I would strongly recommend that you read the first five books in the series, Mask Of Duplicity, The Mask Revealed, The Gathering Storm, The Storm Breaks and Pursuit of Princes before starting this one! However, if you are determined not to, here's a summary of the first five to help you enjoy Book Six…

The Story So Far

Book One – Mask of Duplicity

Following the death of their father, Elizabeth (Beth) Cunningham and her older half-brother Richard, a dragoon sergeant, are reunited after a thirteen-year separation, when he comes home to Manchester to claim his inheritance. He soon discovers that while their father's will left her a large dowry, the investments which he has inherited will not be sufficient for him to further his military ambitions. He decides therefore to persuade his sister to renew the acquaintance with her aristocratic cousins, in the hope that her looks and dowry will attract a wealthy husband willing to purchase him a commission in the army. Beth refuses, partly because she is happy living an unrestricted lifestyle, and partly because the family rejected her father following his second marriage to her mother, a Scottish seamstress.

Richard, who has few scruples, then embarks on an increasingly vicious campaign to get her to comply with his wishes, threatening her beloved servants and herself. Finally, following a particularly brutal attack, she agrees to comply with his wishes, on the condition that once she is married, he will remove himself from her life entirely.

Her cousin, the pompous Lord Edward and his downtrodden sisters accept Richard and Beth back into the family, where she meets the interesting and gossipy, but very foppish Sir Anthony Peters. After a few weeks of living their monotonous lifestyle, Beth becomes extremely bored and sneaks off to town for a day, where she is followed by a footpad. Taking refuge in a disused room, she inadvertently comes upon a gang of Jacobite plotters, one of whom takes great pains to hide his face, although she notices a scar on his hand. They are impressed by her bravery and instead of killing her, escort her home. A secret Jacobite herself, she doesn't tell her Hanoverian family what has happened, and soon repairs with them to London for the season.

Once there, she meets many new people and attracts a great number of suitors, but is not interested in any of them until she falls in love with Daniel, the Earl of Highbury's son. The relationship progresses until she discovers that his main motivation for marrying her is to use her dowry to clear his gambling debts. She rejects him, but becomes increasingly depressed.

In the meantime, the Jacobite gang, the chief members of whom are Alex MacGregor (the scarred man) and his brothers Angus and Duncan, are operating in the London area, smuggling weapons, collecting information, visiting brothels etc.

Sir Anthony, now a regular visitor to the house, becomes a friend of sorts, and introduces her to his wide circle of acquaintance, including the King, the Duke of Cumberland and Edwin Harlow MP and his wife Caroline. Beth does not trust the painted Sir Anthony and thinks him physically repulsive, but finds him amusing. Following an ultimatum from her brother that if she keeps rejecting suitors he will find her a husband himself, she accepts a marriage proposal from Sir Anthony, partly because he seems kind, but chiefly because he has discovered a rosary belonging to her, and she is afraid he will denounce her as a Catholic, which would result in her rejection from society and her brother's vengeance.

The night before her wedding, Beth is abducted by Daniel, who, in a desperate attempt to avoid being imprisoned for debt, attempts to marry her by force. Beth's maid, Sarah, alerts the Cunninghams and Sir Anthony to Beth's plight, and she is rescued by her fiancé. He then gives her the option to call off the wedding, but thinking that being married to him is the best of the limited options she has available to her, she agrees to go ahead as planned.

Book Two – The Mask Revealed

Sir Anthony and Beth marry. The following evening at a function, he has to remove his glove and she sees his hand and its scar for the first time, and remembers where she has seen it before. Having removed his furious wife by force from the company before she can give him away, Sir Anthony admits that he is a Jacobite spy, and that he is really Alex MacGregor. He explains the odd circumstances that led him to follow such a strange double life, and admits that he married her mainly for love, intends to make her dowry over to her and effect a separation, thereby giving her her freedom. She, being of a very adventurous spirit, refuses, stating that she intends to stay with him. He tries to persuade her against this, as his lifestyle is a dangerous one, but eventually he agrees, and they go on honeymoon to Europe together, as Sir Anthony and wife.

He explains that he will be visiting Prince Charles Stuart, son of the exiled King James, as a few weeks ago the Duke of Newcastle, not knowing him to be a Jacobite spy, recruited him on behalf of the Hanoverians, to become acquainted with the prince and report back any useful information.

On the way to Rome, Angus (who has accompanied them as a servant) overhears a private conversation between two French courtiers, in which it is revealed that King Louis of France is secretly planning to invade England, and that one of the men (Henri), intends to give the plans to the British. Alex now decides he must do something to prevent this, but must first carry on to meet Charles and convey the news of the prospective invasion to him. He does, and Beth and Alex are married again in Rome under their real names.

After giving a misleading report of his meeting with Charles to Sir Horace Mann who is the Hanoverian envoy in Florence, Alex, Beth and Angus travel to France, where, at Versailles, Beth becomes acquainted with, and starts to like, the man Henri. Alex, as Sir Anthony, pretends jealousy and challenges Henri to a duel, during which he kills him, as though by accident.

Beth, having not been entrusted with his plans, and also having been kept in the dark about some other things, is very hurt and leaves suddenly, travelling back first to London and then

Manchester, on her own, where she settles in with her ex-servants.

Alex's return is delayed as he is held in prison for duelling. He sends Angus to Rome to stop Prince Charles riding to Paris to join the invasion and thereby raising British suspicion and Louis' anger. Alex then returns home to London, where he is expecting Beth to be waiting for him. When he discovers she has left, he follows her to Manchester, where they are reconciled.

Book Three – The Gathering Storm

Following their reconciliation, Beth and Alex return to London, where Beth engineers a marriage between Anne Maynard and Lord Redburn. The prospective French invasion of England is unsuccessful and shortly afterwards the MacGregors journey to Scotland, where Beth meets the rest of her clan and is initiated into the Highland way of life, which she adapts to very quickly. She also meets her MacDonald relatives, including her grandmother, now a very old lady. During a short stop in Edinburgh, Beth, accompanied by Duncan, unexpectedly encounters Lord Daniel, and after an acrimonious and almost violent exchange, Beth realises he is now her sworn enemy.

On their reluctant return to London, Beth is confronted by her brother Richard, requesting funds from Sir Anthony. Incensed by this, Beth ejects him from her home, whereupon he secretly courts and marries Anne, who is now the wealthy widow of Lord Redburn. Beth is concerned about the safety of Anne, and Lord Redburn's unborn child, whom Anne carries.

Prince Charles lands prematurely in Scotland, and the clans start to rally to him. Alex sends Duncan and Angus to raise the clan but he, as Sir Anthony, feels that he will be of more use gathering information if he remains with his wife in London. He consoles himself with the knowledge that this will be a temporary measure, and he will soon be able to take his rightful place as chieftain of his clan in Scotland and fight for the Stuart cause.

Whilst attending a social evening at the house of the Prince of Wales, Sir Anthony is challenged to a duel by Lord Daniel, which he declines to accept. The prince sides with the Peters and Daniel vows revenge. He begins secretly investigating Sir Anthony's background.

Shortly after this encounter Alex receives a message from Prince Charles, asking him to stay in London gathering information about troop movements, until the invasion is over, and James III and VIII is crowned in London. Alex is distraught, but cannot refuse a direct request from his prince, so reluctantly accepts that he must remain Sir Anthony for the foreseeable future.

Book Four – The Storm Breaks

Alex discovers that he is about to be betrayed and he and Beth flee and join the rebels at Edinburgh, where the Jacobites are victorious in the battle of Prestonpans. The Jacobite army then begins its progress southwards, arriving in Manchester, with more people rallying to their call. At Derby, much against the wishes of Alex and many other members of the clans, it is decided that the army should not march on London, but retreat to Scotland to await French reinforcements.

On reaching Manchester, Beth discovers the child Ann, daughter of her servant Martha who was dismissed by Richard on his first arrival home. The child has suffered badly at the hands of her mother's killer, who Beth suspects is Richard. Alex doubts her suspicions, and Beth is driven to tell him of her brother's attack on her. Alex is enraged that she has not trusted him and this leads to an estrangement between them. The army continues northward and Beth, convinced that their marriage is over, attempts to leave Alex. She is attacked and in rescuing her, Alex realises what he has nearly lost, and they are reconciled.

They continue northwards, where the Jacobite army eventually meets with Cumberland and the government forces at Culloden, while the women, led by Beth, shelter in a barn. The battle is lost, Duncan is killed and Alex badly wounded. Angus, after getting his brother to safety, goes in search of the women.

Their hideout has been discovered by a group of rampaging soldiers. The sergeant stabs Maggie, Beth kills him and whilst running away is recognised by the Duke of Cumberland, who gives the command not to shoot her, but too late. The remaining women are raped and killed and their bodies burnt with the barn.

When Angus arrives he finds Maggie who tells him of Beth's death, before dying herself. Angus searches for but cannot find Beth's body, and assumes it has been burnt along with the others.

He returns to Ruthven, where the surviving Jacobites have gathered, determined to fight on. He tells Iain and Alex the bad news. The MacGregors resolve to continue the rebellion and avenge the death of Maggie and Beth.

Book Five – Pursuit of Princes

Once sufficiently healed, Alex, believing Beth to be dead, briefly joins with Lochiel and the Camerons in an attempt to assemble enough clansmen to continue the rising. However, as part of the Duke of Cumberland's design to destroy the Highlanders' way of life forever, a large body of British soldiers is sent to the Cameron lands in an attempt to both capture Lochiel and exterminate his entire clan. Lochiel and his men, along with the MacGregors, succeed in escaping, but have to acknowledge that for now at least, the rising is over.

Alex returns home and concentrates all his energy on pursuing his blood oath, along with a select number of clansmen. Together they conduct a variety of raids, including a highly successful infiltration of Fort Augustus in which Alex, posing as an English cattle dealer, succeeds in liberating two thousand cattle confiscated from the now starving clans by the redcoats.

Following this, Alex meets with Prince Charles, who is still in hiding in the Highlands, being sheltered by a number of loyal clanspeople and seeking passage back to France, where he hopes to persuade King Louis to assist in a further expedition. Whilst in his company, Alex learns that John Murray of Broughton, the prince's former secretary, has been arrested, and has agreed to inform on his former associates in exchange for his life. Realising Broughton knows the true identity of Sir Anthony, the MacGregors go into hiding in case they are betrayed. Beth's cousin Allan MacDonald joins the MacGregors to fight, and Angus and Morag marry. After five months of hiding in the heather, Prince Charles, along with Lochiel, succeeds in taking ship for France.

After a brief visit home, Sarah returns to London with her baby niece, her sister having died in childbirth. As the baby is illegitimate and has no other relatives, Sarah resolves to bring her up herself.

In the meantime Beth, having been rescued by the Duke of Cumberland, is conveyed to the Tower of London, where she is nursed back to health and lodged in luxurious apartments. Once well, she is interviewed firstly by the Duke of Newcastle and later by Cumberland himself, but refuses to reveal anything about the identity of Sir Anthony Peters. She is sent to the notorious Newgate Prison, in the hopes that a stay in a filthy and overcrowded vermin-ridden cell will encourage her to betray her husband. When this fails to succeed in breaking her resolve, Newcastle sends for Richard, who agrees to interrogate her in an attempt to obtain the information.

Beth has discovered she is pregnant, but following Richard's brutal interrogation, she miscarries, and Newcastle, realising that nothing will now break her, orders her to be kept in solitary confinement and quietly starved to death.

But the redcoat soldier who was guarding Beth prior to Richard's brutal attack confides in his brother, who, being a former servant of Lord Edward, recognises the description of Beth and tells Sarah. She enlists the help of Caroline, and with the assistance of Prince Frederick himself, they succeed in locating Beth and liberating her from her cell.

At death's door, she is conveyed to Caroline's and through the ministrations of her friends, together with the expertise of Prince Frederick's physician she recovers, although, convinced that Alex must be dead, she has no real desire to live. She discovers that Richard is attempting to obtain custody of his wife's son by her first marriage, and that Sarah is also in fear for her life, and is determined to kill him if he visits her. Having no reason to live, but realising that if she takes her own life she will have committed a mortal sin and will therefore never be reunited with her husband in Heaven, she decides to kill two birds with one stone, as it were.

She seeks an interview with the Duke of Newcastle, who agrees, believing she has finally seen sense. At their meeting she denounces Richard as a traitor, stating that he knew Sir Anthony was a spy, but accepted payment to keep quiet. But she refuses to reveal any information about Sir Anthony, and hopes Newcastle will now have her executed.

In the meantime, in the continuation of fulfilling his blood oath, Alex encounters Richard, who is engaged in torturing a woman. Alex badly wounds his brother-in-law, but before Richard dies he tells Alex that Beth is very much alive, and is in Newgate Prison. He reveals gleefully that he beat her so badly that she miscarried their child, and Alex kills him in a rage.

He then resolves to go to London to discover if Beth is, indeed, still alive.

STUART/HANOVER FAMILY TREE

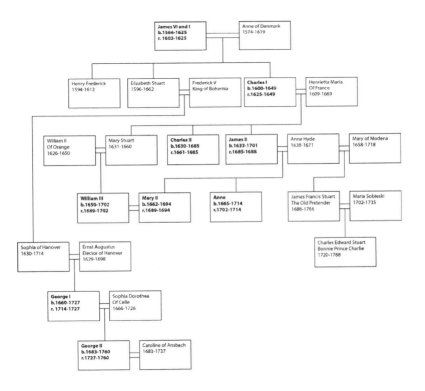

LIST OF CHARACTERS

Alexander MacGregor, Highland Chieftain
Angus MacGregor, brother to Alex
Morag MacGregor, wife to Angus

Iain Gordon, liegeman to Alex
Alasdair MacGregor, clansman to Alex
Peigi MacGregor, wife to Alasdair
Jamie MacGregor, their child
Kenneth MacGregor, clansman to Alex
Janet MacGregor, clanswoman to Alex
Dougal MacGregor, clansman to Alex
Lachlan MacGregor, a child
Allan MacDonald, Beth's cousin

Prince Charles Edward Stuart, eldest son of James Stuart (the
    Pretender), exiled King of Great Britain
Donald Cameron of Lochiel, Chief of Clan Cameron

Lydia Fortesque, a young lady

Edwin Harlow, MP
Caroline Harlow, wife to Edwin
Freddie Harlow, their son
Toby, their manservant

Graeme Elliot, Jacobite soldier
Thomas Fletcher, former steward to Beth MacGregor
Jane Fletcher, his wife
Ann, their adopted daughter.
Mary Swale, former maid to Beth
Ben, former servant to Beth

Sarah Browne, a businesswoman
Mary Browne, her infant niece
Gabriel Foley, a smuggler

Colonel Mark Hutchinson, a dragoon
Bernard, his batman.
Sergeant Stephen Baker, a redcoat soldier

Beth MacGregor, wife to Alex

Captain John Ricky, a sea captain
Mr Johnson, First Mate
Sam, a sailor
Captain Paul Marsal, a privateer
Elizabeth Clavering, Alexander Low, Effie Cameron, Barbara
    Campbell, John Ostler, James McPherson, Flora Cameron,
    Jane McIntosh, Anne Cameron, John Mackenzie, Daniel
    McGillis, Donald McDonald, John Grant – all Jacobite
    prisoners.

Charles de Tubières, Marquis de Caylus

Pierre Delisle, a plantation owner
Antoinette Delisle, his wife
Andre Giroux, their friend
Francis Armstrong, an overseer

Raymond, Rosalie, Eulalie, Ezra, slaves

PROLOGUE

April 30th 1747

Prince Charles Edward Stuart had been sitting in the dining room of his brother's house for over an hour, and he was starting to become annoyed. The table was sumptuously laid for two, the damask tablecloth spotless, the light from the many expensive beeswax candles reflecting off the silver cutlery and crystal glassware. A cheery fire burned in the hearth. The room contained everything necessary for a perfect royal supper. Except for one of the royals.

Really, it was just too inconsiderate of Henry to keep him waiting like this. If he had known he was going to be delayed, he could have sent a message advising his brother as to why.

The fact that he had *not* sent a message stopped Charles from growing too angry at this point. Clearly something unexpected had happened to delay him. Perhaps his horse had cast a shoe, or his carriage lost a wheel – there could be any number of explanations for his tardiness.

Charles had quizzed the servants, who told him that that their orders had been to make everything ready for supper at eight. Prince Henry had gone out a few hours previously, but had been expected back in time for supper, which was ready. Perhaps His Highness would like to eat now? Certainly the master would not object if he did, as the food was in danger of spoiling otherwise.

Charles declined, and said that he would wait in the library for his brother's return, which must certainly be soon. Accordingly a fire was laid, candles lit and a decanter of wine brought, and Charles made himself at home.

1

Although it was spring the evenings were still chilly, and he was grateful for the warmth of the fire. He stood and perused the bookshelves for a few minutes, looking for a volume that would divert him from his mingled irritation and worry as to the whereabouts of his younger brother; but Henry's tastes were very different to his. Charles perused the titles: *La Beaute de Carmel; Synesii Cyrenaei Episcopi Epistolae; Commentaria in Sex Posteriores Prophetas Minores.*

Having no desire to read a dull religious tome or a ponderous volume in Latin or Greek, he threw himself into a chair by the fire and started to make inroads into the wine.

Henry's taste in books reflected everything that was lacking in him. If, instead of learning the history of prophets no one had ever heard of and the excruciatingly boring lives of Carmelite monks, Henry had spent his time studying military history and tactics and in improving his lacklustre personality, he would perhaps have been useful for once in his life, and would have kept the pressure on the French court while he, Charles, was winning victory after victory as he drew ever closer to London.

If he had, their father would probably now be sitting on the throne in St James's instead of languishing in Rome, and would have better things to do with his time than to spend it penning long-winded letters admonishing his eldest son to tread more carefully with King Louis, not to do anything contrary to court rules, and above all always to be diplomatic.

Diplomatic! Charles uttered an expletive that no doubt would have turned his pious, sensitive brother Henry white with shock. He had spent three years tiptoeing round the wily French king, flattering him, toadying to him, although it had galled him to do so. And where had it got him? Nowhere! For that matter, where had thirty years of his father's diplomacy got the Stuart cause? Nowhere!

And yet he, Charles, recognising that the Stuarts would all die of old age if they waited for Louis to help them, had taken action; and that action had almost succeeded in wresting the crown from that German upstart George.

If instead of kneeling in damp musty churches praying for victory morning, noon and night, Henry had persuaded Richelieu to launch the French fleet he had been preparing in December of

'45, Lord George Murray and the rest of the council could not have insisted they turn back at Derby, and he would be in London now, the Prince of Wales, heir to the throne of Great Britain and darling of his people, instead of in a poky house in Paris waiting for his useless brother.

As for his loyal followers, the clansmen...oh God, no. He could not think of what they were enduring now, or he would go mad. He drained his glass and refilled it, staring gloomily into the flames.

Henry had wanted to go to Spain to try and gain support for an invasion of England, but Charles could not have allowed that. True, his own mission, conducted in the greatest secrecy in February, had not gone according to plan, but even so he had made a good impression, he knew that. Lochiel, knowing nothing of Charles' true intentions, thinking he was only going as far as Avignon and that only to spite Louis, had begged him not to anger the French king, and instead to accept Louis' offer of a small expedition to Scotland.

That was understandable; Lochiel was desperate to return to his beleaguered Camerons and take revenge on Cumberland. He, along with most of the other Scottish Jacobites, thought that if Charles could take the Scottish throne for his father, they could break the hated Union and have two separate kingdoms, as they had before Queen Elizabeth had died childless in 1603.

Charles knew he could not go back to Scotland. He told everyone, including himself, that George and his vicious son would never accept the Stuarts ruling in Scotland alone; the only way forward was to topple George from his throne and drive the Hanoverians out of Britain altogether, as they had driven his grandfather out nearly sixty years ago. There was truth in that, but there was also...no. He could not think of that now.

He pulled his gaze away from the fire and looked at the clock. Ten. Two hours overdue. Surely even if Henry's carriage *had* lost a wheel he could have sent a servant back at the gallop to advise the household? A growing anger mingled with his worry. Even so, Charles decided to wait a little longer. Perhaps even now Henry was waiting for the wheel to be replaced, the horse to be shod.

The mission to Spain. Yes, that had not gone as well as he had hoped. The king and queen of Spain had wished him well, had uttered a lot of fatuous compliments and assurances of friendship, and then had effectively told him to leave. Nevertheless, although he had not received the regiments and military assistance to invade England that he had hoped for, the Spanish chief minister Carjaval *had* at least agreed to send arms and three shiploads of much-needed food to the starving Highlanders. That had not been done yet, but Charles consoled himself with the fact that he had still achieved more than his pathetic brother would have done.

Why James kept singing Henry's praises whilst criticising *him*, Charles had no idea. From the moment he could understand language, his father had drummed into him that *he* was the hope for the Stuart cause: the restoration of the Stuarts to the throne of Great Britain rested on *his* shoulders.

When he was five his father had commissioned a full-length portrait of him to be painted, with his hand pointing to a plume of Prince of Wales feathers. A naturally active child, Charles had hated having to stand still for hours. He could still remember the uncomfortable scratchy court costume, the continuous requests for him to stay still. It had been hell, but even at that age he had understood the significance of the plume of feathers he was pointing at, and of the painting, which had been engraved so it could be distributed to his followers; he was the hope of the House of Stuart, it was his destiny and his alone to put his father back in his rightful place.

He owed it not only to his father, but to all his loyal followers, especially the Highlanders, who over the last fifty years had risen time and time again in support of the Stuarts, first for his grandfather, then his father, and, almost two years ago now, for him, the Prince Regent. It was a sign of their steadfastness and their desperation to see the Hanoverians overthrown, that even after thirty years of Hanoverian rule thousands of them had still been willing to risk everything to help him restore the rightful monarch to the throne, one who truly cared about his people and would rule wisely and well, instead of disappearing to Hanover every five minutes and bleeding Britain dry to safeguard his petty German electorate as the current usurper was doing.

Charles had spent his whole life to date training for, and striving to achieve that. No one could accuse him of complacency, or of doing anything other than his utmost to fulfil that destiny. In spite of the lack of gratitude from his father, and the lack of assistance from his brother, he would continue to fight with every means at his disposal to achieve the restoration of his family. What else was there for him to do? He knew nothing else.

For a moment, just one fleeting moment, a vision of a dark and hopeless future opened in front of him. He closed his eyes tightly, then the rage and despair rose in him and he gave a strangled cry, before throwing his glass to the back of the fire.

The sound of it shattering into a million tiny crystal fragments brought a servant, unbidden.

"Your Highness." He bowed deeply. "Can I be of any assistance?"

Charles looked at the clock. Nearly midnight. Had he really been sitting here for over two hours, brooding and staring into nothingness? He yawned, suddenly utterly weary.

"Is there any news of my brother?" he asked the hovering footman.

"No, Your Highness, not yet. Would you care for more wine?"

Charles looked at the empty bottle with some surprise. He didn't remember drinking all that. For a moment he was tempted to call for brandy, drink himself into blissful oblivion at his brother's expense.

"No, thank you," he said, forcing a smile. "I will go home."

"I will arrange for a carriage, Your Highness," the footman offered.

"God, no." Charles laughed. It was ridiculous getting in a carriage to travel to his house, which was next door to his brother's. To hell with protocol. "I will walk," he announced. "The fresh air will revive me. Please notify me the moment you hear from my brother."

The footman agreed and bowed again, before showing the young prince out.

Once outside, Charles stretched his arms, then set off for home at a brisk walk. As he had hoped, the fresh air and activity did help him to ward off the cloud of despair that had threatened to overwhelm him in Henry's tedious library.

It was not over yet. He still had an ace up his sleeve. He would marry. He had hoped to marry a daughter of King Louis, but he realised that if he pushed for that the wily old bastard would probably prevaricate until all his daughters were past childbearing age. And even if he were to achieve a marriage with France, there was no guarantee that Louis would finance an invasion of England even then.

No, perhaps it would be better to look further afield for a suitable bride. Russia, maybe. He could offer for the hand of the Czarina Elizabeth. She was much older than he was, but still of childbearing age, and was no doubt desperate to marry someone who could give her an heir. He could certainly do that! In lieu of a dowry, he would ask for twenty thousand Russian troops, and would use them to invade England and send the Hanoverians packing back to Germany where they belonged.

The crisp night air had done its job now, and he was fully awake. He would sit down this very night and pen a letter to his father outlining his idea. Surely James would find no obstacles to put forward to this? It was an excellent plan! Then he could finally free himself from the grand procrastinator Louis, and at the same time free his beloved, loyal Highlanders from the terrible fate they were now enduring for his sake.

He would make it right. He *had* to make it right. It was not only his destiny, but his duty to do so.

CHAPTER ONE

Liverpool, April 1747

The sixteen women, most of them dressed in filthy rags, stood shivering in a little group on the quayside, waiting to board the ship that was going to take them to hell. They were guarded by a troop of armed militia men. Some of the men proudly sported the uniform blue coat, while the rest wore their everyday clothes. Most of them were very young.

Beth Cunningham, standing in the centre of the group, the only woman wearing a decent, although none-too-clean dress, and the only one in irons, surveyed the enemy and reflected that five well-armed Highlanders could lay waste to the lot of them before they even had a chance to unsling their muskets from their shoulders. Unfortunately, the only well-armed Highlanders left, Jacobite ones that was, were the ones defying the government's disarming act, and they were several hundred miles away with better things to do than attack a group of inexperienced youths.

Beth sighed and stood on tiptoe, trying to see past her taller companions. This was probably the last time she would ever see her native land, but all she could see from where she stood was a jumble of brick-built buildings, which were probably warehouses to store all the provisions that were brought into and carried out of this rapidly expanding town. In the distance, towering above the other buildings was an elegant church spire.

To the other side, in the dock, was a forest of masts. She had never seen so many ships in one place. Maybe it was better to have such an uninspiring view, of a place she didn't know. She was not sure she could have borne her last sight to be the heather-covered mountains of Scotland. At least she was not alone; all the women here, and a much larger number of men were bound for the same fate, and there was a strange sort of comfort in that.

Recognising that sentimentality would only weaken her, she reassessed the restricted view from a more practical point of view. Although there were enough people on the quayside to enable an escapee to rapidly mingle with the crowd, with her ankles and wrists fettered she had no chance of making a run for it. None of the other women were so encumbered, but they might as well have been; kept in filthy cells on inadequate rations for months, they had neither the strength nor, in most cases, the will to make an attempt at getting away.

Beth was fortunate, she knew that. Having been lodged at Caroline and Edwin's for months, she had eaten well, and due to her self-imposed exercise regime was still strong and well-muscled. Following her interview with the Duke of Newcastle at which she had denounced her brother as a traitor, she had been returned to the Tower of London where she had been housed in relative comfort for two days, after which she'd been brought a plain woollen dress to put on, had been manacled, then put into a carriage.

At first she'd thought they were taking her back to Newgate Prison, but instead she'd been conveyed to Tilbury Dock, confined with a lot of other women in a tiny airless cabin on a ship and taken by sea to Liverpool, from where, if the other women were correct and if she was to share their fate, she was to be transported to an as yet unknown destination on the other side of the world. For life. The Colonies, probably. America, where her grandmother had been transported so many years before.

Her thoughts were interrupted by a sudden movement. The militia men moved forward, pushing the women down a gangplank which led onto the ship where they were to spend the next few weeks of their lives. Waiting to meet them on board was some of the crew, dressed in breeches and shirts of varying sober colours, most of them stockingless and barefoot. They were headed by a tall, severe-looking man dressed in immaculate dark blue breeches and frock coat, with cream silk stockings and a gold-embroidered cream silk waistcoat. As the women congregated nervously on the scrubbed wooden boards of the deck, he introduced himself as Captain John Ricky.

"Good morning, ladies," he said. "Welcome aboard the *Veteran*. This will be your home for the next several weeks until you disembark in Antigua, where you are to serve out your sentences as indentured servants."

There was a low murmuring from the women. Antigua? Where was that? He raised a hand, and the women fell silent again.

"It is my aim to ensure that all of you survive the voyage. You will be fed half the rations that my men receive, as you will be resting and they will be working. I apologise that there is insufficient room on board for you to have separate quarters from the male prisoners, but I have ensured you have a little privacy for your ablutions. Do not take this as a licence for you to engage in wanton behaviour. I am a God-fearing man and will tolerate neither immorality nor insubordination. Do I make myself clear?"

Silence.

"Do I have to repeat myself?" he asked coldly.

Several of the women were looking at him blankly. Beth started to translate his speech for the benefit of those who spoke only Gaelic, but had uttered no more than a few words before he interrupted her.

"Wait," he said. "What gibberish is that?"

Beth bristled, but kept her voice calm as she answered him. It would do no good to antagonise the captain of the ship before they had even left port.

"Many of the women do not speak English, Captain," she said. "I was translating your words into Gaelic for them."

He looked at her for a moment, then nodded curtly for her to continue. She spoke rapidly, and when she finished, the women nodded.

"They understand," Beth said.

"You are English, madam," Captain Ricky observed.

"Yes."

"How is it then that you speak this…*Gaelic*?"

"I spent some time in Scotland, and learnt to speak it passably whilst there. I have a facility for languages," she lied, hoping that would stop him asking for more details.

"Your name?" he asked, looking at a paper in his hand.

"Elizabeth Cunningham."

JULIA BRANNAN

He ran his finger quickly down the paper.

"It says here you are a seamstress, from Manchester. Is that right?"

"Yes," she said.

"Mr Johnson," he said, gesturing to the only other well-dressed man on deck.

"Yes, sir?" Mr Johnson said.

"Why is this prisoner in irons? None of the other women are. Is she a troublemaker?"

"I have no idea, sir. She was in irons when I took custody of her this morning."

The captain turned back to Beth.

"Why are you fettered, madam?" he asked.

"I don't know," Beth replied. Interesting. If he knew nothing of her background, she was not about to enlighten him. "Perhaps it was thought I might try to escape."

"Do you intend to try to escape?" he asked. She looked around her. The gangplank had already been lifted.

"No, sir. I have no wish to drown," she said.

He fixed her with a cold grey stare, which she returned with one of cornflower-blue innocence. After a few seconds he seemed satisfied that she had not intended impertinence.

"We have a blacksmith on board, do we not?" he said.

"Yes, sir," Johnson replied. "One of the prisoners, Low, I believe, is a smith."

"Very well. Once everyone is settled in, you will bring him on deck and allow him to strike her irons. Her wrists are already raw. I would not have her die of infection unnecessarily. Which one of you is Elizabeth Clavering?"

Another woman, slightly taller than Beth, with light brown hair tied back with a cord, stepped forward and waited.

"It says here you are a seamstress as well," Captain Ricky said.

"Aye, I am," she replied.

"And a lady, it seems."

"We are all ladies," the young woman said coolly. He bestowed the same look on her as he had on Beth moments earlier. Elizabeth returned his look coldly.

"Do not quibble with me, madam," the captain said. "Or I assure you, you will regret it. I have been told by your husband's sister that you are to petition the king for mercy."

"My husband was hanged at York, Captain, and it's a little late to petition the Elector, even if I wished to do so," she answered. Beth warmed to her immediately.

"Nevertheless, you will do so. And while on board my ship you will show respect for the king, madam, or I will teach you to."

"I have always shown the deepest respect for the king, Captain," she answered. "If you command me to petition for mercy, I will."

"I do indeed. Conduct Mrs Clavering to my cabin, Mr Johnson, and take her statement. Take the others below," he ordered.

They were conducted to a hatch in the deck, and had to climb down a wooden ladder into the hold, which was already crowded with the male prisoners who had been loaded on to the ship before the women. A piece of canvas material had been strung across one corner of the space, behind which was a bucket for the women to relieve themselves in and just enough space for the sixteen females to sit down. They would have to sleep in shifts if they wanted to lie flat, Beth thought.

The men had already settled in, if such a word could be applied to these Spartan conditions. The only furniture, as it were, was a number of buckets which would serve for toilet facilities and which had been moved to one corner and secured with a bit of rope to hopefully stop them spilling their contents when the ship set sail. Other than that there was nothing; no mattresses or blankets. The only light came from the hatch through which they'd just entered, and a few small air vents in the side of the ship.

In the grey gloom, Beth could make out a sea of sparsely dressed individuals, some in breeches and tattered shirts, some in the remains of the plaids they'd no doubt fought in, now ragged. All the men sported beards and long hair, having not had the chance to shave for some time. Some of them wore manacles as she did, although most were unencumbered. There was a low murmur of chatter as people introduced themselves to those who would be their companions through what promised to be a hellish voyage, the soft singsong Scottish cadences mingling with the flat northern English tones of those who had served in the Manchester Regiment.

After a short time Elizabeth Clavering clambered down the ladder, and Beth and Alexander Low, the blacksmith, were called up on deck. While he freed her with a hammer and chisel, Beth took the opportunity to try to obtain information from the crewman who stood guard over them, armed with a pistol.

"Have you been to Antigua before?" Beth asked conversationally. "What's it like?"

"No, miss," he said. "This is my first time. But Sam there has."

Sam, hearing his name, wandered over. Soon they would start to move, and then the deck would be a hive of activity, but for now there was little to do, and chatting with a lovely woman was a pleasant way to pass the time.

"Antigua? It's an island in the West Indies. Near the American Colonies," he added, seeing her puzzled expression. "It's beautiful, miss, and a lot warmer than here, that's for sure! The sea's blue, really blue, and there's bananas that you can pick right off the trees! You ever tasted banana?"

"No," Beth lied, knowing that if she admitted she had Sam would want to know how, and she had no wish to reveal anything at all about her background.

"It's lovely, sweet, it is. I expect most of you'll end up on sugar plantations though. They always need people there, being as the work's so hard." He eyed her speculatively. "Not you, though. I expect you'll end up as a house servant, or maybe even mistress to one of them rich owners, eh, if you play your cards well?" He smiled lasciviously, and for the thousandth time Beth regretted her looks.

"How long will it take to get there?" she asked.

"Depends on the winds and the weather," he said. "Six weeks maybe. Less if we're really lucky, more if we're not. Maybe you and I can keep each other company in the meantime." He smiled again and Beth tensed.

The smith hit one final blow to Beth's leg irons and they fell apart. He glared up at Sam, and the other sailor raised his pistol.

"If you've quite finished chatting," the voice of Mr Johnson came from behind the group, causing the two crewmen to spring to attention. "Thank you, Mr Low. You can go below, and you two can get to work."

Beth and Alexander climbed down the ladder, and the hatch

was closed, plunging the prisoners into near-darkness. Beth felt her way over to the other women, most of whom she'd become acquainted with on the trip from London to Liverpool.

"Did you dictate your abject plea for mercy then?" she said as she sat down in the space they made for her. She rubbed her wrists gingerly. They were chafed, but not too badly.

Elizabeth Clavering laughed.

"I wrote it myself," she said. "It's probably no' quite what the Elector's used to seeing, but to hell with him. Even if it wasna too late, I'd sooner die than beg for mercy from that lump o' shite."

"Do ye think they'll make ye write it again?" Effie Cameron asked.

"They can try, but I'll no' be doing it. I doubt they'll bother. It'll probably be thrown in the sea. Did ye find anything out?" she asked Beth.

"Antigua's an island in the West Indies, somewhere near America, they grow bananas and sugar, and it'll take about six weeks to get there. And sailor Sam would like to become acquainted with me, the fool."

All the women laughed.

"You want to be careful, miss," came a masculine voice from behind the curtain. "I've heard these sailors are none too clean. You might catch lice off him."

The laughter became general. Everyone had lice; it was an accepted part of life in prison.

"I think lice'll be the least o' your worries, lassie," another man commented.

"Lice'll be the least of *his* worries, if he tries," Beth said grimly.

"Did yer mother never tell ye that eavesdropping on ladies in their boudoir is ungentlemanly?" the fiery-haired Barbara Campbell asked primly.

"Begging your pardon, my lady."

"What time do you think they'll serve afternoon tea and cakes?" an English voice enquired.

"Will I ring the bell and ask?"

Beth laughed with the others and settled down to enjoy the banter. If everyone could keep their spirits up, the voyage might just be bearable.

Once the ship set sail, though, it quickly became apparent that darkness and lack of privacy were only a small part of the problems they would face in the weeks to come. Over the last year or so all of them had, to some extent, become accustomed to dirt, vermin, inadequate food and living in cramped conditions with people who they would perhaps not choose to share accommodations with in normal life. They had learned to tolerate the irritating mannerisms and habits of others, to hold their tempers when driven to anger, and to respect others when they withdrew into themselves in an attempt to find some emotional solitude in an environment where physical solitude was not possible.

Many of them had been on a ship before, but there was a huge difference between sailing round the coast of Britain from Scotland or London to Liverpool, and sailing across a storm-tossed open sea. A good quarter of them were seasick to some extent at the start of the voyage, and over half of them whenever the ship hit bad weather. At the beginning, until they found their sea-legs, almost everyone suffered.

When Beth had sailed from England to France with Alex masquerading as Sir Anthony, Angus, acting as Sir Anthony's manservant had been felled by seasickness before the ship had even got out of sight of the coast. But he had, in the main, voided the contents of his stomach overboard, and had spent most of his time lying in a coil of rope on deck, green-faced and sweating, refusing to take to the cabin he shared with his brother for fear of rendering it uninhabitable.

The prisoners on board the *Veteran* did not have the luxury of vomiting overboard, with the result that the buckets started to fill, and the stench was making even those who were not afflicted feel queasy. Even though the improvised chamberpots were tethered to the wall of the hold, their contents still overflowed with every lurch of the ship, meaning that the prisoners, none of whom wanted to occupy the space around the buckets, were even more cramped than they'd expected.

It was with huge relief a few hours after setting sail, that they heard the bolts pulled back, and the hatch lifted, allowing light and, more importantly, air to filter down to the hold. Baskets of food, consisting of slices of rough brown bread thinly smeared with butter, and chunks of hard cheese, were lowered, followed by pitchers of beer. Those not prostrate with sickness reached eagerly for the provisions.

"Make the most of the bread," one of the sailors called down cheerfully. "There'll be a lot of that at first, because the flour spoils after a while."

"Can we come up for some air?" asked John Ostler, a Lincolnshire gentleman who, of all those on board, was the only one not listed as possessing a useful trade. "It is growing unbearable down here."

"I've no orders for that. Only to give you rations, once we were at sea."

"Will ye at least allow us tae empty the buckets, then, man?" asked James MacPherson. "It reeks dreadful down here. There's a good many bodies sick wi' the motion."

There was a brief silence, then the hatch was lowered again.

"They canna leave us like this for six weeks," Barbara Campbell said. "They wouldna gie us buckets if they didna intend us to empty them."

Everyone waited. After what seemed like an interminable time, the hatch reopened.

"All the ladies, and *only* the ladies, may come up to empty the pails," the captain said. "You will be allowed to do this twice a day, weather permitting. Any misbehaviour and the privilege will be curtailed."

The women made their way up the ladder, and the pails were handed up to them to empty over the side. It wasn't the pleasantest job in the world, but at least it would relieve conditions below, and allow them some fresh air. Once the buckets were emptied and passed back down, the women were allowed to stay on deck for a few minutes to stretch their legs, guarded by three sailors armed with swords and pistols. Beth stood by the rail, watching the ship cut through the waves. Above her the sails cracked and billowed in the wind, which also lifted her hair, now almost shoulder length. She inhaled deeply, savouring the fresh ozone scent of the air.

She had been there for no more than a minute before Sam sidled up behind her.

"What do you say then?" he asked.

"What do I say to what?" she replied.

"To us getting better acquainted. Beautiful girl like you doesn't want to be stuck down there for weeks. We could come to some arrangement, like."

"No thank you. I'm quite happy as I am," she replied calmly, still looking out to sea. The boat was racing across the waves. *The sooner we get there the better,* she thought, then realised that the fate awaiting her at her destination was unlikely to be better than life on board ship, possibly a lot worse.

Sam had not taken the hint.

"Come on. I'm asking nicely. Not all the men would. There's some who'll take without asking, if you get my meaning," he said.

She turned now and looked at him, her eyes cold and hard.

"Are there now?" she said. "Well, you tell them that if they do, they'd better enjoy it, because it'll be the last time they ever swive a woman. Or a man, come to that."

He reddened at the implication that sailors went in for buggery, although in fact many of them did, especially when there were no women available. Then he laughed.

"A little thing like you ought to be nice to me. I can protect you from those who'd hurt you," he said, his hand patting the butt of the pistol thrust through his belt.

She looked away from him, out to sea again, made a decision.

"Do you want to know why I was in irons?" she said conversationally. "I killed a man."

"You?" he answered disbelievingly. He looked her up and down. "I don't believe you."

"That's up to you, but it's true. A redcoat sergeant. I put a knife straight through his throat. He choked to death on his own blood," she said with obvious relish.

"Don't have no knife now, though, do you?" he said, but there was hesitation in his voice.

"You don't need a knife to kill someone," Beth replied, smiling. "There was a man, once, Ewen Cameron, his name was. He was fighting in a battle, I'm not sure which one. Anyway, this redcoat soldier got the better of him, disarmed him, and was on top of him, straddling him so he couldn't free his arms. You know, like one of those men you're wanting to protect me from might do?"

She turned to face him again, leaning her back against the rail. Some of the other crewmen were eyeing them; clearly if Sam was successful, the other women would be next to be propositioned. On the other side of the deck near the hatch, which had been closed again, presumably to stop the male prisoners attempting to come on deck, Mr Johnson, who Beth assumed from his dress to be second-in-command, was gazing upward at the rigging, directing the men with a series of hand gestures. Beth took this in at a glance, then focussed on the face of her would-be suitor. He was slightly puzzled, but clearly interested.

"What happened?" he asked when she didn't speak immediately.

"Ewen leaned up, like this," she said, bringing her face to within an inch of Sam's, as though about to kiss him, "and then he tore the soldier's throat out with his teeth."

Sam's eyes widened and instinctively he took a step backwards. Her eyes were pure ice, her mouth hard. He shivered involuntarily. He had no idea if the story was true or not, but her expression left him in no doubt that ravishing her would not be a happy experience.

"You tell that to your friends," she said. "Tell them Highlanders are good at using whatever comes to hand, if need be."

She walked round him and rejoined the other women, who were all looking at her curiously.

As soon as they were back in the hold, Barbara asked her what had happened. She told them, and they all laughed.

"Hopefully he'll think twice before he asks any more of you for favours," Beth said.

"How did you think up that one?" Elizabeth asked.

"She didna," Flora, one of the three Cameron women on board, put in before Beth had chance to answer. "It's true. All the Camerons ken it well. Ewen was Lochiel's grandfaither. It was at the battle o' Inverlochy it happened."

"I couldn't remember the battle," Beth said, managing just in time to stop adding that it was the current Lochiel himself who had told her that story over a bottle of claret one night.

"I met Lochiel once," one of the Manchester men said, "at Carlisle. He was a good-looking man."

"No' as good-looking as Prince Charlie, though," Jane McIntosh said. There was a collective sigh from the women. "He spoke to me once, when we were in Edinburgh. He was awfu' bonnie."

Beth listened in silence as they all talked about the prince, wondering what they would say if she were to tell them that Charles, along with Angus had witnessed her wedding to Alex, and that Angus had won twenty *scudi* off the prince by drinking him under the table afterwards. Alex had looked so magnificent in his borrowed tartan finery.

It had been a wonderful night, one she had resolved she would treasure for the rest of her life. She could not have imagined the pain that memory would bring her now, knowing that she would never see Alex or Angus again.

She took in a deep shuddering breath and wiped away a tear, thankful for the darkness that hid her expression from the others, then concentrated all her mind on listening to the conversation taking place around her, in an attempt to push the memory to the recesses of her mind.

Over the next days, life settled into a routine. They knew when it went dark, because the tiny bit of light from the air vents disappeared. They left the vents open all the time, relishing the small amount of fresh air they admitted. If there was a heavy storm, they'd been told the vents would have to be closed, otherwise they could stay open.

As soon as it was dark, they tried to sleep. As there wasn't enough room for everyone to lie down at the same time, half of them would sleep lying down one night, whilst the others slept sitting as best they could. The following night they would swap. In the morning the hatch would be lifted and the women would go up to empty the buckets. After that breakfast would be served, which consisted of wooden bowls of thin oatmeal gruel, with maybe a small hard biscuit, edible only if soaked in the watery gruel.

At some point in the late afternoon the women would be allowed up to empty the buckets again, and then the second meal of the day was served; a piece of salt pork or beef and a bowl of pease, with maybe some bread or hard cheese, with beer and water served at each meal.

The rest of the time the prisoners passed in talking; there was nothing else to do.

Beth found out that although all her female companions were Scottish, a good number of the men were from northern England like herself, the majority in the Manchester Regiment, captured at the fall of Carlisle Castle and held in prison ever since.

They told her that all the officers had been executed, and she informed them of the good news that three of the officers had escaped from Newgate Prison and as far as she knew had not been recaptured. That cheered them up. They told her that in spite of the conditions on shipboard, they were the lucky ones because they'd survived this far, and some of them were still hopeful that there was more chance of escaping from Antigua than there was from prison, although the months of incarceration had rendered a lot of them, English and Scots alike, depressed and despairing. Which was hardly surprising, given the conditions they'd endured, and the future that beckoned.

Once it became apparent that the men were either too listless or too honourable to try to take advantage of them, the women abandoned their makeshift room, retiring behind the canvas curtain only to relieve themselves, although they still tended to keep together, especially at night.

Over the next week Beth got to know her female companions well, and grew close to two of them, close enough to tell them that she'd been married to one of the most wanted men in Britain, although she did not divulge any incriminating details. Even though they were hundreds of miles from home now, information could still be sent back, and she would say nothing that might risk any of the MacGregors.

Her first impression of Elizabeth Clavering as a strong independent woman was only reinforced once she got to know her better. She had been taken prisoner after the battle at Clifton Moor, where her husband had been fatally wounded.

"He tellt me to leave him," she said, "and I should have heeded him, but I couldna bear to run away when he was still living. After he died, I tried to catch up wi' the others but they'd moved too fast, and the redcoats caught up wi' me. I broke one of the bastard's noses before they took me, though," she added with satisfaction.

She'd been held at York Castle, and because she was a 'lady' had received better treatment than the women Beth had been imprisoned with at Newgate.

"That's where I met Edmund," she said. "He was on his way south from Carlisle to join the prince, and decided to have a bit of fun, so he and his men broke into Lowther Hall while the viscount was away fighting wi' Cumberland, I think. Anyway, they made the servants cook them a meal, but they stayed overlong and were captured. I admired his spirit, stupid though it was, and he admired the way I broke the redcoat's nose. Anyway, we got close. I was still grieving for Dougal, and Edmund was kind. I didna love him though, and when he started talking about marrying, I said no, at first."

By now she'd attracted a small group of listeners, all sympathetic, which encouraged her to carry on.

"Anyway, we drew lots, and I didna have to go to trial, which is why I'm here enjoying the Elector's 'mercy'," she said sarcastically, "but Edmund knew he was going for trial, and that he'd suffer the traitor's death. He didna seem to care at first. He provoked the guards every chance he got, even though I tellt him it wouldna do him any good. Then as time went on he got more and more low. He'd have these outbursts o' temper, then sink into a mood where he wouldna talk to anyone. He said I was the only person who was keeping him from taking his own life. We knew well the trial was a formality – he was for the hangman, so in the end I agreed to marry him. I didna see the harm in it, and if I saved him from suicide and eternal damnation, so much the better. Father John, he was a priest in the prison with us and a Jacobite too, married us. That caused a stramash when the warder found out, I can tell ye, but give him his due, Father John said he'd a clear conscience, because he did it to 'avoid us falling into sin'. That was the last thing I was thinking on, although Edmund said if he got me wi' child they might release me.

"I've nae idea if they would have, but it didna happen anyway. We married in June, and he was hung in November. But at least I made his last months a wee bit happier, and I've nae doubt he's with Our Lord now. He gave a braw speech at the end, as well," she said sadly. "He was a good man, if a little touched in the heid."

The other woman who Beth found an affinity with was about

the same age as she was, plain-featured and with wavy black hair, and could not have been more different from the outspoken Elizabeth Clavering. Anne Cameron hardly spoke at all, keeping herself to herself much of the time and not joining in the spirited conversations that the others indulged in to while away the long hours.

It was when they were on deck one day, about ten days after they'd set sail, that she came over to Beth, who was standing at the rail looking out to sea, as was her custom. The sailors, who at first had maintained a close watch over the women, had now relaxed a little once it became apparent that they were neither going to attempt to storm the ship nor leap overboard en masse, and the female prisoners were left to wander about the deck freely, providing they kept clear of the tangles of ropes snaking along the deck, which were used to train and check the sails.

"It's a fine day," Anne said by way of introduction. It was. For the last few days the sky had been grey, and the day before they had not been allowed on deck due to the heavy rain which had fallen for most of the day. It was all the more of a relief to be able to breathe fresh air now.

"It is. It's good to feel the sunshine on your face," Beth answered.

"I feel bad for the men," Anne said. "It's no' right that they have to stay below all the time."

Beth didn't need to answer this. All the women felt the same way. A lot of the men complained of headaches and sore throats, probably because of the foul air which the small air vents did little to allay, but in the last couple of days two of the men had contracted diarrhoea, which did nothing for the quality of the air and was more worrying, especially as they were now complaining of joint pains too.

"Are you feeling alright?" Beth said instead, sensing that Anne wished to talk about something, but didn't know how to start. "You look sad," she added, although that was her companion's normal expression.

"Aye," she replied. "I heard one of the sailors say that it's the eighteenth of April. Meg died a year ago today. My daughter," she explained in response to Beth's questioning expression. "I was taken at Carlisle, and they let me keep her with me. She was only two months old then. I didna think the castle would fall to Cumberland so quickly. I thought we'd be safe. And then I thought maybe they'd let me go after a wee while, as I hadna done anything wrong except follow my husband. He made me stay at Carlisle, thought we'd be safer there than carrying on in the snow."

"My husband did the opposite," Beth said. "We'd had a fight and I was going to stay at Carlisle, but he told me it wasn't safe, and made me carry on with him."

"They were both wrong, then," Anne commented.

Beth was about to add that, no, Alex had been right, because they'd reconciled and at least she'd spent more time with him, but then realised how tactless that would be.

"Do you know if he's alive?" she asked instead.

Anne shook her head. "You?" she asked.

"No," Beth replied. "But I'm sure he's dead. He'd have found a way to let me know, if he was alive."

They stood in silence for a minute. Above them men swarmed in the rigging, calling to one another, laughing.

"I'm sorry about your daughter," Beth said finally.

"Aye, well. She didna have a chance, poor wee mite. Maybe it was for the best. I wouldna want her to have to go through this, and then die in Antigua, wherever that is. Or have been taken from me and brought up as someone's servant, or worse, and never know her family. She's at peace now, but I miss her every day." She took in a deep breath, fighting not to cry.

"I found out I was with child, when I was in Newgate," Beth said on impulse. "I didn't know until one of the other women told me. I didn't know the signs."

"What...?" Anne began.

"I lost it," Beth said with a tone of finality that stopped Anne asking any more questions. "It was better that way," she added.

She'd told herself that for months now in an attempt to allay the guilt she'd felt at not telling Newcastle before he'd had her tortured, but standing here now, with the wind blowing her hair all over her face, she was certain that she'd done the right thing. No child of Alex's belonged in prison or in a foundling hospital, to be branded as a Jacobite bastard if it had lived. At least it had died without suffering. That was the best she could have done for it, the only thing, given the circumstances. She'd always known that, but this was the first time she'd truly *believed* it.

She felt a great weight lift from her shoulders, and for a moment actually felt happy for the first time since she'd woken up after the miscarriage. She still yearned for death, but if it was not God's will to take her yet, then she would accept that. There must be a reason why she was still alive, after coming so close to dying, twice.

Feeling full of purpose she left the rail and Anne, and walked over to Captain Ricky, who was standing by the larger of the ship's two masts, talking to Mr Johnson.

"Captain," she said. "Could I have a moment of your time, please?"

He broke off his conversation and looked at her.

"Is it important, madam? I am very busy," he asked brusquely.

"It is, I think," she said. He nodded for her to continue. "Are you intending to allow the men to come up on deck at any point?" she asked. "The conditions below are worsening. Many of the men are feeling very unwell, and it would make such a difference to them to have access to a little air and exercise."

"That was not my intention, no," he said. "I will not risk my ship or the safety of my men in order to allow a rabble of traitors to take the air. They should have thought of the consequences of their actions before they followed the Pretender's Son."

His tone indicated that she, being a woman, did not have the intelligence to think for herself. Clearly he did not consider women a threat. She'd hoped he had allowed the women on deck due to compassion, but saw now that she was wrong. She changed tack.

"Two of the men have diarrhoea, and are complaining of backache and joint pains," she said.

"As I have already said—"

"When I was in Newgate," Beth continued conversationally, "there was an outbreak of gaol fever, and a great number of prisoners died. The first symptoms were diarrhoea, then backache and joint pains. Only one woman in my cell died though, and I think that was because I had a little money at the time and used it to buy vinegar to clean the cell and lavender oil to sweeten the air. As I'm sure you know, gaol fever is caused by noxious air, and the air below deck is very noxious at the moment."

Captain Ricky looked at her incredulously.

"As you can see, madam," he said, indicating the ship with a gesture of his arm, "our access to a field of lavender is a little restricted at the moment. Now, if you will excuse me."

"Of course," Beth said. "My apologies. I just thought it would be such a shame if you were to lose most of your prisoners before you reach Antigua. But I suppose it will make no difference to you, as the government will no doubt pay you for us anyway, will they not? I am grateful that you allow the ladies at least to take the air. Thank you, Captain. I am sorry to have disturbed you."

She knew from listening to Alex when talking about his smuggling escapades, that ship owners were only paid for their cargoes when they reached their destination safely. She hoped that also applied to human cargoes.

It seemed she was right. The next day the two sick men were taken on deck and examined by the ship's doctor, who confirmed that the men were merely suffering from dysentery and that their muscle pains were due to the cramped conditions they were living in, especially as they were unable to stand upright, the ceiling of their accommodations being only five feet high.

The day after that the men were taken on deck in small groups and allowed fifteen minutes to stretch their limbs, closely guarded by a number of the crew. This, the captain informed them, would be a daily occurrence unless they offered any violence whatsoever to the crew, in which case they could rot and die as far as he was concerned.

The men made no attempt to storm the ship, aware that in their weakened state and without any weapons they had virtually no chance of success, and that if they did make any such attempt, they would not breathe fresh air until they arrived on land. None of them had any idea how to sail a ship anyway; but they all knew how to fight on land.

Better to submit for now, so that they would arrive in Antigua as healthy as possible. While the men were on deck in groups of twenty, the women were given buckets of sea water and brushes, which they used to wash down the floor of the hold while the remaining men moved around the space as they scrubbed, sometimes taking a turn themselves. The air was still foul, and the food monotonous and inadequate, but it was much better than before and the spirits of the prisoners were raised considerably.

No one knew why the captain had suddenly had a change of heart, and Beth did not tell her companions of her conversation with him; she was just glad that he had taken her veiled warning on board.

In spite of the improvement in conditions some of the prisoners did not survive to reach the West Indies; five of the men and two women died during the voyage, two from infected wounds, one from being thrown against the wall of the hold during a storm, and the remaining three from unknown wasting diseases that they had probably already been suffering from before coming on board. Their bodies were taken out of the hold, and after a few words from the ship's chaplain were thrown overboard.

The remaining passengers were still infested with lice, and had no way of keeping themselves clean and no change of clothing. Bites became infected, and were cleaned with seawater in an attempt to stop them ulcerating, with limited success. But there was no outbreak of typhus or any other contagion, and that was something to be thankful for.

As the weeks passed, the prisoners formed friendship groups based loosely on nationality, clan, or age. By common consent they had agreed not to speak of clan feuds, recognising that this was not the time or place to settle old grievances. Instead of their differences they tried to focus on what they had in common; they all supported the Stuarts, and they were all heading for an unknown life in an alien land.

Nevertheless the strain was starting to tell on them, even though they told themselves that at least they now knew there was an end in sight to their current condition, and that it was getting closer with every day that passed. As they got nearer to their destination the weather, which had been cool and breezy, and often very cold at night, slowly became warmer, and after four weeks at sea the temperature on deck by day was that of a very hot day in high summer in Britain, and even at night it stayed hot and humid, making sleeping in the stuffy hold virtually impossible.

They all dreaded the life they were heading for, indentured servitude just being a synonym for slavery, but told themselves that slaves escaped sometimes, and were set free sometimes too. Anyone who voiced pessimistic views was silenced abruptly; what was the point in becoming miserable about something you couldn't change? They had all made the best of their long imprisonment – that, along with luck in avoiding a fatal illness, was why they were here. They would make the best of what was to come too.

"My grandmother was transported when she was a young woman," Beth told her companions one particularly hot evening as they all sat or lay in the darkness. In Scotland now, and even in northern England, the days would be long, the sun not setting until nine o'clock at the earliest, and rising again around four in the morning. One of the men had commented to a sailor that the nights seemed to be getting longer rather than shorter, and had been told that it was because they were near the equator; that day and night were more or less of equal length all year round. They had all marvelled at this, and had adapted, talking for a short while after dark rather than attempting to sleep for twelve hours, which was difficult in any case, but in this heat impossible.

"Was that after the '15?" one of the men asked.

"No, it was earlier than that, after Killiecrankie." This was a lie, but only a partial one; the massacre of Glencoe *had* taken place after the Battle of Killiecrankie. But Beth had no wish to reveal her MacDonald ancestry to the others; nor did she wish to raise clan matters. Several of her fellow prisoners were Campbells after all, who had fought with the prince rather than against him as the bulk of their clan had. "She was transported to America, and she had a very bad time at first. But she told me that it was partly her own fault, because she couldn't accept the life that God had planned for her, so she fought it all the way. She tried to kill the first man who bought her. She said that she should have learnt when to compromise, because if she had, her life in the Colonies would have been much easier."

"How do ye ken this?" Effie Cameron asked. "Who tellt ye?"

"She did," Beth answered. "The last people who bought her indenture looked after her, even though she insulted them and rebelled. And then they gave her her freedom, and set her up in a little place of her own. She saved for years, and then when she got old, decided she wanted to die at home. So she came back."

There was a short silence while they all absorbed the fact that it was possible to be freed and to go back home. They had heard stories of people returning to Scotland from France, or Italy maybe, but from the other side of the world… no.

"Did she die at home wi' her family, then?" someone asked in the darkness.

"I don't know. The last time I saw her she was still alive and fit and well too. But yes, she was with her family. Everyone thinks she'll live forever, but when she does die she'll be at home, as she wanted. She told me that she nearly died in America, but only because she couldn't accept when she was beaten. I've been thinking about that a lot over the last few days."

By the silence that followed, she realised she was no longer alone in thinking about that.

The following day Captain Ricky informed them that they should, wind permitting, reach Antigua in no more than three days. The general mood on hearing this was one of relief. However bad their new lives might be, it was unlikely that they'd be confined in a hot and humid oversized coffin for weeks on end. And there was always the possibility that they might one day be able to return home. If one elderly woman had done it, why shouldn't they?

Better to think on that, than on the more likely outcome; that they would die as slaves in an alien, hostile land.

CHAPTER TWO

"Do you think you'll be able to do it?" Elizabeth Clavering asked Beth the next morning. The women were on deck, and even though the sun had only risen an hour before, it was already hot. Elizabeth lifted the tangled mass of her hair off her neck in a vain attempt to cool down a little. Not for the first time Beth was thankful that she'd cut hers. Unfashionable as it was for a woman to have short hair, it was certainly more practical, especially in these conditions.

"Be able to do what?" Beth asked, still staring out to sea. She always stood by the rail, but today all the women and most of the sailors who were on deck were also standing there. In the far distance, only just visible over the horizon, could be seen the sails of another ship, although at the moment it was too far away for anyone to discern what type of ship it was.

"Accept that you're beaten? Like your grandmother said."

Beth sighed.

"I don't know," she replied honestly. "She told me that I was like her, had the same spirit, and that she should have stayed at home and brought my mother up instead of shooting a soldier, which was what got her transported. It's a bit late for me to stay at home now, though."

"If you could go back in time, would you have stayed at home?" Elizabeth asked.

"No," Beth said without hesitation. "I wouldn't do anything differently, even if I'd known where it would end. Would you?"

Elizabeth thought for a minute. The other ship was a bit closer now, though still far away. The *Veteran* had two masts and lots of square sails, but this other ship was smaller and had just one mast.

"Yes, just one thing. I would have left my husband when he told me to at Clifton, instead of staying with him. Because we both knew he was dying. I stayed wi' him because I couldna bear for him to die alone, but I ken now that was a selfish thing, because he'd have died happier if I'd have left him and gone wi' the others."

"Would you have been able to forgive yourself for leaving him?"

Elizabeth smiled sadly.

"I dinna ken. But it's done now, anyway. There is no going back. Will ye accept what's to come, though?"

"I don't know. I think I should probably try to, yes. I've done it before, to some extent, at least." She had thought she was making the best of a bad situation in marrying Sir Anthony Peters. And that had turned out to be the best decision of her life. "My grandmother told me that she fought all the way, even against people who would have been good to her if she'd let them. I didn't want to get married but I had to, to get away from my brother, who's the most evil bastard I've ever known."

"Worse than Cumberland?" Elizabeth said, half in jest.

"Yes. Far worse than Cumberland," Beth said vehemently. "Anyway, I had a choice; marry a drunken old man who I knew nothing about, or a younger man who I wasn't attracted to, and who was irritating but amusing to be with and appeared to be kind. Now, from what my granny told me, if she'd been in the same situation at my age she would have refused to marry either of them, and would have tried to carry on fighting Richard and the whole of society instead. But I recognised that I couldn't do that any more, because it was destroying me. And I made the right decision in the end. So maybe I *can* follow her advice. I think it will depend on what happens when we get to Antigua, on who buys my indenture."

"I think you'll fight, just no' in the way of your granny," Elizabeth said. "It seems to me that you've learnt different ways to fight."

Behind the small ship, just appearing over the horizon, was a much larger ship, like the one they were on. At the moment it seemed small due to distance, but it had two masts like this one, so Beth assumed it must be of a similar size. Someone called down from the rigging.

"What do you mean?" Beth asked.

"Well, instead of attacking that Sam straight away when he propositioned ye, ye let him know that ye'd killt a man, and that ye werena afeart to do it again. That was clever. And then ye talked the captain into letting the men up for air. It seems tae me your granny would have challenged him instead."

Beth laughed.

"Not by the time I knew her she wouldn't, no. But yes, when she was young, probably. I didn't know you'd heard me talking to the captain. But I daresay he'd have let the men come up anyway. He seems a hard man, but not one to be cruel for no reason."

"Aye, but—"

Another shout came from the rigging, this time a more urgent one, and suddenly all the crewmen, who had been intently watching the approaching ships, sprang into action.

"Get the women below, now!" Mr Johnson called out urgently.

The women were rounded up none too gently and all but pushed down the ladder into the hold, whereupon the hatch was closed and bolted.

"What's amiss?" one of the men asked. From above their heads came the sound of many feet running, and of heavy objects being moved.

"There are two ships coming towards us, but they're a long way away yet," Barbara Campbell said. "I dinna ken what the fuss is about."

"Everyone was just watching them, and then all of a sudden they said we had to get below," Beth added.

"What kind of ships were they?" John Ostler asked.

"There was a small one and then a big one behind it, like this, I think," Beth said. "I don't know anything about ships, so I don't know what kind they were."

"They could be pirates," John MacKenzie, who had been a captain in Cromartie's regiment, said.

"Pirates!" John Ostler exclaimed. "You mean like Blackbeard?"

"Blackbeard?" Daniel McGillis asked fearfully.

"Pirates are a bit like highwaymen, but at sea," John MacKenzie explained. "My father tellt me about them. It's said that they're all criminals, working only for themselves, and they attack any ship they can, kill all the crew unless they agree to join them, and steal the cargoes for themselves. That noise will be the crew readying the guns to give battle, I'm thinking."

"Mother of God," Elizabeth Clavering said, crossing herself.

"You said there were two ships?" John Ostler asked Beth.

"Yes, the big one had two masts. The small one had one, but just before we were pushed down here, I could see it had a lot of people on it," she replied.

"If they fire on us, they could sink us!" one man said. "If they do, we'll all drown."

"And if we don't then they could kill us all anyway. We've no weapons to defend ourselves with," added another man.

"I'm only fourteen," Daniel McGillis said desperately. "I'm no' ready to die yet!"

"That doesna change with age, laddie," Donald MacDonald replied. "I'm fifty-eight, but I'm no' ready to die yet, either."

The noise from above stopped. It seemed the guns were ready. All that could be heard was the normal creaking of a ship sailing.

John Ostler climbed up the ladder and banged hard on the hatch with his fists.

"What's happening up there?" he shouted. "We can fight with you, if there's a need!"

"To hell with that," one of the Manchester men said in a low voice. "I'm for fighting with the pirates, myself."

A few people laughed, in spite of the tension. John Ostler banged on the hatch again and repeated his words. Everyone listened, but there was no response. Some of the prisoners started praying softly.

"Who's Blackbeard?" Daniel McGillis asked again.

"He's dead now," John Ostler told him. "But he was one of the most evil pirates in the world. My father told me about him. It's said he looked like the devil himself, and if the captain wouldn't surrender, he'd torture him and the crew, and then kill them all. Then he'd ravish—"

"Will ye haud yer wheesht, man?" John Grant interrupted fiercely. "There's ladies on board!"

"Ah. Yes, of course," Ostler said. "They were just stories, anyway. Most likely not true," he finished lamely.

"We'll no' let any harm come to ye, ladies," Grant offered gallantly.

Unless we all drown together, Beth thought. But at least that would be a relatively quick death. Possibly better than being beaten to death by a cruel master or worked to death in the hot sun. She made a decision; if it seemed clear they were going to kill or rape her, she would do her best to jump overboard. She didn't really care about dying, although she felt sorry for the others, who clearly did. At any rate, for the moment there was nothing they could do but wait, and pray.

On deck the sailors were as prepared as they could be. They had six cannons, which were all now in place and ready to fire. Captain Ricky was intently observing the approaching ships through his spyglass. The smaller ship, a sloop, was almost within range.

"Are they hostile, Captain?" Mr Johnson asked, although there were far more men on the sloop than would be needed merely to sail her. As he pondered the implications of that, the larger of the ships, a brig, hoisted a flag, which gave him a definite answer.

"Shit," Captain Ricky said, with great feeling. The flag was red, and in the centre of it was a black skull. He passed his spyglass to Johnson, who raised it to his eye.

"Can we outrun her?" he asked.

"The brig possibly, but not the sloop," Ricky replied. "We're at full speed now, and she's gaining on us." He looked at his men. None of them were experienced fighters. This was a merchant ship. He had only six guns on board, and he had counted twelve on the sloop. He ran quickly through his options. Flight was not one of them, so he could fight, or he could surrender.

If he chose to fight, he would have to completely cripple the sloop before she could damage his ship, which he was unlikely to be able to do. Most likely she would fire chain shot in an attempt to take down the masts. Whether he could sink the sloop or not, unless they escaped unscathed the brig would almost certainly catch them. If he attacked and lost, then, depending on the brutality of the pirates bearing down on him, he could lose ship, crew and cargo, and, alive or dead, be castigated for not surrendering and making the best of it.

On the other hand, if he surrendered without firing a shot there was a much better chance of the crew and human cargo surviving, but then there was the possibility of him being accused of cowardice.

He was no coward, but he was a pragmatist. It might be better to surrender immediately and have a chance of living to negotiate the ransom of the ship and prisoners, than to be remembered posthumously as a stupid hero.

As he was deliberating, the sloop, although still out of range of the *Veteran's* cannon, fired a shot across the bows. It was a bow-chaser; a warning. Several of the sailors cried out, and from the hold below he heard screams, and then more banging on the hatch as the prisoners shouted to be released.

"They missed!" declared Johnson with a mixture of relief and trepidation.

Captain Ricky sighed deeply and made a decision. If even his first mate didn't know what a warning shot was...

"Raise the flag of surrender, Mr Johnson," he said resignedly.

After a few minutes of futile banging on the hatch following the sound of the shot, the prisoners gave up. It was clear that whatever the captain decided, he was not going to trust them to take his side. Which, all things considered, was probably wise, as none of them had any desire to work themselves to death in Antigua, while a good number would be willing to become pirates. After all, they were not exactly worried about falling foul of the law.

It was different for the women, though. They were very aware that whereas the men would probably have two choices; to be killed or given the opportunity to join the pirates, the options for the women were likely to be death or rape, possibly both; although some would probably resign themselves to becoming the pirates' whores, if their lives were spared as a result.

Beth was not one of those women, and Elizabeth Clavering made it clear with her next words that neither was she, and that she believed there might be another alternative.

"There were two women pirates once," she said. "Mary Read and Anne Bonny, they were called. Edmund tellt me about them when we were in prison, once he knew I was going to be transported to the Colonies. He jested that it might be an option for me if I could escape from my employer."

"Many a true word hath been spoken in jest," John Ostler quoted.

"Would you do that? Become a pirate?" Beth asked.

"In a heartbeat. Would ye no' do the same?"

She hadn't considered it, had had no idea that female pirates existed until this moment.

"It would depend on the alternatives," she replied after a minute.

From above their heads came more running and shouting, and then there was a loud bang as the pirate ship apparently collided with theirs, throwing the prisoners against the side of the hold.

"Dear God, have they sailed into us?" one woman asked, when the screams of terror had died down.

"Why would they do that, if they're pirates?" John Ostler asked. "Surely they'd fire at us rather than risk damaging their own ship by ramming us?"

No one answered. None of them had any experience of naval warfare or pirates. All they could do was wait, and try to interpret the noises as best they could. Looking through the tiny air vents was no help, as all the action, whatever it was, was taking place on the other side of the ship.

They all fell silent, not sure whether drawing attention to their presence at this point was a good idea. There came the sound of more footsteps and muffled shouts, and someone fired a pistol, after which there was a cheer and more talking and moving about on deck.

The prisoners were in the middle of a low-voiced discussion as to whether or not they should announce their presence and who they were anyway, just to end the suspense, when suddenly there was the sound of the bolts being drawn back, then the hatch opened. Everyone looked up as a head appeared and then was just as quickly withdrawn. There came an oath uttered in a foreign language followed by retching, then the head reappeared, the nose and mouth covered this time with a handkerchief.

"Bonjour, mesdames et messieurs," the owner of the head said cheerfully, if a little indistinctly. "J'ai le regret de vous informer qu'il y a eu un léger changement de plan, et que vous n'irez pas à Antigua."

The few people who understood French absorbed this, then John Ostler began to translate into English.

"He said that we will not be going to Antigua," Beth said in Gaelic. "He's speaking French."

At this the rest of Mr Ostler's halting translation was drowned out by a rousing cheer from the Gaelic speakers. French! Surely this was good news? After all, the French recognised James Stuart as King of Great Britain, did they not? They were allies!

"Vous êtes écossais?" the man asked, clearly relieved that it appeared part of the cargo could speak French, or understand it a little, at least.

Beth, who happened to be closer to the hatch than John Ostler, looked up at the speaker.

"Some of us are Scots, yes, and the rest are English," she answered in French, "but we are all prisoners because we fought for Prince Charles Edward Stuart."

The man nodded, and disappeared. The hatch remained open. Those who had cheered now reflected that although the pirates spoke French, that did not necessarily mean they had any affection for their native land, if they were outlaws.

"Should we go up?" someone asked after a minute or two.

"Maybe we should wait until they tell us to?"

"Well, they've left the hatch open, so tae hell wi' it," Donald MacDonald said. He started to make his way over to the hatch, but at that moment another head appeared.

"Please, come up," the owner said in heavily accented English.

One by one the prisoners made their way up the wooden ladder, until they were all standing in the blazing sun. They blinked and squinted until their eyes became adjusted to the bright light, and then looked around with interest.

The deck was crowded with men. The *Veteran's* crewmen, including Captain Ricky and Mr Johnson, were standing in a group to one side of the deck. Their hands had been tied behind their backs, and they were being guarded by some of the new occupants of the ship.

The small ship with one mast that Beth had seen earlier was now next to the *Veteran,* secured in place by a number of grappling hooks. That explained the banging and grating noise from earlier. There was still a number of men on the small ship's deck, but the majority of them seemed to have transferred to the *Veteran.* The big ship she'd seen earlier was once more on the distant horizon. Perhaps its presence had just been a coincidence, although Beth doubted it. It was apparent from the lack of artillery fire that

Captain Ricky had surrendered to the pirates without resistance. Surely he wouldn't have surrendered to such a small foe? Although what did she know about naval warfare?

While she was observing the situation, the pirates started to release the grappling hooks in order to free the smaller vessel.

They were an interesting-looking lot. Whereas the now sullen and fearful crew of the *Veteran,* with the exception of the captain and first mate, were dressed in shades of brown, blue and green for the most part, with cream-coloured shirts, many of the pirates were attired in brightly coloured breeches, although in common with the *Veteran* crewmen they were mainly barelegged. They carried cutlasses or hand axes, and round shields reminiscent of the Highland targe, and had pistols thrust through their leather belts. Some of them had scars, some were bare-chested, some wore scarves around their heads, others sported golden earrings. But all of them had two things in common; they were all tanned, their exposed skin a uniform mahogany brown; and they all looked to be experienced fighters.

As the prisoners were taking in the situation, a man who was obviously, by his flamboyant dress, either the captain or a high-ranking officer, came forward, and doffing his tricorn hat made an elaborate courtly bow to the newly liberated Jacobites that Sir Anthony Peters would have been proud of.

"Good day to you. Captain Paul Marsal at your service. I am told," he said, in accented English, "that you are all Jacobite prisoners on your way to Antigua? C'est vrai?"

Beth translated quickly into Gaelic, attracting the attention of the captain.

"This language, it is Scottish, no?" he asked.

"Yes," she replied. "Some of us speak only English, some only Gael...Scottish."

"And you speak all three?"

"Yes."

"Excellent! Then you can be my official translator," Marsal said in French, smiling hugely. "My English is poor, and endeavouring to speak it gives me a headache. I am very grateful for your help, my dear madame." He seized her hand and kissed the back of it in an overblown gesture again reminiscent of Sir Anthony.

In truth, apart from the fact that he wore his own hair, which was brown and tied back with a green ribbon, and his face bore no paint, but was tanned like his crew's, he reminded her of the baronet. Not in looks; where Alex was tall and well-built with slate-blue eyes and regular, handsome features, Paul Marsal was only of medium height, with twinkling brown eyes and a wide mouth that seemed a little too large for his face. But the mannerisms, colourful costume and elaborate gestures all evoked Sir Anthony enough to make Beth's heart clench, and to render her well-disposed to him, even though she had no idea as yet what he was like as a person.

"Are you a pirate, like Blackbeard?" Daniel McGillis blurted out, having observed the heavily armed men with terror. "Are you going to kill us all?"

For a split second Beth contemplated not translating this accurately, but then realised that Marsal certainly spoke some English and probably understood a lot more. Mistranslating the first question asked of him would probably not be wise. She duly translated, and knew she was right when he nodded slightly and smiled at her. Then he adopted a wounded expression and clasped his hand to his heart.

"Pirates! Blackbeard!? You wound me, monsieur!" he declared. "No, no, we are civilised men, operating with our dear country's approval, and have letters of marque to prove it! We have no intention of killing anyone, unless you force us to do so. But I think if you are all followers of the Stuart family then we have much in common, do we not?"

Beth refrained with difficulty from laughing out loud, particularly as she could see Captain Ricky's thunderous facial expression on hearing Marsal's declaration of legality. Clearly he understood French as well. She translated, and was rewarded with looks of relief.

"What do you intend to do with us, sir?" John Ostler asked.

"Well, the first thing I intend to do with you is to enable you all to wash yourselves and your clothes. I'm afraid you really do smell absolutely dreadful," Captain Marsal said. "Now, of course because there are ladies present, it is quite clear that we will have to make some arrangements in order to facilitate this. However before that I think it would be advisable to secure the erstwhile crew of the

Veteran, and what better place to do that than in your previous salubrious accommodations?" He smiled broadly, and after Beth had translated, the Jacobites laughed, their tension draining away as they all started to take the measure of the charismatic Frenchman.

"I object, sir!" Captain Ricky stated. "We surrendered to you of our own free will, to avoid any unpleasantness. You cannot possibly expect us to tolerate such treatment!"

"I am most grateful to you for surrendering, Captain," Marsal replied politely. "It would have been most tiresome if I and my men should have had to resort to violent means. And of course the result of your wise decision is that the fish in the surrounding area will have to seek their food elsewhere today. I am sure that an accommodation that was considered fitting for a hundred and fifty of your countrymen for several weeks will be nothing short of palatial for just twenty-two of you, for two days."

"You cannot expect Mr Johnson and myself to stay down there with the men!" Captain Ricky persisted. "We are gentlemen, sir!"

"As am I, Captain," Marsal said. "But I can hardly expect my men to endure hardships that I am not willing to share with them. I run a democratic ship, sir, and I highly recommend it. Of course tonight I will be making an exception and will occupy your delightful quarters, as you will not be needing them. Escort all of the gentlemen down to the hold, Germain," he continued, gesturing to one of his crewmen.

"Now, let us arrange for you all to wash, to eat, and to make yourselves presentable, after which we will congregate here on deck again later in the afternoon, when the heat is not quite so oppressive for you all. I have been led to believe that your country is cold and wet, so I am sure you will appreciate a lower temperature. Then I will explain to you about your new destination, the beautiful island of Martinique, which we will reach, as I told Captain Ricky just now, in two days, if God is kind." He bowed elaborately to the assembled Jacobites, then turned away. He then issued a series of commands, which were obeyed with an alacrity that made it clear to all that although foppishly dressed and elaborate in gestures and language, Paul Marsal was not a man to be trifled with.

He really *was* like Sir Anthony.

While the men stripped and washed themselves and their clothes on deck, the sixteen females were offered the use of the officers' quarters, where they were given buckets of water, sponges, and soap. One of the men even produced a brush and a comb for them to use. They had to wash their clothes in turns, and in sea water, but they managed to do that and maintain their modesty by half the women washing the clothes of the others out on the deck, while the others washed their bodies and hair in the precious buckets of fresh water they'd been provided with. Then they carefully brushed and combed each other's hair as best they could, killing as many surviving lice as possible. The clothes, spread out on deck under the hot sun dried surprisingly quickly, and within a couple of hours the now clean women were able to perform the same service for the others.

As awkward and inadequate as the washing facilities were, Beth had never appreciated being clean so much in her life.

They assembled on deck again just before sunset, where Captain Marsal informed his much sweeter-smelling, if still ragged audience that Martinique, the island they were to be taken to, belonged to France, and was extremely beautiful, far more beautiful than British-owned Antigua, of course. They were going to Fort Royal, where the island's governor, the Marquis de Caylus lived, an excellent gentleman who was no great lover of King George II, but was a close friend of the Comte de Maurepas, of whom some of them may have heard.

Beth had certainly heard of Maurepas. Alex had told her that it was Maurepas who had authorised the ill-fated ship full of arms and troops *Elisabeth* to sail with Prince Charles when he had travelled to Scotland in July two years previously. If the governor was a friend of the pro-Stuart Comte, surely this boded well for the reception the Jacobites would receive upon landing in Martinique?

Beth told herself that she must not count her chickens before they hatched, but she couldn't stop the thrill of hope that ran through her. Although since her arrest over a year ago she had told herself repeatedly that she did not want to live if Alex was dead, she was young and by nature full of life. It was therefore with a mixed feeling of guilt and exuberance that she realised the future might hold some promise after all. And if she was to have a choice over her future, surely it would be better to make a new life in a country where no one knew her, and where there would be no painful reminders of all she had lost?

* * *

Beth was standing on the deck of the *Veteran*, which she now knew was a brig, as was the ship that had accompanied the *Diamant*, a sloop, when she had appeared over the horizon. Both ships were owned by the man who had given her the information she was now in possession of, and who was standing next to her looking out to sea. They were at the front of the ship, which was named the forecastle or fo'c'sle.

She turned and looked down the length of the ship, which was a hive of activity, and brushed her hair back off her face with her hand. She would be glad when it was long enough to tie back, although if she was going to live for any length of time in this heat, perhaps she would keep it short.

"So," she said, raising her arm and pointing to the left side of the ship, "that is starboard, and the right side is port. And this is the foremast, and the one halfway down the ship is the mainmast."

Captain Marsal clapped his hands in delight.

"Indeed, madame. You are a quick learner. Now, the sails?"

"Er…" Beth was regretting the celebratory glass of brandy she'd just finished, which, having been drunk on an empty stomach, was going to her head rapidly. She should have waited till after she'd eaten dinner, which was being prepared for all the prisoners by Captain Marsal's cook, although they had been warned that at this stage in their journey the fare would not be particularly tasty. The Jacobites didn't care – whatever it was, the fact that it would be eaten in the fresh air would render it palatable. She brought her mind back to the topic in hand; naming parts of a ship.

"Foresail," she said, pointing to the lowest square sail on the nearest mast, "then above that, fore-topsail, then fore-topgallant sail at the top. No thank you," she added to his offer to top up her brandy. She tipped her head to look up at the top of the mast then lowered it again rapidly, swaying as she fought the alcohol-induced dizziness. Captain Marsal put his hand on her arm to steady her.

"Why are they called that?" she asked. "I can understand the mainsail, but why is the second one called the topsail when it isn't?"

"A good question, madame," he answered. His hand was warm and gentle on her arm. "Hundreds of years ago, boats normally had only one sail, so when they added another they thought it was the highest you could go. But once there was the possibility of a third sail, it was believed that only the bravest, or most gallant seamen would have the courage to climb so high. Sometimes there is even a fourth one, and this is called the royal, because normally only the royal standard flies at the top of a ship, when the king is on board. You have a good facility for remembering, my dear madame."

"I had to have," Beth answered, then added before he could ask her why, "Is your brig the same as this one?"

"In many ways," he answered. "Except of course my quarters on *L'Améthyste* are far more tasteful than Captain Ricky's. I have mahogany panelling on the walls, a dresser, comfortable chairs, and a beautiful carved bed with a canopy like so," he made a tent shape with his hands, "made from burgundy silk. I also have a large number of books, and a fine desk. There are several windows as well, so it is very light by day, and cosy and comfortable by night. It is utterly delightful. I would very much like to show it to you when we arrive in Martinique, if you are agreeable."

There was a cool spot on her arm where his hand had been. *He is not Sir Anthony,* she told herself.

"I thought you endured the same conditions as your men," she said. "Do they all sleep in cabins with mahogany panelling?"

Captain Marsal let out a whoop of laughter.

"No, they do not. But were I in the unfortunate Captain Ricky's position, I would not object to sharing the same quarters as my men. When we are planning an expedition, everyone can make suggestions and we make the decision as to where to go together. As the captain, I give the orders once we are underway, and I own the ships. Therefore I have a larger share of any spoils and a nicer place to sleep. But I eat the same food as the other men, and share the same hardships and risks. Any money we make is shared equally, once my share and a payment for any injuries are allowed for. If anyone is killed during an expedition, then his share will go to his family, if he has one."

"It sounds very fair," Beth said.

"And you sound very surprised, if you don't mind me saying so, madame."

"I *am* surprised," she admitted.

"The life of a privateer is often much better than that of a regular seaman," Captain Marsal said. "It is a dangerous life, but an adventurous one. The risks can be great, but the rewards also. But I think you know about adventure and danger, or else you would not be here."

She nodded.

"Yes. So will you return to *Le Diamant* tomorrow?" she asked.

"No, I will stay on board the *Veteran* until we make land," he said. "I will stay in the captain's quarters, as is expected of me. The Scottish and English gentlemen will sleep on the decks. I'm afraid we cannot accommodate them more luxuriously, but I do not think they will object. The ladies of course cannot be expected to sleep on deck. You will all sleep in the great cabin, which is next to the captain's sleeping cabin, and is spacious enough for all of you to sleep in comfort. I regret there are no mattresses, but there is a fine carpet to lie on. I hope you will find it acceptable after your previous accommodations."

Beth looked up at him and smiled. "If we had to all sleep standing on the deck, it would still be better than being down in that awful place," she said.

He raised his hands in horror.

"My dear madame," he cried. "I would never allow ladies to endure such a night, or to sleep in the same room as strangers of the opposite gender! I cannot imagine what Captain Ricky was thinking, to force respectable ladies to endure such conditions."

"I don't think Captain Ricky considers Jacobite prisoners to be respectable, Captain Marsal, any more than he considers you to be. We are traitors in his mind."

Captain Marsal smiled broadly.

"And we are pirates. And yet all of my men are gentlemen, you may be assured of that, and all of you are merely fighting for the rightful monarch to be restored to his kingdom. That is respectable to me."

"You are very kind, Captain Marsal."

"Please," he said, "call me Paul. We are friends, *non*? Or at least I hope we shall be."

Friends. Yes. He seemed to be a kind man, although he must also be a ruthless one. But ruthless men could be kind, as she knew from experience.

"Yes," she said on impulse. "Yes, I hope we can be friends. My name is Beth."

"You honour me, my dear Beth," he said, bowing deeply. His tone was one of complete sincerity. Beth felt the lump in her throat, and blinked back the tears that threatened. *It's the brandy,* she told herself. *It's making me sentimental. He is nothing like Alex.*

They stood in companionable silence for a time, leaning on the rail watching the sun go down. The sunset was very different here than in Britain. In Britain it stayed light for quite some time after the sun had set, but here it was completely dark thirty minutes after the sun had quenched itself in the ocean.

"You would be most welcome to share my cabin, my dear," Paul Marsal said softly, "and my life. I think it is one to which you would be suited."

Beth turned her head to look at him. He was still gazing out to sea. Although it was now almost dark, someone had lit a lantern and hung it from the rail, and by its light she could make out his profile, strong, masculine. Then he turned to face her and the light falling full on his face revealed an expression of the utmost sadness and longing.

He is lonely, she thought. She was lonely too. For a moment, just one weak moment, she was tempted.

He was not Sir Anthony, or Alex.

"I am sorry, Paul," she said gently. "It sounds like an interesting life, but I cannot share it with you. I am married."

His expression changed immediately.

"I am sorry, madame. Had I known, I would never…"

She placed her hand on his arm, silencing him.

"No, please don't apologise. I am not offended. And I am still Beth."

He smiled and placed his hand over hers, which was still resting on his arm.

"Your husband, is he also a prisoner?"

She could not lie to him. He was a gentleman, and had bared a part of his soul to her.

"I don't know. I don't think so," she replied. "In truth, I believe him to be dead. I was taken at Culloden, and have heard nothing of him since. If he lived, he would have found a way to let me know."

"You love him," Paul said, and it was a statement, not a question.

"I will always love him, dead or alive," she replied. "I will never take another man, as a lover or a husband."

"Your husband was a fortunate man, to have experienced such love," Paul Marsal said.

"And I was a fortunate woman," she said. "I do not know if I would be a good privateer."

"It is true that few women take to the life," he admitted. "But there have been some."

"Mary Read and Anne Bonny."

"I am impressed! How do you know of these ladies?"

"One of the other women told me about them," Beth said. A sudden idea struck her. "You should meet her. She is an interesting woman, and very spirited. I think you would like her. When we were all in the hold and we had no notion of what was happening, one of the men said you might be pirates. Elizabeth said her husband had told her about the women pirates, and that she would become one in a heartbeat if it meant she could be free."

"Ah. But you say she is also married," he replied.

"Her husband was executed as a traitor."

"Oh. I am sorry," he replied automatically, but his face was not sad. She had guessed right. He was lonely, and although he was attracted to her beauty he was not averse to considering another woman, if he found her interesting. Elizabeth Clavering was interesting. And spirited, and intelligent.

"You must meet her," Beth said. "I think you will like her. She cannot speak French, but she has English, and I can translate for you, at first, anyway. And you can speak some English, I think?"

"Yes, I can," he replied. "Although I do not like to, because I cannot express myself as well as I can in my own tongue. And of course my translator is so beautiful, how could I refuse her services when they were offered?" He patted her hand, and then released it. She removed it from his arm. "I would be delighted to make the acquaintance of your friend," he said, "after dinner. For now, let us enjoy together the comparative coolness of the evening and the sea breeze."

They stood next to each other, gazing out into the inky darkness of the night, lit only by the light of a million glittering stars and the soft yellow glow of the ship's lantern, feeling the warm sea air soft on their faces and listening to the murmur of voices on the ship, the lilting Gaelic of the Highlanders, the flatter sounds of the northern Englishmen, and the romantic-sounding French mingling together.

Whatever happened when she reached Martinique, right now Beth felt relaxed and free, and as near to happy as she could feel without Alex by her side.

That was enough for now.

CHAPTER THREE

Beth was sitting on a bench under a frangipani tree in the garden of the governor of Martinique's house, waiting for the carriage that would take her to her new life to arrive. It was difficult to believe that only ten days ago she had been lying on wooden boards in a vermin-infested hold with a hundred and forty-nine other people on their way to a life of indentured servitude, or more accurately, slavery.

Now she was wearing a dress of rose-coloured silk with matching slippers, her skin was clean and perfumed and her hair was shining and free of lice. And, more important than that, more important than anything, for the first time in over a year she was truly free.

Her first impression of her new home, as she had stood with all the other passengers on deck watching Port Royal come into view had been that it was the most beautiful place she had ever seen, and the most foreign. Nothing about it reminded her of her homeland, which she considered a blessing. The sea, at home normally grey, or on rare glorious days blue-grey, was here an almost impossible royal blue colour shading to bright turquoise as it drew near to the shore. The sky was also the shade of blue only seen on perfect summer days in Britain. Port Royal, where they were coming in to land, was dominated by its huge fort, Fort St Louis, which stood on a rocky peninsula surrounded by a high and very impressive wall.

Behind the town thickly wooded vibrant green slopes stretched into the distance, and closer to the shore palm trees, of which she had heard but never seen, waved as if welcoming the strangers.

Once off the ship the Jacobites had crowded together on the shore, rendered speechless by the sheer strangeness of it all. Everything was different; the language, the people, whose skin colour came in all shades from ivory through to ebony, the trees, buildings, flowers, weather…there was nothing at all to remind them of home. Everything seemed impossibly bright, vibrant, somehow *more*.

Well, except the clothes. Beth sighed. It seemed ridiculous to her that the white Creole inhabitants of Martinique insisted on wearing European fashions, in spite of the heat. Wearing shift, stays, petticoats, dress, fichu and stockings in the cool English climate could render one uncomfortably warm, but in this heat it was almost a torture.

She flicked open her fan and waved it in front of her face for a few minutes, then gave up. The effort of moving hot air around her head was actually making her warmer than just enduring it would. Even in the shade she was hot, and the heady scent of the frangipani blossoms, wonderful when perfuming a room, was cloying when you were sitting directly underneath the source, sweating freely. She hoped that once she was out of the town people would embrace a more practical attitude to clothing.

Captain Marsal, seemingly oblivious to the heat in spite of wearing breeches and frockcoat of emerald-green velvet and sporting an elaborate powdered wig topped by his tricorn hat, had led the prisoners from the dock, setting a brisk pace along the road to the governor's mansion.

"I sent a message ahead on *Le Diamant* to advise him of our imminent arrival," Paul had explained to Beth as they walked, "and he told us to proceed directly to his house once we docked."

The governor, Charles de Tubières, Marquis de Caylus, came out to meet them all on the spreading, immaculately cut lawn in front of his house. Captain Marsal, tucking Beth's hand neatly under his arm and retaining it when she would have stopped, led her straight up to the governor and bowed deeply. Beth curtseyed.

"Monsieur le Marquis," Paul began, "these are the unfortunate prisoners I informed you of in my letter and this beautiful young lady has kindly acted as my official translator, as she is fluent in

French, English, and Scottish. She has been invaluable to me, and I trust you will make use of her services as well."

The marquis, a slender middle-aged man with a weatherbeaten countenance, eyed her appreciatively.

"Are you agreeable to that suggestion, madame?" he asked.

"I would be honoured to assist in any way I can, Monsieur le Marquis," Beth agreed.

It had been a clever and kind move by the captain, as a result of which, while the rest of the Jacobites had been accommodated all over town in lodgings which ranged from comfortable to barely habitable, Beth had found herself in a beautiful and luxurious apartment in the governor's house itself, where she had lived for the last ten days.

After a warm, jasmine-scented bath into which Beth had sunk in a bliss that was almost delirious, she had been served with a meal that would not have been out of place at the court of King Louis himself, following which a maid had assisted her to dress in a pale green gown borrowed from the marquis' housekeeper. She had then been directed down a sweeping staircase into the governor's office.

"Ah, Madame Cunningham!" he exclaimed. "Please, sit down. I see Paulette's gown is a little generous for your delicate proportions. I will arrange for a dressmaker to visit you tomorrow. Are you feeling refreshed?"

Beth sat down on the solid mahogany chair indicated and looked around with appreciation.

"I am. Thank you, monsieur. Your house is very beautiful. It reminds me of Versailles."

It did. Her own room was painted in pale yellow with white mouldings, the furniture gilded, the cushions covered in cream silk brocade. This room was equally luxurious but decorated in more masculine shades of deep blue, with dark wood furniture. A large mirror hung over the marble fireplace. Beth wondered if there was ever any need to light a fire in its hearth. Behind the governor stood a black man in green livery, while another stood by the door, having opened it for her to enter and closed it behind her.

"You have visited Versailles, Madame Cunningham?" the marquis asked. "Did you take a tour?"

Damn. But it didn't matter. It was common knowledge that she had been there. Regardless of what the marquis intended to do with her and her fellow Jacobites, there was no harm in talking about her time at Versailles.

"Yes, monsieur. My husband and I travelled in Europe after our wedding, and took a tour of the palace. But then we had the great honour of being invited to a soirée by His Majesty King Louis himself. It was most interesting."

"There is a John Cunningham listed amongst the passengers," the marquis said, looking down at a paper on his desk. "Is he then…?"

"Ah. No," Beth answered. "I didn't know there was someone else of the same name on board. No, he is no relation. Cunningham was my name before I married, and I am the only supporter of the Stuarts in my family. My husband was Sir Anthony Peters. I believe him to be dead now, monsieur."

"Sir Anthony Peters?" the marquis repeated, clearly surprised.

"You knew him?" Beth asked, thinking rapidly. She must be very careful now.

"Not personally, no. But everyone knew of Sir Anthony. He was the talk of Paris. Maurepas told me of him. He challenged the king's servant, Monsieur Monselle to a duel, did he not, and accidentally killed him?"

"He did, yes," Beth replied neutrally. It was impossible to tell from the marquis' expression whether he was impressed or appalled by the fact that the baronet had skewered the king's panderer. "It was quite ridiculous. Monsieur Monselle and myself had a shared interest in the poetry of John Milton, and Anthony misinterpreted an innocent friendship. He challenged Monsieur Monselle in a fit of jealous rage. It was most uncharacteristic of him."

"So I heard," the marquis replied, which confirmed to Beth that he had been told Sir Anthony was ineffectual, at the very least. "Well, I must say, Lady Peters, that although I am sure your friendship was purely platonic, Monselle was not a…shall we say, a man of good character? If I was married to a lady as beautiful as yourself, I too would be jealous if such a man occupied your time. But you said Sir Anthony is no longer with us? My condolences, my lady."

"Thank you," Beth said politely. She needed to change the subject, quickly. "If it is not impertinent of me, may I ask if you have reached a decision regarding the fate of myself and my fellow passengers?"

"Of course, that must be your primary concern right now. I have heard of the appalling way those who fought for Prince Charles Edward have been treated by the Duke of Cumberland and his men, and I will not add to your ordeal by prolonging my deliberations. In view of the regard in which King Louis holds King James and his son, there is really only one decision I can make, and that is to treat you all in the same way as you would have been had you sailed to France itself. Tomorrow I intend, with your help as my translator of course, to inform all of you that you are no longer prisoners. You are free."

On hearing this news Beth burst into tears, to her utter embarrassment and horror.

The marquis stood immediately and waved to the servant to bring some wine.

"My dear Lady Peters," he said. "Please, do not distress yourself. I assure you, it is the last thing I wished to do."

He offered her his handkerchief, which she took, wiping away her tears with impatience. The surge of relief, following hard on the reminder of Alex killing Henri, had caught her unawares. She fought to control herself, with some success.

"I am sorry, monsieur," she said, once she could speak. "I am far from distressed. It is just…after two years in prison, I can hardly believe it. It was a little too much for me."

The servant returned with the wine and poured a glass for her, which she accepted gratefully. She sipped at it, taking the opportunity to pull her temporarily scattered thoughts together.

"Won't the British demand our return, once they know where we are?" she asked after a time.

"Possibly. Probably. But I am a man of my word. Once a promise is made, it cannot be retracted. I am sure the British will understand."

He smiled in a way that told Beth he was really looking forward to making the British 'understand'. At that moment she was almost in love with him.

The following morning when the marquis told the assembled crowd of Scots and English, in slightly more formal terms than he had used to Beth, that he was giving them their freedom, he got the same reaction from the majority of them as he had from her the previous evening. This time, however, he was a little more prepared for it and allowed them some time to absorb that they were not about to be sent back to Britain, or on to Antigua, or held in prison here until the British authorities decided what was to be done with them.

Free. They were free to do whatever they wanted. They were all free.

"Now," he said, once they were all capable of listening to him again, "I am aware that you will need a little time to decide what you wish to do, and I will of course arrange for your accommodation in the meantime, and for you all to have food and clothing and a small allowance. I think some of you may decide to go to France, where many of your fellow compatriots are. If you wish to do this, I will happily arrange passage for you, either to France or to anywhere else you may wish to go. I cannot recommend that you return to your native land. But of course it would be your own choice. If you choose to remain in Martinique, then we will see if employment can be found for you. Most of you, I see by the ship's list, have a useful trade. But you do not need to decide today, of course. You are all emotional and need time to take in this information, and to celebrate, I think."

They had celebrated en masse that evening. They had spent over four weeks cooped up in a tiny hold, starving and despairing, and regardless of personality and cultural differences had formed a close bond based on their shared plight. Now they spent one night in the streets and inns of Port Royal, and in spite of the fact that every one of them got roaring drunk, the combination of shared despair followed by shared elation ensured that the only injuries sustained during the evening were due to walking into furniture and falling over due to excessive consumption of alcohol.

Captain Marsal and much of his crew joined the ecstatic throng in their celebrations, the captain being conveyed along the main street atop the shoulders of several of the ex-prisoners. Once back on his own feet he sought and found Beth, who, though having initially vowed to remain sober, was already on her third glass of tafia. She had watered it down, aware that having drunk very little in the last two years her tolerance for alcohol was not what it had been in the past.

"Ah! Lady Peters! I wished to speak with you before we all become too...happy," he announced, bowing with his customary elaborate gesture. He had spoken about her with the governor, then.

"I am still Beth," she replied.

"As you wish. I would like to have met Sir Anthony. He seems to have been an interesting man."

"He was," she agreed, "as are you. It was very kind of you to introduce me to the marquis personally. My accommodations are very luxurious as a result."

"We are friends, Beth, and friends help each other, do they not? I also wanted to thank you for introducing me to the delightful Madame Clavering."

"You are getting to know each other then, in spite of the language difficulties?" she asked. The night they had met, Beth had spent approximately half an hour translating between the two of them before the captain had decided his English, poor as he declared it to be, was adequate to the occasion. Beth, smiling, had left the two of them together.

"We are. You were right, she is a most spirited lady, and a delightful one. And she has kindly agreed to accompany me on my next venture in order to ascertain if she could take to the life." Although he attempted nonchalance his eyes were sparkling, and as she looked up at him he smiled broadly.

"Oh, that's wonderful!" she said, embracing him impulsively. He wrapped his arms around her and was whispering, "Thank you," in her ear when the reason for their embrace appeared behind them.

"So, I leave ye alone for ten minutes and find ye in the arms of another!" Elizabeth said.

Paul pushed Beth away as though indeed guilty and was trying to formulate an explanation in English, when Beth spoke.

"Well, if you leave a handsome and dangerous man, and a Frenchman at that, alone in a street full of free and tipsy women, you've only yourself to blame!"

"Free. Aye, there's a word I didna think to hear in a long time," Elizabeth said, her feigned jealousy forgotten. "Wonderful, is it no'?"

Captain Marsal visibly relaxed as the two women embraced. He really needed to learn about British humour.

"I believe you're going to become a pirate," Beth said once they'd released each other.

"Privateer," Paul Marsal said automatically.

"Of course. A privateer," Beth amended.

"Aye, why no'? I must admit, I've developed a taste for adventure over the last years," Elizabeth said. "I canna really see myself going back to sewing shirts in a wee bothy somewhere, wi' the only highlight a monthly visit to the market. Can you?"

Could she? That was the problem Beth had mulled over in her mind for the next few days while she had gone through the motions of translating for the other Jacobites as they sorted out all the paperwork and administration needed to find jobs in Martinique, or to arrange passage to France.

Each afternoon she ran an impromptu French class on the shady porch of the governor's timber-framed, white-painted house, where she tried to instil basic French vocabulary in all those willing to learn, whilst they drank fresh lemonade and slaves fanned them with huge leaves.

She also attended mass every day while she was staying in the marquis' house. In Britain she had only been able to go to mass a few times a year, due to a combination of the fact that she'd had to keep her faith hidden from her family, and that there were punitive laws in place regarding public worship for Roman Catholics. Here she had no such restriction, and it felt wonderful to sit in the quiet, peaceful church listening to the soothing tones of the Latin service. Every day she lit candles, one for Alex and one for the rest of the MacGregors and MacDonalds. She had no idea how many of them were alive, and what their lives were now like, but it comforted her to pray for them.

During dinner, which she took with the marquis, he regaled her with stories of his eventful life as a commander in the French Navy. He was an excellent raconteur, and she listened with fascination as he told her about the time he had been attacked by the British in the dead of night as he passed the Straits of Gibraltar. He had had only three ships to their four, but had nevertheless prevailed.

"It was ungentlemanly of them, because we were not at war at the time, you know," he explained. "They gave the excuse that they did not know our nationality, which was ludicrous as we were openly flying our colours. I think they expected it to be an easy conquest, but in the end we sent them scuttling away with their tails between their legs, and crippled one of their ships in the process – broke the mast, you know."

"It must have been terrifying for the men, to be attacked in the middle of the night," Beth said, thinking of how frightened they had all been when down in the hold wondering what was happening above.

"Perhaps. But it also gave me an opportunity to get the measure of my crew. You can only tell the real worth of a man when he is under pressure. It was a valuable lesson for all of us."

"Do you miss those days, wish you were still commanding a fleet?" she asked, her mind still pondering Elizabeth's words of a few days ago, and wondering if it was possible to settle for a quiet life once you'd experienced an adventurous one.

The marquis sat and thought for a minute.

"Sometimes," he admitted finally. "And sometimes I regret not marrying and having a family too. But you know, it is not possible to do everything in one life. One must take the opportunities when they arise, as I did when offered the governorship of this beautiful island. And one must also accept when it is time to make way for a younger man. I am nearly fifty. And I am content."

The marquis waved his arm and his servants, or slaves, Beth was not sure which they were, came to clear the dishes. Beth accepted a brandy and they adjourned to the salon.

"I have a proposal for you, Lady Peters, which might suit you. I have an acquaintance, a Monsieur Delisle, who owns a sugar plantation on the windward side of the island near Sainte Marie. They have recently lost a child, and Madame Delisle is feeling a little low in spirits. She was in Paris for a time, but now she has returned she is not settling in well here. Her husband thinks it might lift her mood to have a companion, someone vivacious and intelligent who can help her to readjust to her life here. And of course I thought of you."

"I am not sure I could help anyone adjust to the life here, monsieur," Beth said. "After all, I have yet to adjust to it myself."

"That is true. But you have an enthusiasm and a zest for life that is most beguiling. You are not one to mope about the past, I think. You look forward. I think you might be able to encourage Madame Delisle to take the same attitude, and so embrace your life here together, as it were."

Beth was thankful that he had not seen her standing by the window of her bedroom at night, gazing at the moon and wondering if Graeme, Jane and Thomas, Sarah or any of the MacGregors were also looking skyward and thinking of her. Missing her, as she was missing them so dreadfully.

But he was right. She could not go home; it was too dangerous, for her and for those she loved. She had to make a new life. Why not here? She was tired of adventure, of continuously having to be alert for danger, of never knowing if she would see the sun rise on another morning.

"You do not have to decide now," the marquis said, taking her silence for reluctance. "I only received his letter today. He will not expect me to reply immediately. And you are most welcome to stay here for as long as you please."

He was being kind, she knew that, but she could not stay for long in the house of a bachelor without exciting gossip. And he was a devout man, a man of high morals and very high standing in the community.

"If you do choose to accept, I think you will be happy in Martinique. The people are very friendly and welcoming. And Monsieur Delisle will give you a handsome allowance, as befits your station as a member of the English nobility," the marquis added.

"Rather than as an ex-convict," Beth said drily.

"My dear Lady Peters, you must not think of yourself as such. It is no crime to assist in the restoration of a king to his rightful place."

"I do not think the British Government or my family see it that way, monsieur," she said. "To them I am a traitor."

"Did you ever declare allegiance to the Elector of Hanover?" the marquis asked.

"No," Beth replied. *But I did lie to him, and to his son, and to the whole of the nobility that you feel I belong to.*

"Well then," said the marquis, "you cannot betray someone you have never paid allegiance to."

"You are very kind, monsieur. And in return I must be honest with you before I accept your friend's offer. I am not a member of the English nobility. My father was the second son of a lord, that is true. His brother inherited the title, and the family turned against my father when he married my mother, who was a Scottish seamstress. My husband was not really called Sir Anthony Peters; nor was he a baronet. It was an assumed identity. That is common knowledge in England. His true identity is unknown to the authorities, and I will never divulge it to anyone. And that is why I was transported, when real ladies were not. If your friend still wants me to be his wife's companion when he knows the truth, then I will accept. But I cannot accept a salary commensurate with that of a lady, under false pretences."

The marquis smiled at her.

"My dear, there is more to nobility than a mere title. You are the granddaughter of a lord, therefore you are of noble birth. You display excellent manners, are learned, intelligent, and clearly at home in all echelons of society. Regardless of your family's or your country's opinion, you are well-bred and principled. I cannot think of anyone more worthy of the title 'Lady' than yourself, although I could name a good many who claim such a title with far less justification. But if it makes you feel at ease, then I will tell Monsieur Delisle what you have just told me. If you wish to accept his offer, of course. Please, take the time you need to consider."

"I don't need any time, monsieur. If you consider me to be suitable for the position, I would be honoured to accept your friend's kind offer."

There. It was done. Now there was no going back, no point in spending nights staring at the moon and yearning to sail back to her friends in Manchester or her family in Scotland. She was sick of danger. It was time to move on, to embrace a new life. She was ready to do so.

On Monday the marquis had called her into his study to advise her that Monsieur Delisle had written back to say that he was delighted she had accepted, and that he would send a carriage for her on Wednesday, if that was not too soon.

"No," Beth said. "I think the sooner I embrace my new life the better, although I will miss the others who came with me. But they will soon be moving on to new lives too."

"Indeed they will," said the marquis. "Ten of the men have asked to go to France and will embark in due course. I suspect more will follow. But many have decided to stay here, so I think you will perhaps be able to visit each other, or at least communicate from time to time with them. I will provide you with their addresses once they are settled, if you are agreeable."

"That would be wonderful! And of course you can give them my address too, if you would be so kind."

The marquis nodded assent.

"You might also like to know that the good Captain Ricky has already embarked for Britain with the unfortunate news about his ship. I trust he will not be treated harshly. He really had no option but to surrender, in view of the odds. And I am writing a letter to the Duke of Newcastle to give him the names of those who sadly did not survive the passage, so he may inform their loved ones."

"I doubt he will condescend to perform such a service, but it is kind of you to think of it, monsieur," Beth said. He really was a lovely man. Living in a colony governed by such a kind man could surely only be a positive experience, a peaceful one. She was ready for some peace.

"I will leave you to gather your things together. Are your dresses ready?" he asked.

"Yes. If you will be so kind as to inform me of the cost, I will of course repay you once I receive my allowance from Monsieur Delisle," Beth said.

The marquis looked shocked.

"You will do no such thing, madame!" he said. "Consider the gowns a small remuneration for your services as a translator, and for listening patiently to an old man reliving his youth."

She laughed.

"Your tales were fascinating. I thoroughly enjoyed them, and you are far from old," she said with absolute honesty. She turned and made to leave the room, but then stopped at the door.

"Monsieur le Marquis, may I ask one more small thing of you?

It may seem a little surprising, but I would be obliged if you would perform it."

"Anything, madame."

She told him her request, and although it did seem a little surprising, once she had assured him she was certain of her decision he agreed to acquiesce to it.

Now she sat waiting, and hoping she had done the right thing. She could have requested to go to France, and have thrown herself on the mercy of King Louis, but she was unwilling to put herself in the debt of anyone who wanted to seduce her. Her facial scar had not disfigured her as she had hoped it would, and was now merely a fine red line running from the corner of her left eye across her temple before disappearing into her hair, which had grown over it. Soon, she had been told, it would fade to silver and be almost invisible. There would be too many painful reminders at the court of King Louis anyway. No, she had made the right decision.

She heard the sound of horses' hooves and wheels coming along the drive, and, standing, moved forward out of the shade of the frangipani tree to embrace her new life.

* * *

Although she had resolved to absorb every minute of the journey to Sainte Marie, she had travelled no more than a mile along the road, which was lined with a vast profusion of tropical foliage, all of it strange to her, when the heat combined with the rocking motion of the coach and her fitful sleep of the night before lulled her into a profound slumber that lasted almost the whole duration of the journey.

At first when she woke she had no idea where she was, and gazed muzzily out of the window at the drive along which they were travelling, which was lined on both sides by tall trees casting a dappled shade along the driveway. She shook her head to clear it, then took a drink from the flask of ale that the marquis' cook had provided for her. It was warm, but it quenched her thirst. The air was full of a sweet cloying scent, and she wondered what kind of trees edged the drive that smelt so strongly.

The house itself as they pulled up outside it was lovely. Two storeys high, built of stone and wood with a wide-hipped roof shading the deep wraparound porch, and surrounded by a beautiful garden full of brightly blooming shrubs, it looked very inviting. As the carriage came to a halt, several servants came out of the house to unload and carry her baggage and escort her inside.

"The master bids you welcome, madame," a young black man in full European livery said to her as he led her up the stairs and inside the house. "The mistress is indisposed at the moment, but hopes to join you for supper. The master is expected home at any time, but told me to show you to your room and to bring you anything you want."

"Thank you," Beth said, looking round with interest. She had expected to be taken into a hallway with doors leading off it to various rooms as in England, but instead she found herself immediately in the salon, which was furnished in European style with ornately carved and gilded furniture. The ground floor of the house had no interior walls, the only separation between one area and another being waist-high screens supported by thin wooden pillars. From where she was standing she could see the dining room, one end of the huge mahogany table already set for three, with a centrepiece of bright red and purple flowers.

She pulled her attention back to the hovering footman, and smiled.

"I'm sorry," she said. "Everything is new to me, and I forgot my manners. I am Beth, and your name…?"

The footman looked distinctly taken aback, but recovered quickly. He bowed.

"I am Raymond, madame, and this," pointing to a young woman who had just come running into the room, "is Eulalie, who will show you to your room and ensure that you have everything you need. We will inform you when the master returns."

"Thank you, Raymond. Can you tell me the name of the trees that are planted along the driveway?"

"Yes, madame. They are tamarind trees."

"Tamarind." It was a new word to her. "They have a very strong sweet scent." In fact it was so strong that she could still smell it in the house.

The footman looked puzzled for a moment, and then he smiled.

"Ah! No, madame, I think it is the sugar cane that you can smell. They burnt the fields this morning ready for cutting tomorrow. You will get used to it in time, I think. It is everywhere."

Get used to it? God. It was horrible, sickly and nauseating.

"Does it always smell of sugar here?" she asked.

"I suppose it does, madame. I have been here for over twenty years, and I don't notice it any more."

Her bedroom smelt the same. There was no point in opening the window, because the smell was coming from outside. Thankfully the upstairs area *did* have dividing walls, but they were constructed of wooden planks rather than stone as in English houses. The room was dominated by a large, ornately carved mahogany four-poster bed draped with mosquito netting. Her two trunks, both full of clothes provided by the Marquis de Caylus, had been placed at the foot of the bed, and as Beth lifted the lid of one, three women, all dressed in maid's clothes, came in and curtseyed deeply.

"Madame, we are here to put away your clothes and to help you to wash and change. Would you like some refreshment? Lime water, wine?" the elder of the maids asked.

Beth agreed to some lime water, and allowed the maids to get on with their work while she went to the window and looked out. The house was built on a promontory, and gazing into the middle distance she could see various buildings including two windmills, which she supposed were to do with sugar production. Between the garden of the house and the factory buildings were fields and fields of tall swaying plants that must be sugar cane. To the right of her view were some fields that had been cut. And everywhere there were workers, all of them with dark brown skins, most of the men shirtless in spite of the blazing heat, the women in ankle-length dresses with scarves tied round their heads, and all of them working hard. *Monsieur Delisle must be very wealthy,* she thought, *to be able to employ so many workers, including three maids to attend me where one would have done.* In spite of the heat and the sickly smell, she felt a wave of elation wash over her. She was in a strange land, where everything was new and different. There was so much to learn and she had always had a thirst for knowledge.

She had eaten sugar, of course; Lord and Lady Winter had been very partial to elaborate marchpane subtleties at their parties. But she knew nothing about its production. It would be interesting to learn. She wanted to know everything, everything about this island that was to be her home for the rest of her life.

She made a start on her education at supper. Madame Delisle was still indisposed, her husband informed Beth as they sat down together at the dining table to drink coffee and eat small cakes, attended by two servants. He was a small, rather stout man of about forty with dark brown hair and eyes.

"I am sorry that I did not come to Port Royal myself to bring you here, but it is a very busy time on the plantation right now, and I have to be here to ensure everything goes as it should. My dear Antoinette is unfortunately prone to megrims, which can incapacitate her for two or three days at a time," Monsieur Delisle informed Beth. "She is most upset to be too unwell to welcome you, but I'm sure you understand."

"Of course," Beth replied. She nibbled at a cake, thinking she had never tasted anything so sweet in her life. At least the Winters' marchpane subtleties had contained a lot of almonds; this seemed to be made of pure sugar.

"My wife is of a delicate constitution at the moment. We buried our son only a few months ago, and she seems to have taken his death very badly," her host continued.

"Yes, Monsieur le Marquis told me. I was very sorry to hear it," Beth said. "How awful for you."

"Yes. He was our sixth child to pass in as many years. The climate, you know, it is not healthful for babies. I have assured Antoinette that the next time she is…ah…" he coughed delicately, "I will ensure that she returns to France for the birth, and stays until the child is robust enough to endure our climate."

"I know nothing at all of this country, monsieur," Beth said, somewhat alarmed. It was certainly normal for one or two babies from a large family to die in infancy, but six in six years? And with such obviously privileged parents? "I don't even know exactly where I am in the world!"

"Oh, we can remedy that," he replied happily. "When we have eaten, if you would care to step into my study, I have a map which will show you exactly where you are! Yes, Martinique is most beautiful, and I would not live anywhere else in the world. I have lived here since I was born and it is my home, as I hope it will become yours. My wife was born in Paris and has found it difficult to acclimatise to the tropical climate.

"I had hoped the sojourn to Paris after Jean's death would have helped her to come to terms with it, but alas, it does not seem to be the case. Perhaps you will be able to help her see the beauty of this island. It is full of treasures, which it will be my delight to show you if you are interested. But there are also dangers, many miasmas which flourish in the heat. Of course there is poison, although we have had no trouble in that quarter for a time. And then there are the snakes…do you have snakes in England, Lady Peters?"

"Please, monsieur, call me Beth. It's the name I prefer. Yes, we have grass snakes and vipers, but I have never seen one. They are not common."

"Then you must call me Pierre, and I will tell you immediately about our viper, for it is very poisonous. It only comes out in the evenings and is quite shy, so you should not have a problem, but its bite can be deadly, so you must take care if you walk out in the evenings, and you must not go into the fields after dark. They are more of a problem for the slaves, as are chiggers, little insects which get into the feet and can cause infection. I have lost three slaves this year to viper bites, which is very costly. But of course you will not have a problem with chiggers unless you delight in walking barefoot!" He laughed, and Beth resolved never to walk anywhere without shoes. "My apologies. I do not wish to frighten you on your first day! Come, I will show you where you are in the world, and then if you wish we can sit on the porch for a short time and enjoy the cool evening air, if you are not too tired."

"No," she said. "I slept in the carriage for most of the journey."

She followed her host out of the main house and into a smaller adjoining building, which formed his office. It contained a large desk, currently strewn with papers, sturdy wooden chairs unlike the spindly-legged gilded ones in the dining room, a bookcase and several chests of drawers. Pierre Delisle turned to her and smiled, revealing a set of somewhat blackened teeth, and pointed to the wall with a hand that seemed incongruous with the rest of him, being very slender, almost feminine.

"There, madame…my apologies…Beth, is a map of our part of the world. Here we are," he said, indicating a speck about halfway down a small crescent of specks surrounded by sea.

"But it's tiny!" she said, surprised.

"Yes, we are small, only seventy-five thousand people," he agreed, "and of those, perhaps only fifteen thousand are civilised, but nevertheless Martinique is very important, a large source of income for His Majesty. We produce maybe thirty per cent of the world's sugar," he added proudly. "Here, you see," he pointed to another speck, a little higher up on the map, "is Antigua, your original destination and at the moment a British colony, but who knows in the future, eh? Likewise here," he tapped his finger on a huge landmass above and to the left, "are the American Colonies, also British at the moment."

Beth looked at the map with interest, running her finger down the coastline of North America. "My grandmother was transported here," she said softly.

"Really? Where? Was she with Prince Charles as well?"

"Oh no," Beth said. "She is over eighty now. No, it was a very long time ago. But I don't know which part she was sent to. Your plantation is very beautiful, Pierre. I saw some of it from my window earlier."

"Yes, I have three hundred acres, most of that in sugar, but we also grow much of our food here too, and the slaves have their own plots where they grow food for themselves. You will not have seen from your window, and it is too dark now, but we also have pigs, cows, poultry, and there is a lake which is stocked with fish. Of course we are not far from the ocean either, so we can also enjoy the fruits of the sea."

"How many slaves do you own?" she asked.

"Two hundred in the fields and mill, and another thirty house slaves, although I hope to have more soon. Several of the women are with child and I am praying for their safe delivery. Good slaves are expensive now, more than double the price I paid twenty years ago when I inherited this place from my father. And it is good to have them from birth, in spite of the cost of raising them to an age when they can be useful, because then you can make sure they are not insolent and lazy like many of the negroes brought from Africa are. Some of them are so lazy they will feign illness, even kill themselves rather than do an honest day's work! Luckily at the moment I have an excellent manager who knows how to get the best out of them, but it is a daily struggle."

Beth glanced at Raymond, who was standing by the door in case they should need anything. His face was impassive, his gaze fixed on the wall straight ahead.

"Er…so any children born to slave women belong to you as well?" she asked.

"Indeed. That is why a healthy young woman is so expensive to buy, although I don't know why, as so many of them seem to miscarry their children that they are not worth the price. But I can see I am tiring you, my dear," Monsieur Delisle said, mistaking Beth's shocked countenance for fatigue. "You have had a terrible ordeal in the past weeks and a long journey today, and everything is new to you. That alone can be tiring, particularly for a young lady of gentle birth. We can sit on the porch tomorrow evening, when I hope Antoinette will be well enough to join us. Eulalie will help you to prepare for bed tonight, and then I will assign a suitable negress to be your body servant, with your approval of course." He smiled and raised her hand to his lips. "I will not keep you any longer tonight. Goodnight, my dear."

Once in bed she lay for a long time staring at the heavy net curtains shrouding the bed and protecting her from the mosquitoes which she could hear whining as they flew around the room. Indentured servitude was just another word for slavery. Her grandmother had told her that. Would any children she'd had have belonged to the owner? Was it possible to be so lazy you would rather kill yourself than work? What was it like to watch six of your children die in as many years? And what had Monsieur Delisle meant when he had said there was poison?

It is a new way of life, she told herself fiercely. *Of course it will seem strange to me. The English misunderstand the Highlanders because they don't understand their way of life. I must not judge anyone, either Monsieur Delisle or his workers, until I have learnt about how they live. And I must adjust to that way of life, if I am to be happy.*

She closed her eyes, listened to the unfamiliar sound of the rustling cane, which sounded not unlike waves lapping against the shore, and tried to reconcile the gentle brown eyes and genuine concern of Pierre Delisle for her comfort with his apparently uncaring attitude towards his workforce, until she finally drifted to sleep.

She was awoken early next morning by the clanging of a bell, and sat straight up in bed, instantly wide awake, wondering what was wrong. She listened for a while, but after hearing no sounds from the rest of the house assumed it must be something normal. She got out of bed, and padding over to the window, looked through the slatted blind. It was still dark, although a glow on the distant horizon heralded the imminent rising of the sun. It was already hot and it had rained in the night, which added to the humidity. Even in her thin cotton nightgown she was sweating.

She turned and looked at the clothes for today which had been laid out on the chair for her by Eulalie the previous evening. She sighed. She could not wear all those clothes every day. It was ridiculous expecting people to wear European fashions in this heat. Maybe once she had settled in she could amend her clothing a little. At least she did not need to get dressed until the rest of the household woke.

She waited a while until the sun rose, then after spending a short time working out how to raise the blind, she looked out across the plantation again. The cane fields were a sea of activity, the machetes of the slaves as they cut the cane flashing in the sunlight. A line of mules was being loaded with freshly cut cane, after which they set off in the direction of the cluster of buildings she had noticed the night before. From here Beth couldn't see exactly what they were doing, but she made a resolution to ask Pierre if she could accompany him one day to learn more about sugar production. The bell that had woken her must have been the call to start work.

A little later there came a knock on the door and Eulalie popped her head round it, clearly surprised to see the new madame already up and at the window.

"Good morning, Madame Beth," she said, smiling. "I have brought you some chocolate, and can help you to wash and dress this morning. Monsieur said he will assign a maid for you today."

She came in and bustled round, setting out cups and a chocolate pot on a table in the corner of the room. She poured a cup and brought it to Beth, who accepted it gratefully. "I will go and fetch the water for you to wash, madame," she said, curtseying before disappearing through the door.

Beth sipped the chocolate and grimaced. It was horrible, far too sugary. She couldn't possibly drink it. She got up and put the cup back down on the saucer, then decided to brush her hair while waiting for the water to wash.

When Eulalie reappeared she looked somewhat taken aback that Beth was doing her own hair, but said nothing. She put down the large pail of water, sponge and soap and glanced at the chocolate cup.

"I'm sorry, Eulalie, but I couldn't drink it. I'm not used to so much sugar."

"Could I get you something else, madame? Tea, coffee?"

"Tea would be lovely! But with only a teaspoon of sugar, please. You can have the chocolate if you like it," Beth said.

"Oh no, madame, I'm not allowed to drink chocolate. I'll take it away, and be back in a moment."

By the time she returned five minutes later Beth had washed herself, liberally sprinkled her body with some cologne that had been on the dresser, finished brushing her hair and was already in her shift and stays.

"Ah, thank you!" she said brightly to the maid. "I will need some help tying my laces, I'm afraid. What's wrong?" she asked, seeing the horrified expression on Eulalie's face.

"Nothing, madame," Eulalie replied hastily. "Only…"

"Yes? If I am doing something wrong, Eulalie, you must tell me," she said gently. "I am new to Martinique, and must learn to behave as others do. I'm sure I'll be asking a lot of questions over the next few weeks."

"It's only that it's not normal for white people to wash and dress themselves. I was expecting to wash you and brush your hair, so I was just a little surprised, madame."

"Ah!" Beth said. "But I am perfectly capable, and I'm sure you have a lot of other things to do, especially as looking after me is an extra chore for you right now." She smiled at Eulalie, who smiled back warmly.

"It's no trouble, madame," she said, moving behind Beth and untangling the ribbons of her stays. "In this country the masters and mistresses don't do anything for themselves. That's what we're here for, to do everything so they can be comfortable."

"Everything?" Beth said. "No, I only want one petticoat."

"Everything," Eulalie confirmed. "Are you sure, madame? Madame Antoinette always wears three."

Three? No wonder she's always ill! thought Beth.

"Well, if you don't tell anyone, no one will know," Beth replied, grinning. She looked at Eulalie's costume, a short-sleeved cotton dress and apron. "It's far too hot for three petticoats. In fact if I could, I would rather wear what you are wearing. It's much more practical. Do you think I could have some dresses made up for me?"

"Oh no, madame! You would be the scandal of the island!"

Damn.

Madame Delisle made her first appearance at dinner, which was served at two o'clock at the dining table Beth had seen the previous evening.

The first sight of Antoinette Delisle was something of a shock to Beth. Although her husband was a little stout, Madame Delisle, although extremely pretty, with eyes as blue as Beth's own and light brown hair worn in an elaborate style and heavily powdered, was very overweight. In fact she was the fattest person Beth had ever seen, her numerous chins marring the beauty of her features. Her arms were bare from the elbow and covered in gold bracelets which drew attention to, rather than disguising the rolls of fat at her wrists, and her enormous breasts bulged over the fashionably low-cut bodice of her gown, threatening to spill out at any moment.

Beth greeted her hostess, who apologised for not having been well enough to come down the day before, then sat down at the table, a servant moving forward to push the chair under her. She eyed the bowl of bright orange soup set before her with some interest.

"It's sweet potato," Pierre supplied, noticing her expression. "It is very delicious. I think you will not have tasted it before. I hope you like it, because we eat a lot of it here, in its various forms. It is very versatile."

It was strange, with a slightly sweet, though thankfully not sugary flavour, but it was very pleasant.

"I have found a slave for you who I think will do nicely," Pierre said. "Her name is Rosalie, and she is very clever and quick to learn. She has been begging me for the opportunity to work in the house for some time, so is very grateful. You can meet her later or perhaps tomorrow. Of course if she displeases you, you must tell me immediately and I will set her back to work in the fields."

"I'm sure she'll be fine," Beth said. "Eulalie is very helpful."

"You must be firm with her," Antoinette said between mouthfuls of soup. "You must always be firm with these people, or they take appalling advantage. You are not used to dealing with negroes and they will sense this. You must start as you mean to go on."

"Aren't negroes just like other people?" Beth asked, a little put out.

"Not at all. They are savages, with no morals," she cast a vitriolic glance at her husband, who coloured, "or capacity for reason. The only reason they know is the whip. If you treat them kindly they will murder you in your bed as you sleep."

"That's what they said about my mother," Beth said without thinking, then cursed inwardly.

"Your mother was a negro?" Antoinette asked, eyeing her with profound distaste.

"No," Beth replied, already taking a dislike to this woman whose companion she was to be. This was not a good start. "My mother was from the Highlands of Scotland. The English think of them much as you think of negroes."

"Now, my dear," Pierre jumped in hastily, "you must not alarm our guest, or she will want to leave before she has even settled in! It is true that things are a little different here. I am sure your mother's people are delightful and civilised, but the negro is of a different stamp altogether. They lack intelligence and are incapable of thinking for themselves. They need a firm but kind master. Indeed, that is what they appreciate. And in fact they do very well here – much better than on the British islands, in fact! King Louis, in his divine wisdom, issued a code for the treatment of negroes.

"You will be happy to know that all of them, on arrival in Martinique, are baptised into the faith of Rome and are given religious instruction in Christian ways. It is forbidden for them to work on Sundays, and in fact most of the plantation owners also allow them Saturdays too except at harvest time, when everyone must work as needed. This is not the case on Antigua, for instance, where many negroes are allowed to persist in their heathen, Satanic practices, and where they may be obliged to toil even on the Sabbath! Really, you will discover for yourself that we are all one happy family here!" He beamed at Beth, and smiled tentatively at his wife.

"Some are treated more like family than the family," his wife shot back. The tentative smile disappeared.

"I find your blinds most interesting," Beth said a little desperately. "I have never seen the like before. It took me some time to find out how to raise them this morning."

"Ah! They are Persian blinds!" Pierre responded eagerly, much in the way a starving dog might leap on a bone. "They are most ingenious, are they not? When they are lowered you can use the cord to turn the slats from a vertical to horizontal position, which helps to keep out the heat of the sun whilst letting in enough light for one to read or do other tasks."

The second course, of a fish Beth had never seen before arrived, and she turned her attention to that.

This was not going to be easy.

"He's got two bastards by that negro whore Celie," Antoinette said bluntly later when they had moved from the dining room to the porch, where they were ensconced on bamboo sofas, and supported by several cushions which two slaves had carefully positioned behind Antoinette while Beth had deftly arranged her own. Pierre had escaped with great relief back to his office immediately the dessert plates had been removed, without Beth having had a chance to ask if she could accompany him to the fields the next day. "He thought he could keep it from me, but I'm not stupid. The second brat was born while I was in Paris. When I told him I knew, he had the cheek to suggest that they be brought up in the house!"

"I understand how distressing that must be for you, especially now, after your sad loss," Beth said.

Antoinette looked uncomprehending for a second.

"Ah, yes, of course. We have been very unfortunate. That is just one of the many reasons why I despise this country. I have told him, if he gets me with child again I'm not having it here. Really, the heat is appalling normally, but when you're as big as a house as well…and then for it all to come to nothing when the baby is swept away by some awful miasma. So I told him, if you think you're going to bring up a mulatto bastard to be your heir when you're gone, you can rethink, and that quickly. We'll try again, and as soon as I catch, I'll go to Paris and stay there till the child is old enough to hopefully withstand this damnable place. And then he can have as many bastards as he wants, as long as he leaves me alone and doesn't flaunt them in front of me."

Beth had no idea how to respond to this diatribe, so she sat quietly for a moment. Far from being grief-stricken by the death of her children, Antoinette seemed to consider it merely a nuisance because she was expected to provide more.

"I was hoping to ask Monsieur Delisle if I could ride out with him one day, to learn about the production of sugar, if you do not object," she said finally.

"I don't object, but why ever would you want to do that?" Antoinette asked, genuinely puzzled.

"I thought it would be interesting. I really know nothing about sugar, apart from what it tastes like," Beth said. "I like to learn about new things."

"Well, I'm sure he'll be delighted to regale you with all the tedious details. As long as you don't expect me to come with you."

"I thought perhaps this afternoon we could take a walk round the gardens?" Beth suggested. "There are so many flowers and trees that I have never seen before. I should like to—"

"Damn. Eulalie!" Antoinette shouted suddenly, making Beth jump. "I thought we could sit here for the rest of the day, get to know one another better," she said. "It's really too hot to walk, and if you want to see the flowers I can get one of the negroes to cut some for you and bring them in."

Eulalie rushed out from the house, curtseying and wiping her hands on her apron.

"Yes, madame?" she said.

"I have dropped my handkerchief," Antoinette said, pointing

to the side of the couch. On the floor, a few inches from her pointing finger, was a scrap of cotton and lace. Eulalie bent down and retrieved it, placing it in her mistress's outstretched hand while Beth looked on, aghast.

This was not going to be easy at all.

CHAPTER FOUR

Scotland, late May 1747

Frozen with shock, Angus, along with the rest of the MacGregors watched Alex walk purposefully across the saucer-shaped depression, Richard's blood still dripping from his gore-soaked hand. It wasn't until his brother had disappeared over the edge and was heading down the slope that Angus realised he'd meant what he'd said on emerging from the cave.

"*Mallaichte bas,*" he swore under his breath, before racing to the edge of the depression and looking over it. Alex was striding downhill, careless of the low-growing gorse scratching his legs or the danger of stepping into rabbit holes.

"Alex!" Angus bellowed at the top of his voice. "Stop!"

Although half the clan flinched at the combined volume and desperation of Angus's call, Alex appeared not to hear and continued on his way. Angus hesitated for a moment, then coming to a decision, went after him. As one, the rest of the clan took up a position where they could see what was about to ensue.

Angus caught up with Alex when he was about a quarter of the way down the slope, grabbing his arm to bring him to a halt.

"Alex," he said breathlessly, "Ye canna just go off like that!"

Alex looked at his brother as if seeing him for the first time in his life.

"Did ye no' hear what I said?" he asked. "Beth's alive."

"Richard tellt ye that, did he?"

"Aye." He looked down at the hand that still clutched his shirt. Angus let him go, and he immediately continued on his way.

"He's lying to ye, man! Surely ye ken that? Beth's dead. Maggie saw her shot! It's a trap," Angus said, following behind.

"No," Alex replied. "He knew she'd been shot, in the head, here." He tapped his left temple.

"So do we, but that doesna mean she's alive!" He sped up a little, grasping Alex's arm and bringing him to a halt again. "Maybe someone tellt him. He is her brother, after all!"

"Was," Alex said.

"What?"

"Was. He's dead. Ye need to take him back to the hut and make sure he can be found. I want the Maynard lassie to know she's a widow."

He started to pull away, but this time, instead of releasing him Angus tightened his grip.

"Alex, ye're no' thinking right. Ye canna just go off to England or wherever, like that. That bastard knew ye loved her, and he'd do anything to hurt ye, even if he wouldna live to see it."

Alex turned to face Angus and looked at him properly now, his eyes dark with pain and the remains of his rage against Richard, his mouth hard with determination.

"Angus, I made her a promise. I tellt her I'd come for her. I have to keep it. You can lead the clan while I'm gone. Now let me go. That's an order from your chieftain."

Any other human being, on hearing Alex's tone as he uttered that last sentence, would have obeyed him. When Angus didn't, Alex wrenched his arm free and turned away, intending to carry on down to the lochside.

He managed maybe five paces before Angus ran after him, wrapping his arms round him from behind and dragging them both to the ground, Angus landing on top of his brother, who was face down in the heather.

"And as your brother," Angus said desperately, "I canna let you go. They'll kill ye. I canna let that happen."

Alex's temper exploded immediately and with a strength born of blind rage he succeeded in heaving his brother off his back, and then seeing Angus immediately reaching for him again, hit him full in the face as hard as he could to stop him.

Angus fell backwards for a moment, the force of the blow causing him to see stars, then he threw himself forward again, gripping Alex's legs as he tried to stand and bringing him down in the heather and gorse once more, then punching any part of his body he could reach, desperate to incapacitate Alex enough to stop him dashing off to certain arrest and execution.

Their last serious fight had been over two years before, and Angus had matured considerably since then, both physically and in experience. Both brothers were emotional and determined, and as a result were evenly matched, and what had started as a difference of opinion soon degenerated into a no-holds-barred brawl.

"Christ," Graeme said after a few minutes of watching the vicious fight taking place on the hillside below. "Are you just going to let them carry on until one of them kills the other?"

"No, they dinna intend to kill each other. If that was their intention, they'd hae drawn their dirks by now," Alasdair pointed out matter-of-factly.

Graeme watched as Angus managed to struggle to his feet briefly, his face a mask of red; he aimed a vicious kick at the supine Alex which contacted with enough force to make the chieftain's whole body jerk in pain. Then Alex caught Angus's foot as he took aim again and twisted it hard enough to have broken his ankle had he not gone with the blow and fallen. A series of grunts drifted up the hill as more blows connected and were returned.

"If they carry on like that, one of them's going to get killed, dirk or no," Graeme observed. "I know Alex is your chieftain and all that, but I don't think he'll thank you if you let him kill his brother while he's not thinking right."

Kenneth sighed.

"Christ, Duncan, I miss ye, laddie," he said under his breath, and then indicating to Dougal and Alasdair to follow him he strode down the hill towards the warring brothers, stopping a few yards away from them for a moment to assess the damage. Then he waded in, and grabbing hold of the nearest combatant, which happened to be Angus, he lifted him off his brother and in an impressive feat of strength threw him several yards down the hill, where he landed in an undignified and somewhat startled heap.

"Hold him," Kenneth said brusquely to Dougal and Alasdair, who, not without trepidation each gripped an arm of their bruised and bloody chieftain as he tried to go after Angus, pulling him back down to the ground, while Kenneth walked down to where

Angus was just regaining his feet and grabbed him from behind, pinioning his arms.

Angus struggled in his grip, his chest heaving with emotion, sobbing the same incoherent sentence over and over through swollen, bloody lips;

"Icannaloseyoutoo, Icannaloseyoutoo, Icannaloseyoutoo."

It took a few moments for Kenneth to understand what he was saying, but when he did he closed his eyes for a moment and swallowed, then sank down in the heather, pulling his distraught captive with him.

"*Isd*," he said softly, "We'll no' let that happen. Stop now, stop, for God's sake, laddie." He sat, maintaining his iron grip on the young clansman until he felt the resistance drain away and finally Angus relaxed back into him, his chest still heaving, but now with the effort of holding back the tears. Kenneth relaxed his grip enough for it now to be more of an embrace than restraint, but was ready to tighten it again if he had to.

"Let it out, laddie, there's no shame in it," he said gently, and with that Angus gave up the fight, both with his brother and his emotions, and started to cry in earnest, with great racking sobs. Kenneth turned his body, and Angus buried his head in the big man's chest and wailed like an infant, finally releasing the grief for the death of his brother and sister-in-law that he'd held in for so long.

In the meantime Graeme had made his way down to where Alasdair and Dougal were struggling to maintain their grip on their enraged chieftain, not least because he was commanding them to release him and their inbred instinct was to obey the order.

Graeme had no such instinct. Pulling his pistol out of his belt and cocking it, he pointed it at Alex's head and said, his voice hard and cold, "Calm yourself, man. It's over. Look at him, for God's sake. He's grieving and not thinking clearly. Neither of you are."

Alex froze, his survival instinct telling him that while Graeme would not kill him, he would have no compunction about shooting to disable if he absolutely had to. He looked past the elderly Englishman and down the hill to where Angus was cradled in Kenneth's arms, and his rage drained away as quickly as it had risen.

"Dear God," he said quietly, then he looked at Dougal and Alasdair. "Ye can let me go now. I'm all right. I canna go and leave him like that."

Graeme lowered the pistol and the two clansmen let Alex go. He struggled to his feet and limped down the hill to the two figures huddled on the ground, then knelt down next to them.

"Ye did well, Kenneth," he said. "Let me take him now."

Kenneth carefully relinquished his grip on Angus and transferred him to his brother's arms.

"It's alright," Alex said softly to Angus, who was hiccupping between sobs. "I've asked too much of you. I'm sorry, *mo bhràthair.*"

Kenneth stood and made his way back up the hill to Dougal, Alasdair and Graeme.

"Come on," he said. "Let's away up to the cave." They walked back up to the rest of the clan. Someone had sent for Morag, who had been tending Graeme's new vegetable patch on the far side of the hill, and Kenneth intercepted her as she made her way down towards them.

"He's fine, *a graidh,*" he said, wrapping one huge arm gently round her shoulders and leading her back up the hill. "They've had a wee stramash is all, and need a few minutes alone. It's no' as bad as it looks."

In spite of Kenneth's assurance to Morag, when the two brothers rejoined the clan some time later it did look pretty bad, even to the hardened warriors. Both of them were shirtless at the moment and had been down to the loch to wash the worst of the blood away, so their hair and kilts were dripping wet.

Alex was limping, Angus cradled his left arm in his right, and both men's torsos were covered in rapidly blackening bruises. But it was their faces that seemed to have taken the brunt of the action. Angus's nose was clearly broken, his mouth was split and puffy, and he had a nasty cut above his right eye which was still bleeding, the flesh around it swollen and purple. He sat down heavily on a rock outside the cave, and winced slightly when Morag sat down next to him and put her arm round his waist, her face drawn with worry.

"I'll be fine, *mo chridhe,*" he assured her. "I wrenched my arm is all, and need someone to pull my nose back into place. After a wee dram," he added hastily on seeing Kenneth start to rise.

Alex sat down opposite Angus on the grass, and gingerly massaged his leg.

"Ye've no' broken it again, have ye?" Peigi asked.

"No. I just twisted it is all," Alex replied. "What?" he asked as he looked round at the sea of horrified faces staring at him.

"Have you seen the state of your face?" Graeme said.

"No, of course I havena," Alex answered. "I havena got a mirror. Hurts like the devil, though. I think it was when yon gomerel there tried to mash my cheek into the gorse." He gingerly put his hand up to the left side of his face and it came away bloody.

"I'm sorry, Alex," Angus said indistinctly. Alex waved his hand dismissively.

"We've done the apologies, man, no need for more," he said. "We both lost our way a wee bit, I'm thinking."

"It looks like a piece of raw steak," Graeme elaborated.

It did. The whole side of his face, from temple to jaw, was raw and bloody.

"Your own mother wouldna recognise ye," Janet added.

"Truly?" Alex said. "Have any of ye got a wee bit of a mirror?"

"I have," Morag said. "Shall I fetch it?" She got up and disappeared into the cave, returning a minute later with a small piece of silvered glass. Alex took it and held it up to his face, then to everyone's astonishment, he smiled.

"Aye," he said to himself. "That'll do it."

"That'll do what?" Kenneth asked.

Instead of answering, Alex handed the mirror back to Morag and then looked around.

"Call the others," he said. "I need to talk to you all. And get the whisky for Angus. The sooner his nose is put back, the better."

Once everyone was assembled, the whisky had gone round, and Angus's nose was straight again, Alex started talking.

"First of all, Angus was right to stop me from just walking away like that. I wasna thinking properly, thanks to that bastard." He nodded his head towards the small cave where Richard's corpse still lay. "Kenneth, Dougal, Alasdair, thanks to ye for doing what Duncan would have done, had he lived. That took courage, for we were both of us a wee bit insane, I'm thinking. I can tell ye, I've never missed Duncan as much as I do right now. We both need to grieve for him something fierce, and I think we've made a start on that today. We were wrong to just hide it away and no' speak of him, to each other or anyone else. It's harmed us and done Duncan an injustice, for he deserves to be remembered.

"Having said that, I still made a promise to Beth, and I intend to keep it." He held his hand up as Angus and several others started to speak, and they fell silent.

"I'm going to tell ye what Richard tellt me, and then ye'll at least ken why I have to go to London and find out for myself if he spoke the truth or no'. He said that Beth stabbed a soldier in the throat and was shot in the head, here." He lifted his hand to his temple. "As Angus said, it could be that she *is* dead, and that someone tellt him, although I dinna ken how, for she's unlikely to have tellt anyone her name before she was shot. But it *is* possible he found out. He was her brother, although there was a time when he forgot that, which is why I killed him in the way I did."

"I thought ye did that because of the woman in the wee hut," Kenneth put in.

"Aye, well, that as well. But I'll no' talk of that now. He said that she didna die, and Cumberland sent her to London, had her treated in the hope that she'd betray me. But she didna. So Newcastle sent her to Newgate Gaol, and let Richard torture her..." His voice trailed off, and he closed his eyes, swallowing hard to try to keep the emotion down.

"He said that she was with child, that Newcastle knew it, but still let Richard torture her, and that she lost the bairn because of it. He boasted about it, said that he got to make her pay for everything and that Newcastle hates her, which I've no doubt he does if she hasna tellt him anything." He swiped his hand through his hair, wincing as he touched a bump inflicted by his brother earlier. "I have to find out the truth of it. I canna rest till I do."

There was a shocked silence for a few moments, which Angus broke.

"Do ye no' think he made it up in the hopes that ye'd do exactly what ye're intending?" he asked. "Ye'd been married for three years. What was the likelihood of you getting her wi' child just before she was shot? Graeme, you said ye'd known Richard since he was a bairn. Is it the sort of thing he'd do?"

"It's possible," Graeme said. "Although he was never a good liar as a child. But he knew he was dying, and this could be his way of trying to get you to betray yourself. After all, the authorities have no idea what you look like, but if you turn up at Newgate, or any prison in London for that matter, asking about Beth, you're sure to be arrested."

"Aye, that's right!" Angus said. "Ye canna go, Alex. It's madness."

"I would," Iain said suddenly, causing everyone to look at him. He was sitting on the ground, his long legs bent, his chin resting on his knees, but now he looked up, his eyes moist with unshed tears. "If I thought there was even the slightest chance that Maggie was alive, I'd do anything, anything at all to find out and get her back if I could, whatever the risk. I ken well she's dead, Angus, for ye buried her yourself. But ye didna find Beth's body, did ye?"

"No," Angus admitted. "But that was because the redcoat bastards burnt all the women in the bothy. I couldna recognise anyone."

"What exactly did Maggie say about Beth?" Alex asked.

"I tellt ye already," Angus said. "She was shot and killed."

"Is that exactly what she said?" Alex persisted. "Think, Angus. Take a minute and see if ye can mind exactly what she tellt ye."

Angus sighed, but he closed his eyes and concentrated, recalling the horrific day that he'd spent over a year trying to push from his mind.

"She said that she was holding someone's bairn, trying to stop it from crying, and the sergeant killed it then stabbed her with his bayonet. Beth threw her knife and took him in the throat, then ran. She said that while they were going after Beth she managed to crawl away, which is why they didna burn her wi' the others. 'They shot her in the head. She's dead.' That's what she said. Then she said she passed out for a time, and when she woke the soldiers were raping the women." He shuddered and ran his hand through his hair, exactly as Alex had done earlier.

"But she didna say she'd seen them bury her, or put her body in the bothy. She didna say anything about that, did she?" Alex said.

"No. But she tellt me that Beth was dead, and—"

"So it's possible that she was shot, but didna die, and that Cumberland had her taken to London," Alex interrupted.

"How would Cumberland even ken about it?" Angus argued. "He was too busy watching his men butcher our wounded to go looking at every woman to see if it was Beth! He didna even ken she was there, for Christ's sake!"

"He's right," Kenneth said. "Cumberland wouldna have expected Sir Anthony to be fighting at Culloden – he'd more likely have thought ye both to have escaped to France."

"Even so," Iain persisted. "If there was a doubt about it, about Maggie I mean, I'd have to go and find out for myself."

"Iain, will ye haud yer whisht?" Angus said, exasperated. "Ye're no' helping."

Alex sat deliberating for a few minutes, looking down at his hands, while the clan awaited his decision. Finally he looked up, and to everyone's surprise, he was smiling.

"The last time we had a fight like this one, ye were fashed because ye thought I should have gone to Manchester to bring Beth back," he said to Angus. "And this time it's because ye think I shouldna go to London to bring Beth back. Do ye no' find that a wee bit amusing?"

"No, I dinna," Angus replied. "Because Beth was alive then, and she loved ye. Ye just needed to talk it through, sort out what was between ye. But this time—"

"We dinna ken if she's alive," Alex interrupted. "But if she is, I need to find out. I'm sorry, *mo bhràthair,* but I have to do this. I made her a promise. But now I'll make you a promise, all of you," he added, looking round at his clanspeople. "I'll think it through, and I'll be very careful about it. I'll no' take unnecessary risks, and I'll no' do anything in temper. And if I'm delayed for any reason, I'll write to the post in Glasgow, to James Drummond, and tell ye, in a way ye'll ken, but no one else would."

"And if ye find she's dead, ye'll come back?" Angus said.

"Aye. I'll come back, either with or without her. Dinna fash yourself. I'll no' kill myself if I find that Richard was lying. I'm past that now."

"Ye swear it?" Angus persisted. Normally at this point Alex would have become irritated; his promise should have been enough. But when he looked at his brother, Alex's eyes were gentle, understanding.

"I swear to ye, I'll no' take unnecessary risks, and I'll no' kill myself, whatever I find out," he said softly.

Angus nodded.

"It's no' what I'm wanting, but it'll have to do," he said. "When will you be leaving?"

"No' the night, anyway," Alex replied. "It's too late now, and the afternoon's entertainment has left me a wee bit tired. And sore," he added. "I'll wait a couple of days, think it through a wee bit. So let's get drunk. I think we all need to. I certainly do. We can take that lump of shite back where we found him tomorrow. He's no' going anywhere."

That was the first thing he'd said all afternoon that the whole clan was in accord with.

Two days later the MacGregors gathered once more, to say farewell to their chieftain, who was now dressed legally in the brown woollen frockcoat and breeches that he'd worn the previous summer as Tobias Grundy, but this time instead of a badly fitting wig he wore his own hair, tied back, and the sword at his side showed no signs of rust. He intended to travel down to Glasgow on a garron, the small but sturdy Highland pony, then exchange it for a different mount once there. He had packed a small bag with spare clothes, and for some reason known only to him, the two crutches that Angus had manufactured for him were strapped to the horse.

As he was making his final preparations Graeme approached, leading a garron of his own which was similarly packed ready for a journey.

"I'm ready when you are, lad," he said once he reached Alex.

"Ready for what?" Alex asked.

"I'm coming with you. I thought I could maybe protect you from all those savage Highlanders people talk about. I hear there's a fearsome band of barbarians hereabouts called the children of the mist or some such nonsense. You won't be wanting to travel alone."

Everyone laughed except Alex.

"Graeme," he said, "ye canna come with me. I need to do this alone."

"I know. It's my face, isn't it?" Graeme responded. "I'm not pretty enough for you. Mind, you're no picture yourself at the moment." Alex's cheek had started to heal, but was still a mass of scabs. "Don't worry," he continued, "I've no intention of going to London. But it's time I went home to Manchester. I'm too old to be skulking round in the rain all day and sleeping on a hard floor at the end of it. I want to go back and see what a mess my garden's become while I've been away, sort it out, and then rest in a warm bed at night. I've been teaching young Morag my secrets, and she's got a natural talent for growing things, so you'll not go short of vegetables without me."

"Just to Manchester," Alex said.

Graeme nodded. "Not a step further."

They set off together, riding in silence for a while, both of them caught up in their own thoughts.

"Are ye sorry ye fought for him?" Alex said after a time.

"For Charlie? No," Graeme said. "I wouldn't have missed it for the world. I was in the '15, before you were born and fought at Preston, but of course King James wasn't there, and by the time he arrived it was all but over. This was a different thing altogether, the best chance the Stuarts have had to take the crown back. If we hadn't turned back at Derby, maybe we'd have succeeded."

"Aye, maybe," Alex said. "It would have depended on the Londoners, I'm thinking. And on how Charles conducted himself. And on whether Georgie would have abandoned the throne or fought for it. But I agree, we should have carried on. I doubt we'll get another chance as good as that one."

"Will you rise again for him, if it comes to it?" Graeme asked. "With all that's happened since?"

"God, aye, in a heartbeat," Alex said without hesitation. "But I'm no' sure how many others would. It depends on whether Cumberland's cowed them or enraged them. The MacGregors have got nothing to lose anyway, ye ken, being proscribed. We're outlaws no matter what. Our only chance to lift the proscription is wi' the Stuarts. But to have a chance of succeeding we need French help, and that wily bastard'll no' be giving it, I'm thinking."

"You mean King Louis," Graeme said.

"Aye. And it depends on Charles too, on how he's behaving

in France. It's an annoyance to me that there's no' enough news getting through to me. I think when I get back I must pay Cluny a visit, see what he kens."

"Well, if there's another rising before I'm too old to lift a sword at all, I'd like to join you again, if you'll have me."

"You're an honorary MacGregor as far as I'm concerned, for what it's worth. Ye're welcome back any time, rising or no, man," Alex said.

"That's worth a lot to me," Graeme responded quietly. There was another short silence.

"Sometimes I forget you were Beth's gardener," Alex said. "I think of you more as a father-in-law."

Graeme smiled.

"Thank you, lad. I'd be proud to have you as my son-in-law. And yes, Beth was like the daughter I never had. I loved her."

"What was he like?" Alex asked.

"Her father? He was a good man, kind and generous, but weak. He hated conflict of any kind. I think that's why he let Arabella spoil Richard. It was easier to let her have her own way than to deal with her tantrums and sulks. And then after she died Henry didn't know what to do with him, so he either ignored him or, when the boy did something too bad to be ignored, he whipped him."

"Do you pity him?" Alex asked softly.

"Richard? God, no. He was an evil bastard and deserved what he got. No. He always had a cruel streak in him, from being a small boy. But I don't think it helped that his mother indulged him in everything and could see no wrong in him. He was never punished for anything. Richard was six when his mother died, and he took it very badly. Henry should have taken him in hand then, because he was lost and wild with grief. I think he would always have enjoyed hurting others, but he might have learnt to keep it in check with the right guidance. As it was he was desperate for attention, and the only time he got it after that was if he did something wrong.

"And then of course Ann came onto the scene, and he saw that as a betrayal of his mother, I think. Ann tried to befriend Richard, but he'd have nothing to do with her. Then Beth was born, and both Henry and Ann doted on her. She was an easy child to love." Graeme smiled sadly. "Anyway, needless to say Richard hated her from the moment she was born, and he became completely unmanageable. I think it was a relief to his father when he ran away, but going into the army was the worst thing he could have done in my opinion. It encouraged the brute in him. No, maybe I pitied him for a while when he was very small, just after Arabella died, but a lot of children are neglected. They don't all grow up to be like him. He made his own choices."

This was the most Alex had ever heard the normally taciturn Graeme say at one time.

"Beth and I have never spoken much about Richard," he said quietly. "I ken well she hates him, but when I found out why…" his voice trailed off.

"At Manchester," Graeme said.

"Aye, at Manchester. After that, after we made up what was between us, I tellt her I'd kill him the next time I saw him, and then we didna talk about him again."

"I know what happened," Graeme said. "Or I think I do. She told me they'd argued and she'd kicked him in the balls. He couldn't walk straight for two days afterwards, and he took it out on young Sarah, beat her very badly. At the time I never suspected there was any more to it than that, and, as close as we were, Beth wouldn't have told me or Thomas, because she knew we'd kill him. There's no need to tell me," he added as Alex made to speak. "It's over now, in any case. But no. I'm glad he's dead, and I'm glad he died the way he did. May he rot in hell."

"And I'm glad you were there for Beth, when I was too proud to bend," Alex said.

On the way south they slept in the open when the weather was good, and in cheap inns when it rained, travelling at a more leisurely pace than Alex would have, had he been alone. He used the time to plan his strategy, to practice patience, which he would almost certainly need once he reached London, and to get to know this gruff-natured, thoroughly likeable man better. Just before reaching Manchester they made a small detour and retrieved some more gold from the chest Graeme had buried years before.

"I may well need something to bribe keepers or other officials with, or to change identity," Alex explained in the northern English accent he'd adopted since they'd crossed the border and had maintained, even when alone with Graeme. "I've no idea what I'll need. But I know that money can admit you into almost anywhere."

"Have you got a plan for when you get there?" Graeme asked. "I don't expect you to tell me the details, but I'd be happier knowing you've got some idea of what you're doing."

Alex laughed.

"Yes, I've got a plan, but I'll probably need to adapt it when I'm there. I have no idea where Beth is. Richard said Newgate, but he also said that was a few months ago. That's what I need to find out first, and I think I know how to do that."

"Be careful, lad. All the way here when we've spoken about Beth, you've talked as if she's alive. I want it to be true as much as you do, but remember, whether she's alive or not, she wouldn't want you to risk your life for her."

"If she *is* alive, and what Richard told me is the truth," Alex said, "then she's risked not only her life, but the life of our child for me, and for the clan. I'll do whatever I need to do to free her. I promised Angus I won't take unnecessary risks, and I'll hold to that. But I *will* take necessary ones." He looked at Graeme's worried countenance, and laughed.

"Don't worry, man. Hiding in plain sight and obtaining information is what I'm good at. I spent over three years as Sir Anthony perfecting that, to help the Stuarts back to the throne. But now I've got something far more precious to fight for than the Stuarts, and I'm not about to get myself arrested and executed before I've achieved it. That won't help anyone."

"Well, I'll try not to worry, but I can't promise I won't," Graeme said. "Do you want to stay the night in Didsbury, meet Thomas and Jane? You don't have to tell them who you are."

"No," Alex said. "They met Sir Anthony, and servants are more observant than the nobility. They might recognise my features. And from what you've told me, they're good, honest people. I wouldn't want to put them in a difficult position."

"For all her faults, and she *did* have a few," Graeme said, "Beth knew how to choose the right man. God go with you, Alex. And if you see her, tell her I love her, will you?"

The two men embraced roughly, and then Graeme turned to head along the Didsbury road.

"Graeme," Alex called after him. The older man reined in and turned back. "If you were to get a letter, would the others open it?"

"No," Graeme said.

Alex nodded.

"Well, then," he said. "I'll write to you when I know what's happened to her. Or someone will. It will be an innocent letter, full of uninteresting trivialities. But I think you can read between lines."

"That I can, lad," Graeme replied, smiling. "Thank you."

CHAPTER FIVE

June 1747, Fort William, Scotland

Colonel Mark Hutchinson sank down onto the edge of his bed with a groan of relief. It was all he could do not to fall immediately backwards onto it, coat, sword, muddy boots and all, and just go to sleep. He had never been so exhausted in his life.

Instead of giving in to the temptation he sat forward, rubbing his eyes with his knuckles in an attempt to stop them closing of their own free will. His batman had done a good job; there was a fire roaring in the hearth, a meal of bread, butter, cold meat, cheese and ale stood on the table ready for him, and as Hutchinson readied to stand, the man himself came into the room carrying a steaming basin of water along with various implements used in washing and shaving.

"Welcome back, sir," he said, placing the basin carefully on the table, then coming over to pull the colonel's boots off for him. His nose wrinkled as he inhaled the smell of unwashed sweaty stocking at close quarters. He put the boots in the corner of the room while the colonel removed his stock, took off his coat and rolled down the offensive stockings to reveal a pair of equally offensive feet.

"Here you are, sir," the servant said, placing the basin on the floor. "Put your feet in that and relax. I'll go and get some more water for shaving."

The colonel complied, uttering a sigh of bliss as his sore and blistered feet hit the warm water. By the time the servant returned he was slumped across his mattress, fast asleep. The young batman smiled, and very gently so as not to wake him, he washed his master's feet, applied salve to the blisters, put a cloth over the food to keep the flies away, and left.

An hour later he came back, to find the colonel in exactly the same position, snoring. He shook his master's arm, succeeding with difficulty in rousing him.

"I'm sorry to wake you, sir," he said, once Hutchinson's eyes were open, "but I didn't think you'd want to sleep the whole day away, and if you stay in that position you'll have a terrible stiff neck in the morning."

"No, you're right. Thank you, Bernard," Hutchinson said, shaking his head to clear it of the sleep-induced fog, then sitting up. He got up and walked over to the table, lifted the cover, and then sitting down started to eat.

"Sit down, man," he said between mouthfuls. "No need to stand on ceremony. I'm too tired to discipline you anyway. Bring me up to date on what's been happening whilst I was away. Then you can shave me after I've eaten."

Bernard sat down opposite his colonel and poured a mug of ale.

"God, I hate this bloody country," Hutchinson continued before Bernard could offer any news. "Does it never stop raining? No need to answer that." Actually the last few days had been dry, but today, when he'd been outside the whole day and had needed it to be dry, it had rained. The whole day. Even the weather in this godforsaken country was Jacobite, it seemed.

"You need some new boots, sir," suggested Bernard, eyeing the colonel's bare feet.

"No, those are fine. My horse cast a shoe on the way back and I had to lead her the last five miles in a downpour, that's all. I'd have worn an extra pair of stockings if I'd known I was going to have to walk. So, has everything gone well in my absence?"

"Mostly, sir."

Hutchinson looked up, still chewing.

"That sounds ominous," he said.

"The roof's leaking in part of the barracks, the sleeping quarters. Davis had another fight with Barraclough and cut him in the arm. The sergeant gave them both fifty lashes. And some men have deserted from Inversnaid, sir. Oh, and there's a letter for you, from London."

If it's another order for me to travel halfway across this shitheap to deliver a pointless message to some pompous idiot general, I'm going to hang myself, Hutchinson thought mutinously. He sighed.

"Fetch me the letter, then. Let's get it over with," he said. Bernard got up and went into the tiny adjoining room that the colonel had assigned as his office. "How many men deserted?" he called through as he drained his tankard of ale.

"Thirteen, sir," Bernard said, returning with the letter. "About a week ago."

The colonel broke the seal with his breadknife, scattering crumbs across the table in the process, and unfolded it. Bernard went to the fire and threw some more logs on to it.

"Shit," said the colonel. Bernard looked across at the seated figure of his superior officer, who was now sitting erect. "When did this letter arrive? It's dated April the second."

"It's a few weeks now, sir. We couldn't forward it on to you because we didn't know exactly where you were, and it's addressed to you in confidence so no one else could open it. Did we do wrong? Is it something bad? It wasn't marked as urgent." The servant's brow furrowed with worry.

"No. Under the circumstances, you couldn't have done anything else. Inversnaid, you said?"

"Sorry, sir?"

"Where the men deserted from."

"Oh. Yes, sir."

"You can shave me now, then, Bernard. And after that can you arrange for my uniform to be cleaned for tomorrow? I need a good night's sleep. I'll be damned if I'm setting off today. It's waited since April, it can wait another day."

"I'm sure it can, sir," the batman replied, having no idea what Hutchinson was talking about.

"Then I can deal with this," he tapped the letter, "and the desertions at the same time. Although unless they've been stupid enough to go home, it's going to be the devil's own job to find them. As for this, well, it could actually turn out to be good news, after all."

"Pleased to hear it, sir," said Bernard, still in the dark. No doubt the colonel knew whether whatever it was was good or bad news, and that was all that mattered.

* * *

In fact, as the colonel rode into Inversnaid barracks three days later, he still had no idea whether the information contained in the Duke of Newcastle's letter was even true, let alone good or bad news.

If it *was* true that Captain Cunningham was a traitor, then it would be good news, because he would finally be able to get rid of the vicious bastard. Colonel Hutchinson had been waiting for two years for Cunningham to put a foot wrong, and now it looked as though he might have.

But although Richard Cunningham was savage even by army standards and universally hated by his men, the colonel could not see him as a traitor. From what he knew of him, the captain didn't have the brains or guile to pretend to be anything other than what he was; an ambitious brute of a man desperate to rise to the top.

But there it was. What was it Newcastle had written? *The sister states that Captain Cunningham accepted the money for his first promotion in order to keep silent about the fact that she was a Papist, and that on discovering Sir Anthony was a spy, was bribed once more with the means of promotion to captain.*

Yes, it was possible. Cunningham was hungry enough for promotion to do that. And he had no other way to raise funds. His father had left him penniless, the colonel knew that. And if he had achieved promotion through keeping silence, it would follow that Cunningham would not want Sir Anthony to be arrested in case he divulged what he knew to the authorities. Even if nothing could be proved against the captain, his character would be compromised, which would put an end to all hopes of further promotion.

The colonel thought back to the interview he had conducted with Richard Cunningham after his sister and brother-in-law had disappeared. His shock on hearing that his brother-in-law was a spy had been genuine, Mark Hutchinson was sure of that. When speaking of his sister, Cunningham had seemed to be holding something back, but at the time the colonel had believed it only to be that he'd known his sister to be a Roman Catholic, or some such thing.

Miss Cunningham states that it is always possible to tell if Captain

Cunningham is lying due to the twitching of a muscle in his cheek whenever he utters a mendacity, of which habit he is unaware. Yes, the colonel remembered that. It was quite noticeable, but at a distance of two years, although he remembered the captain's habit, he could not remember at which point in the conversation he had demonstrated it.

He would certainly note it now, though. This was his chance to be rid of the man he had instinctively disliked since he had had the misfortune to command him. And Cunningham's men would have a party if he was proved to be a traitor. If. Unless, after he'd interviewed the man, he had cause to believe there was truth in the sister's allegations, he would not destroy his career. After all, Elizabeth Cunningham was a self-confessed traitor, and it was distinctly possible that she was attempting to besmirch a loyal British soldier. Well, he was about to find out.

Colonel Hutchinson sighed. Sometimes he considered his conscientiousness to be a failing rather than a virtue.

"Gone? What do you mean, gone?"

"He's one of the men who deserted last week, Colonel," Sergeant Baker said.

"*Cunningham?* You are talking about the right man?"

"Yes, sir. Captain Richard Cunningham."

"You oversee the mail, Sergeant. Has any mail arrived in the last, oh, two months for the captain?"

"No, sir. He is not in the habit of sending or receiving letters, so I would remember if he had."

"Anything from London? For anybody?"

"No, sir." The sergeant looked puzzled.

So it was unlikely anyone had informed Cunningham that he was under suspicion.

"So, what happened last week then?" Hutchinson asked.

"We went out on an exercise last Friday, the twenty-ninth, sir. He and twelve of his men disappeared. We assume they deserted."

"We. You said 'we'. Does that mean you accompanied Cunningham on this exercise, Sergeant?"

Sergeant Baker blushed furiously.

"Er, yes, sir. Initially, sir. He stayed behind after we left."

"With just twelve men? In hostile territory?"

"Yes, sir."

There was something not right here. Colonel Hutchinson tapped his riding crop thoughtfully against his boot. Sergeant Baker stood rigidly to attention in front of him. His face was still scarlet, one of the unfortunate side effects of having ginger hair.

"What manner of 'exercise' was this, Sergeant?"

"A pacification exercise, Colonel."

In other words, a raid on a Highland settlement. The men were under strict orders not to carry out such raids with less than thirty men. Unless Cunningham had changed drastically, he would have obeyed those orders to the letter.

"But he sent you and presumably several other men home early?"

"Er…in a manner of speaking, sir."

What the hell does that mean?

"Stephen, how long have we known each other?" Mark Hutchinson said. The sudden informality seemed to flummox Sergeant Baker even more. Beads of sweat broke out on his forehead, even though the interview room they were in was freezing.

"Um…twenty years, sir?"

"Twenty years. And for all that time you have been an exemplary soldier."

"Thank you, Col—"

"And a bloody awful liar," the colonel interrupted. "For God's sake, man, stand at ease. In fact sit down. You're not on trial."

The sergeant sat down. Stiffly. Mark Hutchinson sighed. It seemed that was the most relaxed Baker could manage at the moment.

"I will be frank with you, Stephen. I need to speak with Cunningham on an extremely important matter. Much as I dislike the man on a personal level, I cannot believe he would desert. The army is his life. Nor would he be likely to send a group of his men back to barracks, leaving himself vulnerable. So something happened, and I think you know what it was, or what some of it was at any rate. And I need you to tell me. I think you know me to be a fair man?"

"Yes, Colonel," Sergeant Baker mumbled.

"Talk to me then, and I will hear you out. Informally, and in confidence."

Stephen Baker swallowed audibly, chewed on his lip for a moment, then came to a decision.

"It was my fault, sir. That he was left with twelve men," he said.

Colonel Hutchinson nodded.

"Tell me why you think it was your fault, and what happened."

The sergeant, perspiring freely, told the colonel about the raid on the village, that there had been fifty of them, but only about thirty Highlanders, and most of those women and children. About the fact that they'd killed the cattle and the men who'd resisted, burnt the hovels they were living in and sent the women and children away.

"Some of the men got a little carried away with the women, sir," Baker added.

"Did the captain attempt to stop the men getting 'carried away'?" Hutchinson asked, although he thought he already knew the answer to that.

"No, sir. He encouraged them. That's his way," Baker said. "Anyway, when we were…finished, he was in one of the huts, sir. With a woman. She was screaming. So we waited for a while, and when he still didn't come out I went in to tell him that if we didn't leave soon we wouldn't make it back before dark, and…" The sergeant stopped suddenly. He was no longer blushing; in fact his face had taken on a green tinge.

"And…?" Hutchinson prompted.

"I've never seen anything like it in my life, sir, and I hope I never do again. He…he'd tied her to the roof beams, and he was…he was…Jesus…"

"Just say it, man," the colonel said. *What the hell had he done?*

"He was flaying her, sir. Alive. He'd cut all the skin back from her arms, and it was hanging in ribbons, and she was screaming…I went outside and I'm not ashamed to admit I was sick. And then I think I lost my reason. I told the others what I'd seen and then I got on my horse and I rode away. I think if I'd stayed there I'd have killed him, sir. Anyway, most of the men followed me and we came straight back here. We didn't think much about it when the men weren't back the next morning. We haven't had any resistance from those parts in a while. But then on Saturday afternoon when they still weren't back, I went myself with some other men to see if we could find them. There was a grave outside the hut, fresh, but no sign of any of the other men. So we thought that the captain was worried I'd report him and had deserted along with the others. There are a lot of desertions, sir," he finished. He sat back, seeming almost relieved to have finally confessed.

Mark Hutchinson absorbed this information in silence for a minute. His first emotion on hearing what the sergeant had seen, to his own shame, was relief, because now he knew that whether Cunningham was a traitor or not, his career in the army was over. Rape was one thing; as much as the colonel hated it, he was a pragmatist and knew that when a man was roused to kill all his other base emotions came to the fore as well. But this, if it was true, was beyond the pale.

However, first he had to find out what had happened to Richard Cunningham. He could not just write back to the Duke of Newcastle and say the man had disappeared; he would have to do better than that.

"Is that what all the men think? Is this the first time he's done something like this?"

"Being honest, sir, the men don't really care what's happened to him. They're just glad he's gone. I don't know if it's the first time he's done that, but he's very…er…a very hard disciplinarian and very enthusiastic in his duties."

"Very diplomatically put, Stephen. How far away is this settlement?"

"About three hours, sir."

"Right. I want to see it for myself. Tell the men to be ready in half an hour."

Thankfully it was now dry, and as they picked their way carefully down the steep hillside above the village the sun actually broke through the clouds. Sergeant Baker pointed down to the forlorn little cluster of burnt-out hovels below.

"There it is, sir," he said, indicating the one hut that remained intact.

"And you said the woman had been buried, Baker?" Hutchinson said.

"Well, there's a grave outside the hut, sir, with a little cross made out of sticks. I assumed that maybe one of the men had done the decent thing."

"You think that Cunningham would have waited about while one of his men buried her?" the colonel said. "It's more likely that after he'd finished he'd have burnt the hut to destroy the evidence and finish the job, don't you think?"

The poor sergeant blushed again.

"Yes, sir, now you say it, that *does* seem the most likely thing."

While they were talking they'd arrived in the clearing. Although only a week had passed, the village had an abandoned air about it. He knew that most Highlanders returned to their settlements once they'd been pillaged. But there was no sign of recent attempts to rebuild, or that anyone had come back.

The colonel posted guards around the village, with orders to particularly watch the hillside above for any movement whatsoever, then he and Sergeant Baker walked over to the hut, stopping at the grave. There was a tiny sprig of heather lying on it.

"Was that there when you came here last week?" Hutchinson asked, pointing to it.

"I don't think so, sir."

"Observation, Sergeant. It can mean the difference between living and dying."

"Yes sir."

"Right, let's go inside and see if there's anything else you might not have noticed."

Colonel Hutchinson drew his sword, just to be safe, and stepped through the low doorway.

"Jesus Christ!" he exclaimed, instinctively stepping backwards onto Sergeant Baker's foot. The two men stopped.

"Was *that* there when you came here last week?" Hutchinson asked drily.

"No sir," the white-faced sergeant said, staring in horror at the scene before him.

The soldier's corpse, still in its full uniform, even down to the boots and sword, had been tied by its hands to the roof beams. The colonel, now over his initial shock, went over to it and, waving away the cloud of flies which completely obscured the head, discovered why.

The man's face had been beaten quite literally to pulp, the nose flattened, cheekbones crushed, eyes pulped. Whoever had done this had been enraged; the woman's husband perhaps? Hutchinson raised his sword to cut the ropes binding the corpse's hands, then paused.

"Sergeant, when you came into the hut and saw Cunningham with the woman, is this the way she was tied? Think carefully."

Baker moved forward into the hut, so as to see better.

"Yes, sir. Her arms were spread, like that. That's how I could see the…the skin." He took a deep breath, then clearly wished he hadn't; the hut smelt distinctly of rotting meat.

Hutchinson cut the ropes and lowered the body carefully to the ground.

"It's Captain Cunningham, sir," the sergeant said, looking down at the remains of the soldier.

"How can you tell? Apart from the uniform, that is?"

"The captain has bowed legs, sir. It was something he was very sensitive about. He once had a man flogged half to death for mentioning it. Er…so it became common knowledge, sir."

"That he had bow legs."

"Yes, sir, and not to mention it in his hearing."

But I'm damn sure you mentioned it out of his hearing. No doubt his nickname reflects that, the colonel thought.

Well, it didn't matter any more. The poor bastard was dead. Next.

"You did bring the shovels, Sergeant?"

"Yes, sir."

"Good. Go and get two. We need to dig the body up, make sure it *is* the woman, and not one of our men. Just you and me, Baker. Tell the men to keep a very close eye on the hillside. Do *not* tell them what you have just seen. Is that clear?"

"Yes, sir." The sergeant looked puzzled, but went off to do as he was told. He was clearly confused as to what the colonel intended to do.

As in fact was the colonel. He needed to think this through, and in the meantime did not want any more information to be released about the whole incident than already had been.

Thankfully the body had not been buried very deeply, indicating that whoever had done it had been in a bit of a rush. And it was definitely the woman.

Well, at least I know Baker was telling the truth, Hutchinson thought, looking at the partly flayed corpse they had just exposed.

"No need to disturb the poor woman any more, Sergeant," he said gently. "Let's cover her up again, and then get Captain Cunningham back to barracks. Make sure his head is wrapped up so none of the other men see it. And tell no one anything at this point. Your career depends on it. Is that clear?"

"Very clear, Colonel," Baker said hurriedly.

Back in his room in the company of an extremely large brandy, Colonel Hutchinson pondered the situation, trying to work out what had happened. Before they'd returned to Inversnaid, he had had the men scour the immediate area for any hidden bodies or signs of burial, but nothing had been found. He took a deep draught of brandy and stared into the fire, running through everything Baker had told him and what he'd seen himself, before coming to the only possible conclusion that made any sense.

The men of the village, who had no doubt stayed in the vicinity, had taken advantage of the sudden disappearance of three-quarters of the redcoats plundering their village, and had attacked. The soldiers had run away, leaving Captain Cunningham, who was no doubt still enjoying his sick pleasure with the woman, to the Highlanders' tender mercies. If she'd been screaming continuously as Baker had said, then Cunningham might well have been unaware of the presence of the enemy until they were upon him.

That would explain the tender burial of the woman, the makeshift cross and heather, and also the state of the captain's face, which had clearly borne the brunt of someone's extreme rage and distress. It would also explain why the rest of the men had not returned. Leaving your commanding officer, no matter how much you hated him, to face certain death while you saved your own skin was a serious offence.

Yes, that had to be it. But the next question was, what to do? Colonel Hutchinson knew Sergeant Baker to be an honest man, but even so, until he'd seen the woman's corpse for himself he had been unable to believe anyone would commit such an atrocious act. If it became public knowledge that redcoat officers were torturing women in such horrific ways for pleasure, it would be very damaging for the British Army, whose reputation was not exactly glowing at the moment. There was ever-growing condemnation for the brutal way in which the Highlands of Scotland were being pacified as it was, but if something like this came out, there would be hell to pay. In the wrong hands this information could be catastrophic. The Duke of Cumberland's reputation was suffering as it was; he was far more often referred to as the butcher than the hero of Culloden now.

So, damage limitation was the order of the day. And immediate action was needed.

"Bernard!" the colonel called. The servant appeared within moments. "Get me Sergeant Baker, will you? Straight away."

He finished off his brandy and poured another for himself and his expected guest. When Baker appeared, somewhat breathless from running across the barrack grounds, Hutchinson motioned him to a chair.

"Have a brandy, Stephen. This is an informal interview and will remain between the two of us. I believe you are a man of discretion, but if I'm wrong and I find out, I'll string you up by your balls. Is that clear?"

"Very, sir," replied the sergeant, clearly terrified. The colonel was not one to make idle threats, so when he did threaten you, you took him very seriously indeed.

"Good. Now I don't think I need to tell you that this is a tricky situation. The army's reputation is not of the highest, especially where North Britain is concerned, and if it becomes known that evil bastards like Cunningham are abusing their position to satisfy their perverted pleasures, it will reflect badly on all of us. I also don't think I need to tell you that leaving your commanding officer vulnerable to attack without permission, is desertion of duty, and a very serious offence. Especially when the officer in question is subsequently brutally murdered."

The poor sergeant was white as a sheet. His brandy stood untouched on the table.

"Now I believe that after you and the other men left, the remaining soldiers were attacked, presumably by the men of the village. As the only body we've found is Cunningham's, I have to assume the other men buggered off with alacrity, and left the captain to his fate. Does this seem likely to you, Stephen, in view of Cunningham's standing with his men?"

"Yes, sir," said the sergeant in a very small voice.

"When you came out of the hut last Friday, did you tell the men exactly what Cunningham was doing to the woman? Think carefully before you answer."

"No, sir. I just said that he was torturing her, and I'd had enough of him and his ways."

"Have you talked about it since, including today?"

"No, sir. I've been having nightmares. I just wanted to try to forget it. And then today you told me not to tell anyone anything, so I haven't."

Thank God for that.

"Excellent!" Hutchinson said. "For God's sake, Stephen, relax. Providing you do as I say, I see no reason why we can't just forget all about this unfortunate situation after tonight. Drink your brandy."

Stephen Baker complied somewhat hurriedly, coughing as the strong liquor went the wrong way.

"Now, I think it highly unlikely that the twelve men who deserted are going to talk about what happened. And indeed it seems the only people who know exactly what went on are you, me, and the Highlander who killed Cunningham. So here is what occurred: Captain Cunningham was on an exercise in an area known to have had little rebel activity for some time. When you went into the hut to advise him of the lateness of the hour, he ordered you to go back to barracks, and told you that he would follow on shortly with the remaining men. It was a foolhardy thing for the captain to have done, but as we all know, he was very confident of his ability. Over-confident, we must now sadly surmise. It would seem that once you were clear of the area the men were ambushed and ran away, but Captain Cunningham recklessly refused to retreat and was unfortunately killed in the line of duty. It's a sad business, Sergeant."

The sergeant sat for a moment, silently processing this new state of affairs.

"Indeed it is, sir," he said after a time. "Very sad."

"Good. Now, I'll leave you to arrange the burial of the captain. I have a couple of letters to write before bedtime. Any questions, Sergeant?"

"No, sir."

He put down his empty glass and rose. At the door he turned back.

"Colonel Hutchinson, sir," he said.

Hutchinson looked up.

"Thank you, sir. I won't forget this."

"I suggest you do, Sergeant, as quickly as possible."

After the hugely relieved sergeant had gone on his way, the colonel settled down to write his letters. To the Duke of Newcastle he would write, in the main, the truth, missing out only that Sergeant Baker and thirty of the men had abandoned the captain on their own initiative rather than on his orders. Newcastle would not want the atrocities Richard Cunningham had committed to come to public attention, and would almost certainly be relieved that the colonel had contained the damage. At the same time, Mark Hutchinson very much wanted the duke to know exactly what manner of man Cunningham had been. The bastard was about to be buried with military honours, officially guilty only of a reckless decision to leave himself vulnerable to attack. It was important that *someone* knew what a brute he was.

To Anne Cunningham, of course, he would write the standard drivel that went out to all widows – husband bravely killed in the performance of his duty, very brave, died instantly, etc – the usual platitudes. He doubted she would be overly distraught by the news of her husband's demise.

It was certain that the men who had suffered under Cunningham's command for the last few years would be positively ecstatic at the news of his death. No doubt there would be celebrations in the barracks tonight.

Celebrations which Colonel Hutchinson intended to join them in, although unfortunately he would have to rejoice privately in the comfort of his room.

He refilled his glass and raised it in a solitary toast, his words unconsciously echoing the sentiments of Graeme Elliot, who had known the deceased for far longer.

"Good riddance, you bastard. And may you rot in hell for what you did."

CHAPTER SIX

Summer Hill, Sussex, June 1747

"This," said Caroline, gesturing to an enormous and still-growing pile of soil, "is where the lake will be, and on the other side there's going to be a winding path, wide enough for two people to ride abreast, that will lead through those trees to a building of some sort – we haven't designed it yet – where visitors can relax. There'll be three rooms, including a kitchen so we can have freshly cooked food for dinner parties. Are you tired?" she added.

Edwin, busy looking at the huge expanse of land that comprised their garden, took a few moments to realise that he'd been asked a question.

"No," he replied finally. "Well, yes, but your enthusiasm has woken me up. Once I sit down I'll probably fall asleep, but I'm awake right now. Why do we have to have a kitchen in the garden? We've got one in the house."

"I know, but by the time the servants carried the food all the way down here, it would be cold," Caroline pointed out.

"Can't we just have cold food? Meat, bread, cheese, that sort of thing?"

Caroline looked at her husband.

"No, *Sir* Edwin Harlow, we cannot," she said. "Well, we can, but not if we want to impress the people who can push you up your career ladder. Which we do want to do. Don't we?"

Edwin rubbed his eyes.

"I suppose so," he said without enthusiasm. "But right now I just want to spend a couple of days with you and Freddie, and breathe some clean air for a change." He inhaled deeply. "The air smells green here. It's lovely."

Caroline's brow creased with concern.

"I'm sorry, Edwin," she said. "I'm being selfish. I was so surprised to see you I couldn't resist showing you what we're doing. Let's go back to the house, and you can have a nap. I'll show you the rest later, or tomorrow."

Edwin glanced back at the house, which was a considerable distance away from where they now stood.

"No," he said. "We've come this far, and I really *am* awake right now. I've just had enough of politics and socialising for a day or two, that's all. Carry on. A building of some sort. On the top of that slope?" He pointed to a low hill about a quarter of a mile away. In the near distance Freddie was kneeling down, examining something on the path with the total absorption of the very young.

"Yes. Maybe a Grecian temple, or a gothic building? You can help me decide, if you've got time. If we walk there now, I'll show you the view. It's wonderful. You can see for miles. When the visitors – which we won't invite until you're ready to socialise," she added, "have rowed across the lake and then walked or ridden up the slope, they'll be ready for food. And they'll be able to sit and admire the countryside while they eat. Everyone will be very impressed. And I can't wait to invite Great-Uncle Percy."

Edwin stopped and turned to his wife, who immediately adopted an expression of innocence.

"You *hate* Great-Uncle Percy," he said. "Why would you invite him?"

"Because since you've been knighted he's realised how much he loves his great-niece. And because I'm also going to invite Prince Fred and then make Percy row us across the lake. He won't dare refuse if Fred asks him," she added, the innocent expression spoiled somewhat by the malicious gleam in her hazel eyes.

"We're going to have a *boat?*" Edwin asked.

"You're moving up in the world," Caroline said. "Lord Cobham has a barge like Fred's, with a dragon carved on the prow. We don't need anything as big as that though; it would look silly on our small lake."

"*Small?!*" Edwin said incredulously. "It looks huge to me!"

"That's because you're not used to it. Look at Harriet's place, for example. I think she told me it's a four mile ride around the perimeter, and that's just the garden. She owns half the county. Ours is very small by comparison to that, about one and a half miles, but that doesn't mean we can't impress. Everything just needs to be to scale, that's all. Anyway, Cobham's boat would be too big for Percy to row. But I want something ornate that'll carry half a dozen people or so. Of course we need to finish the lake first. We can think about the boat later."

Having reached Freddie the fond parents, as one, knelt down next to him to see what had captured his interest.

"What's he called?" the little boy asked. Clearly somewhat apprehensive of the large pincer-like appendages on one of the two black beetles he was observing, Freddie was sensibly making use of a stick to stop them running away, blocking their path with it every time they moved a few inches away and forcing them to turn in another direction.

"They're stag beetles," Caroline said. "See, the big one looks as though he's got antlers, like a stag deer."

"Is he hurting the little one?" Freddie asked.

"Er, no," Edwin said, blushing slightly, to Caroline's amusement. "They're…um…"

"Making babies," Caroline finished. Edwin's face reddened even more.

"Ah," Freddie said. "Can I keep them? In a box?" He looked up at his father hopefully, knowing him to be the one most likely to give in.

"No," Edwin said, adding, before his son's face could crumple, "They belong outside, in the grass. They'd be very sad if you put them in a box. You wouldn't want them to be sad, would you?"

"No," Freddie said uncertainly.

"Come on then, let's leave them to…make babies," Edwin continued. "I need you to hold my hand."

"Why?" his son asked, reluctant to leave his new plaything.

"Because I'm tired and I've got to walk up that hill, and I need you to help me go up it."

"You're a wonderful father," Caroline said a few minutes later as the family progressed up the slope at the very slow pace of a three-and-a-half-year-old. Edwin smiled.

"That's another reason I'm sick of politics right now. I don't see enough of you both."

"But you're doing important work," Caroline said.

"Nothing is as important as what I'm doing right now," Edwin replied. They arrived at the top of the slope, and he inhaled deeply as he took in the view that was revealed to them.

"Wonderful, isn't it?" Caroline said.

It was. A glorious patchwork of fields and woodland was spread out before them, reaching as far as the eye could see, broken only by a small hamlet complete with a church whose spire rose above the cluster of houses, the whole rendered picturesque by distance. It was a quintessential English country vista, and Edwin's spirits lifted along with the lark that they could hear singing as it rose higher and higher in the warmth of the perfect early summer day.

"I am so lucky," he said, almost to himself.

"Not at all," Caroline replied practically. "You've worked hard for this."

"It's beautiful," he said, still staring at the view. "But that's not why I'm lucky. If someone had told me that night when I met you at Thomas's dinner party, that nine years later I'd be standing here in my own enormous garden, married to the most beautiful woman in the world, with a perfect son, looking at a wonderful view, I'd have called him a madman. But here I am." He turned to look at her and smiled, his eyes sparkling with unshed tears. Caroline observed this with alarm.

"Let's go back," she said. "You're very tired."

"I am," he agreed, "but I'm also very happy. If it worries you when I tell you I love you, then clearly I need to do it more often."

"You don't need to," she replied. "I know without you telling me."

"Even so," he said, returning his attention to the view. Caroline frowned.

"Is something wrong?" she asked.

"Let's go back," he said. "What else are you planning?"

Caroline's frown remained, but she took the hint and the three of them turned for home.

"I thought we could have a kind of terrace on both sides of the building – maybe one that runs all the way round it," she said, "so that people could have dinner looking at the beautiful view, after which we could have music or some other entertainment, and then they could come to this side of the building and see a firework display. We could set that up on the lawn near the lake, so that the fireworks would be reflected in the water. Yes, that would be very nice. And if anything went wrong with the display there'd be plenty of water on hand to put it out," she added, with the wisdom acquired from attending a great many aristocratic firework displays in her youth.

"Isn't this all going to be very expensive?" Edwin asked as they headed back past the lake-to-be.

"Yes," Caroline said happily, her frown disappearing. "That's part of the point of it. The more wealthy you are, the more impressed people will be. And the more impressed people are, the more likely they'll be to listen to you when you present a bill arguing against public executions or the treatment of slaves in the Colonies, or…there *is* something wrong. What is it?" she asked, noting the look of distress that had passed across his face.

Edwin sighed.

"You know me too well," he said. "I can't hide anything from you. But it'll keep until we get indoors. Let's enjoy the walk back together first."

With an enormous effort Caroline refrained from pestering him to reveal whatever it was that was on his mind. If it *was* the expense involved in this project of hers though, she could alleviate his worries immediately.

"So, as I was saying, when it's finished and people come to visit, not only will they enjoy themselves, but they will believe you to be rich, and wealth implies power, which can only help you. In the meantime I'm enjoying myself enormously here. And no one need know that Harriet's paying for it all. She certainly won't tell anyone."

"Harriet's paying for all this?" Edwin asked.

"Yes. Who did you think was paying for it?"

"I thought…your dowry…" When Caroline had married Edwin her father had refused to pay her £3000 dowry, but now, having seen his formerly despised son-in-law knighted by the king, he had changed his mind and had released it to her, Edwin wanting nothing to do with it.

"God, no. This is going to cost around £20,000 by the time it's finished. Maybe more," Caroline said. "But that's nothing for Harriet, as you know. She's richer than Croesus. She wants me to keep the dowry anyway, 'in case those bloody Tories get in', as she put it. She told me it'll be worth the expense to watch Percy have an apoplexy when he has to row her and Fred across the lake." She laughed. "She has imposed one condition, though. I have to build a hothouse so she can show me how to grow bananas and lemons."

She chattered on about greenhouses and shrubs, and the ha-ha that William Kent had planned to put behind the house so that they could observe animals grazing in the distance without having them trespass on the property and cover the lawn with unwanted manure. This continued until they reached the sanctuary of the library, the cosiest room in the house and at present the only one completely finished, and as soon as Freddie had been passed over to his nurse, Caroline pounced.

"What is it? Tell me now, because nothing could be worse than what I'm imagining," she said.

Edwin sank down into a chair and kicked his shoes off. He looked suddenly utterly exhausted, but as sympathetic as Caroline felt towards him she needed to know the news, whatever it was.

"I've finally managed to find out what happened to Beth after she went to denounce Anthony to the Duke of Newcastle," Edwin said. He had been trying to find out without arousing too much suspicion for months, but had met with a wall of silence. "That's one reason why I'm tired. I took Newcastle's servant Benjamin out last night and got him drunk. Which meant I had to drink too. Not as much as he did, but you know I'm not a great drinker."

"So you're crapulent," Caroline said.

"Not so much now, no, though I was very sick this morning, only managed to get an hour's sleep and then I rode like the devil all day to get here. I wanted to see you and I was going to tell you straight away. But it was so lovely walking round the gardens listening to you telling me all your plans that I didn't want to spoil it."

"Tell me now then," she said.

"Beth didn't denounce Anthony," Edwin replied.

Caroline sank down into a chair opposite her husband.

"Thank God for that," she said. Edwin cast her an astonished look, which she intercepted. "If Beth had betrayed Anthony, for whatever reason, I don't think she could have lived with herself. I know you thought she should, but I didn't and still don't, for her sake if not his. What *did* she do, then?"

"She denounced Richard instead. She told Newcastle that Richard knew Anthony was a spy, but accepted the money to buy a commission in the army to keep quiet, and that he warned them when Lord Daniel found out he was a fraud, so they could get away."

To his further astonishment, Caroline started laughing.

"Oh, that's wonderful!" she said between giggles. "Perfect! I can't think of a better revenge. I didn't think I could love Beth any more than I do already, but this…Richard will have a fit. Does he know?"

Edwin leaned forward, his expression so serious that Caroline stopped laughing abruptly.

"Caro, Beth's been transported for life to Antigua, in the West Indies, as an indentured servant," he said.

Caroline sat for a moment frozen, clearly convinced that she'd heard him wrongly.

"No," she said finally. "No, it's not possible. She's a lady! No noblewomen have been transported! And there's going to be a general pardon soon, you told me so only last week!"

"There is," Edwin confirmed. "It will be published in the next few days."

"Well then, she can come back!" Caroline said. "We can pay for her to come back. I can't believe it. Antigua? Are you sure Benjamin was telling you the truth?"

"Yes, he was. I'm sure of it because this morning he was horrified, said that Newcastle would…er…do something terrible to him if he knew he'd divulged what had happened to her. I promised to keep his confidence, providing he informed me of any more information that came through about her. Which means you mustn't tell anyone, not even Sarah."

"You blackmailed him?" Caroline said incredulously. "You?!"

Edwin reddened.

"I care for Beth very much, you know that," he said. "It was the only thing I could think of to make sure that we find out what happens – assuming he hears anything, of course."

"He could just tell you that he hasn't heard anything, whether he does or not," Caroline pointed out.

"He could. But I don't think he will. He also told me that he admired her courage and thought the duke was very harsh on her. I promised not to say anything about that too. I do have a reputation for discretion, which helped. He trusts me to keep my word and providing I do, I think he will keep his."

Caroline sat back in her chair, thinking hard.

"It seems unfair not to tell Sarah," she said after a minute. "I trust her not to say anything to anyone else."

"I know you do and you're probably right, but we can't take the chance," Edwin said.

"We have to find out who bought Beth's indenture and offer them enough money to put her on the next ship back," she said. "I don't know how we—"

"We can't," Edwin interrupted. "She won't be included in the pardon. There are a lot of exceptions, including Anthony, all the leaders who escaped to France and anyone who was transported before the Act is published, among others. If she came back she'd be arrested, possibly executed. I thought about it all the way here. There's nothing we can do for her."

Caroline covered her face with her hands. A full minute passed in silence.

"I'm so sorry," Edwin said helplessly after a time. "I wouldn't hurt you for the world. But I knew you'd want to know."

She took her hands away from her face. Tears spilled over her eyelashes and ran down her cheeks unheeded. Edwin moved to kneel by her chair and took her in his arms.

"I can't believe that vicious bastard would condemn her to a life of slavery, just because she wouldn't give him what he wanted," she said fiercely into his shoulder. "Flora MacDonald is being treated like a romantic heroine because she helped Charles escape. Lady Mackintosh raised her whole clan to fight for Charles while her husband was out with Cumberland, but she was only in prison for a few weeks! All Beth did was protect the man she loves, yet she's shipped off to be a slave! It's so unfair!"

"It's not the same thing," Edwin said. "Flora MacDonald was

coerced into helping Charles – she said herself that she would have helped anyone, including Cumberland, had he been in the same position. Anne Mackintosh was released to her husband's custody because he was loyal to the king. But Anthony was the most dangerous spy we know of. God knows what secrets he passed on to the Pretender and Louis. He made a fool of everyone, even the king. Beth was his willing accomplice; she admitted that freely. She's as bad as Anthony, in Newcastle's eyes."

"No," Caroline said, taking out her handkerchief and blowing her nose fiercely. "Maybe that's partly true, but a lot of this is to do with her being a woman and daring to stand up to him. He can't have her executed because none of the women have been, so he tried to have her starved to death. Now he's trying to kill her in another way. Didn't you tell me the death rate of slaves is really high out in the West Indies? Higher than in the American Colonies?"

"Yes, but that's not just slaves; over half the new settlers die too. It's one of the reasons why we haven't succeeded in trying to take the French and Spanish islands. Most of the troops we send out die of swamp fever or bloody flux before they get a chance to fight. But it *is* worse for the slaves, yes. That's one of the reasons I'm fighting for better treatment for them. I can't get anywhere by talking about humanity, so I've started looking at economics, to see if it's cheaper to treat slaves well than to buy new ones when they die."

"Newcastle's done this because he wants her dead. This is nothing more than spite on his part. We have to do something."

"I don't see that we can," Edwin said.

"Can we find out where she is exactly, and maybe write to her? At the very least we can let her know that we care for her. And maybe we can pay whoever's got her to release her and let her go to France, or Rome – somewhere she'll be safe, if she can't come home. We could do that!"

Could they? They sat in silence, thinking about it.

"You can't be implicated in this," Caroline said after a while. "Nor can I, for that matter. Newcastle would ruin you if we succeed in thwarting him. And Benjamin would suffer too. But if we can find out where she is I think Fred would help again. And it would do his reputation no harm to do so. I want him to know what Newcastle's done. And then when Fred becomes King, which surely can't be long in coming, I'm going to help him in whatever way I can to destroy that evil bastard."

Edwin regarded his wife with a mixture of awe and trepidation.

"Remind me never to make an enemy of you," he said.

"I haven't loved many people in my life, you know that," Caroline replied, "but Beth is one of those people. I will do a lot, almost anything for the people I love. And she's done nothing to make me stop loving her. As for you, you aren't capable of doing anything to make me stop loving you."

"And Anthony?" Edwin asked softly.

"Yes, I loved him, I'll admit that," Caroline replied. "But if he did leave Beth to her fate to save his own skin, and I find out who and where he is, I'll give him over to the authorities without a moment's regret. But I don't believe he would do that. I think Beth was right. I think he's dead. And so will you be if you don't get some sleep. You look dreadful. Go to bed. We can think this through later. How long are you staying for?"

"I can stay tomorrow, but then I have to go back to London. I'll come back when the session ends on the eighteenth. The king intends to dissolve Parliament then."

"Dissolve it? Why?" Caroline asked.

"Because Fred, as you call him, is causing trouble again. He wants a more active role, and the king refuses to grant him one. So he's trying to influence the boroughs to get as many of his followers into the Commons at next year's elections as possible. And his current supporters are trying to form an alliance with the Tories right now. Which is why the king's dissolving Parliament, to thwart him. And I haven't told you that, either."

"Hmm," Caroline said. "That's interesting. We'll have to tread very carefully here, Edwin. You can't afford to annoy George, but you need to keep Fred on your side too."

Edwin sighed tiredly.

"Let's hope that having Great-Uncle Percy row him across our lake will do that, then, because I daren't express any pro-Leicester House sentiments in Parliament at the moment. The king is not in the best humour about the prince's actions."

"Go to bed, Edwin," Caroline said. "We can talk about that

when you come here for the summer. After all, the elections aren't until next year, and you'll win the seat anyway with Harriet behind you. I think it's more urgent that we try to work out how to help Beth, if we can."

* * *

Martinique, June 1747

Beth was in the middle of breakfast, which she'd elected to eat outside on the porch, the sun having not yet reached its full power, when Raymond appeared to tell her that the master would like to see her in his office once she'd finished eating.

"He was surprised to see you awake so early, Madame Beth, and wishes to know if you are having difficulty sleeping?"

Beth glanced at the clock, which was visible through the open doors.

"Not at all. It's after eight, hardly early," she said. "I wanted to enjoy the morning, before it gets really hot."

Raymond smiled. "It's still spring, madame. It will be much hotter soon. Or at least it will feel much hotter because we have a lot more rain from July to November, which makes the air very humid."

Oh God, Beth thought. She was already finding the humidity unbearable. She finished her pastry and stood.

"Lead the way," she said.

Pierre Delisle was busy writing in his ledger, but looked up as she entered his office and smiled broadly.

"Ah, Beth! You are very prompt. I hope that Raymond did not rush you. I expressly told him to assure you there was no hurry."

Raymond, who was standing stiffly by the door, suddenly looked distinctly alarmed.

"He did assure me," Beth lied smoothly. "But I was eager to know why you wanted to see me."

"I have chosen a negress to be your servant," Pierre said, gesticulating to the corner of the room, "although if you think she is unsuitable, I will find another for you."

Beth turned to look in the direction he was pointing, where a young girl of about fourteen or so was staring at the floor, looking absolutely petrified. Beth smiled and opened her mouth to say hello.

"She is named Rosalie, and if you accept her she will be given a trial with you. She hasn't worked as a body servant before, but Eulalie will help to train her, and if she gives you the slightest reason for dissatisfaction you must inform me immediately and I will deal with her," Pierre continued.

"Hello Rosalie," Beth said gently. The poor girl was shaking like a leaf.

"Curtsey to your new mistress, girl!" Pierre barked. Rosalie sank immediately into a curtsey, only managing to stand again on wobbly legs through sheer effort of will, Beth noticed. She briefly raised a pair of huge, terrified brown eyes to Beth's, before looking at the floor again.

Beth moved forward and took the girl gently by the hand.

"I am sure we will get along very well," she said reassuringly. "We are both new, in our different ways, and we can teach each other. You can teach me about Martinique, and I can teach you how to be a maid. It will be fun!"

"Rosalie," Pierre said. The young girl looked up at him. "You are very lucky to have this chance to work in the house, and I am sure Madame Beth will be a good mistress to you."

Well, I certainly won't be dragging her from the other side of the house to pick up a handkerchief that's two inches away from my fingers, Beth thought.

"As you know, she is new to this country and is not used to the ways of negroes," he continued. "So I will be keeping a very close eye on you. If I see any sign that you are taking advantage of her kind nature, I will have you whipped and sent back to the field gang immediately. Is that understood?"

"Yes, Monsieur Pierre," Rosalie whispered.

"Good. Now Raymond will show you to Madame Beth's room. Go!" he shouted. The girl flew from the room as though shot from a cannon, Raymond closing the door quietly behind them.

The moment they were gone Beth rounded on her employer.

"It's very kind of you to provide a servant for me, Pierre," she said, managing with an effort to keep her voice calm, "but was it really necessary to frighten her out of her wits? I thought the poor girl was going to faint! And I might be new to the country, but I've had plenty of experience in dealing with servants."

"My dear Beth," Monsieur Delisle said in quite a different tone from that he'd used moments before, "I did not intend to insult you. Indeed it was the furthest thing from my mind. I have no doubt of your ability to keep English servants in order, but you will find the negro to be quite a different creature to that you are used to. They are like dogs, brute creatures who need to be constantly reminded who is the master. If you show them kindness, they will bite you."

"In my experience, if you show dogs kindness they will love you for it," Beth retorted. "But we are talking about a human being here, not a dog. I thank you for your advice, but I will train Rosalie in my own way. I will be sure to tell you if I need any help with her."

She turned and walked out of the room quickly, before she lost her temper. What a strange man. Yesterday he had been so kind and considerate; he had told her they were all one big family! Yet today he reminded her of Lord Edward with his pomposity and contempt for servants.

Are all the people in Martinique like this? she wondered. No. The marquis had not been like this; he had been nothing but kindness for the whole ten days she had stayed in his house. But then she had not had cause to speak to him about servants. Slaves.

She stood for a moment with her eyes closed, taking in deep breaths of the hot sugar-scented air, feeling alien. And homesick. She would give almost anything to inhale a lungful of cool fresh Scottish mountain air right now.

No. It's over. That life is finished. This is my new life now. I must remember I am penniless, and Monsieur Delisle is showing me kindness by employing me and treating me as an equal. I must become accustomed to the ways of the people if I am to fit in here. I will fit in here, she told herself fiercely. She opened her eyes and uttered a little shriek.

"I am sorry, madame," Raymond said. He had approached silently while she'd been arguing with herself, and was standing a couple of feet away from her. "I did not wish to alarm you. Rosalie is in your rooms, and Eulalie is showing her how she must behave. I hope—" He stopped abruptly.

"What do you hope, Raymond?" Beth asked gently.

"I hope you will be kind to her, Madame Beth. She is a good girl and hard-working, but not suited for life in the fields, I think. She will do her best to please you, madame," he said somewhat fervently.

"I will be kind to her, I promise," Beth reassured him. "I have never been cruel to a servant, and do not intend to start now."

Raymond smiled suddenly, displaying a set of perfect white teeth. He was very handsome when he smiled. And clearly he disliked sugar as much as she did.

"Thank you, madame," he said. "I am very grateful."

When Beth arrived in her rooms Eulalie was showing Rosalie how to lay out clothes. They both rose as Beth entered, and curtseyed deeply. Rosalie looked only marginally less terrified than she had in Monsieur Delisle's office.

"Thank you, Eulalie," Beth said. "I'm sure you have an awful lot to do, so I will take over now in showing Rosalie her duties. Could you send up some tea, please?"

"Of course, madame," Eulalie replied. As she reached the door, Beth called her back.

"With two cups, please," she said.

Once Eulalie had left the room, Beth motioned to Rosalie to sit down, and then took the seat opposite her.

"Have you ever tasted tea, Rosalie?" she asked.

"No, madame," Rosalie whispered.

"Well, you are about to. And while we drink our tea I want to get to know you a little, and to tell you about myself. It's important that you learn your duties, but it's far more important that you know who you will be working for. Monsieur Pierre was right when he said that I'm new to the country, and that I'm not used to the ways of negroes, whatever they are. I *am* used to the ways of people, though, and I have trained more than one young woman to be a good maid.

"I am patient and kind, but I'm also firm. When I lived in England I had quite a few servants, and they all became my friends. I hope you and I will also become friends. Ah, here is the tea!" she said as the door opened and a young girl brought in a tray, placing it carefully on the table. She set a cup and saucer in front of Beth and then looked confused.

114

"The other one is for Rosalie," Beth explained. "You can leave now. I will pour the tea. Now," she continued as the thunderstruck maid left the room, "tell me about yourself." She poured the tea into Rosalie's cup and then pushed it in front of her. "Help yourself to sugar," she said.

Rosalie sat, frozen. This was clearly such an alien situation to her that she had no idea what to do. Beth sighed. Carefully she placed one lump of the sugar into her cup and then stirred it with a silver teaspoon. Then she sipped it and waited. After a moment, as she had hoped, Rosalie copied her. Beth smiled.

"How old are you, Rosalie?" Beth asked.

"I'm not sure, madame," Rosalie said. "I think I'm about fourteen."

"Were you born here?"

"Yes, madame, I've lived here on Soleil all my life."

Soleil. So she had been born on the plantation, and was therefore presumably unlikely to commit suicide if asked to do a day's work.

"And do you live with your parents?" Beth asked.

Rosalie looked confused.

"Eulalie said I'm to stay here, madame," she said. "I'm to sleep on the floor in case you need me in the night."

"Why would I need...?"Beth began, then rethought. "Do you want to sleep in my room, or would you rather sleep at home? Wherever you normally sleep?"

Rosalie bit her lip and looked around the room frantically as though the answer might be found somewhere in it. She looked about to cry.

My God, Beth realised, *she's never been given a choice in anything in her life. She has no idea how to even form an opinion.*

"Tell me about where you've lived until now," she said instead. "I want to learn all about the plantation. I am going to ask Monsieur to show it to me, but it will help me if you tell me about it first. And then I will tell you about England, and you will see how different it is to Soleil. Have you ever met a blind person?"

"Yes, madame," Rosalie said, perking up now she knew how to answer. "Georges went blind when he got old. He died last winter," she added sadly.

"Oh, I'm sorry," Beth said. "Did you play games when you were a child?"

"Oh yes, madame," Rosalie said.

"This is a game, then. Pretend I am blind, and you have to tell me exactly what your house looks like. And then I'll pretend you're blind, and I will tell you what my house in England looked like. It will be fun, and we'll get to know each other a little."

Rosalie smiled, tentatively. It was a start.

"Adela's cabin is smaller than this room," she began. "The walls are made of wood and the roof is made from leaves, big leaves. There is a table and some stools, and a shelf where Adela keeps her pots and dishes. Adela sleeps in a hammock, but I sleep on the floor with the other children – there are ten of us. The floor is made of dirt and when it rains the water comes under the door and we get wet."

So presumably sleeping on the floor of Beth's room would be preferable to sleeping on the wet muddy ground. Unless...

"Is Adela your mother?" Beth asked.

"No, madame. My mother was sold when I was very small. I don't remember her. Adela doesn't have any children of her own, but she likes them, and she looks after the ones whose mothers have died or been sold."

"Do you think you will be happy to sleep in my room then?" Beth asked, keeping her expression neutral with an effort. "You will be dry, at least, and I will get you a mattress so you don't have to lie on the tiles."

"Oh, yes, madame, I would love that!" Rosalie said happily. "It is cooler here, too!"

Later that evening, while Pierre worked in his office and Antoinette lay on the couch on the porch, snoring gently, Beth listened to the chatter of the night insects and thought about what Rosalie had revealed to her that day about plantation life as she had slowly relaxed under Beth's gentle questioning.

The slaves lived in small cabins, ten or more to a room smaller than Beth's bedroom. Sometimes the cabins were blown down by hurricanes and had to be rebuilt. If the hurricane was very bad and blew the whole cabin away, the slaves would have to live and sleep outside, sheltering from the daily downpours under banana leaves or anything else they could find. On every second Saturday there was no work, except at harvest time or after a hurricane, when everyone had to work very long hours. On the free Saturdays the slaves would tend their little plots where they grew food. In the evening they would tell stories, and sometimes they would play music and dance. On Sundays the priest would come and talk to them about Christ, and if they forgot the words of the creed or the *Pater Noster* he would beat them.

On the surface this didn't seem such a bad way of life, until you realised that harvest lasted from January until June, and that the field gangs worked in the blazing sun, often for sixteen hours or more a day, with inadequate amounts of food. And above all, they had no choice in their lives, none at all.

It was perfectly acceptable for families to be forcibly separated, for mothers and fathers to be sold, never to see each other or their children again.

Ealasaid had told her that indentured servitude was just another word for slavery. At the time, as she had listened to her grandmother's sketchy account of her life in the Colonies, Beth had had only a vague idea of what slavery was.

She had escaped that fate because of a privateer named Paul Marsal. But thousands of other Jacobite prisoners had not.

She needed to know exactly what she had escaped.

"I am sorry Beth, but it isn't possible at the moment. I am far too busy with the harvest to take you on a tour," Pierre said, gesturing to the mound of papers that littered the desk of his office.

"I understand," Beth replied. "I wouldn't expect you to take precious time away from your work, and I know what a busy time the harvest is – it was the same in England. But surely one of your workers could show me? Raymond or Eulalie perhaps? I am really interested to learn how sugar is made!"

"Nothing would give me greater pleasure, I assure you. But I cannot spare anyone at this time. Sugar is not like the crops you grow in England or in France. It has to be cut at exactly the right moment in its growth, and once it is cut it must be processed immediately, or it will spoil. It is a very delicate process. But I don't think it will interest a young lady of breeding. Antoinette has never expressed an interest in seeing it. It is very hot and dangerous work."

"I think it sounds most fascinating, monsieur," Beth persisted.

"And you must remember I am experienced in danger."

"Indeed you are! And it must have been a terrible ordeal for you to be captured by privateers! I would not expose you to more disagreeable sights for the world. When the harvest is over we shall go to Saint Pierre for a few days. It is really most delightful there and far more suited to a delicate lady like yourself."

Back in her room, having been kindly but firmly dismissed, Beth fumed. *Being captured by privateers was one of the best parts of the last few months,* she thought, wondering what Pierre would say if he knew that her experiences over the last two years had rendered her far more suited to a privateering life than one spent sitting on a porch all day listening to Antoinette complain about the heat and her ailments. The harvest would be over soon, and then she would have to wait until next year to see how sugar was produced.

The thought of still being here next year filled her with gloom, which she impatiently pushed to one side. Her current life was far better than the one she'd been destined for on Antigua, she reminded herself. Which brought her back to one of the reasons she wanted to tour the factory – to see what she had escaped, in the hope that it would render the next months or years bearable by comparison.

She sat on her bed, and plotted.

* * *

It was still quite dark when she woke one morning a week after her conversation with Pierre. The bell had rung to call the slaves to the fields, but the house was still in silence. At the foot of the bed on a thin mattress, Rosalie was sleeping soundly. Beth had deliberately kept her awake and busy late last night, inventing chores for her to tire her out in the hope that she would be able to slip from the room at dawn without waking her.

As soon as there was just enough light for her to see to dress, she donned the clothes she had told Rosalie to lay out on the chair; front-lacing stays, one petticoat and a light cotton morning dress. Antoinette would consider her half-naked but she was unlikely to rise before ten, and Beth intended to be back by then. And she didn't really give a damn what anyone thought, anyway. She was always being told she was unused to the ways of the island; she could use that as an excuse if necessary.

Tiptoeing across the room, she opened the door, slipped out and closed it carefully and silently. She walked to the front door in her stocking feet, slipped her shoes on on the porch and then set off in the direction of the fields, where the slaves were already hard at work. As she walked she remembered the last time she had sneaked out of a house on an illicit journey. At least this time she hadn't had to climb down a drainpipe, and she was unlikely to come across a roomful of Gaelic-speaking Jacobites. Nearly five years had passed since then. In some ways it seemed like moments, in other ways a lifetime ago.

She smiled as she remembered how terrified she'd been that night, then pushed the memory of her first meeting with Alex, Duncan and Angus to the back of her mind and focussed on the sight ahead of her as she walked toward the buildings which formed the sugar factory.

The sugar cane was much taller close up than it seemed from the house, about twice the height of a tall man. The slaves, barefoot and dressed in rags, stood in the cane, wrapped one arm round several stems, then swung their machetes and cut it close to the ground. Then they moved on to the next stems, while the children gathered it into bundles and carried it to a line of mules, where it was loaded on to them. Beth stopped to watch, fascinated by the speed and skill of the cutters.

"You should not be here, madame, it's dangerous," a voice came from behind her, making her jump. She turned to the owner of the voice, a slender young white man with long dark hair, dressed in breeches and a shirt that was open almost to the waist. In his hand he carried a whip, and slung over his shoulder was a musket.

"How do they cut the cane without injuring themselves?" she asked.

"It takes time to learn, madame. The cane does cut them because the edges are sharp, but does not harm them enough to stop them working. Sometimes they cut their legs with the machete though. That *is* annoying, because we cannot afford to lose a worker for even a day at this time."

"You are English!" she said in that language, recognising the accent, although his French, like hers, was almost fluent.

"I am," he said, switching to English too. "Francis Armstrong at your service, Lady Elizabeth."

"I prefer Beth," she replied. "But how do you know my name?"

"Word spreads quickly on the island," he replied, smiling. "Everyone knows you are a lady who was cruelly transported by the English and rescued by Monsieur Delisle!"

Beth took a moment to process this version of events, and then smiled.

"I'm sure you know why I am here, then. But what is an Englishman doing in a French colony? You were not on the *Veteran!*"

"No. I am here by choice, my lady. I have contracted to serve Monsieur Pierre for seven years, and then I hope to buy land and settle here. I'm of the Roman faith, and studied in France. I feel more at home here than I would on a British island. But now I must get someone to escort you back to the house."

"Do you have a blacksmith here?" she asked, ignoring his last sentence.

"Yes, but—"

"Excellent!" she replied crisply. "Then I would very much like to see him. I have a commission for him. And as I am here, I am very interested in learning how sugar is produced. So if this someone you are about to get can give me a tour of the factory, I would be very grateful."

"My lady, we really cannot spare someone—" Francis began.

"I know, I understand how busy you are. But it will take no longer to show me the factory than it would to escort me home. Having made my way here alone, I am quite capable of reversing the process. So, if you would be so kind?" she finished, every inch a noblewoman. *If I'm going to be paraded as the plantation's specimen aristocrat, I might as well take advantage of it,* she thought.

The overseer called over one of the slaves, a large, broad-shouldered African, naked from the waist up and sweating freely, and handed him the whip.

"Joshua," he said. "You will make sure the negroes keep at it. I will be back soon and if the work isn't going as fast as it should be, your back will know about it."

"Yes, monsieur," the man said. He took the whip and began

to walk along the line. If Beth had wondered why none of the slaves had stopped work to look at her or observe her exchange with Mr Armstrong, she now had her answer.

The overseer walked along the path with her, explaining as he went.

"The cane, when it's cut, is loaded onto the mules and then taken to the mill," he said. "Everything has to be done quickly and one task follows on from the other, so we must all work at a good and steady speed, so that no one is left with nothing to do."

Inside the mill slaves were feeding the cane through constantly turning vertical rollers which crushed the stalks, resulting in a thick green juice.

"Now I will show you the boiling house, or perhaps it would be better for me to tell you, because it really is very—"

"Dangerous," she finished for him. She turned to a man who was standing by the rollers, closely observing the workers. In his hand he held an axe. "What are you doing?" she asked.

The man bowed deeply. "I watch," he said in broken French. "If hand get caught, I chop, like so." He raised and lowered the axe.

Beth turned to Francis.

"Is that true?" she asked. "He chops the person's hand off?"

"Yes," Francis answered. "The rollers are powered by the wind and we have no way to stop them quickly. If someone gets their hand caught in the roller, then the only way to free them is to cut off the limb. Otherwise they will be dragged through the roller and killed. The rollers are very powerful, my lady, they have to be."

"Does that happen often?" Beth asked, horrified.

"Not often, but yes, it happens, especially late in the evenings when the negroes are tired."

"Is there no way to put up a guard of some sort, to stop that happening?" she asked.

"No. Other owners have tried, but it slows the work down too much, is not practical. Now, shall I take you to the blacksmith?"

"No," she said. "You said there is a boiling house? What happens there? Yes, I know," she continued as he made to object, "it is dangerous. I have experienced a lot of danger in my life, Mr Armstrong. I am sure I can deal with whatever dangers the boiling house holds."

As soon as she got there however, she knew why Francis hadn't wanted her to see it, why Pierre hadn't wanted her to see it.

It was a large room made of stone, with a shingle roof. On one side was a series of copper cauldrons, ranging from very large to relatively small, and each one was set over an oven. The cauldrons were full of boiling juice, and slaves, dressed only in ragged breeches, were skimming scum off the top of each one with what looked like large oars. Steam filled the room, making it difficult to see what was going on clearly.

"Nathaniel there," Francis said, pointing to a thin negro with pockmarked skin, who smiled at her, "is a very skilled worker. He adds quicklime, which helps the sugar to become granulated, but he has to add the exact amount, or it will not work and the sugar will be spoilt. The amount to add depends on many things; the time of planting, the way the cane has grown, the amount of sun and rain, the soil, if it has been attacked by any pests…really, he is a very important man. The juice starts off in the large pot, then it is skimmed, poured into the next one, and so on. Once it is in the smallest, Nathaniel has to determine the exact moment to strike the sugar, and then the fire is dampened and the sugar cools. Let us go outside."

Even standing in the doorway, Beth had felt the heat from the room searing her lungs as she struggled to breathe. After a few seconds her skin felt as though it was going to blister. Never in her life had she experienced anything like the intense heat of that room. It was unbearable. No one could even breathe in there for more than a minute or two, let alone work in it.

Men, women, children were working in there, for sixteen hours a day, six days a week. It was hell, quite literally.

She stood outside, sucking in lungsful of what seemed by comparison to be cool air, although the temperature in the fields was now very warm.

"Are you well, my lady?" Francis asked. "This was why I said it was dangerous, because of the heat. If you are not accustomed…"

"How does anyone become accustomed to that?" she said, aghast. "It's not possible."

"Everything is possible if you have no choice, my lady," he replied with cold practicality. "There is no alternative. The sugar must be processed and that is the only way to process it. The slaves must do it, or die. They know this."

"Do they not die anyway, working in that?" she asked. Her chest was burning, and her hair was plastered to her neck with sugary steam and sweat. She felt sick.

"Some do," he said. "If they get the boiling juice on their skin it sticks and burns through the flesh. Some die anyway, from the heat. But we all have to die. The islands are full of dangers; swamp fever, fluxes, snakebites, maroons…but there are great riches to be made too, for the right men." He smiled.

"But not for them," Beth said, gesturing to the myriad black workers.

"No, not for them. But they are still blessed, because they are all baptised into Mother Church when they land on the island," Francis said, "and have the chance of eternal life in Paradise, which they would not have, had they stayed in ignorance in Africa. The British slaves are not so fortunate, for they are not baptised in any faith at all. So you see, the slaves here are very fortunate and have their own riches to come!"

Back in her room later in the morning, after having seen the blacksmith and instructed him as to the exact type of knife she wanted him to make for her, and promising him cash that she would have to ask Pierre for as an advance on her salary, she thought about what she had seen that day. After a while there came a small cough from the other side of the room. Beth looked up from her musing to see Rosalie, who was standing in the doorway looking very concerned.

"Are you well, Madame Beth?" she asked tentatively. "Can I get anything for you?"

Yes. An extremely large whisky and passage on the next ship out, Beth thought.

"No thank you," she said, forcing a smile. "Come and sit down. I'm very pleased with how quickly you're learning the work. I think you are a natural. Who taught you to massage a scalp like you did when you washed my hair yesterday?"

Rosalie smiled, her eyes lighting up.

"Adela, madame. She said it's a very good way to relax, better than tafia or rum. She said that is the devil's brew."

"It felt very good," Beth said.

"I used to sometimes massage the women when they came back from the fields, if they asked," Rosalie offered. Although by nature shy and quiet, she was opening up to Beth, who was starting to like her very much.

"I went to the fields today," Beth said. "I was very quiet, because I didn't want to wake you."

"Oh madame, you should have woken me! It is not safe to go there alone!"

"I was safe – Monsieur Armstrong showed me how the sugar is made." She caught the unconscious twist of Rosalie's lip as she mentioned the overseer's name. *Interesting.* "I think working in the fields is very hard. I didn't expect the women to be doing the same work as the men. Did you cut cane before you came into the house?"

"No, madame, I wasn't strong enough for that. Only the strongest negroes are in that gang. They plant the cane, and then they cut it. It's when they plant the cane that they ask me to massage them the most, because it hurts the back, here." She put her hands in the small of her back. "I used to help to dig the manure in and pull up the weeds. Monsieur Francis said that next year he would teach me to clay the sugar, but then when you arrived Papa asked Monsieur Delisle if I could come into the house."

"Papa?" Beth, who had been about to ask what claying the sugar was, said.

"Yes, madame. Raymond. He is my papa."

"What's a maroon?" Beth asked that evening as they all sat on the porch after supper. Pierre had elected to sit with his wife and her companion for an hour before returning to his work.

"Runaway slaves," Antoinette said, sipping at a glass of Madeira wine. Beth was not partial to it normally, but as it was the only wine that improved rather than spoilt in the tropical heat, she was learning to like it. "They live in hordes in the forest, and are all murderers and rapists. We live in constant fear that they will come down from the mountains and kill us all as we sleep."

"My dear, you must not frighten our guest so! They are a problem, it is true, but we are well protected here, and my slaves are loyal. Francis told me that you went to the factory today. I must state that I am not happy that you did so without asking me."

"I did ask you," Beth pointed out. "But you said you were too busy. I wanted to ask the blacksmith to make some knives for me, and did not wish to disturb you, so I went alone. Monsieur Armstrong was kind enough to show me the factory, when I asked."

"Really, my dear, you did not need to visit the smith. I could have sent for him. And as I said, it is dangerous—"

"I don't see why it's dangerous, if, as you say, the slaves are loyal. And it's not as though I was actually cutting the cane, feeding it through the rollers or skimming the pots of juice. I was unlikely to cut my own leg off or have to have my hand chopped off to save my life," Beth finished, more bluntly than she had intended.

"Ah, you are upset. And in truth, this was what I wished to spare you," Pierre said, his face a mask of concern. "It is always the way with newcomers. They find our ways distressing until they are more accustomed to them."

"Did one of them have a limb cut off, then?" Antoinette asked indifferently.

"No," Beth said. "Not while I was there, anyway."

"Ah. Good. We really cannot afford to lose anyone at this point in the harvest. They will use any excuse to stop working."

Beth, who had been occupied with trying to fish an unfortunate and now deceased small insect out of her wine glass, looked up.

"Madame Beth, please allow me," Raymond said, leaping forward from his place near the door, where he had been standing in case he was needed. He bent over her glass and took the opportunity to cast her an imploring glance, which she saw. She nodded imperceptibly. "I will change your glass for a clean one," he said.

Beth closed her eyes momentarily, remembered Sir Anthony's training, discarded what she had been about to say, and opened them again.

"Pierre, I am afraid I must ask for a small advance on my allowance, if you would be so kind," she said.

"Of course, my dear. May I ask what you wish to purchase?"

"The smith is making two knives for me."

"Why do you need knives to be made?" Antoinette asked. "We have plenty of knives in the house you can use for cutting food."

"And he asked you for money?" Pierre said at the same time, aghast.

"They are not for cutting food, and no, he did not ask me for money," Beth replied. "They are throwing knives, and have to have a particular point of balance to them. If he does a good job, I would very much like to pay him something. It would make me happy," she finished.

"There is really no need to pay him, but of course if you wish to I will be delighted to advance you the money. In fact I will give you your first month's consideration in the morning. It is not fitting that you should have to ask. I apologise," Pierre said.

"Thank you, Pierre. You are very kind."

"But why do you want such things made?" he asked.

Raymond returned with her wine, and she thanked him.

"My mother was from the Highlands of Scotland," Beth said. "You may know of the Highlanders – they are thought by the British government to be savages, murderers and rapists. Nothing could be further from the truth of course, but it is always so when one people does not understand the ways of another. The redcoats, being civilised, murdered a good number of my mother's clan when she was a child, and so she was taught to protect herself in case of further attack, and she taught me. I am very adept at throwing a knife. I thought it might be useful to have a throwing knife in case I see one of those poisonous vipers you told me about."

"How amazing!" Antoinette said, having missed the thinly veiled inference altogether. "But the snakes move very quickly, you know."

"I am *very* adept," Beth said. "I will show you when I get the knives."

Pleading tiredness due to her early start that morning, Beth made her excuses not long after and headed to bed. As she reached the stairs she passed Raymond, who had been sent to fetch another bottle of Madeira.

"Thank you," she said, her voice low so that the couple on the porch would not hear.

He smiled, knowing what she was referring to.

"You will become accustomed to the ways of plantation life, madame," he whispered. "It takes time, that is all."

"I hope I never become accustomed to what I saw today," she replied. "What is claying the sugar?"

"It is a way of refining the sugar, madame, to make it whiter. You may have seen the clay trays that are used in the boiling room when you were there, before you had to leave."

So Francis had told Pierre about the whole of her visit, then.

"In the boiling room?" Beth said.

"Yes madame. I am sorry, you will excuse me?" he said, lifting the bottle.

"Of course." She started up the stairs, then paused. "Raymond?" she said, still low-voiced.

He turned.

"I swear to you, I will do everything in my power and more to ensure your daughter never has to work in that inferno," she whispered fervently.

He looked up at her, then smiled again, broadly.

"Thank you, Madame Beth," he said. "You are a blessing to us."

He stepped away to the porch, and she continued up the stairs to her room.

CHAPTER SEVEN

London, mid-June 1747

It was late afternoon and the streets were bustling with the usual sorts of people to be found in a reasonably respectable part of the city; maids searching for delicacies to tempt their mistresses' appetites, ladies of means making purchases, accompanied by footmen laden with the parcels they had already bought, young men searching for a trinket to please a young lady, young ladies searching for a ribbon or a perfume to attract a young man. And of course those who were always to be found where there was money to be had; prostitutes, pickpockets and the ever-present beggars, hands held out as they pleaded for a copper.

In amongst this throng was a man, who was making his way down the street with some difficulty, hampered as he was by being possessed of only one leg but two crutches, which he employed inexpertly as he attempted to negotiate the street, with the result that more than one person uttered an exclamation of pain as their ankle or shin came in sharp contact with his wooden supports.

He was tall and well-built, and wore old-fashioned clothes, including a very long full-skirted frockcoat which covered his knees and which was buttoned up in spite of the weather, probably because he was trying to hide his lack of a waistcoat. His dark hair, which was long and tangled, was tied back, and he wore a battered round hat with a wide brim which partially hid his face. Only partially, though. Anyone who got close enough to see under the hat recoiled immediately, which, along with the clumsy use of the crutches, soon ensured that he had a reasonably clear path through the crowd.

Most of the shopkeepers on the street had left their doors open, partly to encourage customers, and partly because it really was a glorious day. The shop which the man was heading for was one of these, which made it easier for him to enter. He ducked his head as he went through the doorway, having to hop a couple of times as one of his crutches slid on the polished floor.

Sarah, who was occupied with a customer, looked up at his somewhat ungainly entrance. Regaining his balance, he leaned against the wall to the side of the doorway and executed an interesting manoeuvre that was clearly meant to be a bow.

"Miss Browne?" the man asked in a gravelly voice.

"Yes," she replied. "Can I help you, sir?"

"I have heard of you. It is said you have some skill with cosmetics," he said. "I was hoping that you might be able to assist me."

"I will try," she said. "In what way?"

By way of answer he removed his hat. His face was in shadow, but she could still see enough to make her step to the side of her customer to shield her from the sight of the man's horribly disfigured features. The left side of his face was a mass of sores. That, coupled with the missing limb, led her to the conclusion that he was an ex-soldier who had probably been involved in an explosion of some sort. Her professionalism in dealing with clients of all kinds ensured that a widening of the eyes was her only reaction. To her relief, once he had shown her the reason for his being there he replaced the hat and turned the ruined side of his face away.

"If you would care to wait, Mr…"

"Featherstone."

"…Mr Featherstone, I will see what I can do for you once I've finished here," she said.

"Thank you. Would you prefer if I waited outside?" he asked politely. She wondered if he had suffered some damage to his vocal cords too; his voice was rasping. Northern English, further north than Manchester, but she couldn't place his accent any closer than that.

"No, of course not!" she said. "If you would care to take a seat, I won't be very long."

"I'll stand, miss, if you don't mind," he replied. "I'm but

recently wounded, and am not very good with these things yet." He gestured to the crutches.

"As you prefer," she said politely.

She continued dressing her client's hair, whilst he leaned against the wall, his head bowed, possibly out of consideration for them, as his position shielded his face completely; or maybe he was just tired. Sarah put him from her mind while she gave her current client her full attention, as was her way.

Once finished, Sarah said goodbye to her satisfied customer and went behind her counter to put her fee away. As she did so she noticed the man move from his position against the wall, accidentally pushing the door closed with his crutch as he did so.

Maybe accidentally. She came instantly to full alert, reassessing him. Very tall, heavily built, almost certainly a military man. Had Richard sent him?

Don't be ridiculous, she chided herself immediately. *Richard would come himself. And if he didn't, he certainly wouldn't send a cripple to threaten me. I could be out of the back door and down the alley before he got halfway across the room.* She relaxed a little, bent down and put the money in her box.

"Do you have any more appointments today, Miss Browne?" he asked. She looked up. "Only my situation is a…delicate one, you understand, and I'd rather we weren't interrupted."

"I have the time to talk to you, Mr Featherstone, and I will see if I can help you," she replied formally, not answering the question. "And I will be discreet, but I will not stop other customers coming in with enquiries, as you did. Please be so kind as to open the door again. It is warm in here."

Instead of doing as she asked, he leaned back against the wall again, reaching under his coat with his right hand as if to scratch his thigh. Or maybe draw a weapon? Sarah stiffened. There was something not right here. Better to be safe and offend him, than sorry. She reached for her pistol, which she kept next to the money box.

"Mr Featherstone," she said, speaking loudly to cover the sound of her cocking the gun, "I—"

She got no further before the man exploded into action. She registered the movement and that he appeared to have regrown his right leg, but managed no more than to raise the gun a few inches before he crossed the room, leapt the counter, knocked the weapon from her hand with a bone-jarring blow and drove her back against the wall, pinning her there with his weight and covering her mouth with one huge hand. She had never seen anyone move so quickly in her life.

"Sarah," her assailant said urgently, the accent the same, although his throat as well as his leg appeared to be miraculously cured, "I've no wish to hurt you. I need to ask you a question, that's all. Once I have your answer I'll leave, I promise. I wouldn't have come, but I think…I hope I can trust you."

Trust? What was he talking about? She didn't know him. She'd never seen him before in her life!

Unable to move, she stared at him, her eyes above his imprisoning hand huge and terrified. Adrenalin flooded her body and her chest heaved as her breathing quickened.

"Promise me you won't scream," he said, "and I'll let you go. I won't stay more than a few minutes."

She scrutinised his face, her mind racing, trying to identify where she knew him from. At very close quarters the apparent mutilation of his face seemed merely to be a mass of partially healed scratches. She disregarded them, took in instead the high cheekbones, the strong, straight nose, the mouth that curled upward slightly at the edges, the eyes, cold and ruthless, long-lashed, blue, with gold flecks in the irises…her eyes widened even further, and she gave a muffled cry of shock. He sighed.

"You recognise me," he said softly, and it wasn't a question. "I've come about Beth…"

The bell jingled and the door opened behind him.

"Hello!" came a familiar voice. "I was passing and thought I'd call in to see whether…" The voice trailed off as the woman took in the broad back of the man behind the counter and the apparent absence of Miss Browne.

Sarah looked at him, saw from his expression a variety of possible options running through his mind, none of them boding well for her, and then she locked eyes with him, trying to convey a complex reassurance with no more than a look and a very slight shake of her head, which was all she could manage due to the vice-like grip on her jaw.

The man she had known in the past as Sir Anthony Peters

leaned away from her slightly, and removed his hand from her mouth. She knew without a shred of doubt, that if she made any attempt to call for help, did anything that would betray him, he would kill both her and her new client in a heartbeat.

She thought rapidly, all the survival instincts she had learned in her life before meeting Beth coming to the fore, and with an inspiration born of desperation, threw her arms around him, embracing him warmly before looking round him at Lydia Fortesque, whose eyes were sparkling with interest at having caught the prim and proper Miss Browne in what appeared to be a compromising position.

"Oh! Miss Fortesque!" Sarah cried, her voice trembling. "You have caught me at such an exciting moment! I must introduce you!"

Releasing him, she squeezed his arm briefly in what she hoped was a reassuring gesture, then moved past him. He did not stop her, which was something. She cleared her throat, tried to calm herself.

"This is…Adam, my cousin, from…Nantwich in Cheshire. I had no idea he was in London! Imagine, he returned home from working in…Newcastle, and discovered where I was. He's come all this way to see me!" she improvised, trying to give him as much information to work with as possible. *Please let him go along with this,* she prayed, knowing that both her life and that of the pretty, vacuous young woman standing looking at them with open curiosity, depended on this man's whim.

There was a moment's silence, during which Sarah was sure Lydia would hear her heart crashing against her ribs in terror, and then the man moved to her side, took off his hat and bowed deeply.

"Pleased to make your acquaintance, Miss Fortesque," he said in a Manchester accent. *Close enough,* Sarah thought. Lydia wouldn't know the difference between Manchester and Cheshire anyway. He stood, displaying the mangled side of his face to her scrutiny.

"Oh!" Lydia cried, recoiling from him.

"We haven't seen each other for…oh…it must be five years, at least!" Sarah said, her voice a little shrill. Hopefully Lydia would put it down to excitement at being reunited with her relative.

"How nice," Lydia said unenthusiastically.

"I'm sorry, Miss Fortesque," Sarah said. "I didn't mean to bore you with my family issues. How can I help you today?" The feeling was coming back into her hand now, pains shooting from her wrist to her forearm. Holding her hand behind her back, she curled and flexed her fingers, trying to ease the pain. She tried to calm herself, to behave normally. *Sir Anthony was kind, caring. He wouldn't hurt me,* she told herself.

This man was nothing like Sir Anthony. Sir Anthony had never really existed.

"I believe you have some new scents, just in from Paris?" Lydia said, breaking into her thoughts. "I hoped to try them."

"Of course!" Sarah replied. Behind her, her new relative stood observing her carefully.

I can't do this, she thought. *Not with him watching. I'll make a mistake, and then we'll both die.* She turned to him, her eyes pleading.

"Go right through," she said. "Make some tea. I'll be finished in a few minutes and then we can have a nice chat."

He looked at her, his eyes still cold, calculating. His lips pursed slightly, considering. And then he blinked, and in that moment transformed himself completely and was her cousin Adam, fresh from the country.

"Tea?" he said, smiling broadly, clearly very impressed. "You have come up in the world, cousin. You're a proper lady now. I've no idea how to make it, though. Have you got one of them fancy pots, and cups and all?"

She could have fainted on the spot from sheer relief.

"Yes I have," she replied lightheartedly. "And saucers too. Put the water on to boil, then. I'll make it when I've served Miss Fortesque," she said.

He disappeared through the door which led to her living area, closing it quietly behind him. No sooner had he done so than Sarah remembered that Mary was having her nap in the bedroom. She told herself that whoever, whatever this man really was, Beth loved him, and Beth would never love anyone who could harm a child. And anyway he was certain to be listening at the door, alert for any attempt on her part to raise the alarm.

Lydia seemed to take forever to try out the different scents, rejecting the Parisian ones and insisting on trying every other perfume Sarah had. Then she prevaricated again, unable to decide if she liked her favourite enough to justify the expense of buying it. Sarah had to resist the urge to give it to her free of charge, anything to get her out of the shop. She might have been able to get away with donating any other perfume to her, as she was a regular client.

But Sarah knew that if she gave her a bottle of the prodigiously expensive *Aqua Melis*, the gossipy Lydia would tell absolutely everyone, no doubt adding in an imaginative and amorous account of the so-called 'cousin' who Sarah was so desperate to get back to. You did not give away a perfume that cost more than a year's wages without arousing a lot of suspicion. Which was exactly what she could not afford to do right now.

By the time she had managed to get rid of the indecisive young woman, shut the blind and lock the door, Sarah was bathed in nervous sweat. She dashed across the shop, noticing that the pistol, which had skittered into the corner when he had knocked it from her grasp, was gone, although she hadn't seen him pick it up. She opened the door to her living room and went in.

The tea had been made, the pot, cups and saucers laid out for two on the table, and his hat and coat were neatly hung on a hook near the fire, but her unwelcome guest was not in the room. She closed her eyes for one horrified second, then picking up the nearest object to hand, ran into the bedroom, coming to a halt just inside the entrance.

He was standing over the baby's bed, staring into it, preternaturally still. The afternoon sunlight coming through the window clearly outlined his profile and picked up the fiery copper highlights in his tangled hair.

She walked over to stand next to him, still clutching the cheap vase she had grabbed as a weapon, and looked down into the bed. The little girl was awake, was smiling and staring at the stranger with long-lashed clear grey eyes. Her father's eyes.

The man Sarah had only ever known as Sir Anthony Peters took a deep shuddering breath, then lifted his gaze from the bed and looked at her, his slate-blue eyes bright with unshed tears.

"Jesus Christ, lassie," he said softly, his Scottish accent breaking through due to his shock. All thoughts Sarah had had of telling him the oft-repeated fiction about her sister and the niece she had adopted flew from her mind.

"Her name is Màiri," she said instead. "People think it's Mary, and I haven't told them otherwise. I thought he'd like it. He told me about her, you see, his wife, and I thought it would be right. Was it right?"

"Aye," he replied. "Aye, it was right."

The little girl lifted her arms to him and laughed.

"Up," she said.

He bent over the bed, and with infinite tenderness lifted the child out. She put her chubby arms around his neck and rested her head on his shoulder. Softly he kissed the tousled dark hair, breathed in her sleepy baby scent.

"*Halò, a Mhàiri*," he said, smiling. "*Nighean bhrèagha mo bhràthair.*" Then he looked at Sarah, the corners of his lips still lifted, and saw the question in her eyes. His smile faded and his eyes misted again. He shook his head, very slightly, but it was enough to give her her answer. She closed her eyes for a moment, struggling for composure, and then she moaned, swaying slightly. He reached out with his free arm and drew her gently into him, and she, who hated physical contact, laid her head against his chest and surrendered to her emotions.

They stood like that for a long time, the man and woman, clinging to each other, united in their grief for the man they had both loved so deeply, while the child who would never know the man they wept for, but whom she so closely resembled both in looks and character, sighed softly, and with her little fists tangled in her uncle's hair, her face nestled in the crook of his neck, went back to sleep.

Later, back in the living room, Alex sat at the table with his niece on his knee, bouncing her gently up and down while Sarah threw away the now cold tea and brewed a fresh pot.

"I'm sorry about your hand," he said, retaining his Scottish accent, albeit less broad than he used at home. It was a little late to pretend he was English now. "I didna mean to hurt you, but I wasna expecting you to have a pistol."

Sarah poured the hot water into the teapot.

"It's not hurting any more," she said. It was, a little, but the pain in her heart was far, far worse. "I bought the pistol in case

Richard came to visit me again. Caroline taught me how to use it so I could be sure to kill him with one shot. I wouldn't have managed it if he was as fast as you, though."

Alex smiled grimly.

"Ye've no need to worry about Richard," he said. "He's dead."

Sarah sat down suddenly and heavily on the chair opposite.

"Dead? Are you sure?" she asked.

He regarded her evenly for a moment, as if making his mind up about something.

"Aye," he said. "I killed him myself. That's why I'm here. I was told by…someone I trust that she was shot and killed after Culloden. But Richard told me that she didna die."

"No, she didn't," Sarah replied. "The Duke of Cumberland had her brought to London and nursed back to health." She watched as the colour drained from Alex's face, and standing, quickly lifted the baby off his knee. He closed his eyes and swallowed heavily, and when he opened them again she was watching him anxiously.

"I'm well," he said. "Where is she?"

"I don't know," Sarah answered. "Edwin's been trying to find out. I haven't seen Caroline for a couple of weeks though, so I don't know if he's discovered anything. Caroline would write to me if he had. She's at Summer Hill." She stopped, saw his look of confusion and realised that he hadn't seen any of them for two years, since the night they'd fled after Lord Daniel found out who Sir Anthony was, or rather who he wasn't. "Tell me what Richard told you," she said. "And I'll tell you the truth, as far as I know it."

He told her, briefly, and then she told him the more honest version, that they'd all believed Beth to be dead or escaped to France, until Tom had come to Sarah and told her what Richard had done. Then she told him about her efforts to find Beth, and then Caroline enlisting Prince Frederick to help.

"Frederick?" Alex said incredulously. "He rescued her? A Jacobite?"

"Yes," Sarah said, "and he came to see her afterwards."

"Maybe there's hope yet, an we canna succeed," Alex murmured to himself.

"I'm sorry?"

"It doesna matter. Go on."

She told him, because he deserved to know, that they'd nursed Beth back to health once more, stopped her from killing herself.

"She said that she knew you were dead, that you'd have come for her otherwise and she wanted to die as well, to be with you. That was when she was very ill, though. When she got stronger she changed her mind, and after that she recovered very quickly. Caroline and Edwin were hoping they'd be allowed to keep her with them until they managed to secure her release, but then she told them that she'd decided to do the right thing and wanted to see the Duke of Newcastle, to talk to him. That was at the beginning of April. We haven't heard anything about her since."

Alex had listened to this in silence, his face closed although his eyes were dark with pain. Sarah had an almost overwhelming impulse to take him in her arms, to comfort him. She had liked Sir Anthony from the start, but she felt closer to this man sitting opposite her, who an hour ago she'd thought would kill her, than she ever had to anyone except Beth herself, and Murdo. *It's because he's linked to Beth,* she thought, *and because Murdo was his servant.*

"Did he know?" Alex asked suddenly.

"Did who know?"

"Newcastle. When he sent Richard to torture her, did he know she was with child? Richard said he did."

"No. He was lying. Beth didn't tell him. She said…" She hesitated, unwilling to cause him even more pain than she already was doing.

"That's one thing I dinna need to do, then," he said.

"What?"

"Kill Newcastle. Because if he'd let Richard do what he did to her knowing she was with child, I couldna have let him live."

Sarah stared at him, her mouth open. The matter-of-fact way he'd said it left her in no doubt that had the circumstances been as Richard had told him, Anthony, or whoever he was, would have killed one of the most powerful men in Britain without any hesitation whatsoever, regardless of the consequences to himself. And it also occurred to her that he trusted her, not only to tell him the truth, but enough to reveal his intentions, or at least some of them. Now, suddenly, she understood exactly why Beth had not betrayed this man, not even under torture.

"Tell me what Beth said," he prompted Sarah gently. "I'm a grown man, and I need to know it all, so I can see what I must do to make it right, if I can."

"Beth said that when she found out she was having a baby, she knew that it had almost no chance of surviving in prison or in a foundling hospital, and that the only way they'd have let her keep it is if she'd betrayed you, which she wouldn't do. So when Richard came to talk to her she deliberately goaded him, hoping he'd kill her and the baby quickly."

"But he didna."

"No. She said he'd changed, had a better control of his temper. If we can find her, she'll be glad to know he's dead though. God knows I am. It's the best news I've heard in a long time. Anne will be happy too. But of course I can't tell her," she finished.

"She'll find out soon enough, I'm thinking," Alex replied. "I made sure he'll be found."

There was a short silence while they both drank their tea and little Màiri chattered incomprehensibly to herself while she played with a ball on the floor. Alex smiled.

"She's beautiful," he said. Sarah took a deep breath.

"Tell me about what happened," she asked. "How he…" She stopped, incapable of saying the word. It was too soon.

"It was in battle, Culloden," he said. "We were waiting for the order to charge, and Cumberland's men were firing the cannons…it was very quick," he added.

Sarah looked at him sceptically.

"That's what they tell all the women," she said, a slight tremor in her voice the only sign of what she was feeling. "He was brave, it was quick, he didn't suffer."

Alex leaned across the table suddenly, grasping her hands.

"I'm telling ye true, lassie. You deserve that. He wouldna have tellt ye about Màiri if he hadna cared for you. He never spoke about her to anyone. He died so quickly he didna even get to finish his sentence. He really didna suffer, and I'm glad of that at least, because so many others did. And I wasna in any way to go back for him afterwards, for I was injured myself."

She looked down at their clasped hands. His were long-fingered and strong, and engulfed hers, as Murdo's had. A single tear ran down her cheek.

"John told me you were all alive when he last saw you," she said sadly. "That was a year ago now. It gave me hope then. And later Beth said that you were all well the day of Culloden too. She told me what Murdo said to her, what he told her to tell me, if…but I thought he would have written to me, at least, if he'd survived. Beth said maybe he didn't want to cause me any problems but she was just being kind, I knew that."

"John?" Alex asked, his brow creasing.

"I'm sorry. There's so much to tell you. John Betts – Beth's stableboy."

"You saw him?" Alex said.

"Yes. He was sentenced to death, but he escaped from prison with two other men, I can't remember their names. He stayed with me until after the others were executed – he wanted to go, to watch them die, said he owed it to them. I told Caroline he was my brother, Jem. I don't think she believed me though."

"You have a lot of problem relatives," Alex observed wryly.

"Not as much of a problem as the real ones were," she answered darkly. "Anyway, he told me that you were all alive when he last saw you at Carlisle. He was going to tell me your names, you, Murdo and Jim, but I told him I didn't want to know, because Newcastle had interviewed me once and might do it again, and the less I knew the better." She saw him open his mouth and shook her head vigorously. "I still don't want to know," she said.

"I'm thinking you already know enough to identify me, name or no," he said softly.

She looked up at him.

"No, I don't," she replied. "I only know that you're tall, English, with dark hair and terrible burns on your face. I can't say you've got one leg because I think Lydia would remember that. But that's all I can tell anyone. I was too frightened to remember anything else."

"Sarah, as stupid as Lydia is, and she is, she'll remember that ye tellt her I was your cousin, if it comes to it."

Sarah thought for a moment.

"I was afraid," she said. "You told me you'd kill us both if I didn't get her out of the shop. It was the first thing I could think of."

"But ye didna run for help when I came in here," he pointed out.

"No. Because you told me that you'd kill the baby if I did."

He let go of her hands, and to her surprise he started laughing.

"Sarah Browne," he said, eyeing her with admiration, "you are a wonderful woman, and I'm proud to know you. Murdo chose right with you."

"He told Beth…he told her that he'd come for me, when it was safe, and marry me if I wanted to," she told him. "I would have, whether it was safe or not. Anyway," she continued, impatiently brushing a tear away, "I haven't done anything special – it's only what any friend would do."

"No," he said. "No, it isna. And you dinna ken me at all. I dinna want you to risk your life for me."

She shrugged.

"I liked Sir Anthony," she said. "He was funny, and he was kind. And he loved Beth and made her happy. That's enough for me. Everything I have now is because of her. And you've come all this way to try to find her. And you killed that evil bastard. That alone would be enough for me never to betray you to anyone."

"You owe me nothing," he insisted, reaching up in his habitual gesture when frustrated to scrub his fingers through his hair, breaking the lace that bound it in the process. Tangled waves cascaded around his shoulders and face. He retrieved the lace from the floor, started combing through his hair with his fingers.

"Wait," Sarah said, "I can do better than that." She stood and walked through into the shop, returning a moment later with a brush and comb. Moving behind him, she gently started to tease the knots out of his hair. He sat for a minute in silence, enjoying the feel of the brush against his scalp. His mother had brushed his hair when he was very young, and he had always loved it. It was comforting, intimate.

"Ye've changed," he said.

"In what way?" she asked. His hair was really beautiful; the colour was glorious, like burnished chestnuts.

"Ye didna like people touching you, as I remember."

That was true.

"I still don't," she said. "But you're different. I trust you. I know you wouldn't hurt me, not for anything." As she said it, she realised something about herself for the first time. She hadn't minded Beth touching her, or Murdo, because she had loved and trusted them completely. And this man was the same. It wasn't that she hated to be touched; it was that she didn't trust many people not to hurt her if they got close to her. She stopped brushing Alex's hair for a moment as the realisation struck her.

I love him.

Not in the way she had loved Murdo; not in a romantic way. But yes, she loved him, fiercely, as she loved Beth. And because of that, she would do anything for him.

She continued brushing.

"Caroline is at Summer Hill," she said. "It's her new country house. Edwin was knighted by the king last year, and Caroline's built a lovely house in Sussex so she can annoy all her relatives, as she puts it."

"Knighted!" Alex exclaimed, smiling. "He deserves that. He's one of the most genuine politicians I ever met."

"I'll go tomorrow," Sarah said, "and see if Edwin's found anything out about Beth yet. You can stay here. I'll only be away a few days." She finished brushing out his hair and tied it back with a piece of purple ribbon. He was very handsome, even with his disfigurement. "What did you do to your face?" she asked. "It looks horrible."

He lifted his hand to the mass of healing scratches that covered the left side of his face and laughed.

"Just before I was due to come here I had a wee stramash – a fight that is, wi' an acquaintance of mine, and he rubbed my face in a gorse bush," he said. "It hurt like the devil at the time, but it also made me look hideous. It gave me the idea for how to disguise myself, but it was nearly healed when I got here so I rubbed my own face in a rose bush yesterday. I knew that if I was missing a leg and my face was ruined, people would only remember that and nothing else."

"Like with Sir Anthony and his makeup and clothes," she said.

"Aye, like that," he agreed. "Ye spoilt it a wee bit for me wi' the leg, but it's maybe for the best. Lydia'll no' remember much about me anyway because I'm your poor cousin and beneath her notice, and it would be impossible to ride in a coach all the way to Sussex wi' my leg strapped up under me. I take it ye'll no' be wanting to ride there?"

"No, I won't," she said. "If I never sit on a horse again it'll be too soon. But you can't come with me."

"I have to, I think," he said. "I owe them an apology for what I did to them as Sir Anthony. I've never felt good about that. And I owe them thanks for saving Beth's life, too."

"You can't," Sarah insisted. "Edwin hates you. He thinks you abandoned Beth to save yourself. If he finds out you're alive, he'll call the authorities."

"Maybe. When I came here, I thought you might too. But ye didna."

"It's not the same thing!" she protested.

"Aye, it is," he said. "If ye tell me where this Summer Hill is, I'll go alone. That'll be best. Ye've already done too much. I didna intend to stay more than a few minutes. I'll leave you in peace now."

"No!" she cried. "You're not going alone. If you have to go, I'm coming with you. And I am not letting my dear cousin Adam, who I haven't seen for five years, sleep on the street or in an inn. You can stay here. I'll go out and get a pie or a chop for us. Please stay here," she finished, and there was a desperation in her tone that stifled his protest before it was uttered. He nodded, albeit reluctantly, and she smiled, vastly relieved. She did not want, could not bear, to be alone tonight.

Màiri, tired of the ball, gripped hold of the leg of the chair Alex was sitting on, and pulled herself up to a standing position. She looked up at him with Duncan's eyes, and her lips curled upward in a smile. Alex leaned down with the intention of picking her up, his mouth curling in an identical smile.

"Papa," the little girl said, quite distinctly. Both the adults froze for a moment, and then he lifted her up, plopped her on his knee.

"Ah, no, *a Mhàiri*," he said softly. "I'm no' your da, my love. She looks very like him," he added, glancing across at Sarah, who was watching the tender scene with tears in her eyes.

"She looks very like you, too," she replied. And then she rose and without a word took her cloak and went out to get the food, leaving him holding all that remained of the brother he missed so dreadfully. He held his tiny niece gently on his knee, and spent the time that Sarah was out telling her about the father she would never know, the tears running freely down his cheeks as he did, while she sat solemnly listening to the soft musical cadence of a language she had never heard before, as though she understood and was absorbing every word he was saying to her.

CHAPTER EIGHT

The next morning Sarah tried once more to convince Adam, as he insisted she continue calling him, Anthony being inadvisable, that he should let her go to see Caroline alone, but he was adamant that he intended to accompany her.

"I've felt guilty about abandoning her and Edwin ever since I ran away that night," he said. "And I didna ken then what they did for Beth, and for you, for that matter. But I'm glad Caroline didna shoot Richard when she could have. If she had I would never have known Beth was alive."

Unable to sleep the night before, the two of them had sat and talked into the early hours, during which Sarah had told him about Richard's attack on her and Caroline's dramatic rescue.

"He wouldn't have been alive to torture her though," Sarah pointed out.

"True. But I'm thinking Newcastle would have found someone else to do the job. Richard was just convenient."

"I hated him," Sarah said.

"Aye, well, he's dead now."

"No, I mean Newcastle. He treated me as though he thought I should be honoured that he was threatening me. He had a list on his desk when he interviewed me and kept looking at it as though it had some terrible secret about me on it. He didn't expect me to be able to read, being a commoner and a woman. It said 'roast beef, potatoes' at the top. I'll never forget that. It's what told me that he didn't know anything, so I could say whatever I wanted as long as I was careful."

Alex burst out laughing, and after a minute her anger dissolved and she started laughing too.

"I called him 'my lord' at least fifty times because I could see it was annoying him," she said, giggling. "In the end he told me that there was a reward of a thousand pounds for any information that would lead to your capture, and asked me to really think. So I sat there for as long as I dared, while he got more and more impatient, and then I said that there *was* one thing."

"What was it?" Alex asked.

"I told him that when you couldn't get violet perfume, you'd sometimes wear lavender. I thought he was going to hit me then; he went scarlet. I was terrified at the time but also really angry, but now it seems comical."

Alex took her hands in his.

"It *is* comical. And you should be proud of yourself, because you made a fool of one of the cleverest men in the kingdom. That's no' an easy thing to do. But never underestimate him. He underestimated you, which made him weak and you strong. If he ever interviews you again you must take it very seriously, because he rarely makes the same mistake twice."

She nodded.

"I will. But everyone seems to think Sir Anthony's either dead or in France with the Young Pretender, so I don't think he'll interview me again."

"That depends on what happens when I see Caroline and Edwin," Alex said. "I really think I should go alone. No one need ever know I was here, if it comes to it."

"Well, I'm coming anyway," Sarah said. "I don't think for one minute Caroline will betray you. And if she *has* heard something about Beth I want to know."

"Aye, but—"

And I want to see the house, because I've only been there once, when they'd just started building it," she continued. "So if you don't want my company on the way, then I'll follow behind."

"Christ, woman!" he said, exasperated. "Did you learn your stubbornness from Beth?"

She grinned.

"I'll get my cloak," she said.

Summer Hill was thirty miles away, a distance Alex could have covered in one day by riding or even walking. But travelling in a coach and with a small child was a different matter, and in the end they had to stop and find an inn for the night, which had just one room available. Any initial embarrassment at having to share it was short-lived due to the complete exhaustion they both felt from travelling along bumpy roads all day after having not slept the previous night. Alex slept on the floor, while Sarah and Màiri had the bed.

The following morning, much refreshed after eight hours of unbroken sleep followed by a hearty breakfast, they set off to walk the last few miles to Summer Hill. It was another glorious sunny day, and the adults tried not to focus on the unpleasant reception they might get when they reached their destination, and instead just enjoy the walk, which was made easier, if slower, by Màiri's fascination with everything she saw.

"I must take her out into the countryside more," Sarah said, watching her daughter's delight in the hedgerow flowers they were passing as they walked down a lane. "I spend too much time working, trying to save all the money I can in case anything bad happens. I think it's because…well, you know where I came from," she said. "I don't want her ever to have to do what I did to survive. But I also need to spend more time with her. She's growing so fast."

Alex, walking by her side, smiled.

"You should," he agreed. He stopped and knelt down in the lane. "*A Mhàiri,*" he said softly, "shall we pick some flowers for the lady we're going to visit?" He picked her up and demonstrated what he meant, collecting a buttercup and some meadowsweet from the hedgerow, and soon the tall man and the tiny child had an accord; she pointed to the flowers, he picked them and told her the name as he did so.

"Why do you call her *a-vaari?*" Sarah asked after a few minutes of watching this, misty-eyed.

Alex passed the collected flowers to her, freeing his hands to pick more.

"Màiri is her name," he said, "but in the Gaelic, if you address her by name, or say hello, then the first letter sound changes and it sounds like a v instead of an m. I dinna ken why, it's just how it is."

"It sounds lovely," Sarah said.

"Aye, but ye must no' use it yourself," he warned her. "Anyone with the Gaelic would ken instantly, and you'd bring suspicion on yourself."

There was so much to remember to forget.

"How did you do it?" she asked. "How did you become Sir Anthony and never make a mistake?"

"I made mistakes, plenty of them, but as long as you stay calm, you can cover them," he said. "You treat it as a game, that helps. It's a wee bit like being an actor on a stage – while you're playing the part you have to believe it completely, become that person. Just as I'm about to become your cousin Adam again, for a short time, at least," he said, switching smoothly from a soft Scottish accent to a broad Manchester one. "Is that Summer Hill?"

Sarah followed the direction of his gaze and gasped. In the distance, where last time she had seen a building site, was a large white three storey Palladian villa, set in acres of lush green countryside. To one side of it was a huge hole, with an equally huge pile of excavated earth near it. Tiny figures could be seen moving to and fro across the grass.

"It's beautiful!" she said, awestricken.

"It is," Alex agreed. "They're moving up in the world. And very well deserved."

"Maybe it would be better if you stayed here," Sarah said doubtfully. "There are a lot of people around. I'll go with Màiri and see what I can find out."

By way of answer he linked his arm through hers.

"Are you ashamed of your country cousin Adam, then?" he asked. "Maybe I can ask if there's a job for me here."

She looked up at him, horror-struck, and then he winked and she realised he was joking. *You treat it as a game.* She sighed, and they continued their slow progress towards the distant house.

They had to ask three workers before they finally located Caroline in one corner of the garden, supervising the planting of some shrubs. When she saw the flower-bedecked threesome coming toward her she waved to them.

"Sarah? Good grief! What are you doing here? Is everything all right?" she asked. She smiled at Màiri, and then looked at the man accompanying them, who instantly removed his hat and executed a somewhat amateur bow.

"Yes!" Sarah replied energetically, noting that several people were in earshot. "This is my cousin, Adam, who was working in Newcastle but came to see me when he found out I'd adopted Mary. I thought it would be nice to take him and Mary out for a few days in the country, so we came to see you. I hope you don't mind."

"No, of course I don't!" Caroline said. "I'm very pleased to meet you, Adam." She showed no reaction whatsoever to the left side of his face, which was still a mass of scabs.

Adam bowed again.

"Your obedient servant, my lady," he said humbly.

"Mary picked these flowers for you," Sarah continued, taking the large bunch of assorted wildflowers from Adam, combining them with her own and handing them across to Caroline, who accepted them as though they were the most expensive hothouse flowers in the world. She knelt down on the grass, heedless of her white cotton gown.

"Mary, are these for me?" she asked.

The little girl nodded, beaming.

"They are beautiful! Like you," Caroline said, kissing the child. "Come, we must put these in water. They will look lovely in the library. And Freddie will be delighted to see you. He's in the nursery right now." She stood again. "The library, nursery and master bedroom are the only rooms completely finished at the moment," she continued as they started to walk across the grass in the direction of the house. "The salon is nearly complete though, and I've ordered some Bohemian crystal chandeliers that Wilhelmina recommended. They'll look wonderful when they're installed. Are you ready for some refreshments?"

"That would be very kind, my lady. Thank you," said Adam, gazing all around in obvious wonder. "You have a lovely house. Is all this land yours too?"

"My name is Caroline. There are no 'my lady's' here, especially where Sarah's family is concerned. Yes, all this is mine, up to the other side of that small hill. You must stay for the night, and then tomorrow I'll show you the grounds. The guest rooms are not finished yet, but we can make you comfortable, at least."

Sarah looked distinctly uncomfortable at being asked to stay the night, in view of the circumstances.

"I wouldn't feel right sleeping in a big house," Adam said. "Where I worked, I used to sleep in the stables of a night."

"Nonsense! I wouldn't hear of a guest sleeping in the stables. Sarah is a good friend to me, and if you've come all the way from Newcastle to see her I expect that you think highly of each other."

"That we do, my la…Caroline," he said. "She's done a lot for me. Trust her with my life, I would."

Sarah flushed.

"What do you do for your living, Adam?" Caroline asked.

"I don't have no special trade, but I can turn my hand to lots of things," he said. "I'm very adep…adapt…er…"

"Adaptable?" Caroline ventured.

"That's it!" Adam smiled shyly. "That's what Mr Allbrow – he was the man what I was working for in Newcastle – said to me."

"And when do you have to return to Newcastle, Adam?"

"Oh no, er…Caroline, I'm not working for him no more. I haven't got no work right now. I'm here to see Sarah, and hoping to find news of an old friend, too."

"Caroline, can we have a talk in private?" Sarah asked somewhat desperately, unable to bear this pretence for much longer. It was one thing to lie to the Duke of Newcastle; quite another to do it to a friend, particularly when the lie was going to be exposed in a few minutes.

"Of course!" Caroline replied. "We can talk in the library. I'm expecting Edwin home at any time, so hopefully you'll be able to meet him too, Adam. The session ended yesterday, and we're both going to spend the summer here. Ah, Toby!" she continued, addressing an extremely elderly and frail-looking man in livery, who was standing at the entrance to the house, and who bowed deeply on seeing his mistress approaching.

"Miss Browne has brought her cousin Adam to visit!" Caroline bellowed, to the obvious alarm of that cousin. "Can you arrange for refreshments in the library? And take Mary up to the nursery?"

"Indeed, Lady Caroline," Toby said. Very reverently he took the little girl's hand, and together they began to make their way at a snail's pace up the beautiful curved mahogany staircase. Caroline led her visitors through a door on the left of the marble-floored entrance hall, and into the library. Adam and Sarah looked around the room with obvious pleasure.

Two of the four walls were lined with bookshelves, on which at the moment stood only a handful of books. There was a white marble fireplace in the centre of one wall, with alcoves on either side also lined with currently empty bookshelves. The visible walls and the ceiling were painted a warm peach colour, with white cornice and mouldings. Under the large sash window stood a writing desk, and on either side of the fireplace was a sofa, striped in peach and white brocade, with a tea table in between. Caroline sat down on one sofa and beckoned her guests to sit on the other. Sarah sat down opposite her friend. On Caroline's invitation Adam took off his coat, placing it across the arm of the sofa, his hat on top.

"Toby's deaf as a post," Caroline continued. "I'm sorry Adam, I should have warned you. But he's an old retainer and I can't bring myself to pension him off. I think he'd die if he didn't feel useful any more. But that means we can talk in private without any danger of him hearing when he eventually arrives with the refreshments. What is it you want to talk about, Sarah?"

Sarah flushed scarlet.

"Er…" she began, then looked at Adam, who was still standing, ostensibly admiring the décor.

Caroline smiled.

"Adam," she began, "if you are hoping to find work here, I always have need of good—"

"Caroline," he interrupted in a completely different voice from that of cousin Adam, more cultured, but still English, "do you not know me?"

She looked up at him, clearly puzzled.

"How should I know you?" she said. "I have never met you before."

He sighed, and then, still standing, shifted position slightly, and in that shifting he seemed to shrink a few inches, and his limbs lost their ungainly awkwardness, becoming loose, languid and effeminate. He bowed, this time expertly and elaborately.

"Oh, my dear Caroline!" he trilled. "I simply could not bear it if I were to discover you have forgotten me, even after such a prolonged absence!"

Caroline froze, her face a picture of shock. Sarah closed her eyes, dreading what was to come. Sir Anthony straightened and

149

waited, with no sign of the tension he must be feeling. When the reaction came, after an endless moment, it was not what either Sarah or Alex had been expecting.

Caroline blinked once, and then standing, she crossed the few feet of room between them and took him in a fierce embrace.

"You're alive!" she cried. "Oh thank God, thank God!"

Still holding him, she leaned back, looking up into his startled blue eyes. Tears brimmed in her own hazel eyes, and she gave him a watery smile. Then she released him and stepped back, as if ashamed of her sudden display of affection.

"You bastard, Anthony," she said, anger in her voice now. "Where the hell have you been? We thought you were dead. *Beth* thought you were dead. Wait," she said commandingly when he made to speak. She turned to Sarah. "Have you told him what she went through for him?"

"Yes. I—" Sarah began.

"Well then," Caroline interrupted, turning back to him, "why didn't you let her know you were alive? You could have found a way, surely? She wanted to die, to join you! I could kill you myself! What the hell—"

"I didn't know!" he said loudly, cutting her off. "I thought she was dead. No, I *knew* she was dead. If I hadn't been sure, I would have found a way to get to her. I didn't know, Caroline, I swear to you!"

There came a light knock on the door, which then opened.

"Sit down," Caroline commanded, and the young man, instantly Adam again in the presence of Toby, obeyed. The three of them sat in silence while the elderly man tottered across the room with the rattling tea tray, placing it on the table between them. There was tea and a plate of tiny currant cakes. The minute Toby had left the room, Caroline spoke.

"You'd better tell me what happened, now," she said. "Because happy as I am that you're not dead, Anthony, I can't say I think well of you. Anthony isn't even your name, is it?"

"No, but it's as good as any, in private at least. I'm sorry, Caroline, truly I am," Alex said. "I didn't want to leave you in the way I did that night at the Winters' without any explanation, but I—"

"I'm not angry about that, you fool," she cut in. "I know why you left so quickly that night. I understand that. I even understand that you were upset about lying to us for over two years, although I can tell you now that Edwin doesn't. He feels used by you and betrayed. What I want to know is why you let Beth rot in prison for over a year. How could you know she was dead, when she wasn't?"

"There are things I can't tell you, Caroline, can't tell anyone," he said. "But someone I trust completely saw the redcoat shoot her in the head, and told me she was dead. That person believed she was telling the truth and I had no reason to think otherwise, until two weeks ago."

"Two weeks ago? What happened two weeks ago?"

"Are you going to give me up to the authorities, Caroline?" he asked bluntly.

"Of course I'm not, you bloody idiot!" she said. "Although I probably should. No, I'm going to listen to what you have to say, and then, depending on what it is, I'm going to see if I can help you. Without putting Edwin at any risk whatsoever," she added.

"I don't want any help," Alex said. "I didn't want Sarah to come here with me, but she's as stubborn as Beth ever was. The last thing I want is to put those I love in any more danger than I already have."

Caroline's eyes softened.

"Go on then," she said. "Tell me what happened two weeks ago, and why you're here. And have a cake. It's a miracle Toby got them here without dropping them. They won't survive the return trip to the kitchen if you don't eat them."

Caroline poured the tea, and Alex ate a cake while he considered what to say.

"Two weeks ago," he said finally, "I met Richard, by chance. We had a...chat."

"A chat," Caroline said drily. "And what was the result of this chat?"

"He told me that Beth was alive. He told me that she was with child, and what he did to her," Alex said. He swallowed, hard, then continued. "He said that she was in Newgate Prison, or was a few months ago. So I came to London, to the only person I knew I could trust." He glanced at Sarah, who blushed and smiled. "I intended just to find out if she knew where Beth was and then leave, but things didn't quite go as planned."

"Lydia Fortesque came in and caught us together." Sarah spoke for the first time, relaxing a little now it was clear Caroline was more surprised than angry.

"*Lydia?*" Caroline said. "Oh God. It'll be all over London by now."

"No, I don't think so," Sarah said. "I told her he was my cousin, and then he showed her his face and she lost interest. But if she does talk, she'll just say that my cousin Adam is horribly scarred. No one in her circle will care."

"What *have* you done to your face?" Caroline asked. "Is that why you wore so much paint?"

"No," Alex said. "This is a disguise. It'll heal in a few days. I rubbed my face in a briar."

Caroline whistled through her teeth in admiration.

"And what about Richard?" she asked. "Does he think you're Sarah's cousin Adam?"

"Richard doesn't think anything," Alex said coldly. "He's dead."

Caroline's eyes widened.

"You killed him?" she asked.

He nodded.

"Well done," Caroline said, smiling. "Someone should have done it long ago. Does Anne know?"

"Not yet, but she will, in the normal way a wife gets to hear of a soldier's death," Alex replied. "Caroline, I need to tell you something. You may not believe me, but I need to say it anyway."

"What is it?" she asked.

"When I became Sir Anthony and friended you both, I did it hoping to find out information that might be useful for the Stuart cause. I hated the Elector so much that I didn't think it possible to like anyone who supported him at all. I thought Hanoverians were all arrogant and pompous."

"Like Edward and Bartholomew," Caroline said, grinning.

"Yes. I was very naïve. I realise that now, because I came to like and admire quite a few of them. But I came to love you and Edwin. Until I met Beth, you were the only people in London I thought of as friends." He leaned forward earnestly. "I swear to you I never passed anything Edwin told me in confidence on to the Stuarts, once we became friends. I continued to deceive you because I had to, but I tried not to do anything that would compromise you if I was discovered."

"You compromised all of us, from the king down, and in doing so compromised none of us," Caroline murmured. "Highbury told me that. He was right, wasn't he?"

Alex smiled.

"Yes, he was right. As I said, when I visited Sarah I intended only to ask where Beth was and then leave. But then I had to become her cousin, temporarily. Sarah wanted to come here alone today, to find out if you'd heard anything about Beth. She told me that you're trying to discover where she is. But I insisted on coming with her because I wanted to tell you myself that I'm sorry. And thank you for everything you've done for Beth."

"And now you have," she said. "I believe you. And I forgive you."

"Have you heard anything about Beth?" Sarah finally put the question they'd come here to ask. To their surprise, Caroline blushed scarlet. She looked down at her hands resting in her lap for a long moment, considering.

Sarah, sitting next to Alex, could sense the almost unbearable tension in him as he waited for Caroline to answer. But he made no move to force her to speak. The silence stretched out, palpable in the stillness of the room. Just as Sarah thought that she, for one, could wait no longer, Caroline looked up, straight into Alex's eyes.

"This is very difficult," she said. "The last time we saw Beth she told us she wanted to see Newcastle, to do the right thing. We took that to mean she was going to denounce you. After that we heard no more of her, and when Edwin tried to find out what had happened it soon became very clear that someone in authority wanted her whereabouts to remain a secret."

"You mean Newcastle," Alex said.

Caroline nodded. She took a deep breath, let it out on a sigh and then came to a decision.

"Beth didn't denounce you," she said. "She told Newcastle that Richard knew you were a spy, that you paid for his commission to buy his silence, and that when Daniel found out about you, Richard warned you so that you could escape arrest.

Then she told Newcastle those were the last words she'd speak to him."

Alex closed his eyes, his mouth a thin line. In his lap, his hands curled into fists.

"What did he do to her?" he asked. The desire to do violence radiated from him and both women felt it, and shivered.

"I will tell you. I have to, I think," Caroline said. "But you must be careful how you act on it, Anthony. Edwin found out by unconventional means, and if that comes to light his career will be over."

"I will do nothing to jeopardise Edwin, or you," Alex said tightly, "but I will know what became of her, and that now." It was a command, and for the first time since he had leapt the counter in her shop Sarah was afraid of him, of what he might do.

"Beth was transported in April, to Antigua, as an indentured servant. For life," Caroline said.

Sarah gasped, but Alex, strangely, showed no reaction at all.

"You are sure of this?" he asked quietly.

"Yes," she replied. "Edwin found out two weeks ago. I couldn't write to you Sarah, I'm sorry, because he asked me not to tell anyone at all. She must be there by now. We're trying to find out who bought the indenture, to see if we can buy it back and pay for her to go to France or Italy, where she'd be safe."

"Thank you," Alex said quietly. He took his gaze away from Caroline and looked down at his hands, still fisted in his lap. Slowly he uncurled them.

"Yes," he said quietly, as if to himself, "I can do that."

"Do what?" Caroline asked.

He stood, suddenly.

"Thank you for telling me, for trusting me. I won't betray your trust, I promise you that. Sarah, I think you should stay here tonight, but I'll leave now. I'll put you in no more danger than I already have. There is no way I can repay what you've both done for me."

He reached for his coat and Caroline smashed her hand down onto it, flattening his hat in the process. Both women stood up.

"Wait a minute," Caroline said. "I want to know what you intend to do. You owe me that at the very least."

"Maybe it's better you don't know," he began. "Then, if anyone asks—"

"To hell with that," Caroline interrupted, her colour rising. "I love Beth and, God help me, I love you too, Anthony. You are not just walking out of here without telling me what you're going to do, and letting me help if I can."

"Caroline—"

"She's right," Sarah said. "I feel the same way. Beth is our friend, and so are you. We have a right to know what you're going to do."

He looked from one to the other, then came to a decision.

"The last time I saw Beth," he said, "I promised her that when it was over, I'd come for her. Now I know she's alive, I'm going to keep my promise."

"You're going to Antigua?" Caroline asked.

Alex nodded.

"I need to plan, but yes. I'll go to Antigua, find who has her, and then I'll do whatever I have to do to bring her back. She has suffered so much because of me. I never wanted that for her. I told her to denounce me if it came to it. She should have done," he said, looking at the two women. His eyes filled with tears. "I can never make this right," he whispered, "but I have to try."

"Oh, Anthony," Caroline said. She walked across to him, and took him in her arms. "She loves you. She told me that, and that you made her happy. She never regretted marrying you, not for a moment."

He wrapped his arms around her, and held her tight.

"Thank you for telling me that," he said into her hair.

The door opened, and Edwin walked in.

He stopped on the threshold, taking in the scene; his wife embracing another man, a tall and very handsome stranger, and Sarah, whose face drained of all colour as she saw him. And then Caroline looked over the man's shoulder and saw him, and also paled. She wrenched herself from Alex's embrace and looked at her husband, read the expression on his face.

"Don't be silly, Edwin, it's not what you're thinking," she said, and sighed. "It's far worse than that. Come in and shut the door."

Ignoring her, Edwin stayed in the doorway staring at Alex, who had now turned to face him.

"What the hell is going on?" he asked.

Caroline walked to the doorway, pulled Edwin inside and shut the door firmly.

"Edwin, this is Anthony," she said bluntly.

Edwin froze for a moment, in much the same way that Caroline had when she had discovered the identity of the visitor. But once the news sunk in, his reaction was very different.

"*Anthony?!*" he said, his colour rising. "*You* are Anthony?!"

Alex held his hands up palms outward, in the universal gesture of submission.

"Edwin," he began, "I—"

"Get out," Edwin said, his voice low, shaking with suppressed anger.

"Edwin," Caroline said, "he thought—"

"I don't care what he thought," Edwin interrupted. He rounded on Alex. "You absolute bastard," he said. "After all you've done, you have the bloody nerve to come here now, and put us at risk again? Have you any idea what we went through after you skipped the country?" he continued, his voice rising. "Have you any idea what Beth went through, is still going through, because of you? Get out of my house, or by God I'll call the authorities right now, and see you hang with pleasure!"

To everyone's surprise, without a word, without even picking up his coat and hat, Alex nodded once, then turned and calmly walked out of the room, closing the door quietly behind him. The three remaining occupants of the room stood looking at the door for a moment. Edwin was breathing heavily, his face still flushed with emotion.

"It's my fault," Sarah inserted into the tense silence. "I let him come with me. He wanted to apologise to you both. I shouldn't have let him come."

"Please leave, now," Edwin said, his voice still taut.

She picked up Alex's coat and hat, and went to the door.

"I'm sorry," she said tearfully. She opened the door and went out, looked round the entrance hall. There was no one in sight. She would have to try to find the nursery and Màiri herself. She brushed a tear away with the back of her hand and started to climb the stairs. When she was halfway up she heard the library door open and turned back. Caroline came out and beckoned to her.

"Sarah, would Anthony leave without you?" she asked.

"I don't think so," Sarah said. "He wouldn't let me and Màiri walk back to the village alone. He's probably waiting outside somewhere, at the gate maybe."

"Good," Caroline said. "Go to the kitchen and get cook to prepare some food for the journey home, and then get Màiri. Third door on the right," she elaborated. "Don't leave yet, though. Let me calm Edwin down. He's very upset."

"I'm so sorry, Caroline," Sarah said. She had never heard Edwin swear before. That he had, and in front of women, showed how enraged he was. Her lip trembled, and tears sparkled on her eyelashes.

"No need to apologise," Caroline said. "Just give me a few minutes with him." She went back into the library.

Edwin was pacing up and down, but the moment he heard her come back in he rounded on her.

"What the hell were you doing, embracing the man?" he shouted.

"Surely you don't think—"

"Of course I don't!" he roared. "I know you wouldn't…you know…but Caro, he's a traitor, for God's sake!"

"Will you keep your voice down?" Caroline hissed. "He's Sarah's cousin Adam, from Newcastle."

Edwin closed his eyes and took a deep breath.

"He's a traitor," he continued after a moment, in a quieter voice. "He pretended to be our friend for over three years and all the time he was using us, laughing at us behind our backs! How could you even allow him in the house, let alone embrace him?"

"He wasn't—"

"He married Beth, made her fall in love with him," he continued fiercely, "and then he left her to face Cumberland and Newcastle, knowing that they'd do anything to break her, and knowing that, poor girl, she loved him enough to defy them, whatever the cost."

"Edwin—"

"He doesn't care about anything or anyone except saving his own skin. He—"

"Edwin, will you shut up!" Caroline shouted, loud enough that Toby, passing through the hall, heard her. She moved across to her husband, took his hands in hers.

"Calm down, and listen to me for a minute," she said. "Hear me out, and then if you still feel the same I'll go out and tell him never to contact us again."

"He's still here?" Edwin said incredulously.

"He won't let Sarah walk back alone."

"I don't see why not. She got him in to see you, what further use does he have for her?"

"Edwin," Caroline said warningly.

"Very well," he said. "I'll hear you out." He sat down heavily on the sofa and leaned back. She sat opposite and told him everything that had passed between them since Anthony and Sarah had arrived at the house. After she'd finished he sat quietly for a moment, taking in what she'd said.

"You told him that she was in Antigua," he said.

"Yes, I did. I know you said I must keep it a secret, but I had to tell him, I think. I know he fooled us all with his impersonation of Sir Anthony, and I know he must be a very good liar, but I believed him when he said he never passed anything you told him back to the Stuarts. I also believe he'll do whatever he needs to do to find Beth. He's hardly going to tell anyone how he found out where she is, is he? He'll reinvent himself, go to Antigua, and bring her back. If anyone can do it, he can."

"Do you really believe he'll do that, go all the way to the West Indies?" Edwin asked. Now the rage had dissipated, he looked tired, careworn.

"Yes," Caroline replied with conviction. "He loves her, as much as she loves him. I'm sure of it."

"How can you be sure of that? Really sure?" Edwin asked.

"Because when I told him that Beth had defied Newcastle and that he'd had her transported, he was angrier than I've ever seen anyone be. He couldn't feign that. In fact he tried to hide it, to stay calm. And because if I had been him, and you had been transported by a vicious pig like Newcastle just for standing up to him, I'd feel the same way.

"I'd feel the same way because I love you as much as Anthony loves Beth, as much as she loves him. I would kill for you, and I'd die for you, without hesitation. We know Beth would die for him, and now I'm certain he would do the same for her. He deserves the chance to find her, to try to take her somewhere safe. They both deserve that. And I want to help them, if I can. But I'll leave that decision to you, as I promised."

She finished speaking, sat back, and waited while he

considered. She was not a person to defer to anyone, particularly if she was convinced she was in the right. Edwin knew that, and had always loved her for it. The fact that she was willing to now told him that she trusted him to make the right decision. He thought for a few minutes, running back through his friendship with Anthony, through everything Beth had said about this man she called her husband, about all the times Caroline had been correct in her judgements of people in the past. Then he scrubbed his hands across his face, and sighed.

"I hope you're right," he said softly. "I hope we're both right. Because he now has the means to destroy us, if he chooses to. You said he's still here?"

"Sarah said he won't leave without her. He's probably at the gate."

He nodded.

"Go and tell him to come back in. Tell him I'm calmer now, and I need to talk to him."

She smiled, and standing, went to the door.

"Thank you," she said. Then she opened it and went out, leaving him sitting on the sofa, wondering if he was insane for what he was about to do, and knowing that he would do it anyway. For Caroline, who he loved. For Beth, who he loved. And for Anthony, who had once been his closest friend, and who in spite of everything he also still loved.

He reached across the table, picked up a cake and ate it, washing it down with the remains of the now-cold tea. Then he sat back and waited for the others to return.

"I was very angry," Edwin said the moment they came back into the room, "but I've calmed down now. Were you at the gate?"

"Yes," Alex said. "I wouldn't leave without being sure Sarah and Mary were safe. Edwin, there's nothing I can say that will make things right between us, but for what it's worth, I'm sorry."

"My wife believes you, and trusts you," Edwin said. "And because she does, I will, too. If you betray our faith in you, I will do everything in my power to have you arrested. That's all I want to say on the matter."

"I understand," Alex said. "I'll be on my way, then. Thank you."

"You cannot go to Antigua, Anthony," Edwin said. "Beth isn't there."

Alex, in the act of turning to leave, stopped.

"But Caroline told me she had been transported to Antigua," he said.

"She was. But last night I had news of her. Sit down, for God's sake, Anthony. And Sarah. I'm sorry for using bad language in front of you, both of you." He glanced at his wife. "That was unforgiveable of me."

"I've heard much worse than that in my time," Sarah said, vastly relieved that Edwin seemed to be himself again. She sat down, and after a moment's hesitation Alex sat down next to her.

"What is this news?" he asked. "Can you tell me, without risk?"

"Yes," Edwin said. "It is no secret that the *Veteran* sailed for Antigua with a hundred and fifty Jacobite prisoners on board. What Newcastle doesn't want people to know is that Beth was among the prisoners. He wants to forget her, and, more importantly, he wants Prince Frederick and Prince William to forget her too. It seems Cumberland is still somewhat enamoured of her, or at least might be if she is brought to his attention again."

Engrossed with the news he had to impart, Edwin failed to see the look of rage that crossed Alex's face at the mention of Cumberland's name, before he composed his expression and waited with apparent calmness for Edwin to tell him where Beth was. Sarah and Caroline *did* see it, and Sarah reached across the space between them to give his arm a reassuring squeeze, and felt the rock-hard muscle of his forearm, tensed in anticipation of bad news.

"Where is she?" she asked bluntly, wanting Edwin to get to the point for Anthony's sake.

"I'm sorry," Edwin said, noticing for the first time the unbearable tension pervading the room. "The captain of the *Veteran* arrived back in England two days ago. His ship was captured by pirates when he was one day away from Antigua, and was taken to Martinique."

"Where's Martinique?" Caroline asked.

"Martinique is another island in the West Indies," Alex said. "Were they French pirates?"

"So it seems," Edwin replied. "We have no further news yet, but Captain Ricky said that the prisoners were brought on deck and he and his men were put in the cargo hold where the prisoners had been kept."

"This could be very good news," Alex said. "France is an ally of the Stuarts. I would expect them to treat any Jacobites kindly; I would hope so, in any case. And it may be easier to get her back if she has not been sold into servitude." He looked at Caroline and Edwin and smiled, a real smile that lit up his eyes. "Thank you for telling me this."

"Do you intend to go to Martinique?" Edwin asked.

"Yes, of course," Alex said. "If Beth is there, then I must go to her."

"If you intend to go to Martinique, you will first of all have to sail to France. And then it could be weeks, maybe months before you find a ship that will take you there."

"That's not a problem," Alex said. "No matter how long it takes, or how far I have to travel, now I know she's alive I will find her."

Edwin sighed.

"Anthony, the Duke of Newcastle is writing to the governor of Martinique this very night, to demand the return of the prisoners."

"Yes, I would expect that," Alex said. "It's a formality that has to be gone through. And I am almost certain that the governor of Martinique will respectfully refuse Newcastle's request. It would be the same if the situation were reversed."

"What is *not* common knowledge," Edwin continued, "is that Newcastle is going to offer inducements for the return of *certain* prisoners, of which it's certain Beth will be one. You must keep this to yourself, Anthony. If they agree, she will be returned to England."

Alex just managed to stop himself from swearing in two languages. He tore his fingers through his hair, freeing it from its ribbon.

"Can you find out if she is?" Caroline asked her husband. Edwin glanced at Alex, then away. "You've trusted him this far, Edwin," she added gently. "It's all or nothing, I think."

"Have you told him why I didn't come for Beth earlier?" Alex asked. Caroline nodded. "Edwin," Alex continued, "I didn't need to come here today. Sarah very kindly offered to try to find out if you had any news of Beth's whereabouts. I insisted on accompanying her because I wanted to apologise to both of you for what I did to you, for betraying your trust in me. I know that in your eyes I'm a traitor, and I accept that. But you were my friends, and although I've done many terrible things in my life I have never betrayed a friend.

"Caroline believes me, which is more than I hoped for. I don't expect you to, but I have to say to you, as I said to her, that I am sorry, for I never meant to hurt you, and although I lied to you because I had to I never passed any information you gave me on to my Jacobite connections. I'm honoured that you've helped me this much, and if you don't want to tell me any more about Beth, I'll understand. I know you hate me and don't blame you for it."

"You're a fool, Anthony or whoever you are," Edwin replied. "I didn't hate you because you lied to me, but because I thought you'd abandoned Beth. Regardless of her mistaken allegiance to the Stuarts, Beth is a very special woman, and she does not deserve what happened to her for refusing to betray you. I thought you weren't worth her loyalty, but Caroline believes you thought she was dead. And now I've calmed down, I think that's true. If you truly are willing to go all the way to Martinique for her, then you must love her."

"I do, more than life itself," Alex said.

Edwin nodded.

"Then don't go yet. I will do what I can to find out what the governor does with the prisoners. How can I make contact with you when I do?"

"He'll be staying with me," Sarah said immediately, "as my cousin."

"No," Alex countered. "You've already done far more than I expected you to. I may have to stay in London for a few weeks, and during that time I think it's safer for all three of you if I keep away from you, in case something goes wrong. If you find anything out, send word to Adam Featherstone at Sam's Coffeehouse on Exchange Alley. Don't write openly though, in case someone reads the letter. Just tell me that the parcel is where I expected, or is in Fleet Street if it's France, or is being returned to the sender if she's being sent back here. I have to go out of London for a few days, but when I get back I'll go to the coffee house every day until I hear from you. In the meantime I'll make preparations to leave for Martinique." He looked from Caroline to Edwin, and smiled. "When I came here today, I didn't know what your reaction would be, but even in my wildest dreams I would never have expected you to help me as you have offered to do. I can never repay you for this."

"You don't need to," Caroline said. "You are our friend. But please be careful."

"I will be very careful, but you must promise me something, you as well, Sarah. If you hear that Sir Anthony Peters has been arrested, do not make any attempt to contact me in any way. Just forget that I ever existed."

"I can't do that—" Sarah began.

"You can't expect us just to leave you—" Caroline said at the same time.

"No!" Alex interrupted, his expression earnest, verging on desperate. "You must promise me this. When I left London as Sir Anthony, I never expected to return, except under one circumstance, which has not come to pass. Every day I stay here increases the risk that someone will discover me."

"But you don't look at all like Sir Anthony!" Caroline said.

"Even so, it's possible something may go wrong. If it does, then I would ask you to do as you were going to, try to help Beth to get to a safe place where she can live out her life in peace. But you absolutely must not attempt to do anything for me, no matter how small. You will not be able to save me, and will only put yourselves at risk."

Edwin nodded.

"You're right," he agreed. "We will do as you say."

"Thank you," Alex said. He stood. "I'll leave now. Will you ensure that Sarah and Mary get back safely tomorrow?"

"No," Sarah said, standing as well. "We'll go back to London with you. People saw us come here together. If we leave separately it may cause suspicion. Once we reach London I won't try to contact you again, I promise."

She had a point. He smiled and nodded.

"You have all been wonderful friends, to me and to Beth,"

Alex said. "Whatever happens, I will never forget that."

"Anthony," Edwin said. "I can see now that you took a huge risk today, because we now know exactly what you really look like, and you did that only to apologise to us. That tells me more than any words could. You may have terrible judgement where monarchs are concerned, but not only have you been our friend, you still are. Do not get yourself arrested, not at this late stage. I don't think any of us could bear that, least of all Beth."

"I will do my utmost not to," Alex said, smiling broadly.

On the way back to the village Alex and Sarah walked in silence, each pondering the events of the last couple of hours. Màiri sat on Alex's shoulder, chattering happily to herself in baby talk.

"They are wonderful people," Sarah said after a time.

"Indeed they are," Alex agreed. "And so are you."

She smiled at this, and they carried on in silence for a little longer.

"Can I ask you a question?" she said.

"Of course."

"Do you trust them?"

"Of course I do," Alex said. "They have the means to have me arrested, as do you. Yes, I trust them."

"Why didn't you speak to them with your proper accent, then?" she asked.

"How do you know that the English accent is not my proper one?" he replied.

She looked at him wryly, and he laughed.

"I trust Caroline and Edwin," he said, "but you're family. There's a difference, ye ken."

For a moment she thought he was referring to his fictitious relationship as her cousin, but when she looked at him he smiled down at her with the same curve to his mouth that Màiri had, and looked at her with the same long-lashed eyes as Màiri's, save only the colour, and she knew that he was, in his own way revealing to her what she had suspected all along; that he and Murdo were closely related. He reached out his hand to her, and shyly she took it.

It was transitory, she knew that. When they got back to London he'd leave her, and she would probably never see him

164

again. But right now it felt very good to be part of his family. She lapsed back into silence, intending to commit to memory every remaining second she had with him, and they continued on their way hand in hand.

CHAPTER NINE

Martinique, July 1747

Once the harvest was over, as promised Pierre took Antoinette and Beth to Saint Pierre for a few days. Beth would have enjoyed the journey more if she had been allowed to ride in the fresh air and take in the scenery along the way, but everything had to be done with great pomp, so they travelled in a stuffy carriage which bounced its way along the bumpy, badly maintained road, while several liveried footmen, including Raymond, rode on the front or back of the coach, and other slaves were either sent on ahead to prepare the rooms their owners would stay in or ran behind the coach as it travelled.

At the speed the coach was travelling, 'running behind it' was actually no more than a leisurely walk. Beth, sitting inside the overheated carriage, with the velvet curtains firmly closed so as to keep out any light which might bring on one of Antoinette's megrims, longed to leap out and walk with Rosalie and Eulalie, who were bringing up the rear. But of course that would never do, so she gritted her teeth and bore it, and by the time they arrived at their spacious apartments in the town, she ached far more from the jouncing of the coach than she would have done from walking.

The first evening they went to a concert and listened to Bach's Goldberg Variations. To Beth's delight, both Pierre and Antoinette declared themselves to be great lovers of music, and as a result she could allow herself to become completely absorbed in the delicate melodies without them being rudely interrupted by her companions.

However, in spite of the undoubted skill of the harpsichordist, the luxurious surroundings, and the comparative silence of the appreciative audience, she did miss a few of the variations completely due to reliving the first time she had heard Bach's music, at Versailles, when Lord Winter had been a most uncongenial companion, and Sir Anthony had, during the interval, challenged Henri Monselle to a duel. Had it really been over four years since that night? In some ways it felt like yesterday; she could still see the shock in Henri's eyes as Sir Anthony's blade drove through his chest, could feel the hurt and despair that had clutched at her heart as she realised that the man she loved did not trust her. And yet in other ways it felt as though centuries had passed since then; so much had happened in the intervening period, both good and bad.

That life is over, she told herself fiercely as she felt tears prick her eyes, and she forced herself to concentrate on the music again. *Henri is dead, Sir Anthony no longer exists, and Alex...* No. She would not think of him. She would think of the future. That was all that mattered now.

The following day Beth was hoping they might go for a walk along the wide tree-lined roads of Saint Pierre and take in some of the beautiful European-style buildings; but instead they clambered back into the stuffy coach and went on a round of social calls, at which there seemed to be two main topics of conversation; slaves and disease. At every house the company talked about the laziness and lack of gratitude of the slaves and the resulting punishments that had to be meted out, the potential for a slave uprising, and who had died recently.

Beth was wondering if every other plantation except Soleil was composed of slaves who just sat around all day doing nothing, until Antoinette joined in, saying that it was the same everywhere, and that Monsieur Armstrong had to wield the whip constantly to get the negroes to do any work at all. Having seen first hand how the Delisles' slaves laboured, Beth then allowed her mind to wander, as she had learned to do so well in her early days with her Cunningham cousins. It was the only way she could be sure not to say something offensive.

As for the second topic of conversation, it appeared that several people of their acquaintance died every week. She was about to dismiss that too as ridiculous exaggeration until she remembered that all six of Antoinette's children had died, and that every household they visited had lost more than one member of the family as well as a large number of slaves to some illness or other; mainly either *vomito negro,* which could carry people off in a day, dysentery, or ague, also called intermittent fever because it came and went, some victims surviving for years, some dying very quickly. That, combined with the fact that even the wealthy planters rarely lived beyond fifty, told Beth that her chances of being reunited with Alex reasonably soon were pretty good. It was a cheering thought.

In the evening they went to a dinner in a luxuriously appointed salon which would not have looked out of place in Paris itself. As Beth entered she was announced as 'Lady Elizabeth Peters', after which numerous guests were presented to her, curtseying and bowing obsequiously, their expressions conveying that they considered it a great honour that the beautiful English aristocrat would condescend to speak to them. She played along, smiling graciously and uttering meaningless pleasantries while she wondered what the Delisles had told their acquaintance about her to make them behave in this deferential way.

Within five minutes of sitting down to dinner she found out.

"I am so excited to be seated next to you, my lady," the elderly woman to the left of Beth said, once she had managed to manipulate the vast skirts of her dress into place and sit down. Beth fanned herself vigorously and smiled at her neighbour, whose white paint and rouge were already starting to run in the heat of the room. All the doors and windows were open, but there was not a breath of wind; the flames of the many candles in the sparkling chandeliers were all vertical, those on the table only flickering due to the movements of the diners. "Pierre tells me that you have been to the Palace of Versailles at the express invitation of His Majesty the King!" the woman continued excitedly.

"Indeed, er…"

"Do please call me Louise!" the old lady trilled.

"Indeed, Louise, I did have that honour when I visited France with my husband four years ago."

Louise clapped her hands with joy.

"Oh, do tell me what the Palace looks like! Is it as beautiful as they say?"

Obligingly Beth launched into a description of the beauties of the Palace; the glorious Hall of Mirrors, so named because it boasted over three hundred prodigiously expensive mirrors, the War Room with its ornate marble panels glorifying the great deeds of the present king's great-grandfather Louis XIV, the incredible decorations by the gifted artist Le Brun, and the Royal Chapel, with its beautiful vaulted ceiling. As she spoke she became aware that everyone in the vicinity had stopped talking and was listening avidly to her. She was just about to continue on to describe the gardens, when Louise interrupted her.

"And is it true that His Majesty became a *particular* friend of yours?"

Further down the table Pierre beamed at her, basking in the reflected glory of his beautiful and aristocratic house guest, who was, it seemed, not only on first name terms with the King of France, but was a *particular friend.*

Beth sighed. It was clear where this was leading. The Delisles had already invented their own version of her history, and their friends obviously believed them. She knew how society gossip worked; denying outright that she had been Louis' mistress would only convince them all the more that she had shared his bed.

Pierre had been good to her; although technically her employer, not for one moment had he treated her as anything other than an honoured guest. The allowance he was paying her was extremely generous, and he had shown her nothing but kindness. Partially falling in with what appeared to be his exaggerated account of her relationship with King Louis was the least she could do. For the rest she would employ one of Sir Anthony's weapons for such situations.

"Indeed," Beth said. "I will never forget the first time I caught sight of His Majesty. My husband and I had been invited to attend mass in the Royal Chapel, and I became so engrossed in the paintings on the ceiling I was just telling you about, that when King Louis entered I quite forgot to lower my gaze to the ground, with the result that I found myself staring straight into his eyes! A terrible breach of protocol! I was mortified!"

"Oh, how romantic!" a pretty young lady on the other side of the table cried. "And was it then that you—"

Her question was interrupted by the arrival of the first course, oysters and crayfish in a spicy sauce, of which large platters were placed at strategic points along the table, from which the diners could then help themselves. Once everyone had chosen what they wanted both the eating and conversation resumed, and Beth was within a few minutes asked the inevitable question, which although delivered *sotto voce* by the questioner, might as well have been bellowed across the room, judging by the number of necks craning to hear the answer.

"And was it then that you became the lover of the king?" the pretty young lady asked.

Well, that was a little more direct than she'd expected.

"Of course not! We were in the chapel, madame! We were there to hear mass, a most solemn occasion. No, I kept my eyes to the ground and my thoughts on Heaven for the rest of the service."

"Of course," her questioner said, annoyed that the directness of the question had not inspired an equally direct response.

"Is it not true, Lady Elizabeth, that your husband challenged the king's personal servant to a duel due to jealousy, because he could not challenge the king himself?" Louise asked.

"Why on earth would he wish to challenge the king?" Beth responded, utterly astonished. "We were honoured to be invited to the Palace! But yes, he did challenge Monsieur Monselle, which was quite ridiculous. He and I were merely acquaintances. We shared an interest in the works of John Milton, nothing more. It was a most unfortunate and tragic situation. Ah! Here is the soup course. I had never tasted sweet potato until I arrived here, and I confess to having quite a weakness for it."

She dived into the soup, completely entranced by it, so entranced that she did not hear the next three questions aimed at her from further down the table, but did, oddly, hear the fourth, which coincidentally was not about the King of France.

"I am learning to," she replied in response to the question about whether she was acclimatising to Martinique, "although I think it will take me a little time to adjust to the climate. It is so different from that of England."

And Scotland. She would give all of this luxury, her safety, even her life, if she could be sitting on a log by the side of Loch Lomond right now, her thumb tucked in Alex's swordbelt, his arm heavy on her shoulder as they watched the sun go down over the water. For a moment the fine table, the crystal, the silver, the guests, faded away as she leaned into her husband, feeling the warmth of his body against the length of her side…

Stop it, she told herself fiercely, dragging herself back to the present. *You will go mad if you let yourself live in the past. It is over. It. Is. Over.*

"I'm sorry?" she said, aware that someone else had asked something that everyone was clearly hoping she would answer.

"I asked if the king's bedchamber was also decorated by Le Brun?"

Oh, for God's sake…

"I really couldn't say, madame," she replied sweetly. "After all, visitors are not allowed to enter the King's and Queen's private apartments, as I'm sure you know."

After another few well-deflected questions, people gave up. It was very clear that King Louis had chosen Lady Elizabeth Peters to be his mistress not just for her beauty, but for her discretion, or possibly stupidity, too.

The rest of her time in Saint Pierre was in the main a copy of the first two days. Only the entertainment differed. Sometimes it was music, sometimes a play or an opera, all of which Beth enjoyed. But she came to dread the inevitable dinners with variations of the same questions to be fended off.

Eventually, on her final evening in Saint Pierre, someone came up with a question which no one thought she could evade.

"Do tell me, my lady, is the king's member really as large as it's reputed to be?" It was asked by a middle-aged rakish man with a long face and a hooked nose who Beth had met three times, and towards whom she had developed an antipathy. The question was greeted by gasps; whilst possibly an acceptable question to be put to a whore, Lady Elizabeth, royal mistress or no, had been a paragon of virtue since arriving on the island.

Lady Elizabeth looked the gentleman up and down with obvious disdain, and then smiled.

"I hate to disappoint you, Monsieur Duval, but I don't believe

King Louis is enamoured of buggery. Indeed I think it may be illegal in France – it certainly is in England. However, as you are so interested, I shall write to His Majesty this very evening, giving him your details and informing him of your desire for him."

For the rest of the evening no one asked her any questions that were even vaguely related to King Louis, and the unfortunate Monsieur Duval gave her a very wide berth indeed. Beth reflected that if someone had asked her that question on her first evening in Saint Pierre rather than the last, she might have at least enjoyed the meals more.

She would not have enjoyed the dancing, though, which went on into the early hours of the morning. It was incredible that women who found the temperature too hot to contemplate going for a walk or a ride outdoors by day were happy to spend hours dancing indoors in furnace-like heat whilst wearing heavy and cumbersome court gowns supported by hoops and numerous petticoats.

* * *

After two weeks the Delisles and accompanying slaves returned to the Soleil plantation, where life returned to normal. After another two weeks of sedentary pursuits in the enervating company of Antoinette, Beth reflected that life with her Cunningham cousins had been exhilarating by comparison.

Her only consolation was her friendship with Rosalie, which was improving daily as the young maid grew more competent at her duties and more confident in conversing, once she realised her mistress was not going to punish her for making a mistake or speaking out of turn.

One afternoon when Antoinette was in bed suffering from one of her attacks, Beth was about to set out for the blacksmith's forge to see if her knives were ready, when Pierre intercepted her as she was leaving the house and insisted on sending a slave to find out for her. She returned to her bedroom in a black mood, pacing up and down the room in a futile attempt to burn off her energy. Then she threw herself onto the bed and picked up the book she was halfway through reading, *L'Astrée*, but after reading the same page four times without absorbing anything, was about to put it down when Rosalie came in, carrying one of Beth's heavy gowns, which had just been cleaned.

"Ah!" said Beth, seizing this chance of diversion. "Do you have any other chores to do today?"

Rosalie looked confused.

"Madame, I am always yours to command," she said. She moved toward the heavy chest in the corner of the room to put the dress away, ready for the next time it was needed to torture its wearer. The way she carried it, with infinite care, gave Beth an idea.

"Would you like to try it on?" she said.

Rosalie's expression gave Beth her answer, even though the maid shook her head instantly.

"Oh no, madame," she said. "I couldn't. I would make it dirty."

"Of course you wouldn't," Beth said, "and we are about the same size. I think it would fit you very well."

Rosalie looked longingly at the heap of turquoise-blue silk draped over her arm. "No, really, madame, you are very kind, but I couldn't."

"Let's play a game," Beth suggested, a tactic which she had employed repeatedly since her first day with Rosalie, and which seemed to help her relax. "You will be the mistress and I will be the maid, and will dress you. I am very bored, and as Monsieur Delisle does not take kindly to me offering to help Eulalie prepare dinner or weed the gardens," both of which Pierre had rebuked her for trying to do in the past week, "then you will be helping me to keep my sanity. Come, take off your gown, and I'll lay out the clothes on the bed."

Half an hour later and with much laughter Rosalie was encased in shift, stockings, stays, pockets, modesty petticoat, panniers, three petticoats, stomacher and gown, all tied or pinned in place.

"Oh, Madame Beth!" she said. "It is so heavy! How do you wear all these clothes for a whole day?"

"I wish I didn't have to," Beth responded candidly. "I have always hated dressing fashionably. I would far rather wear practical clothing like your own. When I lived at home, I did."

"At home in England, madame?"

"Yes." *And Scotland.* "No, don't look in the mirror yet. I don't wear wigs, so I don't have one for you to try on, but you need something to decorate your hair. Here." Deftly she tied a ribbon of the same colour as the dress into Rosalie's thick black frizzy hair, which she kept ruthlessly brushed and pinned into a roll now that she had a position in the house. "There," Beth said, handing her a fan. "Now you may look at yourself."

The rapturous expression on the young maid's face as she observed herself in the mirror was worth all the time spent tying ribbons and laces. The aqua shade of the shimmering silk complemented her dark brown skin wonderfully and she looked like a fairytale princess.

"Ohhh!" she said breathlessly, turning round and looking back over her shoulder into the mirror. "Oh, madame, it is worth feeling so hot to look so good!"

The next two hours were spent with Beth showing Rosalie how to walk, sit, curtsey, use a fan and finally, with much laughter, how to use a chamberpot. For the first time since Beth had listened to Bach in Saint Pierre, she was actually enjoying herself.

When Rosalie was finally back in her normal dress and the gown was put safely away, she untied the ribbon from her hair and moved to put it back in the drawer with Beth's other fripperies.

"No," Beth said. "I would gladly give you the gown, if you had a use for it, but you must at least keep the ribbon. It will remind you of this afternoon."

"You are too good to me, madame," Rosalie said, smiling shyly as she ran her fingers along the length of ribbon.

"When I lived in England, before I married Sir Anthony," Beth said, "I had a maid called Sarah, who also became a friend, as you and I are becoming. On the night before I was due to marry I took her to the opera. I helped her to dress, just as I have helped you and we enjoyed ourselves enormously."

"Oh, madame, that must have been wonderful for her!"

"Not really," Beth said. "The evening didn't go as planned, although it was certainly memorable. But one day if possible I will take you to a play, or a concert maybe, and if I do you can wear that gown."

Rosalie smiled sadly.

"You are very kind, Madame Beth," she said, "but even if Monsieur were to allow it, no slave would be permitted to attend the theatre."

"Are there no free black people in Martinique?" Beth asked.

"Oh yes, madame, but I do not think they would be allowed to attend a theatre with white people."

Beth sighed. Of course not. What was she thinking of? She threw herself down on the end of the bed, standing up again immediately and picking up the book she had inadvertently sat on. She was about to put it back on the shelf when an idea struck her.

"Rosalie," she said. "Would you like to learn to read?"

"No, Beth, I'm afraid I cannot allow that," Pierre said, when Beth put her idea of holding reading and writing classes for the slaves to him.

"But why not? You said there is not as much work now the harvest is over." Although Pierre *had* said this, Beth saw no sign of the slaves having any more leisure time than they had in the cane-cutting months. The bell still rang before sun-up, and the field gangs toiled until long after sunset. There was always something to do; digging, planting, weeding, collecting wood for the boiling house ready for the next harvest, repairing machinery and walls – the list of chores seemed endless. "Surely you could spare them for maybe one hour a week?" she persisted. "It would give me something to do. I want to feel useful."

"But you *are* useful, my dear. Antoinette could not do without you." Pierre sighed. "Even if I could spare the slaves for an hour a week it is not advisable that they learn to read, even if they were capable of doing so, which I really do not believe most of them are. If they could read, then they would be able to read nefarious publications encouraging them to rebel. That will not do at all."

Beth, who had been about to say that Rosalie was learning to read very quickly and after just a week knew the whole alphabet and could write her name, realised this would not now be wise, and changed tack.

"But they would also be able to read the Bible, Pierre!" she said. "How wonderful would it be if they could read the word of God every day, and not only on Sundays?"

"Ah, now I can see that although you are a good Roman, the reformed faith of your home country has been a bad influence on you. It is quite sufficient for the negroes to learn the word of God from someone who knows which scripture is fitting for them to hear and which not. No, I am sorry Beth, you know I will indulge you where I can, but this is not possible."

Back in her room, Beth fumed. No doubt he wouldn't want the slaves to be able to read Galatians 3:28, or Exodus, or numerous other verses that spoke about rights that the slaves of Martinique did not enjoy.

She was still annoyed about it a few days later when Pierre and Antoinette threw a dinner party, to which were invited all the local plantation owners. It was a somewhat informal occasion; dinner, then conversation and cards followed by some music and perhaps dancing.

Beth insisted on helping to choose and pick the flowers that would decorate the dining table, which gave her an opportunity to wander around the garden all day finding out not just about flowers for the table but other plants too, from the extremely knowledgeable head gardener, an elderly wrinkled negro by the name of Ezra.

"You see, madame, this flower, the marya-marya, she is very beautiful, but like many beautiful ladies, she is also deadly," he said of a passion fruit plant over whose flowers Beth had exclaimed. "She has the sticky juice here on these bracts, which insects love, and then she traps them and they die, and so they cannot eat her, because she eats them first! She is very clever! And then this one, with her tiny flowers, which madame will not want for the house, I think, she is very precious, because with her you can cure many things. She is called Snakewort, because she cures the bite of the snake sometimes, and also the dysentery."

"How do you know all this, Ezra?" Beth said after an hour in which she learnt more about plants than she had in the whole of her life in England, and all of it delivered in a fascinating way.

"People tell me as a child, madame, and I listen. Once I know a thing, I know her forever." He beamed, delighted to have a truly interested audience. "Now I teach Nicaise, who is my grandson, because I am very old and soon I must die, I think."

"How old are you, Ezra?" Beth asked. He did look very ancient indeed, older even than her grandmother, who was probably over eighty.

"I am fifty-two, madame!" he said with great pride.

Fifty-two, she thought as she walked back to the house, her arms full of exotic flowers, her head full of knowledge and rage. He had a prodigious memory and intelligence. What could he have achieved, given an education? He could have been an apothecary or a great medical man perhaps. Instead he spent his time and energy stopping the ever-growing tropical foliage from encroaching on the perfect clipped lawn, just so that Pierre and Antoinette could, if they wished, sit on it and drink tea or chocolate occasionally. True, he seemed happy enough; but how could he be if he had no choice in his life? He was one of the lucky slaves – clearly he enjoyed the task he'd been given, or had learned to.

But what of the others, the field gangs, those who toiled in the boiling house?

She thought about this all through dinner, with the result that afterwards as they were about to go into the salon Antoinette took her to one side.

"Are you feeling ill, Beth?" she asked.

"No, not at all!" Beth responded. "Why do you ask?"

"Only you were so quiet all through the meal, and hardly spoke at all. You look well, but I thought perhaps you felt unwell."

For a moment Beth was tempted to say yes, she had a headache and make her excuses, avoid the tedium of the conversation to come, but that would be unfair. After all, her allowance was large and her duties few; but she knew that one of her unwritten obligations was to be the gracious and vivacious English noblewoman when guests called. So far no one had mentioned King Louis, so it was possible that the evening might be moderately interesting.

"No," she replied, smiling. "I wished only to concentrate on the food, which was exquisite. But thank you for your concern, Antoinette. You are most kind."

Once in the salon, where some settled to cards and others relaxed on chaise longues and cushioned chairs to converse, Beth made more of an effort and was soon listening with interest to a neighbouring planter who was explaining how his great-great-grandfather, along with other Frenchmen, had made the island their own.

"It was very dangerous, Lady Elizabeth," he told her. "He was living on what is now a British island, St Kitt's, and was forced to leave. When he arrived here the island was full of Caribs. My great-great-grandfather lived in a little shack he built from leaves and branches, and cleared his land by hand. I'm sure you have seen how quickly everything grows in Martinique already, even though you've only been here a short time. It is very difficult to cultivate such land. But he did it, and in between doing it he led raids against the Caribs. They were savages – it is said that they ate the flesh of men when they could get it, which made it very perilous for anyone to go into the jungle."

"Really, Julien, do you think man-eating savages are a suitable topic of conversation for a young lady? We do not want to drive Beth from Martinique before she has had time to grow used to it!" Pierre interposed.

"My apologies, Lady Elizabeth," Julien said, bowing. "I assure you, there are no Caribs on the island now and have not been for many years."

"No, now we have the danger of the slaves rising and cutting us to pieces while we sleep," Antoinette put in. Pierre raised his eyes to heaven.

"Are you now becoming accustomed to life on Martinique, my lady?" Julien said quickly, before the conversation could turn to the ever-present dangers of malcontent negroes. "It is very different from your home country, I think."

"It is," Beth agreed. "I enjoy the food now; it's interesting to try the fruits and vegetables I had never even heard of before I arrived here. I can cope with the heat a little better. And when I first arrived here the smell of the sugar made me feel sick all the time. It was Raymond who told me that he didn't notice the smell any more. I found it hard to believe that anyone could not notice such a strong odour, but now it no longer bothers me at all. Some things are harder to adjust to, though."

"Beth finds the treatment of slaves difficult to accept," Pierre elaborated.

"Ah," Julien replied. "This is normal, I think, for people who are new to the islands. It is the punishments you have a difficulty with?"

"Not only that, monsieur," Beth said. "I find it difficult to live in such luxury as this," she waved her arm around the room with its ornate gilded woodwork, crystal chandeliers, rich velvet curtains and luxurious furnishings, "while the people who work to provide the money for it live in vermin-infested shacks, work more than sixteen hours a day in appalling conditions, and are beaten regularly."

"But this surely is no different to your country, or my own, in fact?" argued Julien. "The poor in France and England live in very basic conditions and work long hours, whilst the rich enjoy untold luxuries. It is the way of the world."

He had a point.

"That is true," Beth conceded. "But at least they have not been torn from their own country; and if they are in a job that they hate, with a cruel master, they can seek another one and leave. If they are unjustly treated, they have some recourse to the law. They have some choice; a limited one maybe, but at least some."

Julien nodded. "I see your point, my lady, and I have heard this view before. But you are not allowing for the base nature of the negro. Left to himself the negro is a savage barbarian. In his own country he lives in sin, walks around almost naked and does as his tribal leader tells him without question. He is incapable of thinking for himself. At least here, although he may be enslaved he is at least exposed to civilisation."

"That is exactly what the British government say about the Highlanders in Scotland," Beth said. "It is the excuse Cumberland and his troops are using to justify the so-called 'pacification' of the Highlands."

"Ah, yes, I have heard of this," another man put in. "It is regrettable. But I think there is some truth in this view. The Highlanders are a lawless savage people who live by raiding and murdering each other. They speak a sort of gibberish language, and I am told the men wear a short petticoat and nothing else! On a windy day nothing is left to the imagination!"

Several women tittered.

"My mother was a Highlander, sir," Beth said quietly. It was on the tip of her tongue to say *and my husband too, and he was more civilised than all of you.* But no. She had not kept silence for over a year only to divulge secrets over brandy in a salon.

A profound and uncomfortable silence fell upon the room.

"I thought you were of a noble family, Lady Elizabeth," one woman finally ventured.

"My father was the second son of a lord, madame," Beth said. "My mother was one of these Highland savages of whom you speak. I am, I suppose, to this gentleman's way of thinking, a mulatto. That is what you call the offspring of a white planter and a savage barbarian negro, is it not? Tell me, would you accept a mulatto into your society as you have accepted me?"

"It is not the same thing at all, my lady," Julien countered, "and I am sure your mother was an exception."

"No, she was not an exception," Beth replied, her temper rising. "She spoke the 'gibberish', which is rightly called Gaelic, and is a beautiful, poetic language. She came from a clan who, it is true, in common with other clans, look to their chief rather than the government in London to dictate the law and to protect them. They have their own code of honour and loyalty, which they adhere to, and which is the reason why in five months of hiding in their lands with a reward of £30,000 on his head, Prince Charles Edward Stuart was not betrayed to the government."

"I am sure no one wished to offend you, Beth," Pierre said.

With an effort, Beth calmed herself.

"I am sure that's true, Pierre," she said after a moment. "But it does illustrate my point. The reason that the British government, and you, monsieur," indicating the unnamed man, "believe that the Highlanders are savage barbarians is merely because you do not understand them, cannot speak their language. Just because their laws, customs and traditions are incomprehensible to you does not mean they have none. Those they have are not the same as yours, so you believe them to be wrong rather than merely different. And now the Elector and his son are showing the Highlanders what real civilisation is, by butchering men and children, raping women and burning them in their homes!"

"I must protest, my lady!" the unnamed man replied. "I did not intend to insult your mother, and I apologise for that. But if we return to our original conversation, we were discussing the negro. After all, the Highlanders are European, and white. The African is a very different sort of creature from us. They do not think the same way, cannot reason as we do. Left to themselves they are lazy and indolent, lacking in motivation. They do not feel emotions as we do. They are human, yes, but a far more inferior human. To expose them to civilisation, and to Christ, can only be a good thing!"

"But what sort of civilisation are you exposing them to, sir?" Beth retorted, silencing the murmurs of approval that the man's comment had aroused. "A civilisation that says people can be bought and sold like cattle, can be forced to labour twenty hours a day in the most appalling conditions without pay, and can be whipped and mutilated, even murdered at the whim of their owner, with no right to seek justice, no rights at all. A civilisation that allows babies to be torn from their mother's breast and sold, husbands and wives to be separated. It is wrong.

"Maybe I feel this because the attitude towards the negroes and my mother's family is the same. Maybe it is because I was sent here by the British government to be sold into slavery for life, and would, were it not for Captain Marsal and Monsieur le Marquis, be living in the same way as your slaves, with no choice, no rights and no recourse to law. I think you see things differently when, but for the toss of a dice, you would be suffering the same fate. But at least in the eyes of my government I had committed an offence and was being punished for it. The negroes have done nothing wrong except to be African and black, which makes their treatment even worse."

The silence which now descended on the company was even more profound and uncomfortable. Beth looked around at the uncomprehending expressions on people's faces, and sighed.

I might as well have been speaking in Gaelic for all they understand, she thought sadly. They did not want to understand, because if they did then they might have to act on it, and then their way of life would collapse. *It's pointless,* she thought. *Everything is pointless.* A great wave of despair washed over her.

"I am sorry, Pierre, Antoinette," she said, "I did not wish to spoil your evening. If you will excuse me, I think I must be a little unwell after all. I will retire to bed, with your permission?"

"Of course, my dear!" Pierre said, his expression one of mixed concern and relief. She had given him an excuse for her behaviour. *She is a woman, new to our ways, and unwell. She did not mean what she said.*

Beth said her goodnights and left the room. Suddenly she felt unutterably weary. *I cannot go on like this,* she thought. *I cannot become accustomed to this way of life. I do not want to become accustomed to such a way of life.*

She was halfway up the stairs when she heard her name called, very softly. She looked over the banister to see Raymond in the hall, his face lifted to hers. Quickly he ran up the stairs, stopping two steps below her.

"Madame Beth, may I ask, did you mean what you said just now, in the salon?" he asked.

"Yes. I rarely say what I do not mean," she replied.

He smiled.

"You are a good person, my lady," he said. "I wanted to thank you for what you are doing for Rosalie. She is very excited to be learning to read. She loves you very much."

"It is nothing, Raymond," Beth said. "She learns very quickly and it helps me to pass the time as well. I would teach you too, all of you, if it were possible."

He nodded.

"Even so, you are different. You see us as people, I think," he said.

"You *are* people, Raymond. How could I not see you as such?"

"Madame, I wanted to give you a present. But I am worried that you will be offended if I do," he said.

"Why would I be offended by a present? I would be honoured, but really, you do not need to give me anything. I'm happy to teach Rosalie."

"It is not for that." He held out his hand to her, and she took the object from him. It was a small triangular stone, intricately carved. In the dim light from the candle she carried she could see that one edge of the triangle had been carved in the shape of a human profile, and there were what seemed to be Celtic knotwork carvings on the face of the stone. A small hole had been drilled through the top and threaded with a thin leather lace.

"This is beautiful," she said. "Did you carve this? You are very talented. What kind of stone is it?"

"It is not stone, but wood, a very hard wood. It is very old. I did not carve it. It gives protection."

"I think you need protection more than I do, Raymond," Beth

said. "You should keep it for yourself."

"No. It is for you. It will give you protection against disease, madame, and against...other things."

"What other things?"

His eyes slid away from hers and then back again, his expression earnest.

"You must promise me, please, madame, that if anything ever happens, anything bad, you will wear it around your neck or on your wrist. If it is seen, you will not be harmed."

"Is something *going* to happen?" she asked, alarmed now.

"I don't know of anything, no," he said. "But if it does, this will keep you safe. You will make me very happy if you accept it."

"Then I will, and thank you," she said.

He smiled broadly, and then, before she could ask any more questions, he turned and ran lightly back down the stairs.

In her room, she sat on the bed looking at the wooden amulet more closely. Each side of the triangle was no more than an inch long, but the carvings were very fine. *Angus would love this,* she thought. After a while Rosalie came in.

"Oh, Madame Beth! I didn't know you had left the party! You should have called me," she said.

"Do you know what this is, Rosalie?" Beth asked, still looking at the object in her hand. Rosalie came across and bent over.

"Ah, so he gave it to you. He said he wanted to, but was afraid you would be angry," she said.

"Why would I be angry?"

"Because you worship the Christ god."

"You do as well, don't you?" Beth said.

"Yes, madame, I do. But this, this is another god, very old. A god of the ancestors of the people who lived here before the French came. His name is Yúcahu, and he will protect you. My father likes you very much and is afraid for you, and for what will happen to me if anything happens to you. He said that you protect me, and so if he gave this to you, by protecting you it will protect both of us!" She smiled, then seeing Beth's expression, her brow creased. "Are you angry, Madame Beth?" she asked nervously.

Beth looked up into her maid's eyes.

"No, I'm not angry, of course not. It's a very kind gesture.

Rosalie, are the slaves planning to revolt?"

"No, madame!" Rosalie replied immediately. "No, it is to protect you against illness, snakebites and bad luck. I have heard nothing of a revolt. Did my father say that?"

"No. It was just my imagination. Come, help me undress, and then you can sleep. You look tired," Beth said.

Later she lay in the dark listening to the muted sounds of music and laughter from below, running her fingers over the amulet, and thinking.

Rosalie had been telling the truth when she said she knew nothing of a revolt, Beth was sure of that. She was not so sure of Raymond, because she didn't know him well enough to be able to tell if he was lying. She could not blame them if they were planning a rising. She had lived here long enough to know that slaves were whipped and beaten for nothing. She had heard their screams carrying across to the house as they were flogged at the whipping post, had had to resist running across the fields to stop it. She could not stop it. She had no authority over the drivers and overseers who meted out discipline.

The planters were terrified of a slave revolt. The whites were outnumbered by slaves by over five to one, and the whole island was like a barrel of gunpowder waiting for the fuse to be lit. If she told Pierre what Raymond had said to her, he would be arrested, questioned, certainly tortured, and probably killed.

She could not do that to a man, one who was trying to protect her, based only on her own vague suspicions. If she had any proof it might be different.

Might.

Her father had been English and Hanoverian, her mother a Highlander and Jacobite. She had grown up hearing both sides of the story and had finally, after much thought and reading, chosen to take the side of the Stuarts. It had been a reasoned decision, not based purely on instinct and emotion.

She had spoken the truth tonight. She was of noble birth, that was true; but she was also a Highlander, partly by birth and partly by marriage. And the Highlanders were being treated in the same way as the negroes. The difference was only a matter of degree. She felt an obligation to the Delisles, liked many of the planters she had met, even if she held little in common with them; and she felt a great sense of injustice at the treatment of the slaves, but had not lived here for long enough to come down firmly on one side.

I don't want to live here long enough for that, she thought. *But I have to. I must stop thinking about home and the people I miss there. I cannot go back. If I do I will put my friends and myself in danger. And if I go to France or Italy I will just be another Jacobite among the many that King James and Prince Charles now have to support. As a woman I cannot fight, and I would not wish to be a burden.*

At least here she could do *something.* As far as the possibility of a slave revolt went, for now she would do nothing, but she would pay attention. If she heard something more definite, then she would find a way to alert Pierre to the possibility of a revolt without implicating Raymond or anyone else.

She could teach Rosalie to read and write, albeit in secret, maybe find a way to teach others too, in time. It was better to help at least one person to maybe have a better life. And if she could, when she knew more, persuade some of the planters to treat their slaves more sympathetically, then her life would be worth living.

Small victories.

During the days when Antoinette did not need her, and as the temperature rose as July gave way to August, Beth spent more and more time in her room, ostensibly 'resting', a pastime eminently fitting for a delicate young aristocratic lady in such weather. Of course she needed her maid to fan her, and pour glasses of lime or tamarind water for her.

And so Rosalie's education continued apace.

CHAPTER TEN

London, August 1747

After his meeting with Caroline and Edwin, the first thing Alex had done was to return to the field near Manchester where the chest of gold was buried, to retrieve more money. The last time, when accompanied by Graeme, he had taken enough to pay for a stay in London, the adoption of another couple of disguises if necessary, and for generous bribes to prison keepers. He had, however, not taken enough to pay for a trip to France, then to Martinique, followed by a possibly lengthy stay there while he searched for Beth.

This time he made sure that he had more than enough to fund whatever might need to be done. He could hardly return from the West Indies if he were to discover a need for even more money. He could always replace some if necessary; although he doubted that Beth would complain about the amount he had spent, if it meant they were reunited.

Reunited.

He still had to pinch himself on a regular basis to make sure that this was not some dream from which he would awaken to find that she had, after all, died at Culloden. He had a second chance of life with the only woman he had ever loved, the only woman he *would* ever love, and he was ready to do anything, anything at all to find her and bring her home.

He had spent the evening in an inn in Lancashire, where he demanded a private room, then sat up into the night sewing the considerable amount of gold coinage he now possessed into his clothing, ensuring that if he was robbed (unlikely as that was, considering his height, build and, when he wished to display it, air of menace) he would only lose the small amount of money he carried in his purse.

The next day he set off for London, where he rented a room near to the Royal Exchange, within reasonable distance of the coffee house at which he hoped to receive news of Beth's whereabouts. He used the name of Sarah's fictitious cousin, Adam Featherstone, although he abandoned the country bumpkin persona he'd adopted for Lydia's benefit on the spur of the moment; it was not wise to appear to be innocent of the ways of the town, if you wished to remain unmolested. Particularly if you were carrying a small fortune on your person. The amended Adam Featherstone was from Cheshire, and was a man of small means but large ambition, who hoped to learn more of the stock market in the hopes of investing a little money and making a lot.

Mr Featherstone had, in the recent past, he made it known in the taverns and coffee shops he frequented whilst staying in London, been a pugilist of some renown in his native Cheshire, and also enjoyed hunting when he got the opportunity. Having established himself as a man not to be messed with, and openly wearing a small sword, he wandered the streets around his lodgings unmolested.

His lodgings were within walking distance of St Paul's and Paternoster Row, where he could often be found perusing the bookstalls, from which he frequently chose a volume to while away the lonely nights in his room. They were also close to Newgate Prison, which he studiously avoided, knowing that were he to come across the keeper Jones he would be sorely tempted to exercise his pugilistic skills, to say nothing of his expertise with the dirk (which he also wore, though not openly). He did for a time contemplate actually looking the keeper up; it was never difficult to lure a greedy man to a dark and quiet place. But then he reasoned that he must take no unnecessary chances. He had to keep his mind on the main reason for being here, and keep a low profile while doing it.

Nevertheless the temptation to be where Beth had been, however silly and sentimental that might seem, was overwhelming, particularly as the days passed with no word of the disposal of the *Veteran's* prisoners. To that end he took a trip to the Tower, along with a number of other tourists, where he visited the menagerie, paying his sixpence rather than looking for a dead dog or cat to be fed to the animals, which could be presented in lieu of an entrance fee. In keeping with the other visitors, he expressed wonder at the ferocity of the lions and tigers, and joy at the grace of the cheetahs which were led about the grounds of the Tower on leashes for exercise and the wonderment of the spectators. Meanwhile he wondered where Beth had been kept whilst imprisoned here, what her thoughts had been, and how hope must have changed to despair as the weeks and then months had passed without him coming for her as he had promised to.

I am coming soon, mo chridhe, I swear it on my life, he vowed, willing the thought to somehow cross the oceans and reach her, wherever she was.

Later, back in his room he paced up and down, looking not unlike the unfortunate and bored lion in its cage at the menagerie. Four weeks had passed since his meeting with Caroline and Edwin, and still no letter had arrived at Sam's Coffeehouse for Mr Featherstone. He dared not make enquiries about travelling to France at the moment; France and Britain were at war.

France had, only a few weeks ago, achieved a resounding victory at Lauffeldt in which Cumberland's reputation as Commander-in-Chief of the British Army had been badly tarnished, due to him losing his nerve at a decisive moment in the battle and withdrawing his forces. Unfortunately for the podgy duke, at the same time Sir John Ligonier had successfully launched a cavalry attack on the French, which he was then unable to follow up on due to Cumberland's withdrawal.

It was very heartening to Alex to hear that Butcher Cumberland's laurels were being trampled in the mud, but it also meant that any attempt to seek a passage to the enemy country would have to be made discreetly and then followed through quickly in order to avoid arrest as a possible spy or Jacobite. As eager as he was to be reunited with Beth, it would be idiotic after years of evading capture as Sir Anthony, to risk it now due to impatience and a wish to be active.

Instead he went to visit Sarah, partly because he liked her, and anyone who knew Mr Featherstone to be her cousin would expect him to, partly to see his beautiful little niece, even though her resemblance to his dead brother tore at his heart, and partly to obtain reassurance that Edwin and Caroline hadn't changed their minds about contacting him when they had information.

"No, they wouldn't do that," Sarah said as they tucked into a hot steak pie and some boiled potatoes that Alex had purchased from a local cookshop on his way to see her. They were sitting in her little living room around the table. As soon as Màiri saw Alex she made a beeline for him, reaching her arms up to him. She had not lost physical contact with him since, with the result that he was now attempting to eat one-handed, the other being employed in supporting the little girl who was sitting on his knee. Sarah watched him struggling to cut his way through the pastry for a few moments, then pulled his plate across and deftly hacked her way through the crust before pushing it back to him.

"She's completely different with you," Sarah observed, watching as her daughter leaned comfortably back against Alex's chest. He mashed half a potato against the plate, then lifted a forkful to his lips, blowing on it gently until it was cool enough before feeding it to his charge. "She's shy with strangers normally."

"Aye, but I'm no' a stranger," Alex said, lapsing into Scots now they were alone. "She kens we're related."

"You are, really?" Sarah asked softly. He paused with a forkful of steaming meat halfway to his mouth, and looked at her.

"Have you forgotten your cousin Adam so quickly?" he joked in a Mancunian accent. "If I'm your cousin, then it follows I'm hers too."

Sarah didn't pursue the matter. She knew better than that.

"I sometimes wonder if...no, it doesn't matter. It's silly," she said.

"What? Ye can tell me, an ye want."

"I...since you told me about Murdo...I wonder if maybe he knows somehow, about Màiri. There used to be an old woman in my village who said that the spirits of the dead would come back to watch over their families sometimes, and that very young children could see them because they were sensitive to such things."

Alex smiled.

"I dinna rightly ken, but I'm sure of one thing; if he knows of her he'll come to see her, and you too."

"Sometimes she looks into space and smiles, as though she can see someone there. Once she lifted her arms, like she does when she sees you. But I thought you were a Catholic," she added.

"Who tellt ye that?"

"No one. But I know that Beth is, and your cook…Sir Anthony's cook Maggie, she is too. So I thought you probably were as well. Catholics don't believe in ghosts, do they?"

"Aye, well, I daresay if you tellt a priest that Màiri had seen a ghost, he'd warn you that Satan sends such demons in the guise of loved ones to tempt you into sin. But then he'd also tell you that there's no such thing as the second sight, but I've seen proof of that for myself. There are a lot of things we canna explain, but that doesna mean they're evil. If the wee one here sees her father, then that can only be a good thing. There wasna an evil bone in his body."

Sarah smiled, but her eyes were soft and sad.

"My father said the old woman was a witch and in league with the devil. He tried to bring a prosecution against her, but he couldn't get anyone to take him seriously. Everyone knew she was just a harmless old woman whose mind was a bit weak."

Alex raised his eyebrows and Sarah caught the look.

"He was a preacher," she said, "and a vicious bastard who knew a lot more about the devil than any silly old woman."

"Is he dead?" Alex asked.

"I don't know. I hope so. And if there is a God and a devil, I'm sure he's burning in hell right now, and Richard Cunningham with him. Oh! I forgot to tell you, Anne had a letter from Richard's colonel. It seems Richard died during the execution of his duties. He was very brave, and it was very quick. He didn't suffer at all."

Alex's mouth twisted.

"Aye, well, he was brave, that much is true. The man was evil, but he was never a coward, even at the end. Was Anne upset?"

"Of course she was! She's an idiot. No, that's not fair. She's tender-hearted. But she was also very relieved. He was trying to take Georgie away from her. Caroline told me that Beth asked her and Edwin about the law and Edwin said it was possible Richard would win. I think that was one of the reasons why she told Newcastle that Richard was a traitor. And I think another reason she did it was because of me," Sarah finished in a small voice. She put her knife and fork down, even though she'd only eaten a small amount of her meal.

"You?" Alex said.

"Yes. I've been thinking about it ever since Caroline told us what Beth had done. Just before Beth went to see Newcastle I visited her, and we were talking about Richard. I told her that I had a pistol and that if he ever came to the shop again I'd blow his brains out. She told me I couldn't do that, because he was a soldier, and I'd hang. And I told her that I'd take my chance, but I would never let him anywhere near me again. I'm so sorry."

"You shouldna be sorry. You'd have been right to shoot him."

"I know, but if I hadn't told her maybe she'd still be here. She did it to protect me, and I feel terrible about it." Her eyes filled with tears. Alex put his own cutlery down and leaned across the table, capturing one of her hands.

"Sarah, dinna blame yourself. Beth would have gone to Newcastle anyway, to protect Anne and to get revenge for herself and our bairn. It isna your fault. You mustna think that way, no' for a minute. The fact that she was protecting you and Màiri too would have been a consideration, I'll no' lie, but it was no' the only reason."

Sarah looked down at his hand enfolding hers. It was large, long-fingered like Murdo's, but unlike his there was a ridge of scar tissue across the back of it. A tear splashed onto the table.

"She doesn't know about Màiri," Sarah whispered. "I never told her. I couldn't bear to tell her the lie that she was my sister's baby, and I…I thought she might be disgusted with me because I'd lain with Murdo without being married to him. Every time I saw her I determined to tell her, and every time I lost the courage."

"She wouldna have been disgusted with you, any more than I am," Alex reassured her. "I'm glad ye did lie with him, for there's something of him left behind and that's a comfort to me, and would be to Beth too."

"I know that now," Sarah said. "When you find her, will you tell her for me? And let her know I'm sorry I didn't tell her myself?"

He could not promise what he wanted to, that he would bring Beth to see Sarah, so she could tell her herself. That would be too dangerous.

"I will. And when I do I'm sure ye'll be getting a letter of some kind, from somewhere, about it. Maybe no' from Beth, though. Maybe from your cousin Adam's new wife."

He winked, and in spite of herself she smiled.

"I do like you, Cousin Adam," she said. "I wish you really *were* my cousin."

He nodded, then squeezed her hand and let it go. They carried on eating in companionable silence, each wrapped up in their own thoughts.

* * *

Another two weeks of excruciating boredom passed, in which Alex went for long walks, read more books and finally wrote to Angus, something he'd intended to wait to do until he had more definite news to relay. He had already been away from home for over two months, and it seemed unfair to make his brother wait any longer. So James Drummond's Uncle Archie wrote to him, telling him that the package he had gone to retrieve had unfortunately been mislaid, but he had high hopes of being able to locate it soon and would notify his dear nephew as soon as he had more news of it.

The next morning he took the letter to the post and then headed off for his regular morning coffee. Mr Featherstone was now a familiar face, calling in as he did every day to read the periodicals and enjoy a beverage. Although he was not a gregarious man he'd become embroiled in a number of discussions, and had made a few acquaintances in the weeks he'd been patronising the establishment. It was impossible to frequent a coffee house and *not* become engaged in conversation; that was after all the primary purpose of them.

"Found anything to invest in yet, Featherstone?" a fellow customer called as he saw the newcomer signalling for coffee. Mr Featherstone made his way over to join the man, a portly butter merchant who dropped in periodically to get a little respite from his wife and ten children. He usually came early in the morning, as by noon the place would be full of people and the ensuing debates would become lively and sometimes aggressive. At the moment, although at another communal table a group of men were already engaged in a heated debate about the War of the Austrian Succession, the merchant was the sole occupier of this table on the opposite side of the room.

"No," Featherstone replied. "Everything seems either to promise too little return, or too much. The last thing I want is to lose all my hard-earned money on something like the South Sea disaster, or that Darien venture the Scotch lost everything on. I've no wish to lose my independence due to greed, as Scotland did."

"I take your point, sir," the butter merchant said. "But I think it was more than the failure of the Darien enterprise that led to the Act of Union."

"You say so?" Adam commented. "I don't know a lot about the Scotch myself. A strange heathen nation, I've been told, although I believe they're coming into line now, since the rebels were routed." It would do no harm, were Mr Featherstone ever to come under suspicion, for it to be reported that he knew little and cared less about the fate of the North British.

"Indeed sir, you have it. Things are changing there, and all to the good I think. If you ask me—"

The waiter arrived with the coffee, and a paper, which he handed to his customer.

"Letter came for you about half an hour ago, Mr Featherstone," he said. Adam took the proffered missive, glanced at the seal, and then put it in his pocket.

"Don't mind me," his companion said. "Read your letter if you want."

"No, it's from my aunt, who lives down in Sussex. She writes the most tedious news, how many eggs the chickens have laid, that sort of thing. It will wait. You were saying about Scotland?"

"Ah, yes. I really do believe, now that the Highlands are being brought into line, that Scotland will become civilised. Of course it will take some time, but…"

Alex listened patiently while the genial merchant unknowingly maligned his country, his clansmen and his ancestors, occasionally dropping in a question to keep the man talking until he could finish his coffee, order another as was his custom, and enquire as to whether there was any news worth reading in the Gazette.

After an hour, which was the normal amount of time he stayed, Mr Featherstone made his farewells and set off for his lodgings at a leisurely pace. When he got back he exchanged a few pleasantries about the weather with his landlady and then made his way up to his room.

Only then did he show the urgency he had felt for the last two hours, pulling out the letter which had been burning a hole in his pocket since he'd received it, and breaking the seal. He unfolded it, to be confronted by a single line of writing.

There is news. Please call at your earliest convenience.

There was no salutation, and no signature. He could glean no hint as to whether the news was good or bad. *Damn.*

His first urge was to run back down the stairs, hire a horse and gallop to Summer Hill immediately. But if he did that he would attract a lot of attention, not least from his inquisitive and gossipy landlady. Sir Anthony Peters had never been apprehended, because Alex MacGregor knew the importance of reining in his impulsive nature and attending to details.

So he waited in his room for the longest hour of his life, until the landlady went out to market, after which he made his way to the nearest inn with horses for hire, hired one for a week, mentioning in passing that he was going to visit an aunt in Oxford who had been unexpectedly taken ill, then trotted out of London along the Oxford road for a couple of miles before deviating off it and heading in the direction of Sussex.

Only then did he give the horse its head, arriving in the late afternoon at a different inn to the one he had stayed at with Sarah. As much as he wanted to ride straight to Summer Hill, Sarah's cousin Adam was not the sort of person to be able to afford a horse.

So he paid for a room and stabling under the name of Oliver Price, then advised the landlord with a wink and a lewd expression that if his luck was in he might not need the room, but was happy to pay for it, just in case the lady in question was not as accommodating as he hoped.

An hour of very brisk walking saw him standing in the driveway of Summer Hill. He paused just long enough to send up a prayer that all was well, walked up the steps and knocked deferentially at the door, removing his hat and twisting it in his hands while he waited for someone to answer his knock. Anyone observing would have thought that perhaps he was asking for work and was somewhat nervous of the response he would get from the master or mistress.

After a minute a maid opened the door.

"Ah, Mr Featherstone is it?" she said.

"Yes, miss," he replied, bowing.

She grinned and blushed, obviously both amused that this handsome young man was ignorant enough to think he had to bow to her, and flattered as well.

"You're expected. If you follow me," she said, sashaying ahead of him in what was clearly meant to be an enticing manner. She knocked politely on the library door, then opened it. "Mr Featherstone is here, Sir Edwin, Lady Caroline," she said.

So, they were both waiting for him. It was important news then. Alex felt the adrenalin surge through his veins, but gave no outward sign as he moved into the room at the maid's signal. He bowed clumsily to Edwin and Caroline, keeping in character because the maid was still there but noting that they both looked tense, Edwin especially so.

"My lord, my lady," he said.

"You may go, Emily," Caroline said to the hovering maid.

"Yes, my lady. Shall I fetch tea?" she asked hopefully.

"No, thank you. That will be all," Caroline replied in a tone that ensured they were alone within seconds. "Please, Mr Featherstone, take a seat," she said, before walking past Alex to the door, opening it and looking out into the hall. She closed it again.

"We can speak freely," she announced. "Anthony, how are you? Your face has healed!"

It had. As Sarah's cousin had not told Lydia that his facial disfigurement was permanent, he had allowed it to heal naturally, once the need to be a one-legged battle-scarred army veteran had passed.

"I received your message this morning," he replied, too anxious to hear the news to engage in small talk. "You have news of Beth?"

Edwin and Caroline exchanged a look.

"Sit down, Anthony, please," Edwin said.

Alex put his hat on the back of the sofa and sat down on the edge of it. Edwin and Caroline sat opposite him.

"Perhaps tea would be a good idea after all?" Edwin said. Caroline made as if to stand.

"No, tell me the news first," Alex replied, trying to keep the impatience out of his voice.

"A letter arrived this week, from the Marquis de Caylus. He's the—"

"Governor of Martinique," Alex interrupted. "I'm sorry. Go on."

"The prisoners who were on the *Veteran* have all been released," Edwin continued. "The Duke of Newcastle has written a letter demanding that they be returned, but the marquis' letter is dated the end of May, so it isn't a reply to that. It doesn't say anything about whether the prisoners will be sent back, or where they are right now."

Alex ran his fingers through his hair in frustration and disappointment. This was no news at all, in his view. He had known that the governor would not just send the prisoners back to Britain of his own accord. Although they had been released, rather than being held awaiting negotiations, which was something.

What would Beth do? He sat there, thinking furiously. *She thinks I'm dead,* he reminded himself. Would she come back to Britain, in that case? If she did, she would go to her friends in Manchester, or to the MacGregors. But then she would risk capture, and possibly bring danger to her friends too. No. She would not do that. Maybe…

He looked up, aware that both Caroline and Edwin were staring at him anxiously.

"There's something you're not telling me," he said.

Edwin had a rolled-up paper in his hand which he was twisting, much as Alex had twisted his hat on the doorstep when he was being the nervous Adam.

"Er…the marquis said that all the prisoners…ex-prisoners were being treated well, and were free to—"

"For God's sake, man, tell me what it is!" Alex interrupted, his voice rising.

Edwin blanched.

"Edwin, he needs to know. Beating around the bush isn't going to make it any easier," Caroline said.

"Needs to know what?" Alex asked.

"She's dead," Caroline said bluntly.

"Caroline!" Edwin cried in distress.

"I'm so sorry," Caroline said, her tone softer now. "The marquis enclosed a list of those who had died during the voyage or shortly after landing. Her name is on the list."

"Is that the list?" Alex said, very quietly.

"Yes," Edwin said. "Anthony, I—"

Alex held his hand out.

"Let me see," he said.

Edwin handed it over. Alex unrolled it carefully, then scanned down the list of names. It was a short list, comprising only eight names. Hers was at the bottom and had obviously been added after the others, in a different hand.

Lady Elizabeth Peters.

He looked up at the two worried faces across from him.

"Was she listed on the original ship's manifesto as Lady Elizabeth Peters?" he asked.

"No," Edwin replied, clearly taken aback by the unnatural calmness his friend was showing at this catastrophic news. He had paled, but otherwise showed no reaction. "No, she was listed as Elizabeth Cunningham."

Alex nodded.

"She arrived there alive, then," he said softly. He placed one finger on his lips, kissed it, then very gently ran it along her name. He rolled the paper up and placed it on the table.

"Thank you," he said. Then in one quick movement he stood, turned, and walked out of the room, leaving the library door open.

He was halfway across the hall before Caroline caught up with him.

"Anthony," she said, in her distress forgetting he was supposed to be Adam, "you can't leave like that. I'm sorry, but there was no easy way to tell you."

"I needed to know. You did right," he said without turning back or stopping. She followed him across the hall and gripped his arm to stop him as he opened the front door.

"Please," she begged. "Please, don't leave, not yet."

He froze, his body rigid, trembling with suppressed emotion.

"Let me go," he said, in a tone that brooked no refusal.

She lifted her hand from his arm and he carried on immediately, walking down the steps that led to the drive without looking back.

Caroline went back into the library and joined Edwin at the window, where he was watching the man whose identity he did not know, but who he loved anyway, walk purposefully, not down the drive as one would expect but across the lawn at the front of the house, as though incapable of going in any direction except straight ahead. Edwin glanced at his wife, saw the tears welling in her eyes, and put his arm round her, pulling her in to his side.

"I shouldn't have told him like that," she said brokenly. "I should have found a better way than that."

"No," Edwin said. "There's no good way to tell someone that sort of news. You were braver than I, that's all. I thought he took it very well, considering."

"No," she said. "No, he didn't."

Edwin opened his mouth to contradict her, then stopped. Halfway across the lawn, about a hundred yards from the house Alex had stopped at an oak tree which was in his path and which had not been chopped down, partly because it was a particularly lovely specimen, and partly because it would provide natural shade in the summer for tea parties and suchlike. He leaned against it for a minute, his forehead resting on the trunk, his hands braced on the rough bark. Then he stood upright, clenched his fist and hit the tree as hard as he could, over and over again. His accompanying roar of pure agony and despair carried across the lawn, bringing more than one servant to a window to see what was happening.

"Dear God!" Edwin said. As one they both turned and ran out of the room, across the hall and down the steps, intending together to insist that their friend come back, to find a way to console him, although they had no idea how they would achieve that. But before they'd made it more than a few feet across the grass, Alex stepped away from the tree and carried on across the lawn, walking so quickly that they would have had to run at full speed to catch up with him. Edwin would have done just that, had Caroline not gripped the sleeve of his shirt and stopped him.

"Let him go," she said. "We can't help him, not now, at least."

"We can't let him leave like that!" Edwin cried. "God knows what he might do!"

He pulled away, tearing his shirt sleeve in the process. Caroline ran in front of him and gripped his arm with all her strength, bringing him to a halt.

"Edwin," she said, her voice trembling with tears and distress, "we've just broken his heart. You were right when you said you were afraid of what he'd do when we told him. He's beyond reason, we both saw that just now. If we try to bring him back, he might become violent. And if he does, he'll regret it once he comes to his senses. We can't do anything for him now. Let him go. He needs to be alone, I think. By the time he gets back to London he'll have calmed down a little. We'll go to see him tomorrow when he's had time to take in the news."

"We don't know where he's staying," Edwin pointed out, still anxious to go after his friend before he got too far away.

"We'll find him. Sarah will know where he's staying," Caroline said. "He's supposed to be her cousin, after all. She's sure to know."

Edwin stopped pulling away, but was still clearly torn.

"I want to go after him too," Caroline said. "But when I stopped him in the hall, he was shaking with the effort of holding himself together. He didn't want us to see him fall apart and I think, as his friends we have to respect that."

Edwin sighed and gave in, because she was right. They stood together and watched their friend stride away across the grass, both of them heedless of the rain that had started to fall or the servants staring with curiosity at the uncharacteristic behaviour of their employers. They watched as he walked up the incline to the top of the slope on which their Grecian temple or gothic building would one day be situated, and then he continued without pausing to admire the beautiful view, and passed out of their sight.

They stood for a while longer, still staring at the last place they had seen him, as though expecting him to come back and accept the comfort they both longed to give him. They stood until the rain soaked through their clothes and hair, running down their faces, mingling with the tears that both of them had shed.

Then they turned, and arm in arm slowly made their way back to the house.

* * *

The shop was closed, Màiri was settled in her bed for the night and Sarah was sitting with her feet in a basin of hot water sprinkled with dried lavender flowers and rose petals that she'd bought from a street seller on the corner. The relaxing scent of summer filled the room and Sarah sat back in the chair and sighed blissfully. She closed her eyes and was once again walking along a country lane, her hand firmly clasped in a strong warm one, except the strong warm hand of her imagination was Murdo's, not Anthony/Adam's, and the eyes looking down at her were clear grey like his daughter's, rather than slate blue.

She hadn't realised that she'd fallen asleep until the knock came on the door, soft, timid even, but even so, unusual enough to bring her instantly to wakefulness. She moved to stand, forgetting that her feet were in the basin, upending it and tipping scented water and soggy petals across the floor.

"Damn!" she said. "Who is it?" she called, not loudly enough to wake her daughter, but enough for whoever was at the door to hear her. It was the back door that led to the alley, so she reached for the pistol that she kept ready on a high shelf out of Màiri's reach.

"I have something for you," a voice replied after such a long silence that she had started to think the knock had been part of her dream. She put the pistol down and opened the door immediately, expecting Anthony, as she still thought of him, to walk in.

In the dim evening light she could just make out the shape of him leaning against the wall on the other side of the alley, drenched to the skin from the rain that had fallen steadily for the last few hours. Inexplicably, in view of the weather, rather than wearing his coat he carried it over one arm.

"What are you doing out here?" she asked, instantly alert. When he had called to see her the last time he had come to the front door, as anyone would expect her cousin to do. "Is there something wrong?"

"I didna want anyone to see me like this," he said, and the combination of him not having moved away from the wall and speaking in a Scottish accent out of doors, rang alarm bells with her. There was something wrong. Quickly she stepped out into the alley, glancing from left to right to see if there was anyone there. Then she gripped his arm and pulled him out of the alley and into her room, closing and locking the door behind her before turning back to face him.

He stood in the middle of the room, the rain dripping from his clothes joining the water from the upended basin on the stone floor. In the fire and candlelight she could see that his face was white, his expression dazed, and he was shivering uncontrollably. There was clearly something very, very wrong.

Her first instinct, as always, was practical. Going into the bedroom she returned a moment later with a blanket, which she laid over the chair.

"Come on," she said. "You need to get warm." Gently she took the folded coat from his arm and hung it on a hook near the fire to dry. It was heavier than she had expected it to be, but she put that down to the fact that it was wet. As he still stood unmoving, his eyes glazed, she then pulled his shirt out of his breeches, intending to help him lift it over his head, as he seemed incapable of doing anything at the moment.

Then she stopped, assailed by the memory of all the shirts she'd helped men to take off in her past life, having to pretend she couldn't wait to see what was underneath, while dreading what was to come. She took a deep breath, dismissed the memory, and reached for the bottom of the shirt again. His hands moved over hers arresting her movement, and she looked up at him. His eyes had cleared, and his expression told her that he knew exactly what she'd just been thinking.

Sir Anthony always had an uncanny ability for reading people's minds, she thought.

"I'm sorry, lassie," he said softly. "I shouldna have come here the night. It's strange," he continued, speaking more to himself than to her. "Last time I wanted to be alone, but this time...I couldna bear it. And you're the closest I have to family here."

"Then you should have come," she said, "whatever it is that's happened." His hands were warm on hers and she realised that it was shock, not cold that was causing him to shiver. Whatever it was was very bad. She looked down and gasped. His right hand was badly swollen and covered with clotted blood.

"What have you done to your hand?" she cried.

He followed her gaze, staring at his mangled hand as though aware for the first time that he was injured.

"I...I dinna rightly remember," he said.

He released her hands and turning, swiftly lifted his shirt over his head, placing it near the fire to dry. She had a glimpse of a broad, heavily muscled back and long, powerful arms, and then he unfolded the blanket and wrapped it round his shoulders. He sat down on the chair opposite to hers. She hesitated for a moment, torn between the wish to tend his injured hand and the need to find out what was wrong. Then she sat down facing him.

"What is it?" she asked. "It's Beth, isn't it? What's happened to her?" She couldn't think of anything else that would have brought this strong, capable man to the state he was in right now.

"She's dead," he said, as bluntly as Caroline had done earlier that day. He looked up at Sarah and his eyes filled with tears, which spilled down his cheeks unheeded. "She's dead," he repeated in a choked voice. He lifted his hands and covered his face, the blanket falling from his shoulders.

"Oh, God!" he cried. "I canna bear it."

She rose from her chair instinctively and crossed the space between them, kneeling by his side and pulling his head onto her shoulder. He wrapped his arms round her and sobbed, his whole body shaking uncontrollably with grief. Gently she stroked his hair and murmured meaningless sounds of comfort, while the tears poured down her own face, dripping onto his hair. How could someone as full of life as Beth was be dead? It wasn't possible.

Of course it was possible. It was just the sort of thing that the jealous, vengeful God her bastard of a father had believed in, had taught her to believe in, would do; take away the life of someone beautiful and caring just when she had everything to live for, even though she hadn't known it. What had this man done to deserve to suffer such grief, not once, but twice? Nothing.

There was no God. And if there was, she wanted nothing to do with Him.

She sat, her mind full of hatred and pity, love and grief, and comforted this man whose name she did not know, until his sobs turned to hiccups and then shuddering breaths as he fought to regain control of himself. Then very gently she released him, stood up, and pulled the blanket back over his shoulders. She gave him her handkerchief, and he leaned back in the chair, wiped his eyes and blew his nose, still breathing heavily. She put some more wood on the fire, which was burning very low, noting with surprise that enough time had passed for the spilled water to have spread across the stone floor and started to dry.

She picked up the basin, hung the kettle on its hook over the fire to boil some water, and went into the shop to get some salve for Alex's hand. When she came back he was standing and had his shirt in his hands ready to put back on, although it was still obviously wet. The church clock struck eleven.

"I'm sorry, Sarah," he said. "I canna imagine what ye must think of me. I shouldna have come here tonight. It's late. I'll go, and let ye away to your bed."

"Yes, you should have come. And if it was possible to think more of you than I already do, I would. Don't leave yet. Let your shirt dry properly. I'll look at your hand. I'm no Anne, but I can at least wash it for you."

He looked down at his swollen hand, then straightened his fingers carefully, wincing as he did. "I dinna think there's any bones broken," he said indifferently.

She took the shirt out of his hands and hung it back up to continue drying. Then she bustled about, getting two pewter mugs from the dresser and pouring gin from a jug into them, followed by hot water and a spoonful of honey. She stirred briskly and handed him a cup. The scent of juniper rose from the mug.

"Sit down," she said. "I'll tend your hand, and while I do you can tell me what happened, if you feel able to. And drink that, it'll comfort you."

He sat, and drank, and told her what had happened earlier in the day, while she tenderly washed the blood away from his hand and examined it. The knuckles were badly swollen and skinned, and his whole hand was blackened with bruising, but it seemed he was right; nothing was broken, and in time it would heal.

"I canna mind what happened after I left," he said. "I walked across the grass, I remember that, and then I was at the inn where I left the horse. I tellt the landlord some nonsense about the lady no' being agreeable and that I'd decided to go home after all, then

I rode back to London like the devil. I've no idea why I pushed the poor horse so, I didna have anything to come back for. Anyway, I sat in my room for a while, and then I thought I was going to go mad so I came here. I did need to come, but it could have waited till the morning. I wanted to—"

He was interrupted by a noise from the bedroom, then a small voice cried, "Adam!"

"Oh, Christ," he said softly. "I'm—"

"If you say you're sorry once more, I'm going to hit you," Sarah said. She disappeared into the adjoining room, returning a minute later with a wild-haired, sleepy-eyed bundle in her arms. On seeing Alex, Màiri beamed and lunged towards him, causing Sarah to nearly drop her. Alex leaned across and grabbed the little girl, settling her on his lap, where she snuggled in against his bare chest. He pulled the blanket back up around them both, so that only her head was visible. She rested it against him, her eyes already closing again.

"Say goodnight," Sarah said, "and then you have to go back to bed."

"Ah, no, let her bide awhile," Alex said softly. "She's nae bother, and I need to say goodbye to her," he added when Sarah looked doubtful.

She sat down suddenly.

"You're leaving?" she asked.

"Aye, I'm leaving," he said. "I've no reason to stay now, lassie. And I'm a danger to ye every day I stay. If someone finds out ye've no' got a cousin Adam—"

"How would anyone find that out?" she asked. "I don't want you to go," she added sadly.

He smiled, his eyes warm, sad, still red-rimmed from weeping.

"I canna stay, Sarah. I have to try to go on wi' my life. It's what she'd want. Ye tellt me that when she was very ill she said she wanted to die, but then she changed her mind."

"Yes," Sarah said. "It was very sudden. She was eating and drinking because we blackmailed her into it, but then suddenly she got her spirit back, and that was when we knew she was going to get better."

"Aye, well, she remembered," he said.

"Remembered what?"

"That for us, suicide is a mortal sin. If she'd let herself die then she'd no' have gone to Heaven and never could have been reunited with me. She knew well that I'd be waiting for her. And now she's waiting for me, and I must take comfort from that and go on until God sees fit to let me go. I've an oath to fulfil, and maybe I can be useful in some other ways. And when He chooses to take me, then I'll go to her gladly. What's amiss?"

"You really believe that, don't you?" Sarah said. "Do you think Murdo's waiting for me, too?"

"I do. Do ye no' believe in God at all? I ken ye're no' of my faith, but surely you believe that Christ is our Saviour? Did your father no' teach you that, and him a minister?"

"No," she said bitterly. "My father taught me that I was full of sin, and that God hated sinners and would send me straight to hell. He said that everyone was evil, but women even more so because of Eve, and that it was his duty as one who had seen the light and the will of God to drive Satan out of me in the hope that God would take pity on me. I don't know if there is a God or not, but if there is, then He must be evil. What sort of God needs a little girl to be beaten and starved for Him to take pity on her?"

"God isna evil," Alex said softly. "He loves us so much that He sent His only son to die for us, so that we could be forgiven. It's no' just the Catholics who believe that, but the Anglicans too, and other Christians. We've our differences, it's true, but we all believe that. It seems to me that it was your father who was evil, no' God."

Màiri murmured softly in her sleep, and then settled closer in to him.

"The Christ I learned about loves bairns," Alex said, smiling down at the little dark head resting trustingly against his chest. "Suffer the little children to come unto me, and forbid them not: for of such is the kingdom of Heaven. That's what He said."

"That's what...someone told me that once," Sarah said, straining to remember. She knew that biblical phrase. Who had said that to her? Not her father. He never would have said anything so gentle.

"Sarah, I wouldna ask you to bring wee Màiri up as a Catholic," Alex said, "for that would bring you a world of trouble. But I wouldna want you to raise her in the hate of God either. For if you do, then it seems to me that your father will have won, and will have shut you out of the light of Christ forever. Dinna let a twisted man make your mind up for you on this. You must look into it yourself and make your own decision."

"I've never thought of it in that way before," Sarah said.

"You're a good woman and a clever one, and a wonderful mother to this wee lassie," Alex said. "Ye'll do right by her, I'm sure of that."

"I'll look into it, for her sake if not for mine," Sarah said. "But I can't promise you anything."

"No more do I expect you to," Alex replied. "Now you must away to your bed, for it's after midnight. No," he said when she bent to lift Màiri from his lap, "please, let her bide a wee bit longer. She's a comfort to me, and I need that tonight. I'll no' leave her alone."

Sarah smiled. That meant he would stay the night, and in the morning he would still be there and she would have at least a little time more with him.

So she went to bed and lay for a while, wondering how a man who had just lost his wife for the second time, after having his hopes raised and then destroyed, could still believe in a God that would do such a thing. And then she cried for the loss of the woman she had called her friend, who had changed her life forever, and who she would never see again, and for the father of her child, who was also gone forever. She wondered if they were both in whatever Heaven was, waiting together for the handsome, enigmatic man sitting in the next room to pass from this life and join them. And then she fell asleep.

She woke at some point in the dead of night, and seeing the faint yellow light under the door she got out of bed and padding barefoot across the room, she opened it, intending to check on her daughter and maybe bring her to bed.

He was slumped back in the chair asleep, his long hair tumbling over his shoulders, his injured hand resting on the arm of the chair, his other arm wrapped protectively around the child. At some point Màiri must have moved, dislodging the blanket in the process.

The candle was still burning on the table and Sarah stood watching them, the powerful, heavily muscled man, his face peaceful in repose, long lashes resting gently on his cheeks as he slept, and the tiny fragile body of her daughter cradled tenderly against his chest, her dark hair fanned out across his bicep, her equally long lashes fluttering slightly as she dreamed.

She stood watching them for a long time, burning the memory into her mind, knowing that it would have to last her for the rest of her life. Then finally and with infinite care, she tucked the blanket around them both and went back to bed.

When she woke again it was full daylight. She yawned and stretched and looked automatically to the small bed in the corner, although she already remembered Màiri had slept in the living room. But to her surprise the little girl was in her bed, still asleep.

He must have come in at some point during the night, Sarah realised, and put Màiri back to bed. She lay for a moment, hoping to hear sounds of him moving around in the living room, but apart from the distant noises of the street coming from the front of the building, there was silence. He must still be asleep. That was understandable. He'd had a long ride and a terrible shock the day before. She got up, yawning, and wondering what time it was wrapped her shawl around her shoulders, and opening the bedroom door walked into her living room.

It was empty, the fire burnt down to embers and not replenished, the candle snuffed out. Because the living room boasted no window of its own, the only light came from the small barred window of the bedroom, and at first she didn't see the coat still lying on her chair, a dark shape against the light cushions. When she did, her heart soared. He had not left yet then. Maybe he had stepped out, gone to a bakeshop to buy bread, perhaps.

In the gloom she crouched down by the fire, blowing on the embers until they glowed. Then she added a few small sticks and soon she had enough of a flame going to add some logs. Although August, it was still chilly in the room; and having been cold for so much of her life, a good supply of wood or coal was one of the luxuries she allowed herself. She stood up. She would dress and then get some water from the pump in the street, and make tea to go with whatever Anthony brought back.

It was as she turned that she noticed the two mugs and jug were still on the table from the night before. And that all three vessels were full to overflowing.

With gold.

Her forehead creased and she bent over, picking one of the coins up and looking at it. It was a guinea. Twenty-one shillings. That was more than a week's earnings for her – a good week's earnings. She tipped the cup up and gold showered across the table, more than a year's earnings in one cup. What was going on? It must belong to Anthony, but why had he filled the containers with it like that?

She moved to the chair and lifted the coat, noting how much lighter it was now that it was dry. And then she saw that the hem of the coat had been roughly unpicked, the lining torn in places. That was why it had been so heavy the previous evening, she realised. It was the weight of coins, not rain! So he had unpicked the hems and removed all the gold. But why?

As she lifted the coat off the chair a folded sheet of paper which had been pinned to it fluttered to the ground. She picked it up, realising that it was a page from her account book which had been torn out; one edge of the page was jagged. On it her name had been written in a smooth, flowing hand.

She moved back to the fire and unfolded it, reading it by the light of the flames.

> *I trust you*, it said. *Burn this.*
>
> *The money is for Màiri, and for you. Enjoy her childhood, and your life. Take her to the countryside and pick flowers, and think of Beth from time to time.*
>
> *Our name is outlawed and she dare not use it, but when she's older and times have changed, I leave it to you to decide whether or not to tell Màiri MacGregor that her Uncle Alex was proud to have known both her and her mother, and that she has Duncan's eyes.*

A huge lump rose in her throat, and she closed her eyes tightly in a vain attempt to stop the tears from coming. The realisation that he had gone and that she would never see him again hit her like a blow, temporarily rendering the information in the letter meaningless. A wave of loneliness so powerful it made her gasp tore through her, and she sat down heavily on the chair, clutching her stomach and trying not to voice her distress and wake her daughter.

She sat like that for some time, until the worst of the despair passed a little and she could think clearly. Then she picked up the note from the floor and read it again. And again. And again. When she was sure that every word of the note was burned into her brain and her heart, she kissed it and then placed it into the flames, watching until it had burnt completely to ash.

"Duncan MacGregor," she whispered to the empty room, "I love you. I will always love you. I'll make you proud of your daughter, and one day I'll tell her what kind of man you were and what kind of man your brother Alex is, and she will be proud to be Màiri MacGregor." She waited a moment as though expecting a response to her declaration, then shook her head at her own folly.

Then she leaned across the table and carefully counted the gold coins, stacking them in little piles as she did.

Two hundred guineas. At least five years' earnings, probably more.

He could not give her what she craved; no one could bring the man she loved back from the dead. But he had given her the next best things. His absolute trust. A name for her daughter and a sense of family. And security. Whatever happened to her business now, she would not starve and her daughter would never have to do what she'd done to survive. If Màiri ever gave herself to a man it would be through love, not necessity. He could not have given her a more precious gift, and he had known that.

It was why he had come to see her last night, what he had been trying to tell her when Màiri had interrupted him. In spite of his grief and despair, he had thought of her and his niece.

"I will take her to the country," she said aloud. "And I'll pick flowers, and I'll think of Beth, and of Duncan, and of you, Alex MacGregor. And if your God is as good as you say, one day we will meet again."

She put the money away, very carefully, and then she went into the bedroom, to wake Màiri, to dress and to start her day.

* * *

Once back in his lodgings Alex packed a small bag with his spare clothes. He still had a good amount of money about his person. More than enough to get home to Scotland in style. He sat for a while and thought about it.

He could not stay here any longer, had no wish to stay here, had no wish ever to see London again, for as long as he lived. He had only partially fulfilled his oath to Maggie, and he would return home to complete what he had started.

But not yet.

He could not go home yet. He could not bear to see the pity and sorrow in the eyes of his clansmen when he told them that he had lost his wife, again. He could not bear to see them hesitating before they spoke to him, dreading invoking his rage or his grief, or both. He needed to grieve, he knew that. His heart felt like lead in his chest, and at the moment the future opened up like a black tunnel ahead of him, completely devoid of light and hope.

It would pass, he knew that. He had survived knowing she was dead once; he could do it again. But it would take time, and he had already inflicted his despair on his clansmen once; he would not do it again, even though he knew they would want him to. But he needed to be active, and to occupy the time usefully until the ferocity of the sadness in him dulled and he could go home and be Alex MacGregor, chieftain of the clan again, instead of a liability. And extended practice of being the leader would do Angus no harm.

He sat for a while longer, deep in thought. And then he stood, suddenly decided, and moved to the rickety wooden table in the corner of the room. He trimmed a quill, took out paper and ink, and wrote a letter to James Drummond, in Glasgow.

Then he sealed it, put it in his pocket, picked up the bag and left the room. Downstairs he settled with the landlady, answering her queries as to his mashed hand and pallor with a tale about having drunk a little too much on the previous evening, and of having been attacked on his way home by some ruffians. His pugilistic skills (of which, she would remember, he had told her), had stood him in good stead, but unfortunately one of the footpads had ducked, which had resulted in him hitting the wall rather than the face of his opponent.

Yes, of course it would be fine. No bones were broken and he certainly had no wish to stay in this city any longer than was absolutely necessary. He had already hired a horse and intended to ride straight for his home in Cheshire, where a man could walk the streets at night even in his cups, without any fear for his life. But if anyone of his acquaintance were to express a desire to visit London, he would of course direct them to her fair establishment, where he had been made so very welcome. With these promises and a reasonable tip, he managed to extricate himself from the flirtatious invitations of the proprietor without too much difficulty.

He mounted his horse and rode away, stopping briefly at the post office to deposit his letter before riding out of the city, not in a northerly direction, which would take Mr Featherstone to Cheshire, or Mr MacGregor to Scotland, but eastwards, where lay the coast and, he had decided, his immediate future.

CHAPTER ELEVEN

Martinique, August 1747

Still caught in the dream, Beth fought to control the panic that surged through her. Her heart hammered in her chest and for a moment she thought she was going to faint. She swung her legs out of bed and leaned forward, putting her head between her knees until the dizziness passed.

"Are you sick, Madame Beth?" Rosalie asked worriedly. "Should I wake Monsieur and ask him to send for the doctor?"

Before Beth could answer, there came a knock on the door.

"What's happening?" Pierre's voice sounded from the hall. The door opened an inch, admitting a slice of light from the candle he was holding.

Beth sat up again, ignoring the little white lights sparkling at the edge of her vision that told her the dizziness had not completely passed.

"I'm sorry," she said, her voice shaky. "I had a bad dream." She pulled the sheet around her. "Please, come in."

He walked into the room but stopped just inside the doorway, obviously torn between the breach of etiquette he was committing by entering a lady's bedchamber and worry for the welfare of the said lady.

Rosalie picked up a candle from the bedside table and lit it from the one Pierre was carrying. Yellow light filled the room, banishing the shadows.

"You are very pale, Beth," Pierre remarked. "Are you sure you're not sick? Do you have a fever?"

"No, really, I am well," Beth assured him. Although she was

sweating, partly from the dream and partly from the temperature in the room, she actually felt cold and clammy rather than hot and feverish. She had still not shaken off the dream; it seemed more real to her than the room she was in and the two people observing her worriedly.

With a great effort she pushed it away and looked up at her employer.

"I'm sorry," she said. "I didn't mean to wake you. I must have cried out. It was a nightmare, that's all. I will be fine, really. Rosalie, will you fetch me some lemon water, please?" She swung her legs into bed and sat back against the pillows. She hoped that Pierre would leave with Rosalie, but instead he moved further into the room and sat on the edge of the bed.

"What manner of dream was it?" he asked. "Did you dream of a snake, or of a black bird?"

"No, not at all," Beth replied. "Why?"

"One of my friends, his wife dreamt that a snake had come into her husband's room and was eating him. The slaves said that it was a very bad omen, but my friend of course ignored it, being civilised and a good son of the Church. A few days later he died."

"He died?" Beth said, aghast. "Did a snake bite him?"

"No, he had a fall from his horse. I'm sorry. This is not helpful. It was just superstition, I'm sure. Don't worry about it."

"It wasn't about anybody in Martinique," Beth reassured him. "It was about before I came here. I really don't want to talk about it."

"No, of course not. I am sorry. You have had some terrible experiences in your life, far too many for such a young woman. It's hardly surprising if you have a nightmare now and then. And you know that there are some philosophers now who say nightmares are caused by eating rich food. Perhaps that's what it was." He patted her hand gently to reassure her. Rosalie came back with the drink, and Pierre stood.

"Well, if you are sure you are not unwell…" he said.

"No, Rosalie is with me and I don't feel ill at all, just tired," she assured him. She wanted desperately to be alone, to think about what she had dreamt before it faded from her mind completely, as dreams often do.

After he'd gone Beth put on a clean, dry nightdress, then told

Rosalie to go back to sleep. She sat for a while sipping the lemon water, deep in thought, but when she realised that Rosalie was worried about her mistress and was trying to stay awake, Beth blew the candle out and lay down. After a while she heard her maid's breathing even out and knew she was asleep.

She had lied to Pierre; her dream had not been about her past. In it she had been standing on a lawn, a lawn she had never seen in life. To the right in the distance there was a mound of earth, and in the middle of the lawn was a huge oak tree. She had looked down at her feet and seen that they were bare. The grass was cool and wet and it was raining, not as it did in Martinique, torrentially, but as it often did in Britain, a light, drizzling rain. It had been a pleasant dream. She had wiggled her toes, enjoying the coolness of the soft green grass under her feet.

And then she had heard a roar of despair and anguish so loud and so heartrending that it had shocked her out of sleep immediately. There had been nobody else in her dream; the landscape had been empty, apart from the tree and the mound of earth. But the cry was indisputably human.

Indisputably Alex.

She had not dreamt of him since she had set sail on the *Veteran*, five months ago. At first she had missed the dreams of him, which had always been pleasant, reliving times they had spent together; sitting on a log by the side of Loch Lomond, dancing at Versailles while the whole court watched them, lying in the heather snuggled together under his plaid. When the dreams stopped she had missed them terribly, but after a while she had told herself it was better so. She had to move on, start a new life. But this dream had not been a reliving of anything they had been through together, good or bad.

She lay awake for a long time, trying to convince herself that it was nothing. As Pierre had said, it was the workings of a piece of almond cake she had eaten at supper. It was nothing. Alex was dead. It was her imagination, that was all.

Beth had the same dream the next night and the one after that, with the consequence that on the third day she was exhausted and quite happy to sit on the porch with Antoinette playing cards for the whole morning, letting the mundane gossip that so interested her companion wash over her instead of fidgeting and trying to find excuses to do something active to break the monotony.

It was very hot during the days now, and even the constant waving of fans by the slave children brought no relief, merely wafting hot humid air around them, while the poor children were bathed in sweat from the effort of moving the huge woven palm fans for hours at a time.

But this is better than working in the boiling house or the fields, Beth told herself. *They are fortunate.*

She had hoped that this was as hot as it got in Martinique and that, like in Britain, September would see some relief from the high temperatures and heavy rainstorms that left the air so humid it was difficult to breathe sometimes. But when she had asked Raymond, he told her that September would be even hotter than August and there was a higher risk of hurricanes too.

Antoinette chatted away about the disgraceful behaviour of Monsieur Bernard, who not only acknowledged his mulatto bastards, but insisted that they live in his house with his legitimate children. She had been complaining about her neighbour's behaviour for days now, so Beth no longer had to pay attention to be sure of making a suitable response. Instead she let the monologue become background noise and thought about her dream instead.

Three nights. Exactly the same dream, with no variation. This had never happened to her before. Rosalie had told her that dreams could mean someone was trying to snare her with witchcraft, but it would depend on the dream. Was it about someone who had died? Beth had said that it was, although she was reluctant to give details, for no good reason that she could think of. She just felt instinctively that she should keep it to herself. Rosalie said that perhaps the dead person was trying to communicate with her, to pass on an important message. Sometimes to dream of the dead meant there would be news of the living, but whether that was good or bad news she couldn't say. Other people said that if you dreamt the dead person had come back to life, it meant that something important that you had lost would come back to you.

In other words, Beth thought drily, *no one knows what the hell dreams mean for certain.* If they meant anything at all.

She hadn't dreamt that Alex had come back to life. The tormented cry that had shocked her into wakefulness for the last three nights had been uttered by a living voice, not a dead one, nor a resurrected one.

Was Alex alive?

Even while she told herself that she was being stupid, that he was certainly dead, doubts assailed her, filling her mind. Highbury had said there were no prisoners named Alexander MacGregor, but what if he had been imprisoned somewhere where no one knew his true identity and was being held under an assumed name? What if he had been so badly injured that he was incapable of coming for her? If Duncan and Angus were dead too, and there was no one with the ability to find her? *Graeme would have come, or Iain*, she thought. Unless they were also dead. It was possible; Culloden had been a massacre.

On the fourth night she didn't dream of the strange lawn, or hear the cry of distress; but nevertheless she was still shocked into wakefulness in the middle of the night, not by a dream this time, but by a memory.

"He thinks of you, all the time. He doesn't know, you see, that's why." That was what Prince Edward had said when she had told his father that Sir Anthony was dead. At the time she had dismissed it from her mind, and then had forgotten it completely in the maelstrom of subsequent events. Now she sat up in bed in the dark, remembering. The prince was a strange child, 'a sayer of things', someone had said.

She thought back to the cricket match at Prince Frederick's, when the child had told her that Daniel was going to hurt her. After the malevolent young lord had thrown the ball at her, she had been impressed that the prince had foreseen it. But what if he had not been referring to something as trivial as a bruise, but to the fact that Daniel had gone on to discover the truth about Sir Anthony? Alex had thought him to have the second sight, after all.

Had he been telling her in his strange way that Alex hadn't come for her, not because *he* was dead, but because he thought *she* was? No, it wasn't possible. There had been twenty women in the hut that day, and most of them would have seen what happened to her after she killed the sergeant. One of them *must* have told

Alex or whoever else had come for her after the battle.

She was being ridiculous. She hated living in this hot, sticky, boring place, surrounded by luxury she had no interest in and desperately miserable, sullen slaves who she could not relegate in her mind to being part of the scenery. She hated it so much that she was trying to invent reasons to go back to Britain.

She could not go back to Britain. It was too dangerous for her there. Prince Edward was just a little odd. No doubt he had keen eyesight, being so young, and had seen the malevolent look in Lord Daniel's eye from across the cricket pitch. He had made a lucky guess, that was all. She could not travel halfway across the world, risking her life in the process, based on the ramblings of a small child.

She told herself that for the rest of the sleepless night with the result that the next day, after four badly disturbed nights, she was half-dead with fatigue. On any normal day she would have been able to go back to bed at any time, but as chance would have it today visitors were coming for lunch, after which they would go for a drive to the coast, hoping to enjoy a sea breeze.

Normally Beth would have relished any diversion from listening to Antoinette's complaints, and would have thrown herself wholeheartedly into the excursion; indeed she did try to, but by early evening the combination of heat and exhaustion rendered her listless and irritable, with the result that her answers to the habitual questions probing her relationship with King Louis verged on sarcastic rather than merely evasive and by the time she was able to go to bed she had a banging headache, fell into bed the second Rosalie had finished helping her to undress and was asleep the moment her head hit the pillow.

It seemed that she had been asleep for no more than a few minutes before she was being shaken awake.

"Madame Beth!" Rosalie cried. "Wake up!"

She felt drugged and heavy, her eyelids glued shut, and when she finally managed to open them and come to some sort of wakefulness, she was surprised to see that several candles had been lit and Rosalie was already fully dressed. Voices came from the corridor, along with the sound of someone running down the stairs and across the porch outside.

She sat up, rubbing her eyes.

"What's wrong?" she asked, yawning sleepily.

"Madame Antoinette is sick, very sick," Rosalie replied, pouring water from a pitcher into a basin and dropping a cloth into it. "Papa has been sent to fetch the doctor." She wrung it out and gave it to Beth, who had thrown back the covers and was sitting on the side of the bed. Beth wiped her face with it and then stood up, grabbing her dressing gown from the chair where it had been placed the previous morning. She wrapped it round herself.

It must be serious, then. Antoinette was always ill, or always complaining that she was ill. No one, including her husband, thought of her constant ailments as anything more than hypochondria. Pierre would not have sent for the doctor in the middle of the night for one of her megrims.

"Are the guests still here? Did they stay?" Beth asked as she hunted under the bed for her slippers. One particular guest, an elderly man with startlingly black hair, had flirted incessantly with her throughout the evening. His attentions had stayed within the bounds of propriety and seemed harmless, but she didn't want to fuel his ardour by appearing *en déshabillé* if he was still here.

"No, they left a little while after you came to bed. I'm so sorry to wake you, madame, because you were very tired, but Monsieur told me to, once he saw that Madame was...that she wasn't...er..."

"That she was really sick, instead of just pretending to be so," Beth finished helpfully.

"Er...yes, madame."

"Rosalie, I will never be angry with you for speaking the truth," Beth said. "Now, I think you should go downstairs and see if you can do anything to help. I will call you when I need to dress properly."

She walked down the hallway and into Antoinette's room, which was ablaze with candlelight. Pierre was standing at the foot of the bed looking helplessly on as Eulalie attempted to support her mistress whilst holding a basin, into which Antoinette was vomiting weakly. Beth moved forward and sat on the bed, holding the sick woman up until she had finished, then lowering her back down. She was shivering violently, but her face was flushed and she was burning with fever. In spite of the fact that Antoinette had taken to her bed on the slightest pretext every few days since Beth had arrived, this time there was no denying that she was very sick.

"Do you have pain, madame?" Eulalie asked, moving to the window and throwing the contents of the basin as far as she could into the night so that they would miss the porch.

"My eyes and my back," Antoinette moaned through chattering teeth. "It hurts, so much."

"We must try to bring the fever down," Beth said. She tried to remember if Anne Maynard had ever told her how to treat fever, but as far as she knew no one of her acquaintance had ever had more than the mildest fever. She wanted to help, but had no idea what to do.

"Tamarind water," Eulalie advised, taking over. "She must drink as much as possible to sweat out the sickness. Monsieur Pierre, could she have some laudanum for the pain?"

Pierre jumped, as though coming out of a trance.

"Of course!" he exclaimed, rushing from the room and returning a minute later with a small brown bottle. Eulalie took it from him, putting several drops into a glass of wine. Between them Beth and Eulalie managed to get Antoinette to swallow it. Pierre hovered at the end of the bed again, his face a mask of distress. Antoinette slumped back, still shivering. Her nightdress and the sheet beneath her were soaked. Beth went to the chest, rummaging in it and producing a clean nightdress and a sheet.

"Monsieur, if you wish you could try to get a little sleep?" Eulalie suggested gently. "You will need to be fresh when the doctor returns. We will wake you if there is any reason to, I promise."

"Of course, you are right," he said, vastly relieved to be given an excuse to vacate the room.

"There," Eulalie said briskly once he was out of the way. "Now we won't be falling over him. Can you stay to help, Madame Beth, or do you need to sleep as well?"

"No, I'm awake now," Beth said. "Do you know what is wrong with her?"

"It could be swamp fever," Eulalie said. "If it is, then she should recover. It comes and goes, and she has had attacks before. But they were not as bad as this. Or it could be the yellow fever;

when I had it, I too had pains and a fever like this."

"I thought people died of yellow fever!" Beth said.

"A lot do, but some live, too. I was blessed," Eulalie replied. "But we must pray that it is not, that it is just an attack of swamp fever."

Between them they changed the sheets, managed to get Antoinette into a dry nightdress, and then spent the rest of the night alternating between washing the delirious woman's face and limbs with cool water, persuading her to drink as much as they could, and holding the basin while she vomited it back up again.

It was mid-morning before Raymond returned with the doctor, by which time Beth was struggling to keep her eyes open, even though Antoinette was much worse, unable to sleep and in considerable pain in spite of the laudanum.

"You must go to bed for a time, Madame Beth," Eulalie said. "I have had the fever and no one who lives through it falls sick again. But you have not, I think, and you need to be strong so as not to fall ill also."

Beth took her advice. There was little she could do right now. As she was walking to her room the doctor came up the stairs, followed by Raymond. The doctor nodded to her and carried on, but Raymond stopped.

"How is she, Madame Beth?" he asked.

"She's in a lot of pain, and has a fever," Beth replied. "Eulalie thinks it could be swamp fever, or maybe yellow fever."

Raymond's eyes widened.

"Madame, are you wearing the charm I gave to you?" he asked urgently.

"No, not at the moment. Why?"

"Please, madame, I beg of you to wear it. If it is the yellow fever, it is very, very bad. The charm will protect you, stop you getting sick also. You must promise me!" he finished, a tone of desperation in his voice. She reached out and took his hand, touched by his concern for her.

"I am going to sleep for a few hours," she said. "But I will put it on now before I sleep, I promise. And I will keep it on."

"Thank you," he said.

Taking the amulet out and slipping it round her neck was the only thing she did, before falling onto the bed and sinking immediately into sleep.

When she woke it was dark, and for a moment she lay there disoriented, drugged by the deep sleep she had just had. Then she remembered and sat up, fumbling in the dark for the flint and tinder to strike a light. There was a thin yellow band of light under the door which told her that whatever time it was, people were still up and about. Abandoning her search, she wrapped her dressing gown around her and opened the bedroom door. Rosalie was sitting outside it on the floor, and only Beth's natural quick reflexes stopped her falling over her maid.

"Oh, madame," Rosalie said. "I didn't wish to disturb you, so I was waiting here for you to awaken. I will help you to dress." She stood up and pulled a candle from one of the wall brackets.

"What time is it?" Beth asked as Rosalie lit candles in the room and then opened the chest which contained her mistress's clothes.

"I am not sure, but the bell should ring for the field gangs soon," Rosalie answered.

The field gangs? Had she slept right through the day and into the night? No wonder she felt disoriented!

"How is Antoinette?" Beth asked.

"She is the same," Rosalie said. "The doctor has bled her and purged her, but it has not helped yet. He is staying tonight, is sleeping now. Eulalie is still with Madame Antoinette."

Once dressed, the amulet tucked out of sight so as not to attract comment, Beth went to the sick woman's room, insisted that Eulalie go and get some sleep, and then sat on a chair at the side of the bed.

Antoinette was sleeping fitfully, and when Beth put her hand to her companion's forehead it was still hot. She wrung out a cloth in a basin and wiped her face gently. Then, because she didn't know what else to do, she folded her hands and prayed that the sick woman would survive.

At first the prayers, along with the doctor's ministrations, seemed to work. On the third day the fever subsided and Antoinette announced that she felt much better. She ate some soup and expressed a wish to get up on the following day, once she had slept properly. She insisted on being left alone to do so. Hugely relieved, the exhausted, worried household all went to bed.

Two days later Antoinette relapsed, and this time there was no doubt in anyone's mind that it was indeed yellow fever. Her skin and eyes turned yellow, she started to vomit again, a dark bloody stream that soon became almost continuous, and began having violent convulsions. The doctor, and this time the priest were sent for, the priest arriving in time to give the patient the last rites, although Antoinette was incapable of confessing her sins or making any responses by then.

The doctor arrived half an hour after she died. It seemed that several of the guests at the Delisle's party had also succumbed to the fever, although Antoinette was the only one who had perished so far. Which was indeed a miracle, the priest said. Yellow fever was a virulent illness known to wipe out whole swathes of the population, particularly the whites.

It was common knowledge among the white population that negroes, being a different and inferior species to the European settlers, had some degree of natural protection against the fever, much in the same way apes did. It seemed that Monsieur Pierre and Madame Beth had been fortunate indeed, as neither of them sickened.

This was no doubt due to their prayers and righteous way of life, the priest remarked at dinner the following day. He was staying until the funeral was over, which would be conducted within the next two days. Lengthy funeral preparations were not practical in a tropical country.

Beth wondered what the priest would think if he had heard Raymond, just half an hour before, thanking Beth for wearing her charm, as that was no doubt the reason she had not fallen sick, especially as she had spent all of the last day of Antoinette's life at her bedside. Whether it was due to the charm, her godliness or her robust constitution Beth had no idea; she was just happy not to be dying in such a horrible way.

She also felt guilty. She knew she should feel very sad that Antoinette was dead. She was sorry that the poor woman had suffered so and she felt great sympathy for Pierre, who seemed distraught by the loss of his wife. But she had neither liked nor respected Antoinette Delisle, and she realised now, as she sat in the darkened dining room and sweated in the obligatory black woollen dress that was *de rigueur* for mourning, that for her everything had changed.

For at least a month now she had known in her heart of hearts that she would never become accustomed to living in Martinique. In spite of the luxury and the beautiful scenery, she hated too much about it to ever settle here; the heat, the boredom and pointlessness of life for women at least, the lack of freedom of movement, and above all the brutality of slavery.

Antoinette's death meant that she had to act. She could not stay at Soleil plantation now. If she were to remain in Martinique she had two choices; marry a planter or spend the rest of her life as companion to a series of spoiled, bored women. The first she would never do, and even the thought of the second made her want to throw herself off the nearest cliff in horror.

So then, she would leave. She could not go right now and leave Pierre alone in his grief. But once the funeral was over she would start making plans, and as soon as he had recovered from his initial shock at the loss of his spouse she would tell him of her intention to return to...

France. That was what she would tell everyone. She was going to France. They would accept that. France was the mother country, after all, and Beth was known at the court. And in saying that, she would be telling no lies. She was indeed going to sail to France. And then from there she was going home.

Later that night in bed she thought about the enormity of what she intended to do. If she was caught she would probably be imprisoned for life, at best. More likely she would be quietly disposed of.

It was fortunate that she had, on the spur of the moment, asked the Marquis de Caylus to add her name to the list of dead; including it as Lady Elizabeth Peters rather than Elizabeth Cunningham would tell Newcastle when he read it that she had been defiant to the end. She had done it to stop him sending assassins out to kill her, which she suspected he would probably have done if he knew her to be alive and free. He hated her, and the feeling was requited. But she realised now that because she was believed to be dead, no one would be actively looking for her to return to Britain, although if she was recognised once there, which was possible in view of her distinctive hair and features, she would be arrested in any case.

Nevertheless she was going back, regardless of the risk, regardless of the stupidity of quite literally following a dream. Because since the recurring nightmare she could not shake the feeling that Alex was alive and had been in some way calling to her. She had to find out for certain that he was dead. And the only way she could do that was to go home.

To Scotland.

* * *

Three weeks after the funeral, with no sign of Pierre coming out of his profound depression, Beth was growing restless and irritable, and feeling terribly guilty for doing so. Part of her felt deep sympathy for him; after all, he had been married to Antoinette for over ten years and had no children to comfort him. And he was now alone, having no relatives in Martinique.

But at the same time, when Antoinette had been alive the couple had behaved like polite strangers to each other. She had never seen either of them show even the slightest sign of affection towards one another. Even when she was dying, Pierre had come no closer to his wife than the bedroom doorway, retching at the dreadful smell emanating from the dying woman and terrified of contracting the disease himself.

She couldn't help but think that some of his apparent misery was in fact feigned, part of a façade that he felt he must present to his neighbours along with the stiflingly hot mourning clothes. Really, it was ridiculous for people to follow the traditions of France to the letter in this climate! It was all well and good to wear woollen mourning clothes for six weeks in Paris, where the climate was more akin to that of England, but in a tropical climate like this it was sheer hell.

She tentatively suggested to Pierre that perhaps they could revert to silk mourning a little early, but his horrified reaction to the gross lack of respect it would show for his dead wife put an end to that. Instead she spent as much time as she could in her bedroom, where she would sit by the window in her shift staring out at the luxuriant countryside and the slaves labouring in the fields, planning for the day she would leave this beautiful, horrible island forever.

On the first day of the seventh week after Antoinette's death, Beth threw off the woollen mourning with profound relief and, wearing black silk with the absolute minimum of undergarments ventured out into the garden, heading down to a part where some trees had recently been felled, leaving stumps a few feet high which would be ideal for her purposes. Now that she had at least half a plan for what she intended to do with her future, she knew that danger was likely to feature in it, and she might as well prepare for that as best she could now, whilst she had nothing else to occupy her time with.

She put down a bag full of old cracked pots that she'd got from the gardener, took out her knives, of which she now had four, and laid them on the ground. Then she went over to one of the stumps and placed a cracked clay pot on top of it before walking back to the knives. She picked one up, took careful aim and threw. It missed the pot by a couple of inches and disappeared into the undergrowth. Beth swore under her breath and went off to search for it.

There was no greater incentive to speedy improvement than spending twenty minutes hunting through dense foliage for a lost knife. Within a few throws she was hitting the pot every time. Within an hour she was aiming for, and hitting, particular flowers, vines, and within an inch of the same spot on the tree stump, and from an ever-increasing distance. Maybe she could ask Pierre for a target to be made. Then she would not spend half her time trying to locate her knife after it had sliced the vine she'd aimed for in two and sailed on into the undergrowth.

She was sweating freely now, but thoroughly enjoying both the challenge and the exercise. She decided to have one more round of throwing before heading back to the house. The knives would need sharpening, another thing she wanted to do herself. And she would need to start holding books at arm's length again, as she had in the Tower of London; her arms were aching with the unaccustomed exertion.

She bent down, picked up a knife, aimed carefully, and threw. It pierced the tree and stuck there, quivering. Then she picked up the other three knives together and one after the other in quick succession threw them after their companion. She was about to walk over to the tree to see how accurately she'd thrown when applause came from behind her. She turned to see an elderly man with startlingly black hair watching her with open admiration. She remembered him; the last time she'd seen him had been the day before Antoinette had fallen ill, and he had flirted with her all evening.

"Bravo, madame!" he called. "You have an incredible skill! I have never seen the like before."

She smiled and then walked over to the stump, pulling the knives out before joining her admirer.

"Monsieur Giroux, how lovely to see you!" Beth said. She was actually telling the truth. He could only be here at Pierre's invitation, which was a good sign, as the grieving widower had seen no one since Antoinette's funeral.

"Please, madame, you must call me André. I insist," he said.

He offered her his arm and she put the knives in her pocket and took it. They walked back to the house together.

"Where did you learn such a skill, my dear?" he asked as they entered the salon. Raymond was despatched to inform Pierre that his visitor was here, and Beth and André sat down.

"My mother taught me when I was a child," Beth replied. "She was a Highlander and thought it prudent to teach her daughter how to defend herself."

"And have you needed to defend yourself?" André asked.

"In a manner of speaking, yes," Beth replied.

Before he could ask her to elaborate on this, Pierre appeared.

The difference in him was so remarkable that Beth knew at once that whilst Pierre no doubt was saddened by the death of his wife, the majority of his decline had been for show. He came into the room smiling and greeted his friend very cordially. He wore black, as was correct, but like Beth he had abandoned the heavy woollen clothing, instead opting for a black silk outfit. Before long several other guests arrived, and they all repaired to the dining area for dinner.

Although there were no flowers on the table and there was neither music nor dancing afterwards as a sign of respect for the dead woman, the evening was very convivial, with André regaling the tale of how he had come upon Lady Peters skewering a tree, and renewing his flirtation with her.

This time she was not exhausted and irritable, so she accepted both the questions regarding her knife-throwing skills and André's overblown compliments in good part. The evening ended with a game of cards and as she mounted the stairs for bed, Beth realised with surprise that she had actually enjoyed herself, for two reasons; firstly she had been starved of company for the last six weeks, apart from Rosalie, who had come on in leaps and bounds with her reading and writing due to the increased amount of time Beth now had to teach her; and secondly because now she knew that Pierre was not actually going to grieve to death, she could start to put her plan into action.

That thought cheered her up immeasurably.

The following morning she slept late and when she woke up and tried to move, her arms were stiff and dreadfully sore from the previous day's exertion. She was tentatively stretching her arms above her head trying to relieve the ache, when Rosalie appeared with a tray of breakfast for her.

Freshly squeezed orange juice, chocolate, almond pastries. And a slender glass vase, in which resided a single perfect cream flower. Beth stared at it. The petals were thick and waxy, and a faint pink blush tinted their underside. She didn't bend to smell it, because she knew it had no scent. She also knew that it was called an orchid. She knew that because she had seen its twin, in Nice, four years ago almost to the day. Except at that time it had been Angus who had brought breakfast, not Rosalie.

It's a sign, she thought, *that I'm doing the right thing.* A wave of longing to be sitting at breakfast with her husband and brother-in-law, watching them insult each other good-naturedly as only very close relations or friends could, washed over her, bringing tears to her eyes momentarily.

Beth looked up to see Rosalie eyeing her uncertainly.

"Is something wrong, madame?" she asked. "I thought to bring you your favourite breakfast, but if you want something else, then—"

"No, it's perfect," Beth said. "The orchid is very beautiful. I didn't know that Monsieur Pierre grew them."

"He doesn't, madame. It is a gift from Monsieur Giroux. He said that it is flawless like yourself, and that if it pleases you he would very much like to show you his collection of orchids, if you would honour him with a visit one day."

"He told you to tell me that?" Beth asked.

"Yes, madame. He made me repeat it so that I would make no mistake."

So the flirtation was not all harmless, after all. The sooner she left, the better. She picked up the orange juice.

"Monsieur Giroux has the most remarkable black hair. It cannot be natural."

Rosalie grinned.

"No, madame. His body servant colours it for him. But I think he wouldn't want anyone to know that."

"I promise I won't tell him. Do you know how to colour hair, Rosalie?"

"No, madame. But I'll try to find out, if you wish."

"Yes please."

"May I ask, madame, if it is for you?"

"It is, although I would prefer it if you told nobody that. It should be a secret."

"Of course." Rosalie smiled, clearly liking the idea of being entrusted with a secret. It would be interesting to see whether she was able to find out the information without breaking the confidence.

"Really, my dear Beth, there is no need for you to leave. Why, I have come to think of you almost as family. Are you not happy here?" Pierre asked when Beth revealed her intention to leave Martinique. She could hardly tell him how miserable she was here; after all, it was not his fault.

"Of course I am happy," she lied instead. "But I was engaged as a companion to Antoinette, and it wouldn't be proper for me to stay for much longer now there are no other women in the house. People will start to talk, which will do neither of us any good."

"Ah, of course you are right. I should have thought of that. I have been somewhat distracted of late. But it would not do for your honour to be compromised."

"I'm so glad you understand," Beth said.

"However there is a way that you could continue to stay here. You must know how very fond of you I have become in these last months. I would be deeply honoured if you would consent to become my wife," he continued, moving forward and taking her hand in his.

Beth's horror at the proposal must have shown on her face, because Pierre released her hand immediately.

"I understand that this has come as a shock to you, and if I have offended you I apologise," he said. "In France, as I'm sure you know, it would be most unseemly for a man to propose to another lady whilst in mourning for his previous wife. But unfortunately, due to the particular conditions on the island and the precariousness of life, we do not have the luxury of being able to wait for months before continuing with our lives. Nobody would think it strange if we were to marry immediately.

"But I understand that you might need some time to become accustomed to the idea. Or if you would feel more comfortable waiting until the official mourning is over, I could arrange for you to stay with some married friends of mine, so as to avoid any rumours."

Beth was stunned, not just by the proposal, but by the arrogance of the man. It was quite obvious, not only by his words but his manner, that he expected her to be honoured that he wished to marry her. The fact that she might find him repugnant did not even cross his mind. He really believed that her only possible objection could be one of social convention. Her first impulse was to tell him the truth; but she had not spent years under the tutelage of Sir Anthony Peters without learning how to dissemble. And if she was to get everything she wanted, she must not antagonise him.

"Pierre, I am truly flattered," she replied. "If I appear somewhat shocked it is partly as you say, because I'm not accustomed to the speed of life on the island. But also you have forgotten, I think, that I am still married. Indeed, that is one of the reasons I must leave."

"But did you not tell me that you believe Sir Anthony to be dead?" Pierre asked.

"I do believe it. But believing is not the same as knowing. I could not in all conscience marry you when my husband might still be alive. That would be a terrible sin, not just against you and the law, but against God."

"But my dear, you may never find out! And it would be a great tragedy for such a beautiful young lady as yourself never to know happiness again because of such a forlorn hope."

He really thought that she would find happiness with him, that a woman was incapable of being happy unless a man was telling her what to do! No, that was unfair to him. Society in general believed a woman's only function in life was to make a man happy and bear his children. And he would be a good catch for some woman, wealthy as he was, kind, if a little distant, and not unattractive.

But not for her. Alex had spoilt her for any other man. She would never marry again, whether he was alive or not. *Think!* She told herself fiercely. *Keep focussed on what you need to achieve here!*

"You are indeed correct, Pierre," she responded. "And that is one of the reasons why I think I should go to France."

"France?!" he cried. "You mean to leave Martinique altogether?"

"I think it is my only choice. If my husband is alive he will almost certainly have travelled to Paris, or possibly to Rome, where he will be safe. And I am sure that, if he is alive, someone in Paris will know of his whereabouts. If there is no news of him there, then I will be convinced that he must have perished."

"But you do not need to actually travel all the way to France to ascertain that," Pierre objected. "Surely we can make enquiries by letter? I know it will take longer, but I am willing to wait for you, and I can think of several married friends who would be only too happy for you to pay them an extended visit while we wait."

"Oh, no! We could not do that! You know of course that Sir Anthony was one of the most successful spies King James had! I do not know what identity he is now living under, but a letter, if intercepted, could prove fatal to him. I will not take that risk, not for anything. If I discover that he is dead, then I will of course be free to marry again."

She smiled at Pierre in a way that she hoped conveyed that if that were the case he would be her first choice of spouse. It seemed she was successful, because he beamed at her and taking her hand in his again, raised it to his lips.

"Then, my dearest Beth," he said, "we must arrange passage for you as soon as possible, although I am not happy at the thought of you making such a long journey alone. I would love to accompany you, but alas, I cannot leave the plantation for such a long time."

Thank God for that, she thought.

"That is one of the things I wished to discuss with you, Pierre," she said, allowing him to retain her hand. "I had hoped you would permit me to purchase Rosalie, so that she could accompany me. And, for my added safety, I would of course like a man to accompany me as well, and to that end would be very grateful if you would allow Raymond to come too. I don't know how much it would cost to buy them both, but I am happy to pay whatever you ask."

Out of the corner of her eye she saw Raymond, who was standing in the corner of the room as usual, flinch and glance her way. She dared not give him any sign, because Pierre was staring at her in shock.

"Raymond?" he said. "Of course I would be happy to let you have Rosalie as a gift from me, to show my affection for you. You have trained her to your desires and I have no use for her, except as a field slave perhaps. But I could not possibly part with Raymond. If I were ever to sell him, he would fetch at least a hundred and fifty louis, probably more. He is young, healthy and a very experienced manservant."

A hundred and fifty?! She could not afford that. Unless…

"Pierre, I would happily pay that to have someone I could trust implicitly accompany me on my voyage. As you know, I arrived here penniless and the only money I have is the generous allowance you've paid me. I will gladly give all of that back to you if you would allow me to buy him. Once I am in France, I am not without connections and will arrange for the remaining sum to be sent to you."

Pierre smiled, and patted her hand.

"Now, I would not hear of you giving your allowance back to me – you will need that for your trip. I will of course pay for your passage. No, I insist," he said, when she opened her mouth to object. "I will seek for someone else to accompany you."

Damn. She couldn't labour the point right now. She must be content with Rosalie for the moment. But she had no intention of separating father and daughter. A hundred and fifty louis. Where could she get that much money? She had to think of a way. But not now.

"It will be so exciting to have a slave of my own!" she said instead. "How soon can we transfer her to me?"

"I will send for my lawyer tomorrow and we can have the papers drawn up. You will need them in case anyone questions you or accuses her of being a runaway."

"You are very kind, Pierre! Thank you!" She stood on tiptoe and kissed him on the cheek.

She went back to her room feeling like a prostitute. Which was ridiculous, because she had only kissed him and allowed him to briefly embrace her. It was nothing compared to what women did every day of the week to get their way.

But it was not what *she* did. She had absolutely no intention of marrying Pierre, no intention of ever coming back to Martinique, regardless of what she discovered when she got home. And she had every intention of taking Raymond away from here too. There had to be a way to get the money. She could and would repay it when she got back to England. There was a chest of gold buried in a field that could buy an army of Raymonds.

She was so preoccupied with her thoughts and plans that it didn't occur to her to question where Rosalie was until there came a loud banging on the door. Before Beth could respond, Eulalie threw the door open and ran into the room.

"Oh, Madame Beth!" she cried, gripping Beth's arm and pulling her to her feet. "You must come at once!"

Manhandling a white person and making a demand of them was such a huge breach of slave conduct that Beth immediately knew something must be terribly wrong.

"What is it?" she asked.

"Monsieur Armstrong, he is whipping Rosalie! You must stop him!"

Eulalie had hardly finished speaking before Beth was down the stairs, across the porch and running across the fields in the direction of the whipping-post. Eulalie picked up her skirts and followed behind.

By the time Beth came within sight of the post, Armstrong had already administered several strokes to Rosalie's naked back. Too breathless to command him to stop, Beth kept running, cannoning into him from behind with such force that he went sprawling on the ground.

She stopped, standing between him and Rosalie so that he could not continue the punishment, and bent over, fighting for breath. Rosalie, tied by her wrists to the frame, was moaning incoherently. Armstrong clambered to his feet and glared at her. All the slaves in the vicinity stopped working. This was going to be interesting.

"What the hell do you think you're doing?" Beth gasped, when she could breathe enough to speak.

"This negress has been stealing!" Armstrong stated. "I am administering punishment, as it is my job to do."

Beth straightened up. In the distance she could see Eulalie hurrying through the cane fields in her direction.

"Did Monsieur order you to flog her?" Beth asked.

"No, but—"

"And I certainly did not. Your responsibility is for the field slaves, Mr Armstrong, not for the house slaves. How dare you even *think* to touch my maid without first asking my permission?"

"I do not need your permission, madame, to chastise one of Monsieur's slaves," Armstrong replied coldly. "I have his authority to act as I see fit."

"You are misinformed, sir. Rosalie is *not* one of Monsieur Pierre's slaves. She belongs to me."

Her voice, although she did not realise it, was pure ice. Pure aristocrat. Francis Armstrong recognised it, and for the first time his tone expressed some doubt.

"You? I have not been told of this. When did you buy her?"

"That is not your concern. Neither Monsieur Delisle nor myself need to ask permission of you to make a business transaction, I think?"

"No, but—"

"You have exceeded your authority, Armstrong," Beth said, relegating him to inferior status by referring to him by his surname alone. In the background someone laughed, and Armstrong swivelled round, eager to vent his frustrated rage on someone. A sea of blank expressions faced him. He turned back, to where Beth was instructing one of the slaves to cut the maid's bindings. When he did Rosalie slumped to the ground, where Eulalie, who had now caught up, gently covered her naked upper body with her apron.

"Madame, this woman stole some ribbons from you," Armstrong said. "You should be happy to discover this before something more valuable is taken. She was brazenly wearing them in her hair, for all to see!"

"Some turquoise ribbons?" Beth said coldly. "She was wearing them 'brazenly' as you say because I gave them to her as a gift. Did you ask her where she came by them?"

"Yes, but—"

"And did she tell you that I had made a present of them to her?"

"Yes, but—"

"And you did not make the effort to come to me to ask whether or not she was speaking the truth? As in fact she was?"

"Slaves lie all the time!" Armstrong protested. "I cannot go and ask the master every time a slave lies to avoid punishment! No work would be done if I did that!"

"No work will be done by my maid for several days while she heals, because of your erroneous assumption, Armstrong. And you have damaged *my* property, and for no good reason, which I am extremely displeased about. I will be having very strong words with Pierre about you!"

Although it appeared to be a slip of the tongue, she had used Monsieur Delisle's first name deliberately to demonstrate that she was on friendly terms with him, and she saw by Armstrong's change of expression that he understood what she was inferring. He had a choice; lose face in front of the slaves by apologising to a woman openly, or risk her raising hell with the master. The slaves saw it too, and all of those out of his line of vision were grinning.

Beth resisted the urge to grin back at them. She had to maintain her cold, superior expression, which was not difficult as she was as angry as she'd ever been in her life, a cold anger. The two English people faced each other, while in the background Eulalie muttered soothing words to Rosalie.

Armstrong looked away, down at the floor, and she knew she had won.

"I apologise, madame, if I acted wrongly," he muttered.

"You did. And now you will release one of the field hands to carry my maid carefully back to the house," she said.

"But the field hands are not allowed in the house!" Armstrong protested.

"You seriously wish me to call Monsieur Delisle from his work to carry my maid back to the house? Very well. Eulalie. Please go and tell Monsieur that he is required urgently."

"No!" Armstrong cried. "I only meant…I will carry her myself."

"You will do nothing of the sort!" Beth responded. She turned her back in a gesture of contemptuous dismissal. "You," she said, pointing to a young man, "will you carry my maid back to the house? You will receive no punishment if you do."

"Yes, madame," he said. "I won't hurt her, madame."

"Thank you. Come, we are finished here."

The young negro bent, and with great tenderness picked Rosalie up as if she weighed nothing and set off across the fields with her, Beth and Eulalie following behind, walking slowly so as to cause her the least discomfort possible. Even so, by the time they got back to the house the young girl was unconscious from the pain.

When he got to the porch steps the young man stopped uncertainly.

"Follow me, please," Beth said, and led the way up to her bedroom where she instructed him to lay Rosalie on the bed, face down. He bowed to her, turned to leave, then hesitated before turning back to her.

"Madame Beth," he said. "You have made an enemy of Monsieur Armstrong. He is a very bad man."

"I am not afraid of Armstrong," she replied gently. "But I will be careful. If he tries to punish you for following my orders today, make sure I hear of it immediately. In fact, if he takes out his anger at me on any of you, I would like to hear about it."

"I think he will not today, and maybe never." He glanced at her neck, and smiled. "You are a good lady. You will be safe."

He turned and ran lightly down the steps and was gone. Beth

looked down at herself to see what had made him smile. The cord from which the amulet hung was showing. She tucked it back under her fichu. He must know about the amulet and also believe in its protective qualities. Maybe Raymond had showed it to the other slaves when he had found it.

She put the matter from her mind and went to tend to Rosalie.

Eulalie had removed her apron from Rosalie's back and was gently washing the blood away to reveal a number of weals. Armstrong had hit her at least ten times.

"She will be scarred for life," Beth said, tears coming to her eyes. "I didn't reach her in time."

"No, no, Madame Beth, it is not so bad," Eulalie assured her. "It would have been much worse if you hadn't run so fast. The punishment for stealing is a hundred lashes at the very least. Usually the hand is cut off, but Mr Armstrong cannot mutilate a slave without Monsieur's permission."

"But he *has* mutilated her!" Beth said.

Eulalie smiled at madame's naivety.

"Oh, no, madame, I mean he cannot punish in a way that would reduce their worth. Rosalie will be scarred, though not very much thanks to you. But she will still be able to work for you! You told Monsieur Armstrong that she was yours?"

"Yes. I asked if I could buy her. Monsieur is going to gift her to me," Beth said. She didn't elaborate, not wanting anyone to know what she intended yet.

Eulalie started to rub salve into Rosalie's wounds. The maid moaned, and her eyes opened. Then she realised where she was lying, and tried to move. She cried out with the pain, and Beth sat on the side of the bed, taking Rosalie's hand in hers.

"Shh," Beth said. "You must stay still. You are safe now. Eulalie is taking care of your wounds, and then she will fetch something for you to drink to ease the pain and help you to sleep."

"I cannot sleep here, madame!" Rosalie said. "This is your bed! It isn't right. Monsieur will be very angry."

"Monsieur will not know unless you tell him," Beth said logically. "Rest. Everything will be well, I promise you."

Later, when Rosalie's wounds had been dressed and she was finally sleeping, drugged by one of Eulalie's potions with the addition of some laudanum, Beth thought it safe to leave the room for a while. She wanted to go and talk to Pierre about Francis Armstrong's actions, but Raymond intercepted her as she walked across the porch toward his office.

"Monsieur has guests, Madame Beth," he said.

Ah well. Probably better to take a little time, think how to word her complaint against Armstrong in the right way.

"Thank you," Beth said.

"How is Rosalie?" Raymond asked.

"She's sleeping now. Eulalie says she will be better in a few days. I'm sorry."

"Why are you sorry, madame? You saved her from much worse!" Raymond said.

"I didn't reach her in time to stop him hurting her. She will be scarred, I think."

"Madame, you saved her. No one else would have done that. I thank you. And I wished…if I may ask you something?"

"Of course!"

"Do you really intend to take Rosalie to France with you?"

"I intend to take both of you to France with me, if you wish it," Beth said. Almost she told him of her full intention, but reined her tongue in. No. She would tell no one until she was sure she could fulfil her wishes.

"You are very kind, Madame Beth. But I must tell you, Monsieur will never sell me, not until I am too old or sick to serve him. But I would ask you to take Rosalie with you."

"Raymond, you have already lost your wife. I would not separate you from your daughter as well," Beth replied.

"Madame, please. I beg of you, whatever happens, please take Rosalie away from this place with you. She will be happy with you and you will treat her very well, I know. That will not be the case if you leave her here. I will be sad to lose her, but happy that she will have a good life." His eyes on hers were pleading, desperate.

"I promise you, Raymond, that I will take her with me when I leave. But I have not given up yet. I will do my utmost to take you with me as well, if you want."

"I think it will not be possible," he said sadly.

"Few things are impossible, if you want them badly enough," Beth said. "We will see."

Firstly she would fight to get Raymond. And then, if Alex *was* alive, she would find him. Whatever the cost, however long it took, she would find him.

She had been wrong. She did not want a new life; she wanted her old life back. And finally she had the determination, the courage, and most importantly, the freedom to obtain it.

CHAPTER TWELVE

Glasgow, September 1747

Having ridden into Glasgow from Loch Lomond on a sturdy garron, arriving in the evening, Angus paid for lodgings and stabling just off High Street for two nights. The following morning he was up and about early, having a list of purchases to make on behalf of the clan, including pots, tools, stockings, and lengths of linen and woollen cloth to make dresses for the women and much-hated breeches for the men.

In defiance of the Act banning the wearing of Highland dress, the core group of MacGregor men still waging war on the redcoats wore the *feileadh mòr* when fighting, partly because it was a far more practical garment both for protection against the elements and camouflage, and partly because they reckoned that if they were captured the fact that they were wearing outlawed clothing would be the least of their worries.

The rest of the men had, with reluctance and resentment, abandoned the Highland garb. The plaids had been dyed in an attempt to get rid of the outlawed tartan pattern and had been refashioned into coats, skirts for the women and other items of clothing. None of the clansfolk, whether waging war or not had handed in their weapons, which was also required by law. It had been illegal for a MacGregor to carry any kind of weapon for as long as they could remember, and having been in breach of the law their whole lives they saw no reason to break with tradition now that law was general to all Highlanders.

To that end, when Angus set out the following morning to make his purchases and to check for any mail arriving from his brother he wore the required breeches, stockings and shoes, as well as a clean linen shirt and coat. He carried no sword, of course, but hidden about his person was a *sgian dubh* and a dirk, cleverly concealed in a specially added pocket in the lining of his coat. He didn't expect to have to use them, but you never knew, and he would have felt naked without a weapon of *some* kind, anyway.

He spent a pleasant morning shopping, and by dint of fierce haggling managed to save enough money to allow him to buy a slender silver bracelet for Morag. Their first child was due in a few weeks, and she had been a bit irritable and low in spirits lately as the baby was lying in a position which made it difficult for her to sleep. Hopefully this would cheer her up a little.

He dropped his purchases off at his lodgings then carried on to the post, where he asked the clerk if there was any mail for James Drummond.

"For James Drummond, you say?" the clerk repeated. His eyes wandered briefly over Angus's right shoulder, then he dipped his head in a nod. "Aye, there is. A letter came in from London a few days ago, sir." He went through to the back room, returning a moment later with a folded sheet of paper sealed with red wax. Angus handed over his money and took the letter, putting it in his pocket and thanking the man.

He left the building and looked up at the sky. Another couple of hours yet before twilight. He carried on up High Street in the direction of the cathedral, then, seemingly on the spur of the moment, went into a chop house, where he ordered mutton chops and a pint of porter. He sat by the window gazing idly out into the street, and while waiting for his meal to arrive took his brother's letter out of his pocket, examining the seal with some care before breaking it and unfolding the paper.

He had intended to take it straight back to his lodgings to read in private, but things had changed, and he wanted to know the news it contained now, in case it altered his plans for the evening. He quickly scanned the missive, which purported to be a letter from his affectionate uncle, Archie, and which contained some information regarding the mislaid parcel of the previous correspondence, which he had hoped to locate. It seemed innocent enough, should arouse no suspicion if a stranger were to read it.

He read it again more slowly, taking the time to interpret the message. Halfway through the letter his meal arrived and he thanked the server absently, before finishing the sentence and inhaling sharply.

"Is it bad news, sir?" the server asked, hearing the intake of breath and seeing his customer's face contort. Angus looked up, seeing the man as if from a distance, then pulled himself together.

"This?" he said, waving the letter. "No, it's just a wee note from my uncle. I've been having pains in my back. They take me unawares at times, and are very sharp. I'm thinking to see someone whilst I'm here. Would you recommend anyone who kens about such things?"

The serving man thought for a moment.

"Well, there's John MacKenzie down by the river. He's no' a qualified physician though, ye ken, but a good man, even so. He fixed my shoulder the once, when I put it out playin' the fitba'."

Angus listened carefully to the man's directions and thanked him. He put the content of the letter and its import firmly to the back of his mind, having more urgent matters to think about right now. Then he ate his mutton chop and drank his porter, by which time the sun had almost set and it was threatening rain, which suited his purpose even better. He ordered another drink and waited a little longer until the threat of rain became a reality, and then he paid his bill and left, thanking the serving man again and stepping out into the downpour.

Turning his coat collar up he walked briskly along the street, keeping close to the buildings in an attempt to avoid the deluge. At the crossroads he turned down the Drygate, continued straight until he was sure the man following him had turned the corner and could see him, then he turned again, into one of the maze of dark alleys lined on either side by tenement buildings.

Once in the alley he ran at full speed for about twenty yards before diving into the shadows, flattening himself into the recess of a doorway. He reached into his coat, grasping his dirk in his right hand and sliding the *sgian dubh* into his sleeve where he could retrieve it instantly if needed. Then he waited.

Sure enough, after about thirty seconds the short, squat man who had followed Angus out of the post office after the clerk had nodded to him, had waited down a side street opposite the chop house while Angus had eaten his meal, and then had continued following him when he left, appeared at the end of the alley and started to make his way down it. Angus waited until the man had passed him, then followed him for a few paces before catching up to him and grabbing him from behind. There were the beginnings of a struggle, then the man felt the cold iron of Angus's dirk against his throat and stilled instantly.

Angus stepped backwards, taking his captive with him, and set his back against the wall so he could not be attacked from behind by any accomplices the stalker might have following behind.

"Now," he said quietly, "as ye've taken such pains to follow me all day, what can I be helping ye with?"

"I wasna following—" the man began, then gave a low cry as the knife pierced his skin. A thin trickle of blood ran down his neck.

"Ye're in no position to be lying to me, I'm thinking," Angus said. "Why are ye following me, and who tellt ye to? I'll no' ask twice, mind. I'm a busy man." The man stiffened and twisted slightly in his grip as he tried to reach for whatever weapon he was carrying. Angus pressed the blade harder against the man's neck, enough to cause the thin trickle to become a thicker one, upon which he seemed to realise that it was pointless resisting and the fight went out of him.

"Mr Mathieson paid me to follow you," he said, his voice trembling.

"Mr Mathieson? Is he the clerk in the post?" Angus asked.

The man went to nod his head then thought better of it.

"Aye," he said.

"Right. And why did he want ye to follow me?" Angus asked.

"I dinna ken. No, really, I dinna!" the man cried as the blade bit even deeper. "He just tellt me that when James Drummond came in to collect his letter I was to follow you, find out where you were staying, and then go back and tell him."

"He tellt me that the letter came in a few days ago. So ye've waited at the office every day since then?" Angus asked.

"Aye, he said he'd pay me a pound if you..."

"If I..." Angus prompted, when the man showed no signs of finishing his sentence.

"If you were arrested," the man finished shakily. "Please, if ye

242

let me go, I'll go and tell him I lost you, I swear I will."

Angus thought for a moment. It was a shame he couldn't see the man's eyes.

"Ye're lying to me," he ventured. "What if I'd no' come for weeks? Ye wouldna have stood in the office all that time for nothing, in the hopes of maybe earning a pound. There's more you're no' telling me." He felt the man tense, and knew he was right. "You're no' from these parts, I can tell by your accent," Angus continued, "so let me tell you something. This is a part of town, if ye havena guessed already, where I could dismember ye slowly and no one hearing ye scream would even pause in what they were doing to think about it. If anyone were to walk down this close, they'd step round us so as no' to get their shoes bloody. Now, if ye dinna tell me everything, I fully intend to prove what I've just tellt ye to be true. Is that what you want?"

"No!" the man cried. "I...he...Mr Mathieson, he tellt me that there's a Jacobite plot afoot, and there's a spy in London sending coded letters to ye about the gold that was landed by the French, that you're arranging to ship it to England, or maybe to the Young Pretender, so he can pay for an army to raise another rebellion." He was so desperate to tell all he knew now, to save his life, that he was tripping over his own words. "He said that if we could catch you, then we could make ye tell us where the gold is, and we'd all be rich! Please, that's all I ken, I swear it!"

"Yon Mathieson, has he tellt the clerk in London about this plot?" Angus asked.

"No, he said that he didna want the bluidy Sasannachs getting the gold, when he was the one who'd discovered about it."

"That's very loyal of him," Angus said drily.

"Aye, he hates the English. We all do," the man said desperately. "Please, dinna dismember me!"

Behind the man's back, Angus smiled grimly.

"I'll no' dismember ye, laddie," he said softly, and removing the dirk from his captive's throat, he lowered it, changed his grip slightly, then drove it between the man's ribs and into his heart. The man stiffened for a long moment, then relaxed.

Angus lowered him gently to the ground, then pulled the dagger free, remembering the time – was it really five years ago – when he'd nearly fainted on seeing Alex kill a man in cold blood in just the same way. He smiled to himself, remembering his innocence, and how much he had changed in that time.

He'd had no choice but to kill the man; if he'd let him go, he'd have gone straight back to Mathieson to tell him what had happened. As it was, with luck the clerk would wait a while longer for his man to come back with news, by which time Angus would be long gone. He wiped the dirk on his victim's coat, sheathed it and carried on walking down the alley, pondering what to do next.

He had to get out of Glasgow right now, that was certain. If the man had told him true, then Alex was not being watched and was in no immediate danger of arrest. In fact, if he'd read the letter correctly, then Alex was almost certainly no longer in London at all, and unlikely to write any more letters to his nephew for Mathieson to intercept. Even if he was still there Angus had no way of communicating with him, as neither this letter nor the previous one he'd received had told him where Uncle Archie could be reached.

Alex would surely be in no fit state to do anything rational, even if he thought he was. He had almost lost his mind the first time he had thought Beth to be dead. To believe her alive, only to find she *had* died after all, might be more than he could bear.

"Ye should have come home, brother," he said softly to the night. At a time like this Alex needed his clan around him, people who loved him, people with whom he could vent his grief and anger, make mistakes with no repercussions. He did not need to be walking straight into a web of intrigue and duplicity, which it seemed he was about to do.

But Angus could do nothing about that right now. He thought about what he *could* do, reasoning that by killing the man, he'd bought himself enough time to collect both his purchases and his pony. Better not stay the night, though. That would be pushing his luck just a bit too far. He turned right, then right again, emerging back on to High Street. Then he turned left, in the direction of the river and his lodgings.

* * *

To Angus's surprise, Lachlan and wee Jamie intercepted him a couple of miles south of the MacGregor settlement, materialising out of the landscape and waving before heading down the hill to meet him.

"What's amiss?" Angus said, immediately alarmed. "Have the redcoats come?"

"No, nothing like that," Lachlan said. "I'm glad you're back early, though."

"I havena bought ye anything, if that's what you're thinking," Angus said. "Except a length o' woollen cloth for your ma to make ye a nice pair o' Sasannach breeches."

Lachlan screwed up his face in disgust.

"Morag's having the baby," Jamie blurted out.

"What?!" Angus cried. "She canna be! It isna her time yet!"

"Well, she is anyway. Ma shooed us all away, so we thought we'd head south to see if we could meet ye on the way and tell ye."

Angus threw the reins of the laden garron at Lachlan.

"Bring her back," he said, and then he was off, running at full speed towards home.

"Ye should have let me tell him," Lachlan said sulkily to his smaller companion.

"I canna think why he's rushing, anyway," Jamie responded. "Ma said it was women's doing. She'll only shoo him away as well."

"There's nothing ye can do," Peigi said, as he came to a stop outside his house, gasping for breath. She'd seen him running full tilt along the path and had come to the door to meet him. "She'll be a while yet."

"I want to see her," Angus said between gasps. "I've something for her."

"I dinna think—" Peigi managed, before he gently but firmly moved her out of the way and went into the room. He expected Morag to be lying in bed, but instead she was walking up and down dressed only in her shift, supported by Janet and breathing like a train.

"Morag, *mo chridhe,*" he said. "Are ye all right?"

She looked up, then her face contorted with pain and she bent over, groaning. After the spasm had passed she straightened up a little and shot him a look of the purest hatred.

"You bastard," she said. "You keep away from me. You ever come near me again, and I'll geld ye. Get out."

He stopped halfway across the room, stunned by her response to his appearance, which was the last thing he'd expected.

"I want to help," he said, looking at Janet. "Here, let me hold her." He moved forward to take his wife's arm.

"I dinna think—" Janet began, unconsciously echoing Peigi.

"GET OUT!" Morag shrieked. Lunging away from Janet, she picked up the nearest thing to hand, a wooden bowl, and threw it at him. It caught him a glancing blow on the side of the head and then bounced off into the corner of the room.

He got out.

"I did try to warn ye. She's a wee bit fashed the now," Peigi, who was still outside getting some fresh air, said with spectacular understatement when he reappeared.

Angus reached up to the side of his head and winced. His hand came away bloody.

"She threw a pot at me," he said disconsolately. "Why does she hate me?"

"She doesna hate ye, ye loon. Women are all different, but it's a hard time for us. And it's her first, ye ken. She's blaming you right now, that's all."

"But she wanted bairns as much as I do. Did you throw a pot at Alasdair when you had your first?" Angus asked.

"Well, no, but then he wasna daft enough to come upon me when I was in pain. He kept well away until it was over, which is what you're going to do."

"But I need to help her!" Angus cried. "I canna just leave her to get on wi' it alone!"

"She isna alone. I'm here, and so is Janet, and there's others will take over later. This is women's work. Have ye news frae Glasgow?"

"Aye," Angus said. "But—"

"Away and tell the others then. Morag'll be a good while yet, I'm thinking, once the pains start properly."

"Ye mean it'll get worse than that?" Angus said, aghast. "I must be able to do something!"

Peigi reached out and gripped his face between her hands, pulling him down so he was level with her.

"Angus," she said, her face inches from his. "Ye've done what needed to be done. Ye've put the bairn in her. Now go away and let us get it out safely. I'll come for ye if there's a need, but in truth I dinna think there will be. The baby's lying well, and Morag's strong."

She let him go and he straightened up, his face anguished.

"I'll tell her ye love her, and ye wanted to be with her," Peigi said. "She'll appreciate that, later. But no' the now. Go away."

Reluctantly, he did as she asked. When Lachlan and Jamie appeared with the garron, he unloaded it and personally distributed the contents around the village, to pass the time. Then he called everyone together to tell them what had happened in Glasgow. They all sat in the clearing in the middle of the settlement, Angus facing his house so he would see if Janet or Peigi came out.

"Ye're back earlier than we thought," Dougal said. "We didna expect you home until later today."

"Aye, well I had to leave a wee bit suddenly," Angus said absently, his eyes fixed on the door of his house, which was firmly closed. "It isna right," he added. "She tellt me the bairn wasna due for another three weeks, at least."

"These two arrived four weeks early," Alasdair commented, indicating his three-year-old twins, who he was currently in charge of and who were digging holes with a stick for a purpose known only to themselves. His five-month-old daughter was asleep in his arms. "And Jamie was early too, if I mind rightly. They dinna always come when expected."

"Really?" Angus said, relieved.

"Why did ye have to leave early?" Allan asked.

"What? Oh, aye. I bought everything ye all asked for, and then I went to the post, thinking that if there was a letter from Alex I could take it back to my room to read in private. Anyway…"

He related what had happened, from leaving the post office to killing the man in the alley off the Drygate.

"The letter had been opened and resealed carefully," he finished. "I checked it before I broke the seal."

"Is there anything in it that would incriminate us?" Kenneth asked.

"No, I dinna think—" A long, agonised scream came from the house. "Christ!" Angus cried, leaping to his feet and taking two paces towards the house before stopping, torn between wanting to go to her and obeying Peigi. Alasdair, Dougal and Kenneth exchanged a look, then they stood.

"Let's away down to the lochside," Kenneth said, as though suggesting a turn around the garden. "We'll no' be disturbed there."

"But what if she needs me?" Angus said.

Alasdair called his eldest son over.

"Jamie, I'll mind the twins. I want you to stay here. If Janet or Peigi come out, ye find out what's happening and run and tell us. Come on," he said to Angus. "Ye've clearly got news we need to talk about and we canna do that if your mind's in the house there. Ye'll be no use to yourself or Morag if ye wear yourself out worrying. She'll call for ye when she wants ye, or Peigi will."

He was right.

They adjourned to the lochside, out of earshot of the house.

"What does the letter say?" Dougal asked once they were settled. Or as settled as they could be when their temporary chieftain with the news looked as though he was sitting on an ant's nest.

Angus took it out and unfolded it.

"It's very short. 'My dearest nephew,'" he read, "'I am grieved to tell you that the package I came in search of, although I am assured of its safe arrival in London some time ago, has since been irretrievably lost. You will understand my distress at the loss of such a valuable item. As a consequence, although I hope soon to be reunited with you, I intend first to pay a visit to Aunt Charlotte, in the hope that her company may help to reconcile me to my loss. I am ever your most loving and affectionate uncle, Archie.'"

A profound silence settled over the clan as they digested this letter from their chieftain.

"Holy Mother of God, he must be devastated," Kenneth said after a while. "What the hell's he doing going tae Paris? He should come home, where we can comfort him." There was a general murmur of agreement.

"Is Charlie still in Paris, then?" Dougal asked.

"Aye, as far as we ken. The last news we got frae Cluny said he was, but that was a good while ago," Angus said.

Allan sat looking from one to the other, puzzled.

"How d'ye ken he's gone to Paris?" he asked. "Who's Aunt Charlotte?"

"I'm sorry, man," Angus said. "We're so accustomed to you now, I forget ye've no' been wi' us long enough to ken what the letters say. It's a code, in its way. The package he's writing about is Beth. He's telling us that she got to London alive, so it seems that bastard Richard was telling the truth, but that something has happened since then and she's..." He stopped for a moment, and swallowed hard. "She's dead," he continued after a minute, his eyes moist. "Aunt Charlotte is Prince Charlie. He's away to France to visit the prince."

"We canna do anything about that right now," Alasdair said. "Though I think Alex must be half-mad wi' grief. We all ken what he was like when he thought she'd been killed at Culloden."

"He shouldna be going to France now, while he's like that," Angus said, his worry about his brother momentarily overriding his fear for his wife. "I was there wi' him last time. Ye have to have your wits about you all the time. There's at least three meanings to everything everyone says, and ye canna let your guard down for a minute or someone'll stab ye in the back. No' literally," he said to Allan, seeing the young MacDonald's look of alarm.

Iain, as was his custom since Culloden, had sat listening to all this silently, looking at the ground. He rarely spoke these days, and as a result when he did everyone listened.

"It could be the best thing," he said softly. He looked up at them all. "To do something that will exercise his mind. Every day is hard for me since I lost Maggie, but being able to go on the raids, to kill some of the bastards who are destroying our country, it helps a wee bit. I canna imagine what it would do to me to find out she was alive, and then that she was dead again, as Alex has. But I believe the reason he nearly died last time was because he couldna do anything but lie there in bed and think about her. If he *has* gone to Paris, then he'll have to stay alert, and that'll help him over the worst o' the grief. I think he kens that."

He had a point. And he'd had the experience of losing the only woman he'd ever love, too.

"Aye, ye could be right, man," Angus conceded. "I hope ye are. We canna do anything about that anyway. What worries me now is why the post clerk chose to open Alex's letter."

"Maybe he opens everything that comes from London, just in case," Dougal pointed out. "There canna be that many people writing from London to Scotland, apart frae the redcoats. And then when he's read about the package, he's come to the wrong conclusion altogether."

Half of Scotland was talking about the missing gold which had been landed by the French the previous year, and which had subsequently disappeared, been stolen, or was buried in a place unknown, depending on which rumour you listened to. No one seemed to know where it was. Except, in the mind of a Glaswegian post office clerk, one James Drummond, who, in collusion with his uncle was trying to use it to raise the Jacobites again.

"Aye, if yon wee man tellt me true, and I think he did," Angus said, "then it's a good thing that he thought Alex was writing about the gold, because I dinna think he's told more than a few about it, hoping to get it for himself. He wouldna have told anyone in London, because he'd ken that the first thing they'd do is try to capture Alex, and if he was right he'd never see a penny of it once the English got involved."

"In which case it's also a good thing that Alex isna in London, in case the man talks now ye've killed his accomplice," Kenneth said.

"I'm thinking that this Mathieson, once he finds his man dead, will try to find out where the gold is some other way," Angus said, trying to think as his brother would. "He'll no' tell the authorities what he was up to or they'll ask a lot of awkward questions about why he didna go to them in the first place. And James Drummond'll no' be going to Glasgow again for a good long while, so I dinna think we need to concern ourselves, as long as Alex doesna go back to London and write from there. I canna see any reason why he would."

Wee Jamie appeared in the distance running down the hill, and Angus immediately forgot about the letter, Mathieson, and even, temporarily, his brother. He leapt off the rock he'd been sitting on as though shot from a cannon and rocketed up the slope, passing the messenger without pausing.

Jamie carried on to where the others were watching their rapidly diminishing chieftain with amusement, looking disgruntled at not being able to pass his message on to its intended recipient.

"Is it good news?" Alasdair asked immediately.

"Aye, I think so, Pa," Jamie said, sitting down on the vacated rock. "At least there was an awfu' lot o' screaming and cursing and suchlike, and then I heard the bairn cry. And then Ma came out and tellt me to fetch Angus and tell him that everything was well."

There was a communal sigh of relief. The company cheered up immediately.

"Did she say if it was a laddie or lassie?" Alasdair asked.

His son shook his head.

"Ah well, it doesna signify as long as it's healthy," Alasdair said.

"Will I fetch the whisky then?" Allan suggested hopefully.

Kenneth patted him gently on the back, which nearly sent the slender young man sprawling on the grass.

"Aye," Kenneth said. "We can make a start now, and then once we've got the new faither back wi' us we can celebrate properly."

The new faither stopped at the closed front door of the house, suddenly extremely nervous, uncertain as to the best way to proceed. He lifted his hand, and then realising how stupid it was to knock on your own door, opened it and took a step inside. They were living in Alex's house, and Morag was currently sitting up in the bed, which had been brought down from the loft when Alex had been injured and was still there, because if the clan had to abandon their settlement for the cave again, it was easier to dismantle furniture that was on the ground floor, if there was time to do so.

He stood there, not knowing whether he was welcome or not, feeling shy and awkward, a small child again. There was a strong dark smell of blood, and the room was very warm due to the fire blazing in the hearth. Peigi, who was sitting at the bedside, looked up at him and smiled. She stood up and walked past him, squeezing his shoulder as she did.

"I'll just be outside," she said.

After she had gone he still stood unmoving, paralysed with shyness and shame at the pain he'd caused her.

"D'ye no' want to say hello to your son?" Morag asked softly, when it became apparent that he might well stand there forever if she didn't say something.

He moved across to the bed, looking down at his wife and at the small, neatly wrapped bundle cradled against her chest. Then he knelt down and looked with wonder at the tiny puckered face of his first child.

"My God," Angus breathed, awestricken. He looked at her, and his eyes filled with tears. "I'm so sorry, *mo chridhe,*" he said.

Morag's eyes widened with shock.

"Sorry? What for?" she asked. "Did ye no' want a bairn after all?"

"What?" Angus said. "Christ, aye, a bairn, of course! He's…I canna believe he's real. No, I'm sorry I put ye through all that pain. I didna ken how bad it would be for ye. I swear I'll no' touch ye, ever again."

Morag laughed.

"Angus MacGregor, ye're the biggest eejit on God's earth. And I love you." She looked at the cut on his head, which had scabbed, and at the developing bruise around it. "I'm the one who should be sorry. Are ye hurt?"

"No. But ye tellt me I was a bastard, and no' to come near ye, and then when I heard ye crying out, it fair broke my heart," he said.

"Aye, well, I was a wee bit fashed wi' ye then. But no more. I didna mean what I said. Look at what we made. Is he no' the most beautiful bairn in the world?"

He was, without doubt, the most beautiful bairn in the world. He was fast asleep after the ordeal of being born, smacked to shock him into breathing, then washed. His eyes were tightly closed, his little brow creased in a frown, his lips pursed. A fuzz of pale hair could just be seen on his forehead, the rest of his head and body being obscured by the blanket he was wrapped in. Angus's heart swelled with pride and joy, till he thought it might burst from his chest. Tears spilled over his eyelashes, running down his cheeks.

"I canna believe it," he said. "I canna believe he's mine. Ours," he amended. "He's beautiful, God, he's so beautiful. Can I hold him?"

"Of course you can," she said, smiling. "He's yours."

He leant over, and with infinite care picked up the tiny bundle, holding it against his chest.

"Welcome to the world, my son," he said, bending to kiss the tiny nose. *"Tha gràdh agam ort."* He looked across at his wife. "I love you too, so much," he said, leaning across to kiss her as well. She shrank back in the bed.

"I smell horrible," she said. "And I must look awfu' bad. Will ye ask Janet to maybe help me clean myself a wee bit?" He looked at her. Her skin was pale and greasy, and her hair hung in lank sweaty strings around her face. She did, indeed, look and smell bad.

Angus got off his knees, sat on the bed next to her and swung his legs up on top of the blankets. Still cradling his son in his left arm, he wrapped his right around Morag, adjusting position until she was resting against his chest. Then he bent his head and kissed her hair.

"You have never been more beautiful than you are right now, *mo leannan,"* he said with absolute sincerity.

She smiled and leaned into her husband's warm body. Her eyes closed.

"I bought ye a wee something when I was in Glasgow," he said. With some difficulty he managed to reach the pocket of his coat, from which he retrieved a small parcel. He handed it to her.

"Oh!" she exclaimed on opening the tissue-wrapped present to reveal a slender silver bracelet, its links carefully crafted into a Celtic pattern. "It's beautiful!" She slipped it on her wrist and held her arm up to the firelight to admire it. She turned her head and kissed his chest, which was the only part of him she could reach without moving, which she didn't want to do.

"I bought it to cheer ye, because the baby was lying badly and causing ye pain," he said. "I didna ken he'd come so soon. I'd no' have gone at all, an I had."

"Ye couldna have done anything if ye'd been here," she said. "Did all go well in Glasgow?"

"Aye," he replied, not wanting to disturb this perfect moment by telling her that he'd killed a man in cold blood in a dirty alleyway, Beth was, after all, dead, and Alex was careering off to France with his wits no doubt scattered. Time for that later.

"I dinna think he's early," Morag said. "Peigi said he's bonny and full-size. I think we got our dates a wee bit wrong." She held her wrist up to the light again, turning it so the firelight danced across the links. Angus smiled. It had been a good choice of gift. "I canna wait to see his wee cradle. Have ye finished it yet?"

"Almost," he said. "I can finish it tomorrow, if I spend the day on it."

He remembered the previous child he'd made a cradle for, how he'd smashed it to pieces in the throes of grief after the baby it had been intended for had not lived long enough to sleep in it. At that time he had vowed never to make another one. Strangely, it had been Iain who'd come to him, asked him if he was going to make one for his own child.

"No, it doesna seem right. Ye were no' supposed to ken about it, anyway," Angus had said.

Iain had smiled.

"We kent ye were making us something for the bairn, though we were no' sure what," he'd replied. "It was Beth who tellt us, afterwards, about the beautiful knotwork ye carved into the piece she found. Ye should make one. Ye've a God-given talent for the carving, and it wasna you making a cradle that caused the bairn to come before his time. I'd like to see what it would have looked like," he'd finished.

So Angus had made a cradle for his baby. He had not kept it a secret that he was doing so, but he told Morag he didn't want her to see it until it was finished.

"Shall I send Allan for Father MacDonald the morrow?" he asked.

"Aye, that would be wonderful," Morag said sleepily. "Are we still naming him Alexander after your faither?"

"Aye, if it's what you want too," he said. It was the tradition, to name the first son after the paternal grandfather. "If his hair stays the same colour, Sandy'll suit him well, and avoid confusion wi' his uncle having the same name."

"I'd like that. Hello, wee Sandy," Morag said, her eyes closing.

Angus lay there, enjoying the warmth and weight of his wife against his right side and his son against his left.

At this moment, life was perfect.

When Peigi returned a few minutes later, intending to send Angus out while she cleaned the room and the new mother up a bit, the three members of the family were all fast asleep on the bed.

Peigi watched them for a moment, then smiling to herself turned and left them alone, closing the door very carefully behind her.

Then she made her way down to the lochside to join the celebrations, which were already well under way.

CHAPTER THIRTEEN

Fontainebleau, France, September 1747

"God, but it's good to see you, man," Lochiel said, taking Alex's hand and shaking it before pulling him into a brief but fierce embrace. "Sit down and make yourself at home. Will ye take a dram?"

"I will. It's been a long journey, and I'm a wee bit tired, I'll no' deny it."

Alex had paid an exorbitant amount of money to lie in the bottom of a fishing boat along with part of the catch, and had been tossed about so much during the voyage from Dover to Calais that when he'd landed, wobbly-legged, soaking wet and stinking of fish, he'd been aching from head to toe and desperately in need of a bath, clean clothes and sleep.

He had taken a room, paid another princely sum for a bath to be prepared for him, and then sank into it with a sigh of utter bliss. He was covered in bruises from being thrown about, but he was in France, his portmanteau had been wrapped in oilskin and was dry, so he had clean dry clothes to put on, and the landlord had promised a hearty meal would be ready once he was clean and refreshed.

The following morning, having slept rather later than intended, he'd set off southward, deciding to delay visiting Charles until he had more information regarding what he was up to and how welcoming the French court currently was towards the Stuart prince. The last news he'd had was of Charles' disastrous mission to Spain, which had failed to attain the support he had hoped for to launch a new expedition to England, and must certainly have discredited him with the French.

To that end, Alex made a detour around Paris and headed southeast to Fontainebleau, where Lochiel had set up his home in exile along with his family. The Cameron chief would be sure to know what was going on, and would give an honest, intelligent account of it. Added to which Alex liked and respected Donald Cameron enormously, and looked forward to seeing him again.

He sat now in the luxuriously appointed apartments that had been allocated to Lochiel, and listened to the pleasant sound of whisky being poured into crystal.

"You've no' done too badly for yourself, Donald," Alex said, looking around the room they were sitting in.

"Aye, Anne likes it, we're safe, and it's a good place for the bairns. The boys are learning to hunt, and are training in arms now too. I'm no' ungrateful, ye ken, but I'd give it all up in a heartbeat to be going home at the head of my clan, even if I had to live in a bothy when I got there," Lochiel said with great feeling. "Ye ken my father died recently?"

"No, I didna. I'm sorry for it."

"Thank you. Well, I've been the chief since he went into exile thirty years ago, but I'll inherit the title now too, no' that it means anything any more. Even so, I should be with my clanspeople. That's where I belong, no here."

"Ye canna go back, man. The Indemnity Act excluded you, and your lands are forfeit to the Crown," Alex pointed out.

"It excluded the MacGregors too," Lochiel retorted. "Are ye intending to return to Scotland when you've finished your visit?"

Alex laughed.

"I am. But the MacGregors are accustomed to hiding, and no one kens the identity of Sir Anthony Peters. Everyone kens who you are. If ye go back, ye'll be executed."

"Were you no' concerned that Broughton would betray ye, as he has others?" Lochiel asked.

"I was, aye. When I first heard about Broughton, I couldna believe it. If anyone else except your brother had tellt me I'd have thought it was just more scurrilous lies put about by the Whigs. When I got back home we all moved to a safe place, because I kent that if the Elector found out that Sir Anthony Peters was no' only a Highlander but a MacGregor too, he'd have done everything he could to wipe out the whole clan. If Murray had been going to betray me, he'd have done it straight away. But no one has come for us, at least no more than they have for any of the Highlanders, and that taught me something."

"What?"

"Murray's no' as bad as ye think he is." When Lochiel made to protest, Alex held up his hand. "Think on it, Donald. Lovat was condemned by his own actions – he'd have been executed anyway. And the others he informed against, all of them had let the cause down – Traquair, the English leaders who didna rise. And yet if he'd have admitted that he kent the true identity of Sir Anthony, he'd have been able to name his price for the information. But he hasna. He canna have done.

"And the only reason I can think of for it is that when he was taken he was verra sick, and angry because the cause had been lost due to those who wouldna rise. He wasna a soldier, inured to pain as we are; he was afeart of torture and execution, and he had his wife and family to think of. Ye ken how he adored Margaret. So he compromised to save his life and his family's inheritance, but only informed on those he blamed for the failure of the rising."

Lochiel finished his whisky in silence, poured another and sat back, thinking this over.

"Well, I canna dispute what you're saying, except to ask ye a question. I ken how you loved your wife too. Would ye have turned traitor to protect her inheritance, or yourself?"

"No. But I tellt her to betray me if by doing so she could save herself."

"And do ye think she would have done, if she hadna died at Culloden? Because having met her on several occasions, and Margaret too, I dinna think either of them would have turned evidence, even though they were no' soldiers and inured to torture, but women. Which makes it even worse that Murray did. And I…" Lochiel's voice trailed off as he noticed the expression on his guest's face, which was one of extreme emotion that he was trying unsuccessfully to hide. "What is it, man?" he asked, alarmed.

Alex rubbed his hand through his hair. Then he drained his glass, closed his eyes for a moment, and with a huge effort of will, composed himself.

"Beth didna die at Culloden," he said. "That's one reason why I'm here."

"What do ye mean?" Lochiel asked. "Where is she?"

"I think I must tell you what's happened. And then you must tell me true the state of our cause, for that will determine how I proceed. There's no' many I trust now, but you're the most honourable man I know."

Lochiel smiled at the compliment. Coming from the most accomplished spy and now the most wanted fugitive the cause had known, that was praise indeed. He called for more liquor and for food to go with it, then asked not to be disturbed unless the chateau was burning down.

Then Alex told his friend everything that had happened, from when he'd killed Richard, to finding out for the second time that Beth was dead. By the time he'd finished, evening had fallen, Lochiel had lit candles and thrown wood on the fire, and three bottles of fine wine, as well as the remaining whisky, had been demolished.

"Christ, man, I dinna ken what to say to you," Lochiel said. "I canna imagine how you must feel. Ye must stay the night. In fact, ye can stay as long as you want to, take some rest and time to grieve for her. Anne will be delighted to have you here, and the bairns too."

"Thank you, I will stay a few days. Then I want to visit the prince, find out what's happening. We've had no news from him since May. Once I realised that I couldna do anything by staying in London, I thought to come straight here and find out for myself rather than wait for Cluny to let me know."

"Ye've heard nothing since May?" Lochiel repeated, aghast.

"No, the last we heard was that Charles had been to Spain. I canna imagine Louis would take kindly to that, so I thought to come here first to find out how the land lies between them."

"I think we should call for more whisky," Lochiel said. "Ye're going to need it."

Alex had been slouched back in the chair, the combination of alcohol, fatigue and emotion having drained him, but now he sat up, alert again.

"What's amiss?" he said. "Tell me. What's the wee gomerel done now?"

Lochiel made no comment on the disrespectful reference to Prince Charles. They were speaking openly to one another, and bluntness was not out of place.

"It's no' that wee gomerel this time," he replied, "but his brother, and his father, for that matter. Henry was made a cardinal in July."

He could not have heard his friend right. A cardinal? No. Never. Alex's expression told Lochiel what he was thinking.

"Aye, that's what I thought too, when I heard," he said. "I thought it couldna be true. The Stuarts would never destroy their own cause so comprehensively. But that's exactly what they've done."

"What the hell was Henry thinking? Could Charles no' put a stop to it?"

"Charles didna ken about it till it was over," Lochiel said. "He went to Henry's to have dinner wi' him in April, but he wasna there. He sent Charles a letter a few days later apologising and saying he couldna stand the hostility of the French and had gone to see his father. Charles accepted it. After all, Henry was always sensitive, easily upset by malicious talk. The first he knew was when his father wrote to him to tell him, in July."

"Why did James no' stop him, then?" Alex asked, still in shock.

Lochiel leaned forward.

"Alex, it was James who suggested it, James who wrote to Pope Benedict and asked him to put Henry forward as a candidate. When he wrote to Charles to tell him, James expressly said that both he and Henry were determined to make him a cardinal."

"But why? I can understand if James doesna want the throne himself; he's getting old, and he hasna the energy or determination to rule Britain now, I'm thinking. But Charles was brought up to take back the throne for the Stuarts, and to rule, and by God, he'd make a far better king than that German bastard sitting in London right now. The Hanoverians have spent the last sixty years justifying themselves by claiming that the Stuarts would make Britain a vassal of Rome, and the Stuarts have spent the same amount of time denying it. And now James has just handed our enemies the victory, because the British will never accept a king whose brother is a cardinal of Rome!"

"Aye, ye've the right of it. So ye can imagine how Charles felt when he got the letter, how we all felt."

Alex stood up, too angry to be still. He wanted to smash something, release some of his rage, but everything in the room looked very expensive, and in any case it wasn't very good manners to lay waste to your host's living room. Instead he paced the room, fists clenched. Lochiel watched him sympathetically.

"What the hell did we all fight for?" Alex raged, once he could speak coherently. "My clansmen, my brother, my wife died trying to restore James to the throne and he's betrayed us all, the traitorous bastard! And you, you've lost everything you and your ancestors fought for for hundreds of years. Christ, Donald, are ye no' beside yourself wi' rage?"

"I was. I felt exactly as you do now, when I heard. So did we all. The Bishop of Soissons and a lot of the Roman clergy said, in more polite terms, exactly what you've just said, and to James himself as well. But it's done, and we canna undo the damage. I've had time to calm down now. I canna bring my men back. And he's still my king, as Charles is my prince."

"The cause is lost," Alex cried. "I thought that I might come here to find that Louis had abandoned the Stuarts, that Charles had done something reckless, but I never would have dreamed that James himself would be the one to stab us in the back. That's what he's done, Donald, and he's no' stupid. He must ken that himself. What the hell was he thinking?"

"Go and ask him yourself if you want. But I doubt ye'll get a true answer. He's sent a number of letters to Charles since then, none of them wi' an ounce of honesty in them. He seems shocked that so many have objected, no' just those who fought for him, but the Roman clergy too."

"I wouldna go to Rome right now, if my life depended on it. I didna come here to commit regicide, which is what I'd be sore tempted to do if I saw James now," Alex said.

He really was proving his trust in Lochiel, if he was willing to issue such dangerous sentiments in front of him.

"What *are* ye intending to do?" Lochiel asked.

"I dinna ken at the minute. I'm no' thinking right. I canna believe it. What's Charles doing?"

"Right now? He's staying at Cardinal Rohan's country estate, at St Ouen. I havena seen him recently, but when I last did he was very depressed and drinking very heavily, more than normal. And he's taken to hunting in an area no one but King Louis is allowed to hunt in, without the king's permission."

Alex sighed. The prince always had been reckless at times when he most needed not to be. It was clear now that he'd inherited that trait from his idiot of a father.

"I'm sorry I had to tell you bad news, Alex, when ye've already had a surfeit of it," Lochiel said.

"It's no' your fault. And I needed to ken about it. Better to hear it from you, when I can speak my mind freely, than from someone that I canna trust."

"Get some sleep," Lochiel said. "Stay a while, and think it through before ye decide what to do next. We can talk more tomorrow."

Alex took his friend's advice, finally staying with Lochiel and his family for a week, during which he tried to come to terms with the fact that any chance of a Stuart restoration, slim as it had been, was now virtually impossible. Lochiel himself was of the view that a Scottish restoration was still a possibility. King Louis had promised to provide help if Charles would consider another landing in Scotland, but the prince had insisted that any future expedition must be to England.

While Alex might have agreed with Lochiel before, thinking that there was some chance, with French help, of breaking the detested Union and restoring James, or more likely Charles to the throne of Scotland alone, now he thought that even that was unlikely to happen. Although he himself was Catholic, most of the Scots, both Jacobite and Hanoverian, were of the Protestant faith, either Episcopalian like Lochiel, or Presbyterian, and they would no more welcome a king with such close connections to Rome than the English would. To all intents and purposes, the cause he had worked for his whole life was dead.

His wife was dead, and his cause was dead. Now he had only two things left to live for. By the end of the week he had made the decision as to what he would do with his future. Firstly he would return to Scotland, see if Angus was making a good job of acting as chieftain, although he had no doubt his brother was fully capable in that regard. He would finish fulfilling his blood oath to Maggie and Beth.

Then he would leave Scotland, adopt a new identity and return to London, where he would obtain an audience with the Duke of Newcastle and kill him for what he had done to Beth. He did not anticipate too much difficulty in accomplishing that task, because he had no need to plan his escape. All he needed to do was to make sure that he was killed rather than taken prisoner afterwards.

But before he did either of those things he would go to visit Prince Charles, partly because he doubted they would ever meet again otherwise, and partly because Lochiel had asked him to.

"Charles thinks very highly of you, and trusts you," the Cameron chief said. "A lot of the men surrounding him are older, and Kelly is an awfu' bad influence on him. I'm sure he's the one behind Charles' insistence that any new expedition must be to England. Being as ye're of a similar age, and a master of persuasion, maybe you can succeed where we've failed in weaning him away from Kelly."

"I'm no' so sure about that, but maybe I can raise his spirits a wee bit at least," Alex said. He had no idea how he was going to do that when he was feeling so low himself, but he would try. He still owed Charles his allegiance, even if at the moment he felt no loyalty toward his father and brother. And seeing the smile light up Lochiel's face when he agreed to pay Charles a visit made complying with the suggestion worthwhile.

Charles was not the only one who was depressed. Alex had discovered that in the days he'd spent with Lochiel and his family. The Cameron chief was racked with worry and guilt about the terrible consequences visited on his clansfolk as a result of his decision to come out for the prince, and was dreadfully homesick for his native land.

Hopefully the regiment that Charles had succeeded in persuading King Louis to raise for him would give him a new purpose, and allow him to make a life in this country. Lochiel was Colonel of the new Regiment d'Albanie, the Lieutenant-Colonel being Cluny Macpherson, although as Cluny was still in Scotland and unlikely to come to France in the near future, the position was currently empty.

It was on the last day of Alex's stay, just as he was about to leave for St Ouen, that Lochiel offered him the vacancy if he wished to stay in France. It was a great honour, and one that Alex turned down with regret.

"Maybe when ye've completed your blood vengeance, ye can reconsider," Lochiel said. "Ye'd be an asset to any regiment, and I'd be proud to have ye. And any of your clan who wish to join me, too."

Alex had told Lochiel of his intention to fulfil his oath, but not of his plan to kill Newcastle. He would tell no one of that.

"You're one of the most honourable men I've ever made the acquaintance of, Donald," Alex said, "and I'd be proud to serve under ye, if the day comes that I can. I'll write to tell ye how it goes wi' Charles, but in the meantime ye must look to the future. The past is gone and we canna change it by wishing it had been different. Ye've a wife and family to think of, and a chance to make a good life here."

Lochiel smiled, but there was a sadness in his eyes as he said farewell to his friend.

"Ye're right," he said. "And I would ask ye to take your own advice."

And maybe, if Alex had had a wife and family to think of, he would have. But for him there was no future. Only vengeance, and then death.

* * *

If Alex had expected Prince Charles to be deep in a black depression when he arrived at St Ouen, he was surprised. The prince seemed to be in a good humour, and was certainly glad to see his old friend.

"Are you here to stay?" he asked, once Alex had been announced and greetings exchanged. "Has Sir Anthony been discovered?"

"No, Your Highness," Alex replied. "I'm here only for a short time. We had heard nothing from Cluny for a time, so I thought to come and find out what's happening myself."

They were sitting in the gardens of the house the prince was currently staying at, the weather being very clement. Charles nodded.

"Have you been to the court or did you come straight here?"

he asked, clearly trying to discover if Alex had been apprised of whatever the latest gossip was.

"I havena been to the court, Your Highness, nor in truth do I expect to. I've spent a very pleasant week with Lochiel, but apart from that I've visited no one." Alex took a breath then dived in. Might as well take the bull by the horns, as it were. "Lochiel tellt me about your brother becoming a cardinal. I'm shocked, to tell the truth, and sorry for it."

The prince's face darkened immediately, revealing that the good humour was, at least in part, a facade.

"You always did tell me the truth, which is why I value you so. I accept as a prince that many people think to dupe me, but I never expected my own father and brother to do it! They have struck a blow to my very heart," he said passionately, striking his chest with his fist, "and to the heart of our cause. I cannot understand it. I will never understand it! I am finished with my brother – I will never forgive such a betrayal. And I realise now too, that King Louis will never help me to invade England. I am surrounded by traitors."

"But is it no' true that King Louis would look favourably on another expedition to Scotland?" Alex asked tentatively. Charles' face closed down immediately.

Interesting.

"Let us not talk of such weighty affairs right now," he said. "We have hardly exchanged greetings and we are already embroiled in unhappy topics! You will stay here for a few days," he said, his tone making it clear he would brook no refusal, "and tonight we will make merry, as we did in those happy days in Rome. Except of course you have no need to spend an hour painting your face!"

It would not do to try to continue with the subject right now. Alex knew from experience how stubborn the prince was. So he agreed to stay for a few days, and Charles made arrangements for them to dine at home before heading out to the local taverns, just the two of them, for this evening at least.

It was a great honour, and as Alex repaired to his room to dress for the evening in the only outfit he had brought with him which was suitable for going out with royalty, he tried to summon up some enthusiasm. What he really wanted to do was vent the anger he still felt at the destruction of all his hopes, which had not been dimmed by the ride north.

He wanted to kill people, anyone who had contributed to his misery; King James, Henry, the Elector, Cumberland, Newcastle, every redcoat who had ever struck a blow for Hanover. He wanted to laugh and dance in their pooled blood, as it was said the redcoats had in Jacobite blood at Culloden. He felt the killing rage rise in him, and closed his eyes tightly.

Stop this, he admonished himself. *There will be a time for killing, but it's no' now.* Now he had to be happy, sociable. *You can do this; you've done it a thousand times, as Sir Anthony.*

Sir Anthony was dead, but aspects of his personality could be resurrected at need. And now there was a need.

Alex opened his eyes, picked up a silver-backed brush from the dressing table and brushed the tangles from his hair before tying it neatly back with a royal blue silk ribbon that matched his outfit. Then he eyed himself in the mirror, noting the lines that were appearing at the corners of his eyes, and the hardness of his mouth. *The last two years have aged me,* he thought.

Charles had also changed since he'd last seen him on the banks of Loch Arkaig the previous year. He was still fit and athletic, but his face was rounding a little and softening, and there were dark shadows of unhappiness under his eyes.

Alex composed his face into that of a man who was looking forward to an evening of drinking, gambling and small talk, then looked at his reflection again. Yes, it would do. Then he bent down, put his shoes on, and left the room.

Eight hours later the two young men returned to the house, and if Alex had felt a little older than his thirty-one years before he went out, by the time he got back he felt like a decrepit old man. My God, but the prince could drink! True, he had always been able to hold his liquor; to the best of Alex's knowledge the only man who had ever succeeded in outdrinking him was Angus. But four years ago in Rome Charles had drunk heavily, but socially; now there was a dedication, a desperation even to his drinking that alarmed Alex.

Within an hour he had point-blank refused to match Charles drink for drink, stating that if he tried he would have to be carried home before the evening had really begun. They had started at the theatre, followed by an assortment of taverns, a gambling den where Alex was extremely grateful that he was still sober enough to avoid being fleeced of all his money, and, at the end, a brothel, which was a little odd, as neither man had any interest in sampling the wares, neither of them were quite sure how they'd managed to get there, and both of them beat as hasty a retreat as it was possible to do when your body didn't seem to want to do what your mind told it to.

They walked, or rather staggered back along the side of the river, Alex inhaling great lungsful of air in an attempt to sober up, aware of how vulnerable the two obviously aristocratic young men appeared, although had anyone attempted to rob them, his warrior instinct would have overridden his drunkenness immediately and he was, of course, armed with sword and more than one concealed blade, as was his custom.

They had not talked of anything important whilst out, for obvious reasons, but once back in the house Charles invited him to his rooms for a private supper. Alex would have liked nothing better than to lie down and sleep for a week, but he could hardly refuse such an honour.

Once in the room Charles sent for a cold collation, kicked his shoes off, removed his coat and waistcoat, and invited Alex to do the same.

"Let us not stand on ceremony, for God's sake," the prince said, slurring his words slightly. "I am so sick of being treated as a plaything by Louis and his ministers, as a likely husband by the women, and as an idiot by my family. Tonight let us be friends, equals, and above all, honest with each other."

He threw himself into a chair on one side of the fireplace, and Alex, having divested himself of his own coat and shoes, sat opposite him. The food arrived, and then they were alone.

"When I reported on you to Mann," Alex said, "do you remember we agreed that I'd tell him you were going to marry a French princess?"

"Ha! So we did! I had forgotten that. And he believed it! No one would believe that now."

"Do you intend to marry soon, Your Highness? I think you must. You are the only hope for the continuation of the royal line now," Alex pointed out.

Charles sighed.

"I will be honest with you," he said. "I had thought to refuse to marry at all, in the hopes that Papa would make Henry renounce his ridiculous vows and take a wife. But I see that is a hopeless cause. Henry has always been terrified of women. In truth I think he takes after our great-great-grandfather."

"But King James married and had eight children!" Alex said.

"He did. He knew his duty. But he preferred men, nevertheless. As does Henry."

This was a little more honesty than Alex had bargained for, and in spite of his inebriation, he was aware that in the morning Charles would not be happy to have divulged such a confidence, even to someone he trusted implicitly. Better not to comment; he could always claim later that he had dozed off for a moment and missed the indiscretion.

"Do you have a wife in mind?" Alex asked.

Charles smiled, and his eyes sparkled. He leaned forward in his chair.

"Not at the moment, no. But I have met the most beautiful, charming woman!" he said. "We met at Navarre. I was very low, you understand, after hearing about Henry, and my mother's family invited me to stay at their chateau. Louise was there because her husband is away at the war. She has been very ill, but is now happily recovered. We have spent many happy hours walking in the gardens together, and talking of many things."

"You mean your cousin Louise?" Alex asked.

"Yes," Charles said happily. "She is delightful. Really, you must meet her. You will fall in love with her – she is irresistible. Although perhaps it would be better if you do not. You are a damnably handsome fellow, you know, Alex."

Alex had no wish to meet Prince Charles' delightful married cousin, with whom it was clear he was infatuated. Were they having an affair?

Christ, Alex thought, *I canna pretend to have been asleep the whole night!* Why was the prince handing him all these potential bombs? *He is lonely,* he thought, *lonely and unhappy, and he needs to confide in someone who will never betray his trust. And he has no one else, no one at all who fits the purpose.*

It was an honour, and better the prince open his heart to

someone who really *was* trustworthy, than to one who would spread it round the court.

So he sat and nibbled bread rolls and ham, and listened as his companion elaborated on the perfections of Princess Marie Louise of Guéméné, and realised that for good or bad, she had rescued Prince Charles from a deep despondency, from the horror of having to gaze into a bleak and hopeless future.

And having realised that, he could not blame this charismatic, reckless young man for falling in love. He had spent his whole life believing he was the only hope for a Stuart restoration, had done his utmost to fulfil that destiny, had failed, in great part due to the broken promises of others, and then had had all hopes of another attempt swept away by his thoughtless and inconsiderate father.

To hell with it, Alex thought, *let the laddie take his pleasure where he may. I'll no' admonish him for trying to find happiness. He has suffered so much disappointment in his life.*

It was after three before Charles decided it was time for bed, but when Alex stood on shaky legs, hoping they would hold him up for long enough to get him to the room that had been prepared for him, the prince asked him to stay with him, his mood having once more swung to misery, as is common with the very drunk.

"When we were children," Charles said, peeling off his breeches and snuffing all the candles in the room except one, "Henry would often creep into my room. We had our own rooms, because we were princes of the blood royal. But we were still very little boys, afraid of shadows and of monsters that might hide in closets. Of course because I was older I had to pretend to be brave, but it was a comfort to both of us to sleep in the same bed. We would talk into the night, sharing all our childish secrets and hopes." He smiled, but his face was a picture of sadness. "Never would I have believed, had you told me then, that he would one day become my enemy. It is a hard thing to be an adult, Alex, especially when you cannot trust anyone, even those who claim to be your friends."

He moved over to the bed and pulled back the counterpane and blankets.

"Did you share a bed with your brothers too, as a child?" Charles asked.

"Aye, I did, wi' Duncan at least. We were close in age. Angus was too wee, and restless in sleep. We did much as you and Henry did as bairns, although we had to whisper, for we didna have the luxury of our own bedroom." Alex smiled as he remembered the whispered confidences and sometimes the silent fights that had taken place under the covers in the dead of night.

God, but he missed his brother.

"Come, then," said Charles. "We have both lost a brother, in our own way. Tonight, let us be brothers to each other."

Alex, who had been eyeing up the relative merits of sleeping on the floor or the chaise longue, froze and looked at his prince in shock. His feelings must have showed clearly on his face in spite of the dim light, for Charles laughed.

"You mistake me, Alex," he said. "I am not Henry, nor my ancestor James. But I am so—" He bit the word he had been going to say back, but Alex heard it, and identified with it too.

Lonely.

It was an honour, he told himself. In past times it had been commonplace for a monarch to show favour in such a way to a courtier and friend. It was a sign of absolute trust; no one is ever more vulnerable than when asleep.

The two men climbed into the bed, gasping at the initial coldness of the sheets, and lay down. Charles reached across and snuffed out the last remaining candle, plunging the room into darkness, and settled down. Alex expected the prince to continue talking, but instead he turned on his side and was soon asleep.

Alex lay there for a while, listening to the deep and regular breathing of the man whose cause he had embraced so wholeheartedly, who should, if there was any justice in the world, be sleeping in a palace in London, waking in the morning to a bright future. A bright future that he too had hoped for, with his wife in his arms and his clansmen around him, their name and lands restored.

How had it come to this? Two lonely, desolate young men with nothing left to hope for, sharing a bed in a strange house, in a strange land.

I'm drunk, he thought. He was. But it didn't make his thoughts any less true.

He closed his eyes, then opened them again as the room swirled around him and the bed seemed to shift under him. He lay for a while longer then tried again, this time falling into a deep sleep.

When he woke again it was still dark, and he lay for a moment not knowing where he was or how he got there. Then he heard the man next to him moan in his sleep, and the events of the evening and night came back to him. His throat and tongue were parched and he felt the beginnings of a headache pulse against his temples. He contemplated getting up and trying to locate something to drink, but was reluctant to disturb his companion. So he lay quietly listening to Charles muttering incoherently, clearly dreaming, although whether a good or bad dream, Alex couldn't tell at first.

After a few moments of this, it became clear that whatever the prince was dreaming about, it was not pleasant. He spoke in an Italian too fluent and rapid for Alex to follow, and then he flung his arm out to the side, narrowly missing breaking Alex's nose, shouted "No!" and woke up suddenly, breathing hard.

Alex lay silently for another few moments, not wanting to startle his bedmate while still in the throes of the dream. Even though they weren't touching, Alex knew that Charles was trembling like a leaf; the bed was shaking.

"Will I light a candle, Your Highness?" he said softly.

There was silence for a moment, then Charles said, "No. Give me a minute, and I will be well. I'm sorry to have awoken you."

"Nae bother. I was awake already," Alex said. He listened as Charles' breathing started to return to normal, then he got out of bed, locating the wine decanter and glasses by the last embers of the fire and returning with them. He poured, and handed the prince a glass. Alex couldn't see him, but the hand that touched his as it fumbled for the glass in the dark was cold and clammy, and the Scot nodded to himself.

"Ye dreamt of the battle," he said.

"How do you know that?" Charles asked. "Did I speak of it?"

"No, or at least if ye did I couldna understand you. You spoke in Italian, and I'm no' fluent in the language. I dream of it myself sometimes, and wake much as you have."

"You do?" the voice came from the darkness. "I thought...I thought I was the only one. I thought I was..." His voice trailed off uncertainly.

"It's no' a weakness to have nightmares about such things," Alex said. "Many a brave man has such dreams, afterwards. Ye wouldna ken that, I'm thinking, sleeping as ye do in a room alone, but when ye're sleeping in a field or a wee cottage wi' twenty other men who've seen such horrors, it's no' unusual to be woken by someone screaming in the night. I've done it myself."

"You have?"

"Aye. It's no' something we talk about. It's like a secret, but one that we all ken."

He felt Charles slump back against the pillows.

"They are terrible dreams," he admitted. "Sometimes I am afraid to sleep in case they come. You have experienced more fighting than I have. How do you make them stop?"

"Ye canna make them stop, Your Highness. For me, once I accepted that they were part of fighting, like wounds and scars, they didna fash me so much."

The silence went on for so long that Alex thought Charles had fallen back to sleep. He drained his glass, put it down on the floor next to the bed and lay down again.

"You told me earlier that Louis would assist in another expedition to Scotland." Charles' voice came from the darkness, making Alex jump. "That is true. Lochiel is in favour of it, as I guess are you."

"I am, Your Highness. The Highlanders have been treated so badly by Cumberland and his men, that many who did not rise last time probably would now. With French support ye have a chance of taking the Scottish crown. Although it would be more difficult now, wi' Henry declaring for Rome."

"Yes, I know. But you do not think I can take the English crown too."

"No' without a large French army, and Louis willna accede to that."

"I cannot do it, Alex. I know what happened to the Highlanders because of my actions. I saw some of it myself, and I have heard much more since."

"We knew the risks, Your Highness, and we took them gladly, and most of us would again."

There was another silence, and when Charles spoke again his voice was so soft that Alex barely heard him.

"How can you not hate me, for what I have done to your country?" he asked sadly.

Alex sat up.

"Charles Stuart, you are our prince, the rightful heir to the throne," he said. "You came to Scotland because you believed that you could win the throne back from that usurping bastard, and by doing so, give us a better life. We believed that too. It is my firm conviction that if we hadna turned back at Derby, we would have succeeded.

"But even if we'd carried on to London, and failed still, I wouldna hate you, and no man I ken would. You were following your destiny, and we were following ours. Ye couldna ken what would happen if we failed – after the '15 and the '19, we were allowed to go home, to carry on wi' our lives. It's no' you that we hate, but George, and Cumberland, for trying to destroy our way of life forever. Ye couldna have foreseen that; nobody could. Ye mustna blame yourself for what others have done."

"You really believe that?"

"I do, with all my heart."

"Thank you," the prince said.

There came a third silence, and this time Charles did not speak again, and after a while Alex closed his eyes and finally drifted back into sleep.

Alex stayed for another three days with the prince, and although they went out drinking again late into the night, Alex slept in his own bed when they got home, and neither of them made any reference to the conversation they had had on that first night.

When Alex was leaving, Charles came down to the courtyard to say farewell to him.

"Are you sure you have to go so soon?" the prince asked. "You are welcome to stay as long as you wish."

"I think ye'll enjoy the company ye're expecting more if I'm no' here, Your Highness," Alex said, smiling. Charles had told him the previous day that Princess Louise was about to come and stay with her great-uncle, the ageing Duc de Gesvres, who conveniently happened to reside next door to the house Charles was staying in.

"Not at all," the prince protested, but his eyes were alight with joy at the thought of seeing his cousin again, and Alex knew it was the right decision to go now. They were very different, these two young men, but two things they did share; they were both desperately unhappy, and both of them had been brought up to be rulers of men, each in their own way.

The prince had no men to rule and looked unlikely to acquire any in the near future, if at all. Alex, however, did. He had a clan at home and he needed to return to them, at least for a while, until his purpose was fulfilled.

Let the prince seek happiness where he can, he thought.

"Farewell, Your Highness. May we meet again in happier times," Alex said. He bowed, turned and prepared to mount his horse, but Charles' hand on his arm stopped him.

"Before you leave, Alex, I need to thank you. You cannot know what you have done for me. I will never forget it," Charles said fervently. Alex nodded. There was no need for words; both of them knew to what he referred. "If you ever need my help, you have only to ask," the prince continued. "I would give you this as a token of my affection for you."

Alex took the item that Charles handed to him. It was a snuffbox made of wood covered with gold, with an enamelled lid. It seemed innocuous enough until Alex opened it. Underneath the first lid was another, painted with an exquisitely detailed miniature of Prince Charles Edward himself. It was entirely possible to open the two lids together as though they were one if offering a pinch of snuff to a Hanoverian, or to reveal the owner's true loyalties to a fellow Jacobite by showing the portrait first.

It was a perfect gift for one who had been Sir Anthony Peters, who had concealed his true identity under a veneer. Alex smiled, and an intense wave of love for this star-crossed young man washed over him. Although it broke all the rules of courtly etiquette, he reached out and took the prince in a warm embrace, which was returned.

"Thank you, Your Highness," he said. "I will treasure it forever."

He broke the embrace, mounted his horse, and rode away. At the gate he looked back, and as he did the prince raised his hand in a final wave before turning and going back into the house.

For the rest of his life, through all that was to happen, Alex would never forget his last sight of that lost and lonely young man on whose head so much responsibility had been placed by an unappreciative father, who had abandoned him at a time when he needed a father more than he ever had before.

And because of that, Alex would never cease to love the man he had hoped one day to call his king, but who he knew now, deep in his heart, never would.

CHAPTER FOURTEEN

Fort Royal, Martinique

"Elizabeth! Beth!"

Beth had just dismounted from the carriage that Pierre had kindly loaned to her so that she could travel to Fort Royal, with the dual purpose of shopping for her trip to France and visiting the Marquis de Caylus to say goodbye and thank him for all he had done for her.

She looked round to see Elizabeth Clavering waving frantically and hurrying up the street towards her. The two women embraced, then Beth held her friend at arm's length and surveyed her. The last time they had met Elizabeth had been dressed in borrowed clothes which had been too big for her. Now she was wearing a beautiful emerald-green silk dress, heavily embroidered with gold thread, with matching shoes. Her hair was elaborately styled and powdered, and emeralds sparkled in her ears and at her throat. Beth, dressed in a pretty but serviceable pink cotton dress, her hair, now grown below her shoulders, tied back with a ribbon, felt positively dowdy by comparison.

"You've done very well for yourself," she said. "You wouldn't look out of place at Versailles!"

Elizabeth laughed.

"Aye, I suppose I am a wee bit overdressed for taking a stroll through town, but when I'm at sea I wear breeches and shirts like the men, so I make the most o' things when I'm on land."

"It's good to see you," Beth said, and meant it. "So how is life as a pirate suiting you?"

"Privateer," a male voice said from behind her. She jumped,

turning to look into the laughing brown eyes of Paul Marsal.

"I stand corrected, Captain Marsal," she amended, curtseying deeply. He responded with an elaborate courtly bow, while Elizabeth looked on with amusement.

"My name is still Paul," he said, smiling at her. "And it is delightful to see you, Beth. I thought you were living near Sainte Marie now."

"I am, but I am about to leave, "Beth replied.

"To leave? Do you have another place to stay?" Paul asked.

"No. I am leaving Martinique," she replied, causing matching expressions of surprise to appear on her friends' faces. "It is a long story," she added, "but I intend to sail for France as soon as I can. I came here to see the marquis, amongst other things."

"I am sure the marquis will be as delighted to see you as we are," Paul said.

"I'm not certain of that," Beth replied, looking along the drive at the distant house. "I'm afraid I need to ask him for a favour."

"Why are ye afeart o' that?" Elizabeth asked. "Yon man was much taken wi' ye, was he no'?"

"He said he was, but he has already done so much for me. I hate to ask him to loan me money, but I have no alternative."

"Ye're needing money to pay for your passage tae France?" Elizabeth asked.

"No. My employer has kindly offered to pay for that, and I have the allowance he gave me to live on when I first arrive in France. No. I wish to buy a slave." She looked around at the busy thoroughfare. This was not the place to discuss such things. "It's complicated," she finished.

"Is the marquis expecting you to call on him now?" Paul enquired.

"No," Beth said. "I was going to ask if I could make an appointment to see him, and then do a little shopping before going to my hotel. I have taken a room for a week."

"Excellent!" Paul said, taking her arm and tucking it under his. "Then you have plenty of time to visit the marquis tomorrow. Tonight you are going to be our supper guest on *L'Améthyste*, which by happy chance is just over there." He pointed to the forest of masts in the harbour, presumably some of which belonged to his ship. "You can tell us your complicated story and we can tell you ours, and give you a little advice too, perhaps. Are you agreeable?"

As he was already turning in the direction of the harbour and showed no sign of relinquishing Beth's arm, it seemed he had already assumed her response would be in the affirmative.

Which assumption was indeed accurate.

They dined in the captain's quarters, which were, as Beth remembered him describing to her in May, very tasteful. The mahogany panelling, bookshelves and burgundy silk upholstered chairs and curtains made her feel as though she was sitting in a library in an English country house. Only the temperature told her otherwise.

They sat at the dining table eating crayfish soup followed by oyster pie and orange pudding from silver plates, washing it down with fine wine poured into crystal glasses. While they were eating, Beth related to her interested audience the events of her life since she had last seen them.

"I don't know your opinion of slavery," she said after explaining why she was so desperate to buy Raymond, having already received the papers confirming her ownership of Rosalie.

"Well, it is a very profitable business," Paul commented. Elizabeth leaned across the table and punched him in the arm. "My dear!" he exclaimed. "You see the maltreatment I have to endure from my darling wife. Whatever was that for?"

"Beth is serious, ye loon," his darling wife said.

"And so am I. It *is* a very profitable business. Not one that I actively engage in, but I have captured ships with cargoes of slaves in the past, and have sold them on at a profit." He glanced at his wife. "But no more. My wife holds the same view of slavery as it seems you do," he continued.

"Aye, well, when ye've come as close as we did to being one, it gives ye a different view o' the business," Elizabeth said.

Beth nodded.

"It does," she agreed. "So you see why I need to buy Raymond. I don't want him to lose his daughter as well as his wife, but I haven't got a hundred and fifty louis. I told Pierre that when I get to France I have connections and will be able to send the money to him, but he said he will look for someone else to come with me and Rosalie. So I want to ask the marquis if he will lend me the money. If he will, then I can hopefully persuade Pierre to let me buy Raymond. I think he will see it differently if I have the actual gold, rather than just the promise of it."

Dinner over, they moved to the cushioned chairs in the corner of the room near the beautiful canopied bed, and Paul poured them glasses of cognac.

"But that's enough of my problems," Beth said. "I've talked all the way through dinner, and you've been very patient. Tell me what you have been doing for the last six months."

Elizabeth and Paul exchanged glances, then Paul spoke.

"Well, first of all, Elizabeth and I married, because as you can see, I have a beautiful bed, and was anxious for her to become acquainted with it and indeed with me, in a way that would not have been proper without the requisite vows being exchanged."

"Ye're a damned liar, Paul Marsal!" Elizabeth cut in. "Ye tellt me that marrying ye was the only way to guarantee my safety on board!"

Paul cast her a look of exaggerated anguish that Sir Anthony would have been proud of, and which made Beth's heart contract.

"Well, that was also a consideration," he agreed. "'Love and war are the same thing, and stratagems and polity are as allowable in the one as in the other.' Don Quixote," he added, on seeing the ladies' quizzical looks.

"Ye see, ye did well to reject him," Elizabeth said. "Never trust a pirate."

"Privateer," Paul and Beth said together, then they all laughed. It was clear that Elizabeth had made the right choice, and was very happy with both the life and the man she had embraced. Beth relaxed. She had not felt this much at home since she had left Caroline and Edwin's the previous April.

"After our marriage celebrations we set sail on a little voyage, to give my bride a taste of her new life," Paul continued.

"Which is an awfu' lot like being married to a Highlander, except at sea," Elizabeth interrupted. "So after we married, he and his men spent three days lying on deck in a drunken stupor and then armed themselves to the teeth and ambushed a puir wee ship sailing frae Liverpool wi' a cargo o' fine furniture, clocks and jewellery for the rich planters of Antigua."

"I failed to notice you objecting at the time to us attacking the 'puir wee ship', my dear," Paul commented acerbically. "In fact the emeralds you are so attractively displaying came from that very ship, as I remember. She was most shockingly bloodthirsty," he added in an aside to Beth, winking.

"Aye, well, I didna take kindly to being called a Scotch whore, no' by a squint-eyed Sasannach bastard," Elizabeth said.

"She ran him through with her sword," Paul added happily. "A most excellent baptism into privateering. We shall not bore you with the details, but we profited well from the voyage, and Elizabeth has taken to the life like a fish to water. I am very proud of her."

"We've made two more trips since then, and now we're waiting for the end o' the hurricane season, and enjoying our ill-gotten gains," Elizabeth said.

"And with that in mind I have a proposition for you, my dear," Paul said to Beth. "What do you say to us providing the funds for you to purchase this Raymond you are so keen to have?"

Beth's eyes widened.

"Oh no, I couldn't possibly!" she said. "When I told you about my problem, I did not think for one minute that—"

Paul leaned forward and took her hand in his.

"I do not think that you were trying to inveigle the money from us," he said. "It is not in your nature to be duplicitous, I think."

No, it was not, although she had had to be, many times in her life, and would no doubt have to be again. But not with these people, who, although only briefly acquainted with them, she classed as friends.

"No," she said, "I cannot accept such a gesture. You have already done far too much for me."

Paul waved his free hand in a gesture of dismissal, while firmly retaining hers with his other.

"I insist. You say you have contacts in France who will provide for you once you reach there?" he asked.

Beth opened her mouth to say yes, then closed it again. She could not lie to this man who had saved her life. Well, she could, but she did not want to.

"I did say that, to Pierre," she admitted, "but it isn't true. I have no intention of staying in France, but no one must know that."

"What do you intend to do then?" Paul asked, a concerned look on his face.

"I am going back to Britain, to look for my husband," Beth said.

Paul let go of her hand and sat back in the chair.

"I see," he said.

"But ye tellt me that ye thought Sir Anthony to be dead," Elizabeth said.

"I thought he was," Beth replied. "But I don't know for certain. And then I had a dream that led me to believe he might be alive."

She saw Paul and Elizabeth exchange a glance that told her they both thought she'd lost her mind.

"I know it sounds ridiculous," she said, "but I can't rest and carry on with my life until I know for certain whether he's dead or alive."

"Ye'll no' have a life to carry on wi' if the British catch ye," Elizabeth pointed out logically. "And they could, before ye even get to France, because they're blockading the French ports at the minute, making it awfu' difficult for merchant ships to get in or out."

"I didn't know about the blockade," Beth said, "although I do know what will happen if the British catch me. But it's something I need to do. And I really don't like Martinique. I don't want to spend the rest of my life sweating profusely and having to sit and listen to small talk while surrounded by miserable slaves. I'd rather go home and risk capture. But I will be very careful. And I have a deal of money hidden in England. When I said I had connections, I meant only that I have access to funds to repay the marquis, or you if you really do insist on helping me, and I will be sure to do that before anything else, so that if I am taken it will not disadvantage you."

"What will you do if you find out for certain what has become of your husband?" Paul asked. His expression was serious now, all trace of joviality gone, and he was looking at her with a calculating eye.

"If he is alive, then I will stay with him. If he is dead...I don't know," she said honestly. "I have friends. If I can stay with them without endangering them, I will. If not, I will find a way to be useful to the cause."

"And if he's alive, but seriously wounded, maimed, no longer the man you married? Will you still stay with him?"

"Of course I will!" Beth retorted indignantly. "He is my husband! I love him, and will care for him no matter what, as he would care for me."

Elizabeth looked at Paul, her eyes alight.

"Ye have to tell her that—"

He raised a hand imperiously, and she fell instantly silent. Never taking his eyes from Beth's, he steepled his fingers under his chin and continued.

"And what of your slaves, Rosalie and Raymond? Will you also take them to England with you?"

"I will not take them anywhere," Beth replied. "I mean to free both of them before I leave this island. That is my sole reason for buying them."

He looked at her for a moment longer, and then he nodded, his expression changed, and he adopted his customary light-hearted jovial persona once more. He smiled. Beth realised that she had passed some sort of test.

He really is like Sir Anthony, she thought.

"Then, my dear Beth, I will be delighted to advance you the money to buy this man Raymond," he told her, "and also the sixteen hundred livres you will need for their manumission. It's a tax that has been imposed to discourage slaves from being freed."

Elizabeth clapped her hands in joy.

"Thank you," Beth replied. "I promise you, the moment I arrive home the first thing I will do is ensure the money is returned to you. But you must tell me how to do that."

"Oh no, you mistake me!" Paul said. "I mean not to make you a loan, but to give the money to you. Call it a thank you gift for introducing me to my wife, with whom I am delighted." He blew a kiss to Elizabeth, who blushed becomingly.

"But it's an enormous amount!" Beth protested. "You can't—"

"Indeed I can," Paul interrupted. "I can do whatever I wish, and I wish to give you the means to purchase this fortunate man. This sum you consider enormous, I could lose, have in fact lost, in one night of cards. With this, I make four people very happy, no, five, for you say this Rosalie is his daughter, *non?*"

"She is," Beth said. "But—"

"Then it is a bargain! Five people made happy, my debt to you repaid, and all for the price of a card game. We will speak no more of it. I will procure the money for you tomorrow and bring it to your hotel. Then you can say your farewells to the marquis with a happy heart."

"Are ye going to tell her about—" Elizabeth began again.

"Indeed, now I am satisfied, I am," Paul interrupted. "When do you wish to sail for France?"

"As soon as I can," Beth said. "But I must get the transfer papers for Raymond, and then the manumission papers for them both. I don't know how long that will take. And if as you say the British are blockading the ports, I suppose it might be more difficult than I expected to find a ship that is going there, and will take me."

"I assure you, it will not be difficult at all for you to find a ship that will take you to France," Paul said. Beth's eyes lit up.

"Really? You know of a ship that's going to France soon?"

"Indeed I do, as do you. You are sitting on it."

Beth looked at the smiling couple blankly for a minute. *I've had too much to drink,* she thought.

"You are sailing to *France?"* she said finally. "But I thought you only did…er…business around the islands?"

"Not at all. We do business wherever it is profitable. At the moment the price of sugar is rising, because it is becoming increasingly difficult for merchant ships to successfully export it. The same rule applies to goods coming back. I plan to take advantage of that, and hope to sail in December. And I have a yearning to show Elizabeth a little of my home country, because it is very beautiful. I believe she will love Paris, and will look very much at home in her finery there." He raised his glass to his wife in a toast.

"And you're happy for me to come with you?"

"I am. We are," he said. "But now for a moment, as tedious as it is, I must be serious. In the last months Elizabeth has learned how dangerous my profession is. The rewards can be great, but the dangers also. The life of a privateer is usually short but merry, and the ending can be brutal. I must advise you, for your own sake, that it would be safer for you to stay in Martinique until this war is over."

"And when is that likely to be?" Beth asked.

"Who knows? The countries of Europe can always find a reason to make war on each other."

Beth put her glass down and leaned forward.

"I too will be serious," she said. "When Sir Anthony married me, I had no idea that he was anything other than he pretended to be. When I found out and told him that I wished to stay with him, and join him in his endeavours to restore the Stuarts to the throne, he refused. To illustrate what might happen if I persisted in staying with him, he took me to a hanging, which I had never seen before, and then told me how much worse it would be for me, were I ever caught. And still I insisted on staying with him, and he was right. When I was caught, it *was* so much worse, worse than I imagined it could ever be. But I have never regretted for one moment that I insisted on staying with him, and if I had to do it all again, I would, without hesitation. Does that reassure you?"

Paul laughed out loud.

"What a fortunate man I am, to find not one, but two women of such courage and daring! Yes, that reassures me."

"Good. Then I would very much like to come with you, and I accept all the possible dangers, only asking that you do not take any unnecessary risks on my behalf."

"Then we have a deal," Paul said. "Let us refill our glasses and raise a toast to good friends. And then let us get very drunk together, as all true pirates are expected to do at every possible opportunity."

"Privateers," the two women said together.

"Indeed," Paul replied.

They laughed, raised their glasses and proceeded to get very drunk indeed, with the result that later none of them were capable of even finding their way out of the cabin, let alone seeing Beth back to her hotel. So she and Elizabeth, on the insistence of the gallant captain, slept in the beautiful carved mahogany bed while he snored the night away on the floor.

It was a fitting way to celebrate a meeting six months previously which had transformed the lives of all three of them, and which would hopefully transform the lives of two more, when Beth returned to Soleil in a week's time.

* * *

"I am sorry, Beth, but I really do not think I can part with Raymond," Pierre Delisle said. "He is indispensable to me. But I can find you another suitable male slave, and will sell him to you for a much more reasonable price."

Damn, damn, damn. Beth could hardly explain to Pierre the real reason why it had to be Raymond. She sat on the porch with her employer, sipped her lemon water and thought furiously. In the background the subject of their conversation, dressed in full livery, stood immobile, awaiting his master's summons.

"But he will be more reasonable because he is not as well trained!" Beth cried, as inspiration struck. "It is crucial that I am accompanied by a very highly trained footman. It will reflect very well on you too."

"How could it possibly reflect well on me for you to take Raymond to France?" Pierre asked, confused.

"I will tell you, Pierre," Beth said. "But you must promise me that you will keep this between ourselves."

"Of course!" he agreed, his eyes shining, eager to hear what he had no doubt, judging by the look on Beth's face, was a juicy piece of gossip.

"You will know of course, that I do not speak about such things in general company, although I have been much pressed to," Beth continued. "It is not advisable for one in my position to be indiscreet, you understand."

She had him now. He was desperate to know what she was about to confide to him. And then he would assure her of his discretion and tell everyone the moment she was gone. She knew it, and it made the lie much easier to tell.

"You will, I am sure, have realised that I had a certain…understanding with His Majesty," she said. "That was some time ago, of course, but I have reason to believe that when I arrive in Paris, His Majesty will be generous enough to look on me with favour once more."

"I am sure he will. You are a most beautiful young lady," Pierre replied.

"Thank you," Beth said, blushing prettily. "You are very kind to say so, but there are many ladies of great beauty at the court, all of them seeking the king's favour. I am sure he would look very favourably upon me if I could present him with a most unusual gift."

Pierre looked at her, completely at a loss. She sighed inwardly.

"Black servants in France are very unusual," she continued, "and a negro of Raymond's carriage and training would be a rare gem indeed."

"You mean to give Raymond to King Louis as a gift?" Pierre asked.

"I see we have an understanding," Beth replied, smiling. "I will of course give all the credit for his upbringing and training to you, Pierre. It can bring nothing but profit to you, I am sure."

"But…slavery is prohibited in France!" Pierre said.

Was it? Damn!

"I know, but we are speaking of the King of France, not of a commoner! The king is above the law, answerable only to God for his actions. He will be delighted to have such a present, and you and I both will be looked on most favourably as a result. What do you say, Pierre? I can give you the gold immediately."

In fact, Paul had insisted on giving Beth three hundred louis in case Pierre drove a hard bargain, telling her to give any remaining cash to Rosalie and Raymond to help them make a new life. Beth had no intention of paying a penny more than the price Pierre had quoted to her, and from the gleam in his eyes as he took this information in, she was sure she had just succeeded.

"Ah!" he said. "Now I understand. I see now that Jacques, who I had intended to recommend to you, would not be satisfactory at all! But you really think Raymond is capable of performing his duties to such high standards? After all, life at court is very different to that of a plantation!"

"I will have six weeks, maybe more at sea to teach him," Beth said.

"Hmm," replied Pierre, thinking. "I have had an excellent idea, which I think you will approve of. Instead of selling Raymond to you, I could write a letter offering to transfer him straight to the king myself! You would only need to pay a small consideration for the time I must spend training another body servant. This would leave you with more money with which to attire yourself appropriately for court, and if Raymond was not pleasing to the king, he could be returned to me!"

And then you could be sure to take all the credit for Raymond, in case I fail to tell the king who trained him, Beth thought.

"Oh no, that would never do!" she said. "The training will be very hard; Raymond will have to spend long and tedious hours repeating the same gestures, learning the same lessons over and over, until he performs them perfectly! And I alone will be responsible for this. You know what negroes are like, how lazy and impertinent they can be. As obedient as Raymond is now, once he is free of your discipline there is no telling how he will behave when he has to obey a woman! I must have complete authority over him so that I can administer punishment as I see fit. If I do not have ownership of him, my position will be undermined."

"I do take your point, of course," Pierre said doubtfully. "But—"

"I am quite happy to sign anything you wish, assuring you that if he does not please the king he will be returned to you at no charge to yourself. Indeed, if I find that my husband is indeed dead, as I do believe him to be, I will accompany Raymond home myself, if you are still amenable to making a respectable woman of me," she said, blushing furiously, clearly deeply embarrassed at her own audacity. "Indeed, Pierre, I wish to please the king only because he can find out whether or not my husband lives. Once I know the truth of that, I shall leave the court as soon as I can." She cast her eyes to the ground to compound the impression of being a woman desperate to fly to his arms, even above those of the king, should her husband not be alive.

Pierre softened immediately.

"I understand completely. How could I refuse you anything, when you give me such hopes of making me the happiest of men?" he said, seizing her hand and kissing it fervently while she fluttered her fan in front of her face, a picture of feminine delicacy and confusion.

The delicacy and confusion lasted until she reached the privacy of her room, whereupon she threw both the fan and herself onto the bed, suddenly unutterably weary. She had forgotten how tiring it was to dissemble. How had she managed to do it almost continuously for over two years?

Because she had had Sir Anthony beside her, supporting her, covering her mistakes and treating it all as a game. And because once they were alone, as Alex he had reassured, protected and loved her.

She closed her eyes tightly in a vain attempt to stop the tears which threatened. *God,* she thought, *I am so lonely. I cannot bear this for much longer. Please, please let him be alive. Let all this not be in vain.* Tears trickled down the side of her face into her hair and she rolled onto her side, curling up in a foetus-like position, trying to comfort herself.

Which was how Rosalie found her, fast asleep, when she came into the room an hour later. Very quietly she tiptoed out again, closing the door silently behind her.

"Madame Beth is asleep," she whispered to her father, who stood in the corridor. "We will have to thank her later." Father and daughter looked around, ascertained that they were alone, then embraced, their eyes glowing with happiness.

Later, when Beth awoke, they would assure her that it was not all in vain and she would be comforted by that. But it would not abate the loneliness.

Once Beth had the papers confirming Raymond as her possession she relaxed a little, and spent the remaining two months at Soleil in preparing for her voyage. To that end she ordered two court dresses to be made that she had no intention of wearing, and some serviceable woollen clothes in dark materials that she did. She also exercised her arms, took long walks around the grounds, perfected her knife-throwing skills, and incorporated Raymond into the literacy lessons she was giving Rosalie. As she'd expected, Raymond was a very fast learner. The rest of his time was spent training the slave who would replace him when he was gone.

She didn't tell either of her new purchases that she had no intention of taking them on a perilous trip across the ocean; that she intended to free them. She could not take the chance that they might not be able to resist confiding such momentous news to one of their friends. One of the many lessons she had learnt from

Alex was that if you wanted to keep something secret, you must tell no one. She *had* told Paul and Elizabeth of course, but that had been necessary.

In her last week before sailing she would move to Fort Royal and stay in a hotel there, where she would also obtain the manumission papers setting them free. Then she would tell them both. She couldn't wait.

* * *

As a result of her impatience, the first thing she did in December, after saying her tearful farewells to Pierre and obtaining a room at the hotel in Fort Royal, along with a pallet for Rosalie to sleep at the foot of her bed and a tiny closet for Raymond that wasn't even large enough for him to lie down properly, was to head off into town to get the manumission papers drawn up.

She had spent twenty minutes at the hotel arguing that she wanted proper rooms for her slaves, not cupboards or pallets, until Raymond had gently interrupted and assured her that he was very happy to be in the hotel at all, as normally male slaves would sleep in the cellar or with the animals outside. Then she had reluctantly accepted the situation.

It took a whole day to get the papers drawn up, signed and witnessed, but finally she had them. When she got back to the hotel she ordered a large cold meal to be served in her room along with three bottles of expensive wine. As soon as it arrived she sent Rosalie to fetch Raymond.

While she was waiting for them to come back, she tried to calm herself. She couldn't remember the last time she had been so excited about anything. She cast her mind back to how she had felt when the marquis had told her she was free, how the prisoners had at first sobbed and then rejoiced when the good news had been given to them all. It would be wonderful for them.

Raymond and Rosalie sat silently on the edge of the bed for so long after she told them they were free that Beth thought they hadn't understood what she was telling them.

"Those are the papers telling you and anyone who questions you that you no longer belong to anyone at all. You can make new lives for yourselves, do whatever you want to do."

Rosalie looked at her father uncertainly, while he stared at Beth.

It is not that they don't understand, she realised. *They don't believe me, because freedom is something they never even imagined they could have.*

She stood up from the chair where she'd been sitting and went across to them, knelt down in front of them and took one of their hands in each of hers.

"Raymond, this is why I insisted on buying you rather than accepting a letter transferring you to King Louis. I had to have the ownership papers so that I could set you free in law. I am giving you your freedom, as the Marquis de Caylus gave me mine when we landed here."

She smiled, and Rosalie smiled back at her uncertainly.

"Madame Beth," Raymond said, his voice husky with the emotion he was not yet showing, "why have you done this for us?"

"Because I could," she answered simply. "If I could buy every slave on the island and set them free, I would. No man should live in bondage to another. I have spent years of my life fighting for a cause that would have given me the right to worship openly in my country, to use my rightful name. That cause has failed. This is a little thing, but it makes me very happy to give you both the freedom to choose your own futures."

"This is not a little thing, madame," Raymond said. He stroked his finger lightly over the paper he was not yet able to read properly. "This, this is everything. I…I have no words…" His voice broke, and like a dam breaking the tears spilled over his lashes and ran down his cheeks. He brushed them away, embarrassed, and then took his daughter in a fierce embrace, and the two of them broke down completely.

Very quietly Beth got up and left the room, recognising their need to deal with this overwhelming news alone.

When she returned a short while later they had both succeeded in composing themselves a little, but their eyes were shining and brimming with happiness, and Beth's heart soared.

"When the marquis told us all that we were free," she said, "we were like you. But then once we accepted it, we celebrated together. I know that it would be frowned on if we were to all go out together tonight, and that you wouldn't be allowed to go into the taverns with me. So I thought that we could celebrate here, together." She pointed to the dishes of food and the wine. "We will have to share the glass," she said, "unless you're happy to drink from the bottle, of course! But if you want to just be together to celebrate, then I understand. I can go elsewhere for the evening."

"Oh, madame!" Rosalie cried. "You are our angel! We can never thank you enough! Of course we wish to celebrate with you. I can't...we can't believe it's true."

They shared out the food, and in the absence of sufficient glasses clinked the bottles together and drank.

"It feels wrong to be eating food with you, at the same time, and the same table," Raymond said after a few minutes.

"Well, you will have to become accustomed to it, so this is a good place to start," Beth said. "Oh, I almost forgot! I have something else for you!" She went to the drawer and pulled out two leather bags, giving them one each. "It is a little money to allow you to make a start in life, and you must not thank me for this because it is from a friend of mine."

Raymond opened the bag and gasped.

"Madame, this is not a little!" he cried. "This is a fortune! We cannot accept this. You will need money yourself, when you get to France."

"I have money of my own," Beth replied. "This is for you, and my friend would be very unhappy if you refused it. So would I."

He sighed, and, never having experienced how to argue with a white person, gave in.

"How can we ever thank you for this?" he said. "There is nothing we can do for you to pay you back."

"Yes, there is," Beth replied. "You can call me Beth instead of madame. And you can go and live your lives and seek happiness, as I have...as I am doing. That will be thanks enough."

"Then, Beth," he said, "I promise you that we will do just that."

"Good," she said. "Now let's eat and drink, as friends and equals."

The next day they went for a walk together down to the harbour. Beth hadn't seen Paul or Elizabeth yet, but had sent a message to tell them she was in Fort Royal and asking them to call on her whenever they wanted.

The three companions sat by the harbour looking at the multitude of ships, some of them swarming with figures, loading, unloading or performing various maintenance tasks.

"Do you know which is the ship you will be sailing on?" Raymond asked.

"I don't, I'm afraid," Beth replied. "I know it is a brig, so has two masts, and is called *L'Améthyste*, but I couldn't identify it from here, no. But when I go I hope you will come and wave me goodbye, and meet Captain Marsal and his wife, who are my friends."

Raymond and Rosalie exchanged a look, then Rosalie spoke.

"We would be very happy to meet your friends, ma...Beth," Rosalie said. "But we cannot wave you goodbye."

Beth was surprised by how disappointed she felt that there would be no one to say goodbye to her as she left this island forever. *I'm being ridiculous,* she told herself. They wanted to start their new lives straight away, maybe wanted to leave Fort Royal immediately.

"Of course," she said. "I understand."

"We cannot wave you goodbye, Beth, because we are coming to France with you," Raymond added.

* * *

"So, Paul, you must refuse them permission to sail with you, because they just will not listen to me," Beth said two evenings later, having argued with Raymond and Rosalie for much of the intervening time. It seemed that Raymond did know how to argue with a white person after all.

They were in a tavern in which Paul was known, and in which he'd asked for and got a private room. The three of them sat around a scrubbed wooden table, on which was a candle, a jug and three glasses.

"I'm afraid I cannot do that, Beth," Paul said.

"Of course you can!" Beth replied. "I've told them that France is nothing like Martinique, that it's cold, and that having never lived anywhere else, they will suffer terribly. I also told them that they don't need to worry about me, because you are my friends so

I won't be alone. But they still insist that they wish to come with me. So you must tell them they can't come. They'll have to listen to you."

"Why do you no' want them to go to France with ye?" Elizabeth asked.

"They're only coming because they feel an obligation to stay with me, and it's dangerous, as you said, and because when I get there I can't look after them, and they can't come to England with me. Please, Paul, will you come with me now and tell them?"

"As I've said, Beth, I cannot do that," Paul repeated.

"Why not?" Beth asked, puzzled.

"Because Raymond and Rosalie came to see me this morning, and I agreed to take them to France with us."

"You did what?! How could you?" Beth cried.

"I could because I'm the captain of *L'Améthyste* and I make the decisions as to who goes on board and who doesn't. And I also could because they gave me very good reasons for wanting to go, and they were not the reasons you have just given to me."

"What reasons did they give?" Beth asked.

"They told me that Monsieur Pierre had mentioned that slavery is illegal in France. I confirmed that it is. They said that in Martinique, if they are arrested for any reason then they could be enslaved once more, and they would rather risk the dangers of the voyage and adapt to a new country than be slaves again.

"Raymond also said that if Monsieur Pierre finds out that rather than selling him to King Louis, you have actually freed both him and his daughter – which I might say is highly likely to happen, as gossip is the mainstay of the island – then he will be very angry, and will seek revenge. They will never be safe if they stay here. I agreed with them. So I told them they were welcome to come, and that they can have free passage if they are willing to work."

These were very good reasons; Beth could not dispute that.

"They didn't tell me that was why they wanted to go to France," she said softly.

"No, they didn't," Paul said. "Raymond was very honest with me. He told me that you didn't want them to go, that you assumed they felt an obligation to accompany you from gratitude, and that they didn't know how to refute that without you thinking they were not grateful for what you've done for them."

Beth fell silent, looking down at the table, and after a minute Paul reached out and took her hand, stroking it lightly. She looked across at him.

"Beth," he said gently, "you are a very kind woman, and what you have done is wonderful and will change their lives forever. But Raymond is a grown man and has been through many hardships. He knows his own mind, and although Rosalie is only fourteen, she too is stronger than you think. They have been treated as ignorant children their whole lives by the planters, and in order to survive have had to pretend that's what they were. I think you are confusing what they seem to be with what they are. You, who have had to wear many masks in your life, should understand that better than anyone."

"I never thought about it in that way," she said, reddening. "You are right."

"Don't be ashamed; you are not used to slaves. In your time here you've seen only a very little of their way of life. But you are willing to listen and to learn, and that's a good quality. Of course, there is another reason why you should not try to stop them accompanying you."

"What's that?"

"You have no rights over them. You have set them free, but are trying to stop them exercising that freedom."

To his surprise, she started laughing.

"Touché, Captain," she said. "I used different words, but that's what I said to my husband when he told me he'd married me to set me free. You are right. I concede defeat, and will tell Raymond and Rosalie that when I see them later."

"Good," said Paul. "Tell them also to have some warm clothes made – you can help them with that - and that we hope to sail in three days."

Three days. Three days and she would be on her way home. To hell with the risks. Better die young whilst truly living, than grow old merely existing.

And now she had the freedom to do as she wished, thanks to this charismatic captain who reminded her so much of Sir Anthony. And thanks to her, Raymond and Rosalie also had that freedom.

It was fitting that they should embrace the start of that freedom together.

* * *

The cargo of sugar had been loaded, and the crew all dragged out of whatever drinking establishment they were frequenting. Two of them had then been thrown in the sea to sober up, after which another crewman had had to reluctantly jump in to stop the most inebriated of the two from drowning.

"Seth really is an exceptionally ferocious fighter, and worth saving," Paul explained to his bemused companions as the unconscious man was dragged on board and then pummelled on his back. He brought up an impressive quantity of seawater, groaned, and then curled up on deck and went to sleep. Paul sighed.

"Take him below to let him sober up," he said to two other crewmen. "He can take a double watch tonight as punishment. I really don't want to have to flog men at this stage," he explained to Beth and Rosalie. "In fact I avoid it altogether if I can, because they're then out of action for a day or so, which means the other men have to do his duty as well as their own."

The matter-of-fact way he said this made Rosalie wince. Paul eyed her curiously.

"Rosalie was flogged in October by the overseer. I had given her some hair ribbons, but he thought she had stolen them."

"Mada...Beth rescued me," Rosalie said. "But I will never forget the pain. It was terrible."

"Well, mademoiselle, I assure you that I only flog my crewmen if they really deserve it," Paul reassured her. "There are many other ways to punish a man that do not stop him working, but are very effective. I do not anticipate any problems with my men on this voyage though. We have all known each other for years, and it is in all our interests to reach France safely. I will endeavour not to flog anyone while you are on board." He winked at Rosalie, who giggled.

It was lovely to see the two former slaves starting to come out of their shells as the realisation that they were truly free sank in. At the moment Raymond was on the quay helping to load provisions for the journey. He had been ecstatic to discover that there were two black crewmen on *L'Améthyste*, and that both of them had formerly been slaves. They had struck up a friendship, and the three of them were laughing and chatting as they picked up crates of chickens, preparing to carry them on board.

Accommodation for the passengers had been allocated; it had been agreed that Beth and Rosalie would sleep in Paul and Elizabeth's cabin on mattresses on the floor. This was to ensure that neither of the two women would have to deal with any unwanted advances during the night.

"Because of course I cannot marry all three of you," Paul had joked, "nor have I the space to allocate you a private cabin with a lock. And while I trust my crew, you are both very attractive ladies and they are men, not saints. I don't think it fair to expose them to such temptation. You will be safe enough by day. I would ask you not to be too friendly with them, that is all, give them no encouragement. I do not wish to have to kill one of my crew for assaulting you. They all have unique talents and to lose one would cause all of us problems." He had said it light-heartedly, but Beth had known that he was in earnest. She had resolved to have as little interaction with the crew as possible, not wanting to attract any unwanted attention.

Chores had also been allocated; Beth and Elizabeth would do any sewing and darning that needed to be done, and would help the cook with preparing meals. Rosalie would ensure that the captain's cabin was kept pristine, and would wash clothes for the crew. Raymond would help out wherever needed, with any chores that required muscle but no skill, as he knew nothing about ships.

While Paul looked out to sea assessing the weather, Beth watched Raymond and his companions on the quayside, realising that she had never heard him laugh once in the six months she had lived with the Delisles. It was good to hear his rich deep laughter now, and she smiled.

In the distance she could see two men in what appeared to be a military uniform of white breeches and frockcoats with blue facings, silver frogging and silver-laced tricorn hats. They were heading along the quay in the direction of *L'Améthyste* and she watched them idly, thinking how self-important they looked and how hot and uncomfortable they must feel.

When they reached the three black men they stopped and

asked a question. Beth couldn't hear what it was, but by the change in stance of the crewmen it was clear the soldiers were not passing the time of day. Rosalie came to stand next to her on deck. Raymond was saying something to them, but his head was lowered and he had adopted the submissive posture that Beth had been familiar with at Soleil. The two other men were clearly arguing, gesticulating towards the ship. One of the soldiers looked in her direction, then back at the men.

She was just pondering whether to stroll down onto the quay and eavesdrop, when suddenly the two soldiers moved to either side of Raymond, and taking an arm each, started to lead him away. One of the crewmen turned to the ship, put his fingers to his mouth and issued a piercing whistle. Paul turned, but by that time Beth was already halfway down the gangplank, her skirts hitched up around her knees and running at full speed.

She caught up with the three men halfway along the quay, running round to the front of them and stopping, so that they had to halt or push her out of the way. Seeing that she was dressed expensively and tastefully, the soldiers chose to stop.

"Where are you taking this man?" she demanded.

"What concern is that of yours, madame?" one of them asked in return.

"This man is my…" She hesitated, having been about to say 'friend', but on doing a lightning reassessment of the possible situation, changed her mind. "Slave," she said. "I consider theft of my property to be very much my concern."

The soldiers exchanged a look.

"Madame, this negro is called Raymond, is he not?"

"That is his name, yes," she replied.

"Raymond, belonging to Monsieur Delisle?"

"There you are in error, sir," Beth stated. "Monsieur Delisle sold him to me. He is my negro. Kindly release him at once."

"You have the papers to prove that?" the second soldier asked.

Beth gave him a look of such contempt and disgust that he flushed and looked away.

"You are calling me a liar?" she said icily. "If you would care to accompany me to the ship I will show you the bill of sale. And then you will apologise for insulting me, sir."

"Madame, we mean no offence," the other, somewhat older

soldier said. "But we have been ordered to arrest this man."

"What on earth for?"

"Last night we discovered that a number of negroes have been organising a rebellion, and this man has been named as one of the ringleaders. We are taking him for questioning."

"Raymond? Organising a rebellion?" she said with utter incredulity. She looked at Raymond, who was standing silently between the two men, gazing down at the ground. "And who has named him?"

"We are not at liberty to disclose that," the older soldier said. So they knew who it was.

"Raymond, look at me," Beth commanded crisply. Reluctantly he looked up from the ground and met her gaze. She saw his expression, the hopelessness in his eyes, and remembered what he had said the night he had given her the amulet.

"It will give you protection against disease, madame, and against...other things."

Other things. Like a slave rebellion. She could not ask him if the accusation was correct as she had been about to do, in case he answered truthfully. *Oh, Raymond, no,* she thought. And then she flung the thought as far away as she could, and turned back to the soldiers. Over their shoulders she could see Paul approaching at a trot.

"Really, this is quite ridiculous," she said, looking intently at the military men. "Was it the overseer, Armstrong, who made this accusation?" The blank look on their faces gave her her answer. "No. Then it was most certainly the negro Jacques."

Aha.

"I see by your expression sir, that it is indeed Jacques who has given this false information against my slave. This is nothing more than petty spite. The fact is that initially Monsieur Delisle was reluctant to sell Raymond to me, as he is such a skilled and faithful servant. He proposed that I take Jacques instead. I told him that Jacques would never do. No doubt the man has a grievance because he is not skilled enough to go to France, and Raymond is. There," she said firmly. "Now that is explained, you may release him. We sail with the tide."

"I am sorry, madame, but we have strict orders to take the man into custody. He will not be sailing with the tide, or with any other tide until the accusations have been thoroughly investigated."

"I see," Beth replied. "Very well. You must do your duty, I understand that. Captain Marsal, you will have to arrange for my bags to be unloaded. I regret to say that I will not be able to sail with you tonight. Now sirs, I must have your names, rank and regiment to include in my letter."

The two soldiers were taken aback.

"Letter?" the younger one said.

"Yes. If I cannot sail tonight, then I must write immediately so that Captain Marsal can take my letter to King Louis with him. Captain, can I trust you to personally deliver it to His Majesty? He will be most disappointed to find I am not coming to France, but hopefully he will understand that these men must do their duty."

Paul Marsal's eyes were sparkling, but his expression was serious as he replied.

"Of course, my lady. I would be honoured."

"Excellent!" she said crisply. "So, sirs. You will give me your names, so that I can tell the king who has prevented me from sailing to France today."

"I...we are not preventing you from sailing to France, er..."

"Lady Elizabeth Peters," she supplied. "Indeed you are, sirs. Because this slave is my particular present to Louis...His Majesty, and I have no intention of going to him empty-handed. It is most unfortunate, but there it is. I will wait in Martinique until you have found out that I am not a liar, as you currently believe me to be. Now, shall we go?"

She set off in the direction they had been taking before she'd stopped them. After a few steps she turned back, to see the two soldiers still immobile, with their captive between them.

"Do you intend to interrogate your prisoner on the quayside?" she asked.

"Er, no, mada...my lady. I...perhaps there has been some mistake?"

"You are quite right. There has. But as you are so insistent on taking the word of a spiteful negro over mine, you must proceed as you think fit. Raymond, stand up straight, boy! I will explain the situation to Monsieur le Marquis myself. If you are not released immediately, you certainly will be when the king hears of how displeased I am to be called a liar to my face."

"My lady!" the younger soldier protested. "We did not call you a liar!"

"I think that perhaps…in this case…if you would be so kind as to make a short deposition confirming the innocence of your negro, we might be able to make an exception?" the older soldier suggested, his tone pleading.

Lady Peters looked extremely annoyed at this imposition on her time.

"It is most inconvenient, but if it means that we can sail with the tide, I would consent to that to have this unfortunate business over and done with," Beth replied with great condescension.

Within twenty minutes they were back on the ship, and a note had been written and signed with a flourish.

"Bravo, my lady," Paul said admiringly as the two soldiers made their way down the gangplank. "You were magnificent. I have never seen the like."

"Thank you, Captain," Beth replied. "Sir Anthony taught me well. But now I need a very strong drink."

However before any alcohol could be imbibed, there was a small matter to attend to.

Beth and Paul sat side by side on burgundy-upholstered chairs, while Raymond stood in front of them like a naughty child, his head bowed. Elizabeth was on deck supervising the loading of the remaining provisions.

"For God's sake, Raymond, sit down," Beth said, gesturing to the chair behind him. He did as he was told, still looking at the floor.

"I'm right, aren't I?" she said. "Jacques did accuse you out of spite, but the accusation is true."

Raymond sighed.

"Yes, madame, it is true," he said.

"Is that what you meant when you said the amulet would protect me from other dangers?" she asked.

"Yes. Everyone involved knew that the lady with the amulet was not to be harmed. I am sorry, I am not the person you believed me to be. I have disappointed you." He looked at her now for the first time, and his eyes were bright with tears. "I swear to you, Rosalie knew nothing of this, and I would have her remain ignorant of my part in it," he said. "I will do anything you ask, but I beg you, please take her with you. Let her have a new life away from here!"

Beth looked at Paul, but he remained silent, his face inscrutable.

"You will do anything I ask?" she said. "Would you then tell me who is involved in this plot and when the rebellion was to take place?"

Raymond's eyes widened in alarm.

"Madame Beth, I...I cannot do that. I cannot betray those who trust me. They would be tortured...you have no idea what would be done to them. Please, do not ask me to do that."

"But Jacques betrayed you," Paul spoke softly for the first time.

"Yes Captain, he did. He has lost his honour. But I will not lose mine. I put myself in your hands. You may sell me back into slavery if you wish, or kill me. I will kill myself if you ask it. But I cannot betray those who trust me. I am sorry."

Beth smiled. He had just proved himself the man she believed him to be.

"Raymond, I would like to tell you something about myself," she said. "Paul, you already know this. I was brought here as a prisoner, because I and my husband engaged in a rising against the man who calls himself King of Great Britain. My husband was one of the most wanted men in Britain, and I am here because I would not betray him under any circumstances. I know what it is to be oppressed. I am not disappointed in you. Quite the opposite, in fact. For my part I am proud of you for seeking to free yourself. I do not wish you to kill yourself, or to become a slave again. I wish you to come to France and start a new life with your daughter, and to never feel unable to meet my eyes, or anyone else's again. I cannot speak for Captain Marsal though. Captain, are you happy to have this rebel on board your ship?"

Paul laughed.

"You are the most innocent of all my crew, Raymond. Really, you don't want to know what they have done. I am delighted to have you on board, sir, not because you were attempting rebellion, but because you would not betray your fellows. Loyalty is a trait I value highly. May I suggest that we put both this unfortunate incident and Martinique behind us, just as soon as the tide allows?"

The captain's suggestion met with the approval of all three occupants of the room.

Four hours later, *L'Améthyste,* with its full complement of crew and passengers, sailed out of Fort Royal. Beth, Raymond and Rosalie stayed on deck, watching the beautiful tropical island recede. None of them felt anything but joy when it disappeared from view completely.

Then as one, they turned from the rail, toward the distant horizon and a new life.

CHAPTER FIFTEEN

The trip from Martinique to France went wonderfully for the three passengers, in the main because the cabin Beth was occupying and the food she was served at mealtimes was far superior to that on the trip out, but also because the other two passengers were experiencing freedom for the first time in their lives, and really starting to grasp the idea that their opinion would be sought about things and that they were allowed to say no if they were asked to do something they didn't want to do.

Having said that, at the moment they had no desire to refuse anything that was requested of them, because everything that *was* being asked was reasonable. The chores they'd been allocated were fair, and Raymond was thoroughly enjoying learning about the sea, while Rosalie was enjoying learning absolutely everything Beth could think of to teach her that might help her once she landed in France. This included further mastery of reading and writing, basic number work, and how to dye beautiful silver-blonde hair a hideous mud-brown colour.

Beth had intended to wait until they were a day or so from their destination before attempting to disguise her most outstanding feature, but an incident which occurred in the first couple of days of the voyage made her revise her plan.

Having been told by Elizabeth that she wore men's clothing when at sea, Beth had had a pair of breeches, a shirt and waistcoat made in her size, thinking that it would be wonderful to roam around the deck without cumbersome skirts blowing around her legs. She had donned her new outfit with excitement and had emerged on deck into the morning sun, managing all of thirty seconds in public view before Paul had gripped her shoulder, turned her round and marched her back into the cabin.

"What on earth are you thinking?" he said, once the door was closed. "You cannot walk around deck dressed like that!" He made a gesture with his hand that took in her outfit of green cotton breeches, cream stockings, white linen shirt with full sleeves, currently rolled up to the elbow, and a plain fitted green waistcoat.

Beth's face fell.

"Why not? Elizabeth wears men's clothing at sea, she told me so!" she countered.

"That's true, but there's a difference," Paul replied. "You must change, immediately."

"I don't see the difference," Beth persisted. "Just because she's your wife doesn't mean that—"

"Yes, it does. Partly, at least," Paul interrupted. He wiped his hand over his face. "Sit down," he said in a tone of voice that made her obey without question. "Part of the reason that Elizabeth can wear breeches and shirts on deck is because she is my wife and therefore out of bounds to any man. They all know that anyone who makes even the slightest lewd suggestion will be castrated and fed to the sharks. Yes, I have told them that the same applies with regard to you and Rosalie as well. They believe Rosalie is twelve, and her father is on board which also gives her protection, but you are a different matter."

"Why? My face looks the same whether I wear a dress or breeches. I had hoped that the scar would disfigure me, but unfortunately it's healed really well," Beth said ruefully, lifting her hand to the thin silver scar that ran from the corner of her eye into her hair.

To her astonishment Paul started laughing.

"I have never heard a woman express disappointment at not being ugly before," he said.

"You don't know how many problems it's caused me in my life," Beth replied, smiling in spite of herself at his amusement.

"Listen, I will be honest with you," he said, once he'd recovered. "I love Elizabeth, but she is not beautiful, in either face or figure. She is very thin, and when dressed in male attire resembles a young boy. Whereas you, my dear Beth, resemble an extremely beautiful young woman with the body of Venus. The male clothes only emphasise how long your legs are, how small your waist and how perfect your breasts, and were I not a monogamous man I would be unable to keep my hands off you. And I am not being denied my conjugal rights for weeks, as my crew are. I cannot allow you to walk around in front of the men dressed like that. It is unfair to them and dangerous to you. I am sorry, but I have to keep discipline and order on my ship, and you are a walking mutiny, because if, or rather when, one of my crew molests you and I throw him overboard, the others will resent that, and you."

Beth sighed. She had thought that wearing dresses would be a constant reminder that she was female, and that masculine attire would help her to blend in more. Clearly that was not the case.

"You put your point very well, Paul. I won't wear them again while on board your ship."

"I would highly recommend that you don't wear them when you are *not* on board my ship, either," Paul suggested.

The breeches and shirt were relegated to the bottom of Beth's trunk, and two days later she asked Rosalie to help her to dye her hair. Although Rosalie had learned the method and obtained the ingredients, she was at first nervous about changing the colour of her former mistress's hair, until Beth said she couldn't care less what it looked like as long as it wasn't silver-blonde any more. So, with regret, Rosalie covered Beth's lovely tresses with a paste made of crushed black walnuts, and a few hours later she appeared on deck with hair of a mud-brown colour that enhanced the blue of her eyes, but did little for her complexion.

"I thought it might help your crewmen to keep their minds on their work, and I realised that I need to know how often I'll have to dye it to keep it brown when I'm in Britain," Beth said when Paul and Elizabeth asked her why she'd done it. She hadn't told Raymond and Rosalie of her intention to travel to Britain yet, although she had decided to tell them once they landed in France.

"You do look very different," Elizabeth observed, "and I must admit that when I saw you in Fort Royal, it was your hair that drew my attention and tellt me it was you. I've never seen hair of such a pure blonde before."

Beth was very heartened by this. Hopefully it would help to

keep her safe as she travelled around the country in search of Alex.

Apart from a short period when the ship was becalmed, which resulted in some rationing of food and water, the voyage went very well until they neared the French coast, some six weeks after setting out from Martinique.

It was late afternoon on a very dull and gloomy February day. The clouds overhead were black and had been threatening rain all day, but had not as yet fulfilled that threat. Raymond and Rosalie, both on deck hoping to see the first sight of their new country, were wearing every item of clothing they possessed, and were horrified when Beth told them that it wasn't a particularly cold day for the time of year.

"I did warn you that you would struggle with the cold, not being accustomed to it," Beth said sympathetically.

"We…we will become accustomed to it," Raymond said through chattering teeth. He was shaking as though he had the ague. "It is better than being a slave. If we remember that, then everything else will be easy to deal with."

Beth smiled. That was a very good way of thinking about things.

"When will we see France, Monsieur le Capitan?" Rosalie asked.

Paul, standing a few feet away from them, didn't answer, being preoccupied with looking through his spyglass at the distant mist-drenched horizon.

"*Merde,*" he said softly.

"What is it?" Elizabeth asked, coming to stand beside him.

"A British ship," he said. "She is some way off, but she's seen us."

"Can we fight her?"

"No, my bloodthirsty bride, we cannot fight her," he replied. "Well, we can, but there is nothing to gain by doing so, and much to lose, not least our lives." He handed her the spyglass, and addressed Beth, Raymond and Rosalie, who had overheard the conversation and were looking very anxious.

"She is a frigate with thirty-two guns to our eighteen; and we don't know if there are more ships with her that are not in sight yet. Don't worry, my friends," he said to his three passengers, "we are in little danger. As long as we stay leeward of them, we should be able to outrun them. And they may lose interest when they see we are a lone ship. They will be looking out for fleets of merchant ships trying to enter or leave France. A single brig will hopefully not be interesting enough to chase."

He shouted a series of sharp orders across the deck, which resulted in a great flurry of activity from the crew. Raymond disappeared below decks, having been beckoned by a crew member. "But we will take precautions, just in case," Paul added, winking at Rosalie, who looked absolutely petrified. "Do not fear, mademoiselle," he said. "I will get us safely into port, but I think you should go below decks now. Not because anything terrible is about to happen," he added quickly, on seeing her eyes widen even further, "but because it is about to rain very heavily."

Sure enough within a few minutes the rain began, reducing visibility even further. Beth accompanied Rosalie to the cabin, but returned to the deck a couple of minutes later. The rain was sweeping across it in sheets.

"I'm accustomed to rain," she said to Paul as she went to stand by him on the quarter deck. She pushed her dripping hair off her face. "I lived in Scotland for a time."

He nodded, but continued to watch the approaching ship.

"Can we outrun her?" Beth asked.

"Yes," Paul replied, "depending on the wind. Right now she is out of cannon range, and I intend to keep it that way. My concern is that she is unlikely to be alone, and if another frigate comes upon us from, say, that direction," he pointed into the grey gloom, "then we would be in trouble. I had intended to take us to Calais, because I know that would be convenient for you to try to take a ship to England, but I think there is a strong likelihood that if I continue with that course, we will be intercepted. Would it inconvenience you terribly if I were to make for Rochefort instead?"

Beth had no idea where Rochefort was, but the extreme politeness of his request under what could rapidly become desperate straits, made her laugh.

"Captain Marsal," she replied formally. "As long as I do not have to see a smirking redcoat or the inside of an English prison before I've had a chance to look for my husband, you can make for the moon if you wish."

"I don't think it will come to that, my dear. Rochefort it is. It is a good way south of Calais, but I will provide you with the means to travel north. Have you told Raymond and Rosalie of your intentions yet?"

"No," Beth replied. "I thought I would wait until we land. I think they'll want to come with me, but of course that is impossible. I expect to spend a little time in France helping them become acquainted with their new home though."

"But you do not wish to," he said.

She didn't. Now she was so close to home, she didn't want to waste another moment doing anything but searching for news of her husband. Every part of her wanted to find out, once and for all, if Alex was alive or dead. *In my heart I want him to be alive so badly, I'm starting to convince myself that he is,* she realised. She must not allow herself to believe that. If she did and he *was* dead, then she might never recover. And while she would have to take chances, she could not afford to be reckless in her haste. She had to be patient, a quality she had never really possessed.

"I am responsible for them," she said, evading answering his question. "I will see them settled before I leave them."

Paul smiled.

"Well, we will see. Let us make land before we plan further. Now, I suggest you go below. You can do nothing here, and I think you will have a surfeit of bad weather in the weeks to come. Enjoy the comfort of a dry cabin while you can." He made one of his elaborate bows, and, recognising it as a dismissal, Beth took his advice and made her way back to the cabin.

By the time night fell they were a good way ahead of the British ship, but Paul mounted a double night watch, taking the first shift himself along with Raymond. When he came into the cabin shortly before midnight, drenched to the skin, he was surprised to find the three female occupants still awake, and lanterns lit. They were playing cards in an attempt to while away the time, and as he opened the door they all looked up at him as one.

He walked in dressed only in breeches, his hair trailing in sodden rats' tails down his back.

"Ach, ye're drookit, man!" Elizabeth said, abandoning the cards and going over to a chest. She took out a cloth and threw it to him and he started rubbing himself down briskly, in an attempt to both dry and warm himself.

"I apologise for my state of undress, ladies," he said politely. "My other clothes are in the galley where it is warmer, although I doubt that they'll dry before I have to go back on deck. I assume you're all awaiting a weather and pursuit report?"

"We can tell the weather report by looking at you," Beth replied drily, "but yes, what of the pursuit?"

"We were still well ahead of the frigate when I saw it last, but the rain means visibility is very poor. As long as no other ships converge on us, we will make land safely, sometime tomorrow, maybe the day after, God willing."

"At Rochefort," Beth said.

"Yes. It's a good choice given our present circumstances, because Rochefort is a French naval base, and it is inland – we will have to travel six leagues along the river to get there, which means that there is no danger of the British firing on us in the harbour. They will not pursue us once we reach the river mouth. It will be too risky for them, and as we are only one small boat they will leave off chasing us. I am sure of it. My men will rouse me if there is need. So we can all sleep soundly tonight. Goodnight to you, ladies."

He set a good example by putting his nightshirt on, stripping his breeches off underneath, getting into bed and falling asleep immediately.

"I assume he's telling us the truth, then," Beth remarked, amused.

"Aye, probably, although he slept like that when we were being chased by four Dutch ships too," Elizabeth replied. "But, truth or no, we canna do anything by no' sleeping, I'm thinking." It was good advice, and they all followed it.

They sailed into the port of Rochefort two days later, having successfully shaken off the British ship and negotiated the serpentine loops of the Charente River. As they were unloading the cargo, the crew discovered that in the previous October there had been a second major naval battle at sea between the British and French, that the British had won a resounding victory and were now blockading France's colonies, with the result that Martinique, among other French possessions, was unable to receive or send any provisions at all.

"It seems that we left Martinique at the perfect time," Paul said. "I think God is looking kindly on us. And it means that we will get a very good price for our sugar. Raymond; myself and the crew have had a meeting, and decided that you have worked so hard during this voyage you deserve an equal share of the proceeds."

Raymond, astounded, started to protest that he had worked much slower than the others, but Elizabeth interrupted him.

"Never say no to money, laddie," she advised him. "They wouldna offer it if they didna think ye deserved it. Just say thank you."

"Thank you, monsieur," Raymond said, his eyes shining at the thought of actually earning money for working, a completely new concept to him.

Beth looked on, worried, and later approached Paul to express her concerns.

"Yes, I think they have a good deal to learn if they are not to be taken advantage of most cruelly," Paul agreed. "But they are very fast learners. They have expressed their intention to travel to Paris, and Elizabeth and I have decided to travel with them and to make sure they are settled properly once there, so that you can set off on your quest as soon as you want. My wife wishes to see the city of my birth, and I very much desire to show it to her. I think a visit to Versailles will be a wonderful experience for her, and a chance for her to display her finery."

Beth smiled.

"It will indeed," she said. "She will love it there, I think. I have never seen anything like it, before or since."

"I forgot, you have been there, several times. Will you then accompany us? Paris is after all, en route to Calais, in a manner of speaking."

"I'll gladly accompany you part of the way," Beth replied. "But I cannot come to Paris itself, no. Even with my hair as it is there is a good chance I would be recognised and that it would be reported both to King Louis and the Elector that I am not in fact dead. Unfortunately part of Sir Anthony's persona was to be at the very centre of every gathering, which meant we were extremely visible to the whole court."

"Ah, that is a shame, for I would like very much to show you some of the beautiful places you certainly will not have seen. But *c'est la vie!* At least we will have the pleasure of your company for a few more days. I am sorry that I cannot help you to travel to England. But I dare not put my men in such danger – they would not agree if I suggested it in any case, and I have no contacts that I can call on who would be willing to attempt such a voyage."

"I think I do have such a contact," Beth replied, hoping that was true. "I will find a way."

"Indeed, I believe you shall. You have the most remarkable will, although I urge you to be very careful. But first you must tell Rosalie and Raymond that you do not intend to stay in France."

He was right. She had put it off because she was dreading it. She was sure they would want to come with her, and she had to dissuade them whilst giving them as little information as possible, for their own sakes as well as hers. But the time had come. Better to get it over with.

"But I thought that we were all going to stay together, maybe live in Paris!" Rosalie cried when Beth told her and her father that in a few days they would have to separate.

"Are you not then a friend of the king?" Raymond asked.

"No. Well, that is, I am acquainted with the king, although I wouldn't call him a friend. Part of what I told Pierre was true, and part of the gossip also, which I know you overheard, Raymond," Beth said. "My husband and I did visit Paris, and he did fight a duel and kill a servant of the king's. But it was not because I was having an affair with him. Louis certainly showed an interest in me, but I would never have been unfaithful to Sir Anthony."

"Because you loved him," Rosalie said, sighing wistfully. Beth smiled. Soon she would be sighing over her own first love. Hopefully he would be deserving of her.

"Yes," Beth confirmed. "I cannot come to Paris, because I would be recognised."

"But you told Monsieur Pierre that you were travelling to Paris to find out whether your husband was alive or not," Raymond said. "Do you not then intend to seek him out? And followers of your King James are in no danger in France, are they? So why do you not wish to be recognised?"

She had hoped he would not know that. But of course he did. How many years had he spent standing silent and unobserved in the background while the society of Martinique gossiped about the latest news from France? He probably knew almost as much about the Jacobite rising as she did.

She was silent for a moment, while she pondered how much she could tell them. Not Sir Anthony's true identity; she would never tell anyone who didn't already know that. But she could trust them with her own secrets.

"It is very important that I not be recognised. I did not tell Pierre the truth," she said. "When I was with the marquis in Martinique, I asked him to add my name to the list of those who died on the voyage. The authorities in England believe that I'm dead. It's crucial that I am not recognised by anyone who may pass on the information that I am very much alive."

Raymond's brow crinkled in a puzzled frown.

"I am not staying in France, Raymond," Beth said. "It is unlikely that my husband will be in Paris, or that there will be any news of him there. I intend to travel to England, and once there I will be able to find out whether my husband is alive or not, because I will go to people who *will* know."

"This is why you wished to change the colour of your hair," Rosalie said. "It was not because of the sailors."

"No, it was not, although I think it helped. My hair colour is the reason I was arrested – I was recognised by the…by an enemy. It will help me, I think, when I go back. And I will keep away from London, where I am also well known."

Raymond smiled.

"Now I understand," he said. "You cannot take us to England, because if you do we will draw attention, being black, and that will be dangerous for you."

"Yes, and for you too. France and Britain are at war. I think you will be safer here, and happier too. You speak French, not English, and can make a good life here. Paul has told me that he intends to see you settled, which reassures me. I will miss you. But I have to do this."

"And if your husband is dead? You also have no intention to make Monsieur Pierre the happiest of men?" Raymond asked.

Beth laughed.

"No, I have no intention of ever going back to Martinique. I would die first."

"This is very good news to me, Beth, because Monsieur Pierre was not a good man, and not a man who would make you happy," Raymond said.

"What will you then do, if the news is bad?" Rosalie asked.

"I will stay with the people who are dearest to me, and make the best life I can without my husband. But I cannot tell you where that will be."

"But how will we know if you find him?" Rosalie cried. "I couldn't bear not to know!"

"Hush, child," Raymond said to his daughter. "You have borne many things worse than this. We will trust in fate. But I would ask you to make me one promise, please?" he added, turning back to Beth.

"If I can, I will, yes," she said.

"I would ask you to wear the amulet that I gave you at all times, until you are safe," he said earnestly. "I spoke true to you when I said that it gives very strong protection."

She smiled, and reaching up to her neck, touched the leather thong that the charm was strung on.

"It has carried me this far safely," she said. "I promise you, I will not take it off until I am safe. And I will treasure it for the rest of my life."

"That makes me very happy. Now, let us enjoy the days we have left as we travel together, and we will not speak of this again."

Later, in bed in the room in Rochefort they had taken for a few nights while the arrangements to sell the cargo were made, she held the amulet in her hand and looked at it by candlelight. It was a strange thing, ugly and beautiful at the same time. Could it really protect her?

People of her faith wore crosses or medallions of their favourite saints for protection. It was not something she had ever done, mainly because she had spent most of her life in a country where it was unwise to advertise her faith. She remembered her mother's rosary, how precious it had been to her, doubly so after Alex had rescued it from the fire for her, for it had reminded her of two of the people she had loved most in the world. That was lost to her forever. But she had this strange little carving to remind her of Paul and Elizabeth, who had become true friends, and of Raymond and Rosalie, who loved her, and who she had come to care deeply for as well.

And I will need all the protection I can get in the next weeks, she told herself. *It can do no harm to wear it.* She smiled and tucked it back inside her nightdress. Then she lay down and went to sleep almost immediately, relishing the feeling of being out of danger.

It was an unfamiliar feeling, and one she would not enjoy for long.

* * *

Calais, France, February 1748

As Beth walked around the Courgain district of Calais, she realised she had a problem. Well, in fact she had a lot of problems, but only one that was immediate.

She couldn't remember the full name of the tavern that Gabriel Foley stayed in when engaged in smuggling operations in France. This was because it had only been mentioned to her once, and that in passing, by Duncan, some four years ago. She had racked her brain all night after arriving in Calais and taking a room in a mid-range area of town, one where she was unlikely to encounter any wealthy travellers of her acquaintance from her time as Lady Elizabeth Peters, but equally one where she was unlikely to be robbed and murdered the second she walked out of the door.

The tavern she was looking for had the word 'cat' in it; that was all she remembered. She had asked the hotel concierge if he knew of such a tavern, and he had replied that he knew of several, and asked why she wanted to know.

She could hardly say that she wanted to meet a notorious leader of a gang of smugglers to enquire about passage to England, so she told him that she'd been advised it was an excellent place to eat, but she could not remember the colour of the cat in question.

The concierge had informed her that there were several inns with the word 'cat' in them, but none of the ones he knew of were particularly fine eating establishments, and the three that were in the fisherman's quarter would not be safe for a young lady to frequent, no matter how fine the cuisine. He had helpfully recommended a number of excellent eating establishments in the direct vicinity of the hotel though, with the result that she was at least possessed of a full stomach as she entered the area he had told her was unsafe, the one she thought Gabriel most likely to be found in.

Three taverns.

She was dressed poorly, in a rough shapeless woollen dress and a shawl which she had wrapped round her head and shoulders against the cold, and to hide her face as much as possible. In her pocket she had a few sols, and in her shoe a couple of livres in case she needed to bribe a tavern keeper.

The first one she came upon was 'Le Chat Bleu', as proclaimed by a rusty sign hanging outside. She took a breath, braced herself and went through the door. Although it was only just twilight, the place was doing a good trade and was full of what, by the smell, were indeed fishermen, confirming that she was definitely in the right area, at least.

Not the right inn though, by the looks of it. There was a considerable lull in the conversation as she marched belligerently into the room, scanning it as though looking for a familiar face, which was exactly what she was doing.

"Can I help you?" the landlord asked.

"Yes. If that lazy drunken pig of a husband of mine is here, you can tell him if he isn't home by the time the clock strikes the hour, he can find another place to sleep tonight."

"You are not from these parts," he said, recognising that she had an accent, but not that she was English. All the nights spent listening carefully to Raymond and Rosalie's accents were hopefully about to pay off.

"No. We came in from Martinique a couple of months ago," she said. "Thought he could be a great sugar planter, the fool. All he got was swamp fever. Jacques Fernier, about so high," she raised her hand a few inches above her head, "thin, cross-eyed, ugly bastard. Black hair." She peered into the corners of the room, frowning.

"I don't know anyone of that description, Madame Fernier," the man said, which was not really surprising, as Beth had made it up on the spot. "But if such a man comes in, I'll tell him what you said."

Back in the street, she heaved a sigh of relief. Neither the landlord nor any of the customers appeared to doubt either her story or her accent. It was a good start. Unfortunately none of the customers resembled either Gabriel Foley or any of the accomplices she remembered. One down. Of course he might not be in Calais at all. In fact he was more likely to be in England. She had not seen or heard of him in over two years. He might have acquired new associates, stopped smuggling, be in prison, or dead.

She would not think like that. She had all evening. Her story had been believed and could be used in every tavern in Calais, if necessary. If Foley was not to be found, then she would seek another way to cross the Channel. She continued walking around the narrow cobbled streets of the Courgain quarter. Periodically she would enter an inn that had nothing to do with cats, thinking that Foley might have changed his tavern of choice, and that at the least it would give her practice in being an aggrieved wife.

After visiting Le Chat Noir and Le Chat Rouge with no success, her spirits fell. But as she had nothing better to do with her evening than walk round freezing, refuse-littered streets looking for a fictional husband, she decided to make her way back to her room by another way.

She almost missed it. The only reason she didn't was because as she was walking past the ramshackle building someone struck a light in an upstairs window, causing her to look up and in doing so see the rusty sign stuck to the wall. It was in the shape of a heraldic device, the centre containing a vaguely oval shape which had once been a seated cat. Beth knew that because the tail, curled round the bottom of the oval shape, was distinctly feline. Underneath was painted in faded yellow lettering 'Le Chat D'Or'.

There was nothing even vaguely golden about either the building or the sign. But then she remembered the unremarkable building in Blackheath where she had last seen Gabriel Foley, and took heart. Lifting the latch of the wooden door, she pushed it open and walked in.

She was greeted by an L-shaped room. To her right was a long wooden table littered with glasses and bottles, flanked by benches, on one of which lay a man, fast asleep and snoring. The other bench held a seated man who seemed to be as comatose as his companion, his head pillowed on his arms on the table. The only illumination came from a couple of candles on the table, which had been pushed into the accumulated wax drippings of many other candles to keep them upright, along with one on the bar, which was on the other side of the table. Directly ahead at the end of the L shape was a wooden staircase, the first few steps of which were visible, the rest shrouded in darkness.

Near the steps were half a dozen men, who stopped whatever they'd been doing to stare at her. This was clearly not a place in which the fictional Jacques Fernier would drink. It was, however, the place in which a beak-nosed man was, the same man who had opened the door to Beth and Maggie in England over two years previously. Beth's spirits soared, and she walked towards the group of men.

One of them, a youngish man who shared the cross-eyes of the fictitious Jacques, moved forward to intercept her.

"You're not welcome here, madame," he said in bad French.

Ignoring him, she addressed the beak-nosed man.

"I need to speak to your leader," she said in French. "Is he here?" The man took a step forward, but then the cross-eyed man moved, blocking her view of the man she'd spoken to.

"I said, you're not welcome here," he repeated in a more threatening tone.

"Yes, I heard you," Beth replied dismissively. "Please tell your leader that Mrs Abernathy wishes to see him, urgently."

The beak-nosed man's gaze drifted to the top of the stairs, and with that she knew that Gabriel Foley was indeed in the building.

"Show your face please, madame," he asked politely.

Beth unwrapped the shawl from her head, the cross-eyed man gasped with admiration, and the beak-nosed man nodded slightly and took a step toward the stairs.

"What do you want with Mr Foley?" Cross-eyes asked. "Won't I do, instead?" Beth made to move past him, but he put one hand on her shoulder to stop her, the other reaching down between her legs, grasping a fistful of skirt and cupping round her private parts.

"I ain't had a woman this week," he said, his fingers fumbling for better purchase through the thin woollen material. Then he froze as he felt the knife against his neck.

"How unfortunate for you," Beth said icily in English. "And if you don't remove both your hands from my person right now, you will never have another woman in your life, which promises to be extremely short. Please tell your leader—" She stopped as in her periphery vision she saw the man who had been leaning over the table moving towards her. Her free hand dipped in her pocket and then as fast as lightning, she threw. There came a squawk of pain and the figure moved out of her sight.

She calculated quickly. She could still hear the man on the bench snoring, and she would hear if anyone else came into the inn. So the only danger was from the man she had just wounded with her second knife. All the other occupants of the room were in sight apart from the beak-nosed man, who had disappeared whilst she was preoccupied with the cross-eyed man and who she assumed had gone upstairs. She palmed her third knife, ready to use it if she had to.

The cross-eyed man had acquiesced to her demand and was no longer touching her. He made to step away from the knife at his throat, but she pressed it up under his chin and he froze again.

"I don't know how important this man is to you, but if you want him to stay alive, none of you will move," she said.

"His importance depends on whether he has a good explanation for assaulting a young woman who has come asking to see me, without first finding out whether she was under my protection," came a deep voice from the top of the stairs. A pair of strong legs encased in fine woollen breeches and cream stockings came into view, followed by the broad chest and thick arms of Gabriel Foley. "Put the knife away, please, Mrs Abernathy."

Beth removed the blade from the chin of her assailant and replaced it in her pocket.

"Now," Gabriel said, "do you have a good explanation, Michael?"

"She didn't mention you by name, Mr Foley!" Michael said. "I didn't know that she knew you! I just thought she was some whore looking for business!"

Gabriel nodded thoughtfully, and looked to Beth.

"I didn't use your name, because I didn't know if it would compromise you in any way to do so," Beth explained. "I recognised the face of your man there," she pointed to the beak-nosed man, who had come back down the stairs and resumed his position with the others, "and asked to see his leader, hoping that it would be you. If it hadn't been, I had a plausible reason ready."

"I see. So then, Michael, can you explain why, if you thought this lady to be a common whore, you saw fit to divulge my name to her for her to spread around the streets of Calais along with the pox. No disrespect intended, Mrs Abernathy."

"None taken, sir," Beth replied, highly amused.

Michael flushed red.

"I...er...I..." he stammered.

"Let me help you," Gabriel said conversationally. "You seem to have two choices. One: you have no respect for women who ask to see me and may therefore be my friends, and by extension have no respect for me. Two: you think it reasonable to give my name to any random person who walks into the room, therefore risking the arrest and execution of all of us. Which is it?"

There was a ghastly silence, while Michael's complexion changed from scarlet to white.

"You seem to have lost your tongue," Gabriel said when the silence seemed set to go on forever. "No matter. I don't really need an answer."

Michael started to smile, his face showing utmost relief, and then Gabriel's right arm moved forward and the smile froze. The young man's eyes widened and then became glassy as he fell to the ground. Gabriel looked down at him briefly, then bent and wiped his bloody knife on the man's shirt. He stood up and smiled at Beth, who, with a considerable and hopefully invisible effort of will, smiled back.

"Get rid of him," he said to the room in general, then gestured to Beth to precede him up the stairs. She walked towards the steps, then turned back to look at the man who had moved behind her, who was holding a reddened cloth over his face.

"Are you badly injured?" she asked. "I'm sorry, but when I saw you move I couldn't take the chance that you weren't going to hit me."

"No," the man said hurriedly, his voice muffled by the cloth.

"It's only a flesh wound. I'll be fine."

She turned back and went up the steps, noticing that Gabriel had paused to exchange a few words with the beak-nosed man before following her.

"Second door on the right," he said quietly. She opened the door and went in, noting with pleasure that, unlike the main room downstairs, which had been as cold as the street, this room was warmly lit by a brazier burning in one corner. There was a table with two chairs under the window and a mattress with some blankets in another corner. She heard the door close behind her and turned to see Gabriel standing with his back to it, the pistol in his hand pointed at her heart.

"I mean no offence, Mrs Abernathy, but having just heard of your ability with knives, I'd be obliged if you would take yours out of your pocket very slowly and hand it to me," he said.

Understandable. She obeyed him, and he took it from her. The pistol didn't move.

"Do you have any more about your person?" he asked. On seeing her hesitate, he spoke again. "I will say now that I mean you no harm, and although I have no idea why you have come to see me, or in fact how you knew I could be found here, I will endeavour to assist you in whatever business you have, within reason. If you are honest with me, I will be with you."

In a moment, he had accepted two more knives from her, then he invited her to sit down and poured two glasses of brandy, handing one to her before sitting in the vacant chair.

"Before we discuss your reason for being here, may I ask if you intended to kill the man, or merely wound him as you did when you threw the knife?" he asked.

"I intended to warn him not to come any closer by throwing the knife past his nose. But I only saw him from the corner of my eye and had to keep my gaze on Michael, so my aim was inaccurate," Beth said.

Gabriel whistled softly and admiringly between his teeth.

"Is he badly hurt?" she asked.

"No. You have taken a small slice off his nose, that's all. Remarkable. You are clearly not a lady to be trifled with, Mrs Abernathy."

"No more are you, Mr Foley."

He smiled and raised his glass to hers.

"Now, I assume that you have dyed your hair to that hideous colour because you wish your identity to remain a secret. Firstly, I must ask you the question which concerns me most closely, however, being of a somewhat selfish character. How did you know where to find me?"

"I didn't, really. A long time ago one of my husband's friends was trying to contact you. When he came back, unsuccessful, he told me that it was because you were in Calais, and mentioned the name of the tavern you frequented. I was the only person he mentioned it to," she added. "I thought it of no importance at the time, and when it became of importance I could only remember that the tavern bore the name of some sort of cat. I have spent the evening going to every possible colour of cat inn, hoping to see someone I recognised. I had no idea whether you were even in the country. I just hoped you might be."

Gabriel nodded.

"So, you are in luck. I am here. What is it you'd like me to assist you with?"

"Before I tell you, can I ask if you have seen Mr Abernathy recently?" she asked. She tried to keep the eagerness from her voice, but his change of expression told her that she hadn't completely succeeded in doing so.

"I regret to say that the last meeting I had with anyone of your acquaintance was when you yourself came with your cook to warn me. The payment for the arms was made, and since then I have had no dealings with your husband at all."

"Would you tell me if you had?" she asked.

Gabriel laughed, a rich, deep, infectious laugh.

"If I had, Mrs Abernathy, I would have asked you why you wished to know, but as I haven't, I can tell you the truth immediately."

"Then I do wish to ask you for help, sir. I need to travel to England, secretly. I can pay you for your assistance," she said.

He waved his hand in dismissal, but she didn't know of what.

"I assume then that you intend to look for your husband. Does he want you to look for him?"

"If he is alive, I'm sure he does," she said. "I mean to find out if he is alive or dead."

"And you came to France because you thought him to be here?"

"No." She hesitated for a minute, thinking of how to tell him enough to make him help her, but not enough to allow him to identify her, and through that, Alex. *If you are honest with me, I will be with you.*

"I cannot tell you how I come to be in France, only because it might endanger my husband to do so. Let me only say that I am here involuntarily, and that if I can get back to England, I will never contact you in any way again, under any circumstances. And I must tell you before you decide whether or not to help me, that I cannot return openly to England and there is danger to you if I am discovered in your company."

"That's more honesty than I expected," Gabriel said. "It seems not to be in my interest to assist you! However, danger isn't something that unduly worries me. If it did, I would not be in the line of business I am."

Beth smiled.

"But the risks you take are calculated," she said. "So it's only fair to tell you that there is risk to being discovered helping me, so that you can decide if you wish to."

"And if I say no, what would you do? Would you abandon your attempt to cross to England?"

"No," she replied. "I will do whatever I have to to return. I would row across the Channel if I was capable. If you cannot help me, then I will seek another way."

"Even though it would be very dangerous for you to do so?"

"Danger is not something that unduly worries me, Mr Foley," she said.

He laughed again.

"In approximately four days," he said, "weather permitting, a sloop will be going to England. It will contain four hundred casks of very fine French brandy. Or, if you wish, four hundred casks of very fine French brandy, and one cask of Mrs Abernathy. It won't be very comfortable for you, but I can make sure there is sufficient air for you to breathe, food and drink, and blankets to cushion you from any injury. You will be my personal cask of brandy.

I will be accompanying the sloop, so will make sure that you arrive safely, failing shipwreck or being boarded by the navy, in which case it will be every man or woman for themselves. And as I cannot trust every member of the crew, this being a joint venture as it were, concealing you in a barrel will mean only a very few people will need to know you are aboard at all, which will be safer for you. Do you have accommodation in Calais?"

"Yes," she said, surprised by the question.

"Good. One of my trusted men will escort you home. Take a couple of days to think about it, if you wish."

"I have already made my decision," Beth said. "I will come with you. If I can afford it. What is your price?"

"Do you remember the last time we met?" Gabriel asked.

"Yes, of course I do."

"Well, because of your courage and consideration in riding to warn me, both myself and several of my men are sitting here free, instead of swinging from a noose at Tyburn. You have paid for your voyage in advance, Mrs Abernathy. I only wish it could be more comfortable for you. But it will be better than swimming, at least, especially at this time of year. Keep whatever funds you have to help you in your search for your husband. I truly hope you find him. He is as remarkable a man as you are a woman."

"I could say the same for you, too, Mr Foley. Thank you," Beth said.

"You are most welcome. And now that you have an interest in keeping me alive, you may have your knives back. May I trouble you for a demonstration of your throwing skills?"

Beth was only too happy to oblige, with the result that twenty minutes later, while she was being escorted back to her room by the beak-nosed man, Gabriel Foley was standing before a very indifferent oil painting of a bowl of fruit, which now had a slit through the stem of the apple, the very centre of the orange, and the thin blue stripe decorating the earthenware bowl the fruit was in. He shook his head in admiration.

"A shame you're so devoted to your husband, Mrs Abernathy," he said softly to himself. "You would make a wonderful Mrs Foley, otherwise."

Back in her room Beth went to bed, happier than she had been in a long time. She felt a little sorry for Michael, but only a very little, managing to dismiss him from her mind with ease. She lay for a time, planning. Once she landed in England, she would make her way north as quickly as possible, taking the cheapest form of wheeled transport possible, and staying in indifferent inns. The chances of her meeting anyone who knew her were infinitesimal, and as she was believed to be dead there would be no descriptions of her in circulation.

She turned her mind to Paris, wondering how Paul, Elizabeth, Raymond and Rosalie were. Their final farewell had been heartrending, all the more so because they all knew that the likelihood of them ever meeting again was very remote. Beth had given Rosalie the beautiful turquoise dress which she had tried on in Martinique, and which matched the ribbons that had resulted in the scars she carried on her back.

"When you are settled in Paris, I would like you to wear this dress and go to the opera one night, or to a play if you prefer, and think of me, as I will think of you," Beth had said.

Rosalie had promised faithfully that she would do that, and that she would treasure the dress forever, and one day would tell her children about the wonderful lady who had given her and her father their freedom.

Beth fingered the amulet that she still wore around her neck, and that she would continue to wear, as she had promised Raymond. It had served her well so far. She had not really expected to find Gabriel Foley in Calais; she had only attempted to do so because she had thought the slight chance that he would be there worth the effort of searching.

She had thought that when she left her friends the unbearable loneliness would descend on her again. But even though she had been alone since the coach carrying her had turned the corner on the outskirts of Paris, taking her new friends away from her forever, she was not lonely.

She had a purpose, and while she could actively follow it she would not be lonely. She refused to contemplate how she would feel were she to find out Alex was indeed dead.

Take therefore no thought for the morrow: for the morrow shall take thought for the things of itself. Sufficient unto the day is the evil thereof.

Wise words, and ones she intended to follow. She turned over in the narrow bed, and still grasping the amulet in her hand, went to sleep.

CHAPTER SIXTEEN

Scotland, March 1748

The two groups of MacGregor men had jogged steadily for a few miles, but now that they were nearing home they slowed to a walk, chatting whilst eating their provisions of bread and cheese, and handing round a couple of flasks of ale they'd taken from the redcoats they'd encountered the previous day, who were now sleeping peacefully and eternally under a foot of peat and some carefully arranged heather.

Angus brought up the rear with all but three of the clansmen who were still engaged in the business of ambushing British soldiers, either for the sheer love of killing the enemy, or in the fulfilment of the blood oath they'd sworn. A few months ago they had finally abandoned the *feileadh mòr* in favour of the legal breeches and stockings. They still carried illegal arms, of course; but if a large group of redcoats was to appear on the horizon, they would have time to abandon them in the heather and gorse, becoming a small group of innocent Campbells out hunting for food and unlikely to be arrested. Since the Act of Grace had been passed in June the military presence had been scaled back somewhat, and those soldiers who were still stationed in Inversnaid, Fort William and the other barracks were no longer raiding the villages and isolated homesteads with the frequency and savagery they had eighteen months previously.

Which was making it harder, though not impossible for the MacGregors to find redcoats to kill. Angus had already decided that as soon as they reached the requisite number to call the oath fulfilled, he would tell Alex that he wanted to stop the ambushes.

He had changed in the last months, partly due to becoming a father, partly due to the sheer weariness of killing, and partly because of the three men walking together in front of his group.

Alone of all the clan, Alex, Iain and Kenneth had opted to continue wearing the illegal belted tartan kilt of the Highlander which would identify them immediately as outlaws even from a distance, and which they could not abandon in the heather and gorse.

This was the outward demonstration of an inner problem that Angus had been thinking on since shortly after his brother had returned from France the previous October. At first Angus had been overjoyed to see Alex back with his clan. The first thing he'd done of course was to show off Alex's new nephew and namesake, about which Alex had been genuinely delighted. Then he had told him the clan news, and the decisions he'd made as stand-in chieftain.

Alex had called a clan meeting the day after he'd returned, had accepted the commiserations about Beth's death coolly and then had changed the subject before anyone could request details about what had happened in London, instead telling them about his visit with Lochiel and Charles, and stating that he now believed any chance of a further attempt at restoring the Stuarts was minimal, but that for himself he intended to continue killing redcoats until his oath was fulfilled, after which he would decide what to do next.

And then Alex had retired behind a wall of emotionless detachment that no one, in spite of numerous attempts, had managed to breach in five months. Outside of conducting clan business, which he did as efficiently as ever, he never laughed, rarely smiled, spoke only when necessary and spent the evening hours staring into the fire, his face hard and devoid of expression.

Initially Angus and Morag had thought to remain in Alex's house after his return. There was certainly enough room for them all and Alex had told them they were welcome to stay. But the change in the MacGregor chieftain was so profound it cast a gloomy atmosphere over the household, so that after a couple of weeks of attempting and failing to engage him in conversation, or indeed in anything of a light-hearted nature, they had moved out, leaving him to stare into the fire alone of an evening.

Now, listening to the laughter and chatter of the men with him, and contrasting it with the grim silence of Alex, Kenneth and Iain ahead, Angus felt the unbearable sadness that comes from watching someone you love profoundly die by degrees, whilst being helpless to prevent it. In fact, this was even worse than that, for Alex, still young, strong and physically healthy, might well live for many years. But inside he was all but dead, and Angus could see no way to bring him back to life again. He had thought about it all through the long winter nights, and had discussed it with his wife, already pregnant with their second child. Neither of them could come up with any solution.

Finally he had gone to see Kenneth, who had listened intently while Angus poured out his worries about his brother and his concerns for the clan. He ended up saying more than he'd intended to; but then Kenneth had always been there for him, solid, dependable and completely trustworthy, and had loved and protected him for as long as he could remember, whenever Alex or Duncan had not been around to do so.

"Duncan's dead, and I've come to terms with that now," Angus had told the older man, "but Alex isna, yet I feel like I'm grieving for him as though he is. What can we do to make him happy again?"

Kenneth had smiled, but without humour.

"Ye canna do anything for him, laddie, no more than ye can do anything for Iain, or myself for that matter, although I'm a different case frae they two. Iain and Alex are just passing their time here until they can join Maggie and Beth. It's worse for Alex, for he had the hope of her being alive, and he canna find a way back from the second blow, except for the killing. It's the only thing keeping him going, the hate. I can understand that, for I've felt it myself."

"But you've laughed and danced since…" Angus hesitated, afraid to speak the name no one ever uttered to the giant MacGregor's face.

"Since Jeannie died. Aye, I have. And sometimes I've felt the pleasure of being alive, and felt guilty for it because the woman I loved is in the grave, and I put her there, which makes it worse, although I ken it had to be done. I'm about ready to move on wi' my life now, though. But they two, no, they canna do it, and it grieves me too, but there's nothing to be done."

"So why are you still wearing the kilt, and still keeping wi' them on a raid, if ye can move on? Ye ken the danger of wearing the tartan, man."

Kenneth had stood then and clasped Angus by the shoulder, gently for him, although it still left bruises.

"Because they're fighting recklessly with no regard for their lives, and perhaps it would be kinder to let them die in battle, but I canna do it. I'm protecting them as best I can, and praying every night that they'll find a reason to live other than hate. Ye'll no' be telling them that, though."

Angus hadn't told them that. But it had made him love Kenneth even more than he already did, and it reassured him that the giant clansman was still looking after Alex and by doing so was looking after him too. Because as damaged as Alex was, Angus could not imagine a life without him in it. He had always had a somewhat unrealistic belief that he and his two brothers would grow up together, get married, have children who played and squabbled with each other, and then, in some far-off distant future, surrounded by grandchildren, would die, old and fulfilled.

Duncan's death had shaken that belief badly. But until last October he had still had Alex. There must be something he could do to get him back. He would think of a way. He had to think of a way.

But now, as they made their way along the track that led to home, the snow melting and winter turning to a watery spring, Angus was still no closer to finding a way to breach Alex's formidable emotional defences.

About two miles from home they were met by Lachlan and Jamie.

"What's amiss?" Alex, the first to reach them, asked.

"Nothing!" Lachlan replied. "It's just Ma sent us to see how far away ye were, that's all. *Isd!*" he added to Jamie who, hopping from one foot to the other with excitement, had been about to speak.

"Well, it's clearly something then," Alex observed.

"It is," said the irrepressible Jamie. "But Ma said she'd hang me from the roof beam an I tellt ye."

"Then ye mustna tell me," Alex said. "Learning when to keep a secret is a very important lesson for a clansman, and I'm proud of ye for keeping silence. Away hame and tell your ma we'll be back soon."

"They could have walked back wi' us," Dougal said, the group at the rear now having caught up.

"No they couldna, because Jamie would have tellt his secret, and then been upset about it," Alex replied.

"Seems like it's good news, anyway," Angus said.

"Aye," Alex said indifferently. "Well, we'll find out soon enough."

They carried on together, six of them discussing what it might be, three of them, as was their custom, keeping their speculations, if they had any, to themselves.

When they arrived back at the settlement, the clansfolk were sitting silently on the ground near their chieftain's cottage. Janet was standing next to the bench outside Alex's house, and sitting on the seat was a very old, wizened and filthy man dressed in rags, who none of them recognised. As Alex neared them the old man made a move to stand, but Janet laid a hand on his shoulder and he subsided.

"I tellt ye," Janet said belligerently, looking up at her chieftain with tears in her eyes. "I tellt ye, but ye wouldna believe me."

Alex's brow furrowed slightly, and he looked from her to the stranger on the bench. His thin greying hair hung matted and verminous to his shoulders, he had a long unkempt beard, and the tattered remains of what had once been a shirt revealed a skeletal body covered with scars and sores, some weeping, some scabbed.

Angus stepped forward and was just about to recite the formal offer of hospitality to a stranger, as Alex showed no sign of doing so, when to his surprise his brother showed an emotion, for the first time since he had greeted his tiny namesake.

"Jesus Christ," Alex said, dropping to his knees in front of the man and clasping him very gently by the shoulders. "Simon?" With great care, he drew the man into an embrace, heedless of the suppurating wounds and the lice. "Dear God, man," he said, his voice breaking, "what have the bastards done to ye?"

The skeletal figure laid his head on his chieftain's shoulder and started to weep.

Angus looked at Janet in shock. Simon? This couldn't be Simon! Simon was at least thirty years younger than this man and stockily built, with thick brown hair. It wasn't possible that this man could be Simon.

"I tellt ye," Janet repeated, her voice almost a whisper now, tears running down her cheeks. "I tellt ye he wasna dead, that he'd come home. Ye wouldna believe me, none of ye." Her face crumpled and Kenneth moved forward, scooping her up as though she was a child and hugging her.

"It's as well ye didna say aye to me when I proposed to ye, then," he said. "I'd have made a bigamist of ye, and a cuckold o' him. We'd have had a blood feud on our hands."

"Put me down, ye big loon," she said, laughing through her tears.

Alex was talking to Simon very softly, so softly that no one else could hear what he was saying. Then he shifted position slightly, and lifted his clansman off the bench, his face registering shock at how little he weighed.

"Janet," he said. "Ye were right, lass, and I'm sorry we doubted ye. Ye'll be moving into my house until Simon's recovered." When she opened her mouth to object, he shook his head and she subsided into silence. "I've a comfortable bed, which he'll be needing, and a good fireplace wi' a chimney to keep the room warm for him. Get the bairns and the belongings ye're wanting. I'll move into your house for the present. Lachlan, away and fetch some water for warming and some cloths. Peigi, bring some of that comfrey salve of yours." Then he turned and without another word carried his fragile burden into his house, closing the door behind him.

Angus turned to the rest of the clan, who had all clearly been expecting some sort of a speech from their chieftain, a welcome for Simon, a request to know what had happened to him, a declaration of an imminent celebration for the return of a man who all of them, excepting only one, had believed to be dead and rotting or buried somewhere on Culloden Moor.

"This is wonderful," he said. "I canna believe it. I dinna think any of us can. Janet, I'll say as Alex did; I'm sorry we doubted ye, and I've never been so glad to be wrong in my life as I am right now. Away and fetch the bairns. We'll find out where Simon's been the last two years and we'll celebrate his homecoming soon enough, but let's wait until he's well enough to enjoy it too, shall we?"

There was a chorus of agreement, and then the clan dispersed. Angus knew without a doubt that by the end of the day Janet would be overwhelmed with clothes, salves, food and anything else that the others could provide to aid Simon's recovery.

Within an hour Simon had been carefully washed and shaved by Janet and Alex, his hair, which was matted beyond combing, shorn off, and all his clothes burnt, which got rid of the vermin. Then salve was applied to his sores and his bloody and infected feet were bathed in whisky, the fact that Simon was too weak to do more than moan softly at the pain that caused being noted by the company with an exchange of worried looks. Angus in the meantime made some stew. Simon, placed gently in the bed by Alex, managed two spoonsful before drifting into sleep. While Janet sat by his side, stroking his hand, Angus beckoned Alex out of the house.

"D'ye think he'll live?" Angus said bluntly as soon as they were out of earshot. "I've never seen anyone look like that and be breathing still."

"Aye, he'll live, if anything I can do will make it so," Alex replied with a ferocity that surprised Angus, who had grown accustomed to his brother speaking emotionlessly, if at all.

"Where do ye think he's been?"

"In prison," Alex said. "He tellt me so, but I'd have kent it anyway. Sarah tellt me that Beth—" He stopped abruptly and his face closed down, becoming grim and hard again.

"I wanted to say, I think it wise if the bairns stay wi' me and Morag for a few days, until Simon's a wee bit stronger," Angus said after it became apparent that Alex was not going to divulge what Sarah had told him about Beth.

"Aye, that's a good idea," Alex agreed, his voice steady again, his feelings back under control.

But for a moment he had showed emotion, then and earlier too, when he had first recognised the ancient cadaverous creature to be Simon. That was a good sign, surely? Whether it was or not,

Angus grasped onto it in the way that a drowning man would grasp at anything that floated past him.

Later in his house, as Morag bustled around cleaning and he kept an eye on Simon and Janet's two children, who were playing on the floor while he rocked the cradle containing the sleeping Sandy, Angus thought about the crack he had witnessed in Alex's seemingly impenetrable armour.

It would take time, maybe a lot of time, but the brother he had known and loved his whole life would come back to him. They just had to keep him alive long enough for that to happen.

If anyone in the clan could stop Alex being killed in a fight, the enormous red-haired Kenneth with his unnatural strength and unstoppable ferocity in battle was the one to do it. Angus would help him as best he could, and would continue to pray for something to happen to break down Alex's defences and bring him back to life again.

To paraphrase Alex, it would happen, if anything he could do would make it so.

Over the next few weeks Simon started to recover, sustained by his wife's devotion and determination and the support of the whole clan, who rallied round to make sure that the only task Janet had to concern herself about was the care of her husband. Meals were brought to the house three times a day, firewood and peat delivered, several changes of clothing were provided for when Simon was well enough to get dressed, dirty washing was taken away and returned a few days later, clean and dry, and the couple's two children, four-year-old Simon and three-year-old Jean were brought by Angus or Morag for short visits to become acquainted with the father neither of them could remember, then taken away again the moment Simon showed any sign of tiredness.

Under this deluge of care and love Simon put on a little weight and his sores started to heal, although his feet still gave cause for concern. After three weeks he could sit up and had started to show a real interest in life again, but still could put no weight on his feet.

When he'd expressed a fear that he'd never walk again to his chieftain, Alex had dismissed it, telling him that after Culloden

Lochiel had been unable to walk for a long time, but was now completely healed and leading a regiment in France.

"Ye'll walk again, laddie, dinna fash yerself," Alex said. "Give it time. You're feeling it more because we're all sound now, but Dougal took a good while to recover from his wound, and I was walking wi' a crutch for months after Culloden."

"But I wasna wounded at Culloden," Simon said. "No' even a scratch."

"Aye, ye were. The wounds and scars ye've got now are from Culloden, even if ye didna get them on the day. Ye're just a wee bit behind the rest of us in the recovery, that's all."

One day towards the end of March, when the sun actually held a little warmth in it, Alex called a clan meeting.

When everyone arrived, Simon was once again sitting on the bench, but looking considerably better than he had the last time he'd sat there. Although still very thin and with his feet bandaged, he wore a clean shirt and breeches, and had put on weight. His hair was starting to grow back, a mixture of its original brown and grey, and his eyes had life in them now.

Next to him Janet was sitting clasping his hand, and Alex stood in the doorway.

"I've called ye all together, because I ken that ye're all very curious to find out what Simon's been doing the past two years, and he tells me he's feeling strong enough now to talk about it a wee bit. If he gets tired, though, or just doesna want to talk more, I'll end the meeting and ye'll all understand why." That last was delivered as an order rather than a request. Alex knew only too well how difficult reliving traumatic experiences was, let alone talking about them to others.

The previous evening when Simon had expressed a wish to tell the others what had transpired, Alex had sat down next to him.

"Are ye sure ye're ready?" he'd said.

"Aye. Everyone's been so good and patient wi' me. They deserve to ken what happened."

Alex had not been leader of the clan for so long without getting to know his clansfolk well. It was obvious that on one level Simon felt inferior to the others in some way, partly for not having sustained a wound at Culloden, and then for allowing himself to be taken prisoner when the others had either died or escaped in spite of their injuries.

Alex had told Janet to go off and visit her children, and then had talked to Simon, who, once he had no need to put on a brave front for his wife, admitted that he was also worried he'd never be able to walk again and would be a liability to the clan for the rest of his life.

"I was so desperate to get home, that I didna think any further than that," Simon said. "Perhaps it would have been better if I hadna come back. Janet could have married again, a whole man."

"Simon, ye loon, Janet wouldna ever have married again. She was convinced ye were alive, and never wavered for a moment from that conviction. It's no' just a story she's telling ye. And I firmly believe ye'll walk again, but even if ye dinna, ye're no liability. Ye're one of the bravest men in the clan, braver than I am."

Simon had looked at his chieftain in shock.

"No," he'd started, but Alex had gently laid a finger on Simon's lips.

"It wasna your fault ye were taken. It was just bad luck. Dougal would have been taken or maybe killed, but a redcoat helped him off the field and tellt him to hide. I'd have been taken too if Angus and Kenneth hadna been there to carry me away. We all got to come home and heal together, but you've had two years of hell, man, and survived it. And how ye managed to get home, the way ye were, I canna think. There isna a one of us that doesna admire you for that. And now ye want to talk about it all."

"I should tell ye all, for ye've been so good to me," Simon said.

"Aye, well, I should tell ye all what happened to me in London in October, but I canna find the strength to do it, and I doubt I ever will," Alex said softly. "And that's why I say ye're a braver man than I am. And it's why if ye find it too hard tomorrow, ye must tell me. Promise me."

Simon had promised, and his chieftain's words to him had boosted him a little, although he still believed that Alex was just being kind, but he sat upright, and for the first time since his return found the courage to look his clansfolk in the eyes as he spoke to them.

"First I want to thank ye all for the help ye've given me and Janet these last weeks," he said. There was a general chorus of 'nae need' and 'ye'd do it for us' or words to that effect, which was true. He looked round at them and smiled shyly.

"It's time tae tell ye what happened," he said. "Alex tellt me last night that Dougal was wounded, but was rescued by a redcoat. And ye're perhaps thinking that man was the only decent one of the enemy on the field, but I owe my life to another.

"As I tellt Alex and Janet, I wasna injured at all in the battle. I dinna ken where the rest of ye were, but I ended up in a big crush of men trying to get to the redcoats, too crushed tae swing our swords even, wi' the guns o' the British playing on us. I lost my footing for a minute in the mud and went down and the others ran over the top of me. I think someone caught me in the head, for I lost a few minutes somewhere, and when I came round there was a heap of bodies on top of me, and not a one alive.

"I managed to push them off me, but when I could see what was going on, everyone was running away, and it was clear that the day was lost. I kent well that if I'd have tried to get up and run too, I'd have been dead, for the redcoats were nearby, laughing and stabbing at anything that moved or groaned. Maybe I should have at least tried to kill a few of the bastards, but I thought it better to hide and wait for them to pass on, so I could get away to Ruthven and hopefully join ye all to fight on."

"Ye did right. Ye'd have thrown your life away to little purpose otherwise," Alex said.

"Aye. So I pulled someone's body over me and lay there as still as I could, listening to the redcoats laughing and suchlike, and then after a time they moved on and I couldna hear them any more, so I thought it safe to move and see if I had a chance to escape. And when I heaved the body off me, I looked straight into the face of a soldier. I'd lost my sword when I fell, and anyway he had his bayonet ready, so I just closed my eyes and waited for him to finish me."

"But he didna?" Allan asked, his face rapt.

"Of course he didna, ye wee loon, or he'd no' be here the day," Alasdair said, to general laughter and Allan's embarrassment.

"No, he didna," Simon answered, as though the question had been perfectly reasonable. "When I opened my eyes again, he was

JULIA BRANNAN

still standing looking at me. He was nobbut a boy really, and he was a Scot, too, a lowlander by his accent. And then he said, 'I canna do it. I canna kill any more,' but soft, to himself, like. Then he asked me if I could walk, and when I said I could, he looked around and tellt me to be quick. So I got up and we both ran off behind they walls that ye said should have been pulled down to the right of us, and we sat there for a while in the rain.

"He tellt me that he hadna wanted to enlist really, but his brothers had so he felt he should too, and he wanted to stop the papist Charlie frae winning, but that he hadna kent it would be like this, and tae hell wi' the war, he was going back to Glasgow. He said he thought that if he kept his head down when he got home, it might be thought he'd died on the field, for there were so many dead it wouldna be possible to identify them all. He was a redcoat, but he was a kind young laddie."

"Aye, the dragoon who took me away, he was a good man too," Dougal said. "The redcoats were no' all bastards."

"I've met many good supporters o' the Elector in my time," Alex put in. "Two in particular, who I call friends, and would kill or die for."

At that astounding sentence from a chieftain who was currently slaughtering every redcoat he could find with neither remorse nor mercy, the whole clan as one moved their focus from Simon to Alex. He reddened slightly.

"Go on, man," he said softly to Simon.

"Aye. So we're sitting there having a wee blether and waiting for a chance to get away, when along comes another redcoat, an officer of some sort, because the puir wee laddie stood to attention and when the officer asked what the hell he was doing talking wi' the enemy, he thought fast and said that I'd surrendered to him, and that he was going to take me to Inverness as a prisoner. So the officer said that they'd been tellt to give no quarter and he must kill me and have done with it, and he drew his sword. And the laddie, Archie his name was, stood in front of me and said he couldna kill me or let anyone else, for he'd given his word of honour that he wouldna.

"And the officer tellt him he was a stupit wee loon and no' worth shit, but if he was determined, then he'd take me to Inverness wi' the other prisoners. Which tellt me that Archie

336

wasna the only one who'd refused to give no quarter. But I couldna escape then, so I was taken to Inverness wi' hundreds of others. I'll never forget that laddie, though. I hope he got back to Glasgow."

"So is that where ye've been, Inverness?" Dougal asked.

Simon shook his head, and wiped his hand across his face.

"Have ye had enough?" Alex said, instantly concerned.

"No, I'm well, just a wee bit tired, but I'd rather tell it all, now I've started," Simon replied. "There's no' so much to tell, really. When we got to Inverness there wasna any room in the prison, so we were put on a ship. A man came and asked our names and regiments, and I said I was Simon Anderson and that I'd fought under Glenbucket's, because I kent I couldna say my name was MacGregor.

"We were kept on the ship for a long time it seemed, and then we were tellt we were being taken to Newcastle for trial, but when the ship got there we couldna stay, I dinna ken why, so we carried on to Tilbury. And then we thought we'd at least get to go on shore, but we were kept on the ship. I canna begin to tell ye how bad it was," he said.

"Ye dinna need to," Angus commented. "We saw ye three weeks ago."

Simon shook his head.

"No, it was worse than ye can imagine. I was one of the lucky ones," he said. "We were kept in the hold, and at first there was so many of us we couldna lie down. We werena allowed up on deck at all, and we had to piss and shit where we were. The food was thrown down to us and we just had water to drink, and not enough of that. Then the fever came and it took a lot of us, so once the bodies had been taken away those of us left could lie down, at least. When the guards leaned in to throw the food down to us, you could hear them retching from the stink, but we'd grown used to it then and we couldna smell ourselves, thank God.

"When we got to Tilbury and they tellt us that we were staying in the ships until our trials, I prayed harder than I ever have that I'd get the fever too, because I couldna stand the thought of living worse than an animal for months, maybe years, only to be hung at the end of it."

"I'm glad that ye didna get it. Ye mean the gaol fever?" Alex said.

"Aye. I did get it, though, but I didna die. I've never felt such pain in my life. I thought my head was going to burst open, and all my body was on fire. I thought I'd died at one point, and was in hell. But then I got well again, and realised that I was alive, but it was hell all the same.

"One day a soldier came, and they brought us up on deck. Some of the men couldna manage to crawl up the ladder, but those of us who could were tellt that we were to draw straws, and that out of every twenty, one of us would stand trial and the others would receive the king's mercy if we signed a petition saying that we were guilty of treason for rebelling against our lawful king. So we drew straws and I was one of the nineteen, but I said I wasna signing anything, because I'd risen *for* the rightful king and that the Elector of Hanover wasna the lawful king of Scotland, or England for that matter."

Simon's next words were lost in a great cheer from the assembled clansfolk, and he took the opportunity to drink some ale. Alex leaned over and asked him a question, but he shook his head and waited until everyone was quiet again.

"I thought then that they'd hang me anyway, but they didna. We were tellt that the so-called king's grace was that we'd be transported to the Colonies for life, or some of us might be given the chance to enlist in his army instead. A few of us tellt the soldier to tell the Elector to go and fuck himself wi' his grace, and I think he'd have had us flogged, which would have killt us, for it was all we could do to stand, but no one would come near us because we reeked so bad and we were alive wi' vermin, so they put us back down in the hold.

"We found out later that the soldiers signed for those that wouldna in any case, but at least we kept a wee bit of pride. But those that signed, we didna blame them. Living like that, it takes the fight out of ye, some quicker than others, that's all.

"So we waited to be transported, and more of us died, and then one day we were tellt that there'd been an Act of Grace, and we thought it was another load o' shite about being slowly killt in a different way. After that every few days men were taken up on deck and didna come back. I thought they were being strangled or suchlike and thrown overboard.

"Until it was my turn and I was tellt I was free, and given two shillings. Then I walked home. I kept away from the towns, because I looked bad, and I ken that the English have no love for the Scots. I spent the money on food, and then I stole some, because it being winter there wasna anything to be had in the fields, and I wasna strong enough to hunt. I washed myself in the rivers at first, but by the end I didna have the strength to do anything but just keep walking.

"I wanted to wash in the loch here before anyone saw me, to be clean at least, but then I saw Peigi and Janet on the track and my body just gave up and I couldna carry on."

"Ye walked all the way frae *London*, in just your shirt?" Alasdair asked. "Wi' no shoes at all?"

"Aye," Simon said. "I wanted to get home, and I did it. It would have been easy if I'd been in my strength at the start, but we'd been starved for so long. I really believe they thought we'd die trying to get home anyway and save them the trouble of burying us. When I started walking, I tellt myself that I'd be damned if I'd die in England, and that gave me the strength to get to Scotland, then once I was there I kept saying that it wasna far now, so I might as well keep on. I'm so glad we dinna live in Aberdeen or some such northerly place."

"I canna believe ye made it at all," Kenneth said. "I thought I was the strongest in the clan, but Christ, man, to walk so far, an' ye a skeleton before ye started…" He shook his head in wonder. "Ye're a miracle, that's what ye are."

"That was a brave thing ye did, Simon, telling yon soldier that the Elector could fuck himself," Allan said. "I'm no' sure I could have done the like, in your position."

"He's a MacGregor," Dougal commented. "They've tried to kill us all for over a hundred years, but while we've men like Simon, we've nae need to worry they'll manage it! We're no' so easy to kill!"

There was a great roar of approval, and this time when Alex leaned down to ask him if he had had enough, Simon didn't even hear him.

He was too busy looking around at the sea of admiring faces, and realising that what Alex, and, separately, his wife had told him was true. They were not just being kind. No one thought him a coward for allowing himself to be taken prisoner. No one except himself thought he was a lesser man for allowing himself to be treated like vermin for two years by the British. Quite the opposite; they thought him a hero, and the admiration on their faces was quite clearly genuine.

Alex leaned down again, and this time Simon *did* hear him.

"I tellt ye so," he said softly. "Ye should believe your chieftain when he tells ye a truth. Ye're a brave man, Simon, and I'm proud to call you my clansman. Now, are ye tired?"

"Aye," Simon replied, his eyes bright with unshed tears. "I'm a wee bit tired. But let's have the party soon. I dinna need to be able to dance to enjoy it, not now I ken that..." His voice broke with the effort of holding the emotion back.

Alex gave one of his now rare smiles, and bending, lifted Simon in his arms and took him back into the cottage, thereby bringing the meeting to an end.

* * *

Manchester, England.

She stood for a short time in the lane leading to her destination, plucking up the courage to take the final steps. She was being ridiculous, she knew that; her welcome was assured. But still she dreaded the bad news that might be awaiting her there. If she loitered too long though, she might attract unwanted attention. So she pulled herself together, straightened her shoulders and walked briskly down the lane, stopping at the gate of the house she was heading for.

Last time she had been here the garden had been only partly tamed; now it was completely so, with vegetable beds neatly laid out, some showing shoots, while along the edge of the little path leading to the door daffodils were already blooming. At the right side of the house, his back to her, a young man was wielding a spade to good effect; a young man she didn't recognise, and who most definitely was not Graeme. Her heart sank as she opened the catch on the gate and made her way up the path.

She knocked on the door, hoping that someone she knew would answer. She didn't want to have to introduce herself to a complete stranger, not here, in a place she thought of as her second home. So when she got no answer to her knock she made her way round to the back of the house via the left side of the house. Maybe the occupants were in the back, it being a fine day.

She was in luck; in the back garden were a woman and a little girl. The woman was taking washing from a line and handing it to the child, who was putting it in a large basket on the ground. As she saw the visitor approach the woman turned, her arms full of a sheet she had just unpegged from the line.

"Hello," she said cheerily. "How can I help you?"

The visitor responded by taking the hood of her cloak down, revealing a head of brown wavy hair and a pale face, blue eyes underscored by dark shadows of fatigue. She smiled.

"Hello Jane," she said.

Jane froze for a moment, then dropped the sheet she was holding onto the child, covering her in washing. The child giggled, enjoying this new game.

"Beth?" Jane said hesitantly, as though unable to believe what she was seeing. "My God, is it really you?" All the colour had drained from her face and Beth moved forward, putting a hand on Jane's arm to steady her.

"I'm sorry," she said. "I didn't mean to shock you. Is it safe for me to be here?"

"Safe?" Jane repeated, still stunned. "I...we thought you were dead. Sarah wrote to us and said that you were transported to the Colonies and had died."

"Ah," Beth said, realisation dawning. "I can explain that." She bent down and lifted the washing off the child. "Hello, little sunflower," she said, using John's pet name for Ann.

The little girl beamed up at her.

"Hhhrrrr!" she said.

"You've done wonders for her," Beth said, looking up at Jane. "I hardly recognise her."

This wasn't strictly true; the hideous scarring inflicted on the child's face by Richard in his attempt to kill her rendered her instantly recognisable. But apart from that, this sturdy, well-nourished little girl with shiny curls was a far cry from the filthy emaciated urchin Beth had dropped off at the house almost three years before.

Beth straightened up and Jane lifted her hands, cupping her former mistress's face and staring intently at her.

"It really is you!" she said. "I can't believe it! Are you here to stay?"

"If you want me to, I can stay for the night."

Jane leaned forward, kissed Beth soundly, then embraced her.

"You can stay as long as you want. You can live here, if you like. I can't believe it. I have to tell Thomas. He's in the kitchen. Come on," she said, her voice trembling with emotion. Leaving the remaining washing on the line and the basket on the floor, Jane led the way and Beth followed her into the kitchen, which was, as always, warm and welcoming, and smelt of freshly baked bread.

Thomas was sitting at the table polishing a pair of shoes, but looked up as the two women entered, and, like Jane before him, froze at the sight of Beth.

"Look who's come back to us," Jane said, her voice shaking with tears and excitement. "She's not dead at all!"

Very carefully Thomas put down the shoe and the brush, and stood up. Then he reached out and pulled Beth into an embrace so crushing that she could hardly breathe.

"Beth," he said into her hair. "Oh, this is wonderful." He stepped back, holding her at arm's length, taking her in. "Your hair…" he said.

Beth reached a hand up.

"I dyed it," she said. "My hair is my most recognisable feature. I know everyone thinks I'm dead, but even so, if someone recognises me…if I'm arrested, I'll be executed."

"Sit down," Jane said. "Are you hungry?" Without waiting for an answer she bustled about, putting together a meal.

"Why would Sarah tell us you were dead?" Thomas asked. "She wrote to us last year, said one of her clients found out you'd been transported and died. We've all been in mourning for you."

Once the food was on the table they all sat down, and Beth told them briefly what had happened, about Captain Marsal attacking the transport ship and taking them all to Martinique, about the governor setting all the prisoners free, and about her asking him to add her to the list of dead.

"I made a very powerful enemy when I was in prison, because I wouldn't reveal Sir Anthony's identity," Beth explained, "an enemy rich enough to send assassins out to Martinique to kill me, so I thought I'd be safer if it was believed that I'd died. I wasn't planning to return to England then, but even if there are notices out for the other prisoners who were freed, there won't be about me, which is good. I'm sorry. I couldn't take the risk of writing to tell anyone I was alive, in case the letter fell into the wrong hands."

"No, of course you couldn't. But I'm so glad you decided to come back!" Jane said. "I'll light a fire in the drawing room. You can sleep there tonight and then tomorrow we'll work out something more permanent. You *are* staying?"

Part of her wanted to say yes, desperately. She had been so lonely for so long, and now she was with people who cared for her, the thought of setting out alone again on a dangerous journey with, most probably, terrible news at the end, made her feel sick. A wave of sadness washed over her and she knew that she would have to leave soon, or her courage might fail her.

"I can stay tonight, maybe for a couple of days," Beth said. "But I have to go then. I have something to do."

"What do you have to do?" Thomas asked. "Is it something we can help with?"

"No, it isn't," Beth replied. "I have to find out what happened to…someone. That's why I came back."

"Beth, you look tired and you're very thin," Jane commented. "At least stay until there's some flesh on your bones. This someone, whoever it is, can wait until you're properly rested."

"It's Sir Anthony or whatever his name was, isn't it?" Thomas said, his voice hard. "It's him you're looking for."

"Yes," Beth admitted. "I have to know if he's alive or dead."

"Why? He abandoned you, didn't he, when you weren't of any more use to him? I know you loved him, but he's never tried to find you, has he? Why are you risking your life to look for someone who left you to rot in prison?"

"He didn't abandon me…he wouldn't," Beth said. "He promised me he'd come for me, and he wouldn't have broken that promise unless something had happened to stop him."

To say Thomas looked sceptical would be a vast understatement.

"Well, if that's the case, then he must be dead. And if he's alive, he's not worthy to kiss your feet. So why waste your time? You can stay here, with people who really love you. We'll keep you safe."

Beth's eyes filled with tears.

"I can't, Thomas. I want to, but I can't. It's too dangerous for you, for one thing. And I know you hate Anthony, and I understand that, but you don't know the whole story. I can't tell you, either. I'm sorry. But I have to find out whether he survived Cul...whether he's alive or not. It's burning me up, and I can't go on with my life until I know."

"He was alive this time last year, at any rate. I can take you to him, if you want," a voice came from behind her. Beth turned to see the familiar, if somewhat facially altered figure of her former gardener standing in the doorway.

"Graeme?" she said, standing up. "He's alive?"

Graeme smiled.

"As far as I know he is. Christ, lass, but it's good to see you," he said.

She burst into tears and he moved forward, catching her as she fainted dead away.

She was sitting on Graeme's lap, supported by his arm, her cheek pressed against the worn leather of his waistcoat. She inhaled the familiar scent of leather and green growing things, and was transported back to when she was a child and had sat on his knee after a long day of playing in the fields, listening to the conversation of the adults going on over her head as she drifted off to sleep. Then she remembered the last time she had sat like this, after Richard had hit her and driven John away. And then she became aware of what had happened just before she fainted, and opened her eyes, to see the young man who had been digging in the garden and a young woman sitting at the other side of the table, looking at her with concerned but elated faces.

"She's coming round," the young man said in a strong Manchester accent.

Graeme looked down and shifted position slightly, allowing Beth to sit upright while still retaining the support of his arm.

"I know I'm ugly now," he said conversationally, "But I'm not used to women swooning on me. Hurt my feelings, it has."

Beth smiled

."I'm not used to swooning myself," she said, her voice sounding distant to her ears as she attempted to shake off the disorientation of the faint. "I must have become a delicate young miss after all."

Graeme snorted disbelievingly.

"Here," he said, holding a glass of brandy under her nose. "Drink that. We'll have you climbing trees and falling in the pond again in no time."

She took the glass and drank, then leaned back into him, revelling in the familiarity and comfort of the man who knew her better than anyone. Anyone, that was except...

"You said he's alive?" she said. "Where...?" His hand tightened warningly on her shoulder, bringing her to full consciousness and reminding her that there was a room full of people who, although they loved her and were trustworthy, did not know, and should not know anything more about her husband than they already did.

She looked across the table.

"Ben?" she said, "and Mary? You've grown up! Last time I saw you you were children!"

The couple blushed in unison.

"We have, miss," Mary said. "And Ben and me's going to be married, as soon as we're old enough!"

"Not for a good few years yet," Thomas said with mock sternness.

"When I arrived here I saw you digging and I didn't know who you were. I thought you'd replaced...I thought you were dead," Beth said, looking up at Graeme.

"Hmm, well, it was a close thing," Graeme said. "The redcoat bastard tried his best to do the job, but made a mess of it. Sorry, Jane."

Beth laughed out loud. Until she'd arrived here, it had seemed to her that the whole world had changed, profoundly and irrevocably. But here in this tiny corner of England, Graeme was still swearing and Jane was still shocked by it. And she was still Beth Cunningham, the master's daughter, and their friend.

"Oh God, I'm so glad to be here," she said. "I've missed you all so much. I thought I'd never see you again! It's so good to be home!"

Then she burst into tears and was joined by Jane and Mary, while the men all tut-tutted and made comments about the foolishness of women and suchlike. But when Beth, still ensconced on Graeme's lap, looked up at him, his one remaining eye was moist.

The following day, after a good night's sleep and a hearty breakfast, Graeme announced that he was going to show Beth the garden, as though he owned a vast estate that would take a day to ride around rather than a vegetable patch, a herb bed, and a henhouse. Nevertheless the others took the hint and kept out of the way while Beth accompanied Graeme to the end of the yard, where the ramshackle shed had been replaced with a neat painted henhouse. Outside it were several chickens pecking about in the grass. The log was still there, where she'd sat a lifetime ago, listening to Sir Anthony telling her he was afraid while Graeme and Thomas had watched from the kitchen window. Automatically, she looked down the yard at the house.

"I knew then, when I saw him grab you up off that log, that he was the only one for you, and that there was a lot more to him than met the eye," Graeme said, reading her mind. "Sit down. We've a lot to talk about."

They sat down. The previous evening they'd spoken of the things that they could talk about with the others; that Richard was dead, but not who had killed him; that John had escaped from Newgate Prison, as told to them by Sarah, but not where he was now, because no one knew that. Beth had told them about her time in the Tower, in Newgate, what Richard had done to her, how her friends in London had saved her life, and of her, pointless as she now knew, attempt to discredit Richard which had led to her transportation. She told them about Martinique, and Paul and Elizabeth, about Pierre, Antoinette, Raymond and Rosalie. It had been a very long evening and she had been emotionally exhausted at the end of it, but it had felt good to be able to talk about anything she wanted to.

Almost anything she wanted to.

Now she sat on the log with the man who had been a second father to her, while he told her about Duncan's death and held her as she cried brokenly, stroking her hair and murmuring words of comfort until she was able to pull herself together. And then he told her about Alex's injury, how they'd feared for his life after Angus had told him Maggie's dying words, and how he'd slowly come back to life, fuelled by the wish for revenge.

He made her laugh with his account of the cattle raid and the exploits of Tobias Grundy, George Armstrong and the idiot John, who'd pissed in the soldier's mouth. He told her how Richard had died, and what he'd told Alex before he died, and at that she'd cried again, not for Richard but for Alex, because, even before Graeme told her, she knew that he'd believed her alive, only to find out she was dead again. Because he must have come looking for her.

"He came for me, didn't he?" she said.

"He did. I came with him as far as here," Graeme explained. "I've never seen a man so determined in my life. We all thought that Richard might be lying just to hurt him, but he never doubted for a minute that you were alive. Angus tried to stop him and Kenneth pulled them apart, and then I threatened to shoot Alex to bring him to his senses. I wouldn't really have shot him," he added hurriedly, seeing Beth's look of alarm. "Anyway, we got here, and he took some of your money and then carried on to London. I came here and read the letter you'd sent telling us you were alive, but it was too late to go after him to tell him.

"It was September when I got a letter from him, or rather from my business acquaintance Adam Featherstone, telling me that the package he'd gone to enquire about had unfortunately been lost at sea, and that he was going on a short trip and then would continue with business as before. I knew then that you were dead, and I was trying to think of a way to tell the others without giving away that I knew about Alex, when Jane got a letter from Sarah two days later saying that you'd been transported and died on the way to Antigua.

"I'll be honest with you, Beth, I haven't heard anything of him since then. I don't know what the short trip was, and I can't imagine how he must have felt, thinking you were dead for the second time."

Beth sat quietly for a while, thinking this over.

"I don't know what the short trip would be, but you said he'd taken the revenge oath, and that you hadn't reached the number when he left?"

"No. I wasn't keeping an exact count. Angus was, but we were a good way short of the two hundred."

"Then the 'business as before' is his oath. He would keep that, no matter what. Which means that he went home after his trip. So I have to go to Scotland. That's where he'll be," she said.

"If he's still alive," Graeme pointed out gently.

"If he's still alive," she agreed. "But if he isn't, then if the MacGregors don't know, no one will. So I'll stay here another day or two, because it's lovely being here and because I need to go and get some more of that gold you buried, and then I'll leave. In fact I think we should tell the others about the money and bring it back here. Now Richard's dead, and as far as the authorities are concerned I am too, no one's going to look for it. I expect they think Sir Anthony gave it all to the prince to buy swords. I'll take as much as I can carry without raising suspicion, and you can all have the rest. I'll write to tell you what happens, whether I find the 'package' or not."

"No you won't," Graeme said. "Before you fainted so clumsily into my arms yesterday, I told you I'd take you to him, and I will."

"You don't have to," Beth said. "I know the way. And you've got cabbages and things to plant, surely?"

"Ben can manage that," Graeme said. "I'm teaching him everything I know, so he can take over the heavy digging when it gets too much for me. Not yet," he added, cutting the retort about old men off before it could be uttered. He really *did* know her. "And I got very fond of the purple popinjay, once I got to know him properly. I'd like to see him again. And that big redheaded bastard that kept trying to make me wear a skirt. I want to see what he looks like in breeches now it's against the law for the Scots to dress like women."

Beth laughed so hard at that that she almost fell off the log. And from Graeme's point of view it had the desired result; it stopped her raising any further objections to him accompanying her.

CHAPTER SEVENTEEN

Scotland, April 1748

Angus was sitting part way up the hill above the MacGregor settlement, ostensibly to get a little peace to complete his birthday present for Morag. His excuse was partly true; it was virtually impossible to concentrate on carving an intricate and detailed wooden model of a fox, with Simon and Janet's small but intensely curious and energetic children asking him questions every few seconds. It was a lovely sunny day too, a perfect one for sitting outside. Up near the top of the hill, in the saucer-shaped depression which led to the cave, Alex, Iain and Kenneth were talking, probably planning the next raid.

Some of the other men had gone off to practice their fighting skills and had asked Angus to join them, but he'd declined. Truth be told, he didn't need the practice and was sick of fighting anyway. It was one thing going on a cattle raid, killing redcoats who were raping and slaughtering villagers and burning their homes, or killing in battle as he had at Prestonpans, Falkirk Muir and Culloden; but it was quite another waiting outside the towns to ambush soldiers who had broken their officer's curfew to go and have a few drinks or meet a sweetheart. Which was what they were now having to do to meet their tally.

He had tried to resurrect the rage and hatred he'd felt when he'd found the charred remains of the women after Culloden, when he'd held Maggie in his arms as her life had ebbed away, helpless to save her. But he had realised that it was impossible to maintain a killing rage for two years, especially when you had other things to live for, like your wife and son and another baby soon to come.

One hundred and ninety-two. Eight left to kill to fulfil the oath.

Very carefully he carved the features into the tiny face, hunched over on the ground, focussing completely on his task for a while. Morag would love this. He had already made her an owl, an otter and a wildcat, which were all proudly displayed on a shelf out of the children's reach.

The eyes and nose complete, he reached down, picking up the flask of water and the bannock he'd brought with him, and whilst eating stared out across the loch thinking about the other reason he'd wanted to be alone today. He needed to think about the clan meeting Alex had called two days ago, and the private talk he'd had with Angus after it.

Alex had called the meeting because he'd had a letter from Cluny MacPherson, who was still living in a cave on the side of Ben Alder and who had received a communication from Prince Charles which he was passing on to relevant and trustworthy clan chiefs.

"Charles is telling his followers to be ready to rise again at short notice, because he believes that when the Elector dies Cumberland will try to seize the crown from Frederick. He says that if that happens, the whole country will be thrown into turmoil and it would be the perfect time for another rising."

There had been a moment's silence as everyone processed this.

"What do you think, Alex? Ye ken them all better than most," Iain said.

"Better than Charles does, I'm thinking," Kenneth added.

Alex had scrubbed his hand through his hair, which hung loose around his shoulders and which he only tied back now when on a raid so it wouldn't obscure his vision at a crucial moment.

"I dinna ken for sure," he'd said. "It's possible, but no' likely. George hates Frederick and always has done, and Frederick has caused him a lot of problems – Leicester House where he lives is virtually a rival court to George's. And Cumberland is definitely his father's favourite son. But in fairness to Cumberland, he's never shown any signs of wanting the crown for himself; he's a military man, as we all ken to our cost. And the brothers, though they're no' close, havena taken against one another.

"If ye ignore the fact that the whole family have no right to the throne, then Frederick's the rightful heir to George. And if ye add to that the fact that Frederick already has sons of his own to carry on the line, whereas Cumberland isna even married yet...no, I think Charles is clutching at straws. The only chance would be if George names William Augustus as his heir; in that case he might make a bid, to fulfil his father's dying wish."

"Of course for this to happen, George has to die first," Angus pointed out.

"True."

"But he's an old man, is he no'?" Allan asked.

"He's sixty-five, aye. But he's no' in his dotage yet. Remember he led his troops at Dettingen five years ago. But also, Fred is quite popular, and rightly so, for he's a good man. He'll be a fine king when the time comes," Alex said, to everyone's surprise. He looked around at the shocked expressions on his audience's faces, and smiled.

"I didna say he'll be the rightful king," he explained. "But he'll be a good one. And I owe him a debt, so I hope I dinna have to fight against him one day, although I will of course, if I have to, for I've sworn my allegiance to King James."

"What debt do ye owe him?" Peigi asked.

Alex's face closed immediately, telling everyone that it was something to do with Beth, although he didn't utter a word to suggest that.

"So then," he said, ignoring the question completely, "I dinna think we need to do anything other than what we already are. If there's a rising we could be ready in a matter of days anyway, if it came to it. I just wanted to tell ye what Charles said."

Once the meeting had been declared over, everyone had dispersed except for Angus, because Alex had expressed a desire to have a private word with him. They went to Simon and Janet's house, as Alex was still living there, having dismissed Simon's assurances that he was well enough to move back to his own place.

"I'm fine where I am," Alex had said. "You make the most of the fine bed and the good fire. We'll see how you are at the end of the month."

Alex sat down on a stool near the small central fire, from

which a lazy curl of smoke rose to hover in the roof space before making its way eventually through the thatch. He beckoned Angus to sit opposite, then sat looking into the fire, clearly thinking of how to word what he wanted to say.

In the past Angus would have waited for no more than ten seconds before becoming restless and pressing his brother to speak. The fact that he now sat quietly for a good three minutes patiently waiting for Alex to say something, spoke volumes of the change in him.

"We've nearly reached the total to fulfil our oath to Maggie and Beth," Alex said at length, still staring at the fire.

"Aye," Angus replied. "Eight left to kill."

Alex nodded.

"What will ye do after that?" he asked.

Angus's brow furrowed. Surely it was obvious?

"I'll go back to what I was doing before," he said. "Well, before the rising, that is. Except for having Morag and wee Sandy, of course." He smiled warmly at the thought of what that life would be like. He was ready to settle down. There would be raids, of course, but that was just part of normal life. "Is that no' what we'll all be doing?" he added.

"I canna," Alex said softly. "I canna go back."

He looked up from the fire then, and the expression on his face broke Angus's heart.

"Ah, shit, Alex, I'm sorry, I shouldna have said that. It was thoughtless of me," Angus said. Alex waved a hand dismissively.

"Dinna fash yourself. I'm no' so easily hurt. I made my decision a long time ago, after...I just wanted to be sure ye were ready, to see it for myself, and ye are."

"Ready for what?" Angus asked.

"Once we've finished the killing, I intend to call a meeting and formally declare you the chieftain of the clan. But of course I have to have your agreement to it. I ken the clan will be happy – no' a one of them has brought a complaint to me about how ye led them when I was away."

Angus wasn't so sure that the clan would be happy with that decision. He certainly wasn't.

"Alex," he said, leaning forward earnestly, "I dinna want to be the chieftain. I never have. I never thought to do it; it was always you, and if no' you, Duncan. I havena the wisdom for it. Ye've always said I was reckless, and ye've the right of it."

"Aye, well, ye've changed a lot since Culloden."

"We all have."

"That's true. But ye've changed for the better. In some ways. I miss the carefree boy ye were, I'll admit that. But ye'd have grown up anyway, in time. I'm sorry it had to happen in such a way, though."

"Maybe, but—"

"And ye're far more fit than I am now," Alex interrupted.

"What? No!" Angus protested. "Ye're just grieving, again. I ken it's hard for ye, especially having had the hope that…well, ye ken. But ye'll recover. Ye just need time, that's all."

Alex leaned forward too, then, bracing his elbows on his knees and looking at his brother, his expression intense.

"Angus, listen to me," he said, "for I'll no' speak of this again with ye after today, and never with anyone else. When I thought Beth dead the first time, the only thing that kept me going was the blood oath. I tellt myself that I'd recover, that I could go on, afterwards. But it was a lie. When I looked to the end of the oath, all I could see was darkness. So when I found out she was alive, it changed everything. I dinna think I realised how dead I'd been inside until Richard brought me back to life. But ye ken what happened in London. And now I canna go back to normal. There is no normal any more. There's nothing."

"I dinna ken what happened in London, Alex," Angus pointed out gently. "I ken that ye found out she was dead after all, and today ye tellt us ye owe Frederick a debt, which I assume is to do wi' that time, but that's all. Did he find out that she'd died?"

Alex scrubbed his hand through his hair again.

"Ye dinna have to talk about it," Angus said hurriedly.

"Aye, I do. I see that now. For if I dinna, ye'll no' understand why I must do what I'm going to do, and because ye need to ken why I want ye to be chieftain, that it's no' so I can go and grieve to death as I wanted to after Culloden. I'm past that, at least. But this is between you and I alone."

Angus nodded, at which Alex stared into the flames again, this time for so long that Angus wondered if he'd changed his mind, or somehow fallen asleep sitting up. When Alex finally spoke, he jumped, startled by the sound.

"I'll no' go into the details," he said, "and there's some things that are no' mine to tell. When I got to London I found out that Beth had been transported to Antigua, but that the ship was captured by French pirates and all the prisoners were taken to Martinique. I had to wait in London then, because my informant didna ken if Beth and the others would be released and if they were, whether they'd stay in Martinique. It's a French island, and as we're at war wi' the French I thought it likely she'd be freed. But I couldna go half way round the world only to find out she'd been sent to France or some such nonsense."

"You'd have sailed to the Colonies?!" Angus exclaimed. Even the thought of going on a ship made him feel nauseated.

"I'd have swum there, if I'd had to. We're no' all seasick like you," Alex replied, smiling. "But even if I was, aye, I would have done. Because she thought I was dead. She believed that was the reason I didna keep my promise to her. What that bastard Richard tellt me was true. She was in the Tower, and interviewed by Cumberland and Newcastle, but she didna give me up, didna give any of us up. So they put her in Newgate Prison, which is a hell hole, and when she still wouldna talk Newcastle sent Richard to her. They didna ken she was with child, no' till…afterwards, when she lost the bairn. Newcastle refused to allow her to be treated properly, and she was left in a cell to starve to death.

"None of her friends or family knew she was even in London. But then Sarah found out, and she went to…some other friends, ones with influence and in the end it was Prince Frederick himself who rescued her, and who picked her up out of the filth and saved her life. From what I was tellt, she was worse than Simon, couldna even sit up or feed herself when he found her."

"That's why you owe him a debt," Angus said, awestricken. He had never heard Alex use the royal title of any of the usurper's family before. That he had now showed how high his opinion of the man was.

"Aye, that's why. He sent his own surgeon to her as well, and they brought her back to life, against her will, for she tellt them she wanted to die, to…to…" He stopped speaking, and took a huge, shuddering breath.

"To be with you," Angus supplemented.

Alex stood abruptly, and for a moment Angus thought he was

going to stop the story there, and if so, he would not have pushed him to speak of it again, for he could see what a toll this was taking. He waited while Alex walked up and down the room then stood by the doorway for a while, breathing deeply. Then, having recovered a little, he sat back down and continued.

"Aye. She recovered, in time, and then she found out that Richard was threatening Sarah, and that stupit wee fool Ann that married him. So she decided to go and tell Newcastle that Richard was a traitor, that he knew I was a spy but accepted a commission in the army to keep quiet. She believed that he'd be court-martialled, and she was probably right. If he'd lived, that is.

"But she still wouldna say anything about me, so Newcastle had her transported, because he wanted her out of the way, and he couldna do anything to her in England because Prince Frederick had taken an interest. He no doubt hoped she'd die, either on the voyage or soon after, and he got what he wanted. He must be feeling verra pleased wi' himself right now. And that's why I've tellt ye all this, so ye'll understand why ye must agree to take over the chieftainship after the oath is fulfilled."

Angus thought for a minute, but was none the wiser. He opened his mouth to ask the question, but Alex, observing him closely, had already read his mind.

"When we've fulfilled that oath, I've another to do. I mean to go to London and stab that bastard through the heart," he said.

Angus's eyes opened wide.

"What?! Ye canna kill the Duke of Newcastle! He's one o' the most powerful men in the land! Ye'll never get away wi' it."

"I dinna mean to. I just need to see him, alone. Ye mind Sir Anthony could go anywhere he wanted, and Tobias Grundy rode out of Fort Augustus wi' two thousand cattle. It'll no' be difficult to get a private interview wi' the man. As for afterwards, I dinna much mind. If I can, I'll provoke the guards into killing me. If no', then I'll be executed anyway. Either way, there'll be an end of it, and I'll be happy for that. But I'll be a lot happier if I ken I'm leaving the clan in good hands."

Angus wanted to scream that he would not take on the chieftainship, that he would not let Alex go and kill himself in this way, that it was stupid and pointless. But he didn't, because he knew that if their positions were reversed, and it was Morag and her unborn child who had suffered and died because of a vindictive bastard, he too would want to kill him, whatever the cost. With every bone in his body he wanted to stop Alex from leaving; but he couldn't. So he gave his brother the only gift he could.

"Aye," he said. "I'll take over the chieftainship, after the oath is fulfilled."

Then he stood, and walking unheeding straight through the small fire, kicking the embers across the dirt floor of the cottage, Angus seized his brother, pulling him up off the stool and embracing him with a strength born of love and despair.

And then he let him go, turned and walked out of the cottage without another word.

So now, two days later, he sat on the side of the mountain carving a fox for the wife who was both worried about him and upset with him, because he had told her only that he'd spoken with Alex, which she knew anyway, and that he had been told things in confidence, that he had to think about what he'd been told, and needed time to do so.

He finished the bannock and the water, and then stared across the loch some more. Then he picked the little carving up again and started fashioning the tail. He had to watch the brother he had loved and worshipped since he was a tiny child walk out of his life, never to return. And there was nothing he could do to stop him, just as there had been nothing he could do to stop Duncan from being killed at Culloden. Better never to have had brothers than to have to suffer the loss of them. No, that was a stupid, self-pitying way to think.

The knife slipped, slicing off both the end of the fox's tail and the skin on the top of Angus's finger.

"*Magairlean!*" he cursed, throwing both the carving and the knife on the ground and sucking the tip of his finger. That was what came of not concentrating. The whole damn thing was ruined now. What a fucking horrible week this was turning out to be. Nothing had gone right. Nothing *would* go right.

He closed his eyes and took a few deep breaths to try to calm himself down, recognising that if he didn't he was in danger of going in search of someone to pick a fight with, just to release some of the pent-up emotion burning through him.

When he opened them again he saw wee Jamie heading towards him. He sighed. The last thing he wanted now was to talk to anyone. Unless it was to start a fight. You could not start a fight with an eight-year-old. Angus took another deep breath and composed his face into what he hoped was a pleasant expression.

"What's amiss?" he said as Jamie got closer.

The boy stopped and looked at him.

"What's wrong wi' your hand?" he asked. Angus looked down. His whole finger was red.

"Nothing," he said, wiping it on his shirt. "Just a wee cut, that's all." Jamie nodded.

"Ye said a bad word," he commented.

"Aye, I did. Dinna tell Morag, though, or she'll gie me a hiding," Angus said, winking at Jamie and making him laugh. "So, why are ye here?"

"I was away up the hill to tell Alex there's people coming along the lochside, frae over there." Jamie waved his hand vaguely to the left.

"How many people? What kind? Redcoats?" Angus asked, instantly alert.

"No, there's just two o' them, with a wee garron. They're no' redcoats. Lachlan's watching. He sent me to tell Alex, or you if I couldna find him. He said to come quick."

What the hell was he talking about? Angus stood up.

"How far away are they?" he asked. He might as well investigate. The carving was ruined anyway.

"A good way, maybe half an hour? They're walking."

"Come on then, show me," Angus said.

They jogged off down the hill together, then along the track a short way, before heading into the trees so as not to be seen by the strangers. After a while they heard a buzzard call suddenly and as one the man and boy dropped to the ground. Lachlan joined them a moment later.

"What's going on?" Angus said softly.

"There's two people coming down the track there. One of them's that Sasannach mannie, but I dinna ken the lassie."

"Ye mean Graeme?" Angus said, utterly confused. "Wi' a lassie?"

"Aye."

"Are ye sure? Graeme's away hame. Why would he come back, and wi' a lassie?"

"I dinna ken," Lachlan whispered. "Look, there they are."

Angus crouched behind a tree and watched as the two people came into view. One of them was, most definitely, Graeme, who was leading by the reins a small Highland horse loaded with baggage. The other was a young woman, small and slim, with brown wavy hair. As they passed the place where Angus and the two boys were concealed she turned to say something to the older man, but even before he'd seen her face Angus knew who it was, even while his brain was telling him it couldn't be.

"Holy Mother of God," he said softly, crossing himself.

"What is it?" Lachlan said, alarmed. "Is it a fairy?"

Angus just stopped himself from laughing out loud at that.

"No," he whispered. "I canna believe who it is, but no, it's no' a fairy. I need ye to do something, Lachlan. I need ye to walk down the path to them, and tell them that the man they're looking for is up the mountain, and offer to show them the way. It's Alex they're wanting to see."

"How d'ye ken that?" Jamie asked. "Who is she?"

"Never you mind. Ye've seen her before when ye were a wee bairn, too wee to remember. You can come back wi' me. Can ye do that, Lachlan?"

"Aye, of course I can!" the boy said.

"Go then, and dinna tell them I tellt ye to say it, just act as though ye thought of it yoursel'."

Lachlan shot off, heading through the trees until he was ahead of the couple before making his way down to the track and strolling casually along, as though about to meet them by chance.

Angus grabbed Jamie's hand and backtracked through the woods and back up the mountain at a run. The ruined fox and knife were still there, and he lay flat on the ground next to them, beckoning the boy to do the same so they wouldn't be seen.

"What's happening?" wee Jamie asked, thoroughly confused.

Angus was shaking with suppressed excitement. This was unbelievable. But unless all three of them had gone mad, he had to believe it. The miracle he'd prayed for for so long was happening.

"*Isd,*" Angus said softly. "Just watch. It's a game. I'll tell ye later."

They lay and watched as the two adults and the boy, who was now leading the garron, made their way slowly up the hill. Graeme stopped at one point to get his breath, and then they carried on. Angus waited until they'd passed where he and Jamie were concealed, and then waited again until they were about half way between him and the top of the slope. Yes, that was about right.

He rolled onto his back and very loudly mimicked the sound of a buzzard calling, as Lachlan had earlier, followed in quick succession by a crow cawing, twice. Then he rolled back onto his stomach and waited.

As he'd known, within a few seconds of their agreed warning call there was a very slight movement at the edge of the saucer-shaped depression; it was Alex, but Angus only saw him because he was expecting to, and knew exactly how his brother moved. The couple below continued, unaware that they were being observed.

And then the slight movement became a big one as Alex stood and looked down the hill, and Angus knew that he too could not believe what he was seeing, was convinced he was imagining it, or seeing a ghost.

The ghost stopped and looked up and then laughed, a joyful laugh that Angus had thought never to hear again and which brought tears to his eyes.

For a long moment Alex stood frozen, perfectly outlined at the top of the hill, his hair and kilt blowing around him in the freshening breeze. And then Beth raised both her arms to him and the spell was broken and he came running down the hill barefoot, heedless of the heather and the gorse, heedless of the unevenness of the ground.

When he reached her he was running too quickly to stop, and with one arm he swept her off her feet and carried on, slowing as he went. And then he toppled into the heather, taking her with him in a flurry of skirts and tartan. They rolled on for another few feet and then stopped. Angus heard Beth laugh again, followed by the deep tones of his brother's voice, although he didn't hear the words.

And then Angus looked away, because regardless of the fact

that they were on a mountain in full view of anyone who cared to look, this was a private moment; the most private moment that there had ever been. The most wonderful moment that he had known in all his twenty-three years, excepting the birth of his son.

Angus stood and waved to Graeme, who had watched Alex run past him taking Beth with him and had observed with obvious amusement the big Highlander's attempts to slow down; and then he too had turned away.

He made his way across to Angus, who was standing with tears pouring down his face, a still-bemused little boy sitting at his feet, and the older man's expression told Angus that he too considered this to be one of the most wonderful moments of *his* life. When Graeme reached him, they both looked at each other for a second, and then by unspoken mutual agreement they embraced roughly, slapping each other on the back as men do when united by profound emotion, before stepping away again.

"Well," Graeme said to Angus, paraphrasing a sentence he'd uttered over three years previously to Thomas at the kitchen window in Didsbury, "I think that's what you'd call a reunion."

Angus smiled broadly.

"Aye," he agreed. "I think it is."

When the two men and the child arrived in the village Lachlan was nowhere to be seen, but the garron, still loaded, was tied up outside Alex's house, which was a hive of activity. As they approached Morag emerged through the front door, her arms full of bedding. She laid it on the bench outside and looked at them.

"Graeme," she said. "It's a wonderful thing ye've done."

"I didn't do anything," Graeme replied. "Nothing would have stopped her coming back. I just came with her to make sure she didn't get herself in any more trouble. And I'd a mind to see if there's anything left of the beautiful garden I put you in charge of."

She laughed.

"There's no' so much growing at the moment, no. I've been growing other things." She patted her stomach, causing Graeme to grin. "I've turned the soil and dug the shit in, like ye tellt me to. Ye can help me with it, if ye're staying a while."

Graeme glanced back up the hill, and everyone except Angus

thought he was looking up to the current site of the vegetable garden.

"Yes," he said. "I'll stay a while, if you'll have me."

"Right then," Morag replied, turning to her husband. "Now ye're here, ye can help me wi' the mattress." Without waiting for an answer she ducked back inside the house. Angus followed her. Inside Peigi was sweeping the floor while Alasdair was making up the fire. "We thought they'd want to be together in their own house the night," Morag said. "If ye'll help me get the mattress outside, we can gie it a good shake and air it a wee bit. We havena the time for more, I'm thinking."

"Ye ken she's back," Angus said, a bit disgruntled at not being the first to deliver the wonderful news.

"Aye. Lachlan tellt us that Graeme was here wi' a beautiful lassie, and that when ye saw them ye went white as snow, and then Alex nearly killt her by running at her frae the top o' the ben like a madman. It's Beth, is it no'? She isna dead after all. Like Simon."

"No, she isna dead." Angus forbore from saying that the cases of Simon and Beth were somewhat different. Everyone except Janet had *assumed* Simon to be dead; but they hadn't been told, twice, by reliable people that he was. He took one side of the mattress and together they manhandled it out of the house.

"Simon and Janet are going back to their own house," Morag said. "They said it's about time, anyway." They shook the mattress out, leaving it on the ground to air, and Morag picked the bedding up off the bench. "I'll away down the loch and wash it," she said. "It's a good day for it."

Angus took the bedding from her and accompanied her down to the lochside.

"Is she well?" Morag asked quietly when they were out of earshot of the rest.

"Is who well?"

"Beth, ye loon, who else?" his wife answered.

"Aye, I think so," Angus said, putting the sheets down on a rock and watching appreciatively as Morag kilted her skirts up to keep them from trailing in the water, in the process revealing a tempting amount of shapely leg. "I didna see that much of her."

"I should hope not," Morag said drily, following his gaze. He looked up and their eyes locked. The day suddenly seemed to get considerably warmer. "Simon said he's well enough to have the bairns back now," she added, "so we've the house to ourselves the night. Apart from Sandy, but he's too young anyway."

"Too young for what?" Angus asked

"For understanding what his Ma and Pa are doing in bed."

A great smile spread across Angus's face. The day that he'd thought could not get any better just had. The last few weeks had not been conducive to romance, with tiny inquisitive faces liable to intrude at any moment.

"D'ye have to be washing they things now?" he asked, suddenly impatient.

"Aye," Morag replied firmly, "I do. Ye can help me wring them out, and we can spread them to dry. Anyway, I want to be there when they come down off the mountain."

She had a point. Angus wanted to see Alex and Beth when they arrived in the village too. And the faster the sheets were washed, the sooner…

"Here, let me help ye, then," Angus said eagerly. They washed the sheets together, Angus more of a hindrance than a help. But it was nice to be alone together.

"Ye'll be able to help me wi' chores a lot more, now ye've no need to be looking for redcoats to kill," Morag said as they twisted the sheets to wring as much water as possible out of them.

"What do you mean?"

"A hundred and ninety-two. Ye've no need to be killing ten for Beth now. So that means ye've two to count towards the next stupit oath ye decide to take," Morag pointed out.

She was right. He did not have to kill any more redcoats. Nor did he have to become the chieftain, because Alex no longer needed to go to London and kill the Duke of Newcastle.

This was the very best day there had ever been, not just in his twenty-three years, but since the dawn of time.

From the look on Beth and Alex's faces as they walked into the village some time later, they both shared Angus's sentiment. Their faces were scratched, Beth's dress had a long tear in it, and Alex was limping slightly. There was blood on his shirt, though not enough to cause concern. Both of them had bits of vegetation tangled in their hair.

And both of them were glowing as if a light had been kindled inside them, which in a manner of speaking it had. Their hands were clasped as though welded together as they came to a stop in front of the gathered MacGregors, who were all standing, with the exception of Simon, who, being still unable to, was sitting on the grass.

Everyone looked to Angus, who moved forward, trying and failing to remember the formal speech of welcome.

"*Fàilte dhachaidh, mo phiuthar-chèile,*" he said instead.

Welcome home, sister-in-law.

Beth's beautiful blue eyes filled with tears, and she started to walk toward him, no doubt to embrace him, but Alex remained still and refused to relinquish her hand, bringing her to a sudden stop.

"Tomorrow," he said simply. Then he bent and, lifting his wife into his arms, turned and walked into the house, quietly closing the door behind him.

His clan stood silently outside for a moment, then as one they let out a great cheer, which set all the birds in the trees around the village to flight.

Kenneth and Iain had observed Alex's headlong dash down the mountain and the reason for it, and had made their way down to the settlement by a circuitous route so as not to disturb the couple. They walked over to Graeme now, Kenneth laying one heavy arm across the Englishman's shoulder, causing him to sag somewhat.

"I'm tellt ye're staying a while," Kenneth said. "There's room in my wee house for ye, an ye dinna snore."

Graeme lifted the giant's arm and stepped away, looking the enormous Highlander up and down.

"And to think," he said conversationally, "I came all this way just to see you dressed like a proper civilised man, to find you still wearing skirts like a girl. I could have saved myself a deal of walking if I'd known."

Kenneth laughed, a huge booming guffaw.

"I canna wear they tight Sasannach breeches anyway," he said. "I'm in proportion, ye ken. It'd no' be fair to the rest o' the menfolk to be showing everything I've got."

"I'm no' so sure of that," Peigi chimed in. "We see everything ye've got anyway if there's a breeze, or ye bend down."

"Aye, well, some people are so wee they dinna need me to bend down," he threw back at Peigi, who, although not exactly small, was by no means the tallest of the women. "They can see me in all my glory anyway."

"Aye, there's truth in that," Peigi agreed, "and I can tell ye, Graeme, I'm no' the only thing that's wee around here." She looked pointedly at the appropriate region and everyone burst into laughter.

"Never argue wi' a woman," Kenneth said, sighing good-naturedly. "I should ken that by now. Come on, man," he addressed Graeme. "Let's drink a dram or two to the happy couple. And you too, Iain," he added, gripping the other man's arm when he would have moved away. "Ye shouldna be alone, man, no' the night, at least."

Iain opened his mouth to protest, then closed it again. Kenneth was right. Tonight was not a night to be alone with such conflicting emotions; joy, sadness, envy. Tonight was a night to get very, very drunk, and to forget what would not be coming back to him, ever.

The three men walked away together as the rest of the clan dispersed, Angus following his brother's example by lifting his wife off her feet, carrying her giggling into his house, and closing the door quietly behind him.

Once inside the house Beth turned to her husband, her face earnest.

"Alex," she said, "I'm sor—" He placed a finger gently on her lips, silencing her.

"No' the now," he said softly. "No need for words. For today, let's just be together."

She nodded agreement, and they looked at each other and smiled. Then they undressed each other very slowly, neither of them speaking, focussing completely on the moment, every sense heightened.

As he disrobed her he felt the roughness of her woollen dress, the hardness of the boned stays, and the crisp feel of her shift as he pulled it over her head. He looked with curiosity at the amulet which nestled between her breasts, then lifted it gently over her head, placing it carefully on the table. Then, without touching her skin, he stood back, indicating that it was her turn.

She carefully undid the buckle of his leather belt, then watched as the soft worn wool of the *feileadh mòr*, that he looked so good when wearing but so much better without, fell to the ground. She reached for his linen shirt, standing on tiptoes to lift it over his head; but he was still too tall and had to bend forward to help her.

Then they stood facing each other for a moment, committing each other to memory, glorying in the sheer beauty of each other's bodies, the scars incurred through their battles whilst apart only adding to that beauty, because those battles had, finally, led to this day. This perfect, perfect day.

Then, still without speaking, he picked up the hairbrush from the small table near the bed and moving behind her brushed her hair, removing the bits of leaf and twig carefully, relishing the soft silky feel of the brown waves, that in his mind were still purest silver-gilt. When he had finished, he knelt and very carefully feathered a series of soft kisses up the side of her neck.

She sighed then and would have melted into his embrace, but forced herself to hold back, instead taking the brush from him and performing the same service for him, until the burnished chestnut waves rippled over his broad shoulders, gleaming and lit with coppery fire. And then she gently moved his hair to the side and kissed his neck until he turned and with one smooth movement stood and lifted her, moving to the bed, where he sat down with her across his lap and buried his face in her hair, inhaling the sweet feminine scent of her, a scent he'd thought never to smell again. Now she clung to him, running her hands softly up and down the muscles of his back, feeling him shiver deliciously at her touch.

They had an unspoken agreement to be gentle and slow after the violence of their reconciliation, in which both of them had been bruised, not just by the fall into the heather but by the fierceness with which they'd clung to each other, sobbing and laughing, and muttering incoherent words of endearment.

But then he lifted his head and their eyes met, and suddenly his lips were on hers, fierce, demanding, and she answered his need with her own. He fell backwards onto the bed, taking her with him, rolling so that she was under him. She reached up to pull him down to her, but he braced himself on his elbows and resisted, although his eyes were dark and smoky with desire for her.

"It's been so long," he said breathlessly. "I want to be gentle, but—"

"Don't be gentle," she said. "I don't want you to be gentle. I want you inside me, now."

"But I dinna want to hurt—"

"Now," she repeated desperately, wrapping her legs around his waist and reaching down with her hand to find him and guide him into her. He gave in, to her need and his own, sheathing himself inside her soft warm flesh in one smooth movement, making her gasp. And then he stopped for a second and looked at her, and they both smiled.

"*Tha gràdh agam ort, mo leannan,*" he said softly.

"I love you too, so very much," she replied.

Then he started to move inside her, very slowly at first, while she clung to him, tightening her legs around his waist, pulling him into her, their bodies melding as one as they moved in perfect synchronicity, building up speed as the blind passion overtook them both. He drove into her while she arched against him, throwing her head back and screaming with the ecstasy which overtook her, driving everything else from her mind. Even so she felt the liquid heat of his release, heard his incoherent moan as he climaxed, and laughed from sheer joy, a joy she had not felt for over two years and had thought she would never feel again.

She was come home. They were come home. And they would never be separated again, in life.

Afterwards he rolled over onto his side, taking her with him so they were still joined, and she lay, her head against his chest, listening to the thundering of his heart quieten to a steady, comforting beat. She nestled into him and his arm closed around her, heavy, protective, and they both slept for a while, limbs entwined.

When they awoke it was almost dark. Very gently he disentangled himself from her, ignoring her sleepy moan of protest, and got out of bed. He made up the fire and lit candles until the room was bathed in a soft golden light. Beth, awake now, leaned up on one elbow, watching him as he moved about the room.

"Why are you lighting so many candles?" she asked.

He looked across at her and smiled.

"Aye, well, I've grown accustomed to ye now," he said. "I thought I'd read a wee while until it's time to sleep properly."

She reached back lazily with one arm and launched a pillow at him, which he caught neatly in one hand, while picking up a bottle of wine that someone had thoughtfully placed on the table with the other and returning to bed. He sat up, plumping the pillow behind him, and she sat with him, his arm round her shoulder while they passed the bottle back and forth. He bent his head and dropped a kiss on top of hers, and she snuggled closer in to him.

"D'ye mind the first time we made love, and I made to snuff the candle?" he asked. "Ye tellt me that ye wanted to see me, to know it was me with ye."

"Yes," she replied softly. "I remember that."

"'The dark can lead to imaginings', ye said," he continued. "If I wake in the night, I want to see ye there beside me. I still can hardly believe ye're real. I dinna want the imaginings the dark might bring."

She closed her eyes tightly at that, but even so a single tear squeezed out through her lashes, rolling down her cheek. She kept her head averted, hoping he wouldn't notice, but then she felt his finger lightly brush the teardrop away and remembered that he had always been able to read her mind.

"I'll always be here beside you," she said, "for as long as you want me to be."

"Forever, then," he replied matter-of-factly.

She leaned further into his warmth, running her fingernail down the middle of his chest, down his hard, flat stomach and into the soft chestnut curls below.

He grunted and stirred and she giggled with delight, carrying the movement along the hard velvety length of him. He reached down, imprisoning her roaming small hand in his large one.

"Dinna be so eager," he murmured. "Slowly this time. Verra slowly."

He bent his lips to hers and, with infinite tenderness, proceeded to show his wife, by actions rather than words, just how wonderful forever was going to be.

Having spent the whole night making love, they both slept very late into the next day, waking sometime in mid-afternoon.

They lay there drowsily for a while, limbs entwined, listening to the sounds of the clansfolk who, judging by the number of times someone said *"Isd!"* fiercely, were attempting to go about their duties quietly so as not to disturb the chieftain and his wife.

Finally Alex turned on his side, raising himself onto one elbow and wincing slightly as he did.

"Are you hurt?" Beth asked.

"No," he replied. "Well, aye, a wee bit. I hit it on a rock yesterday when we fell. It was either that or land on top of ye, and I didna think ye'd thank me if ye'd walked all that way only to have me squash you flat."

She laughed.

"You could have broken your neck, charging down the hill like that," she said, half-joking.

"Aye, well, if my last sight had been your face, I'd have died happy," he replied, reaching out and stroking the hair back from her face before leaning down and kissing the tip of her nose.

"I wouldn't have been happy if you'd killed yourself, you bloody fool," Beth said. "For so long I thought you were—" She stopped herself from finishing, but the word hung between them.

Dead.

Alex sighed, and lay back down.

"If anyone but Angus had tellt me," he said softly, "I wouldna have believed them. I would have come looking for ye anyway. I'm sorry—" Now it was her turn to place a finger on his lips, silencing him. When she removed it, he said, "It's tomorrow."

"It is," she agreed. "And we need to get up, to go and tell everyone some of what's happened to me in the last two years. But you mustn't ever apologise to me for believing Angus. It was the right thing to do, and I'd have done the same in your position."

He nodded.

"I agree, if you agree no' to apologise for adding yourself to the list of dead," he said. "It was the right thing to do too, and it means you're safer now for it. We've both suffered badly through thinking the other to be dead."

"We have. But now we're together again, and I don't want our future to be blighted by our past. Life is so short, let's enjoy it."

They kissed, and then they lay for a while longer, revelling in the simple joy of just being together. And then they got up, dressed, smiled at each other, and hand in hand walked out of the house to face the late afternoon sunshine, and the rest of their lives together.

CHAPTER EIGHTEEN

Swiss Confederation, September 1748

The man and woman stood in the graveyard of a small church nestled on a slope on the outskirts of Geneva, while down below on the road the postilion waited with their hired carriage. Monsieur Dubois had made his money from the clothing business, he said; and certainly the couple were dressed expensively, if not ostentatiously. They were from Normandy, although Madame Dubois had a strange accent. When the postilion had commented on this she told him that she had spent some time in the West Indies, but the climate had not suited her and she was very glad to be home.

They were a pleasant couple, and clearly very much in love, which made the elderly postilion smile, remembering his own youth and a red-haired beauty, long dead, who had once captured his heart. He settled back to reminisce and took out his pipe and a pouch of tobacco to while away the time until his services were required again.

In the graveyard M. and Mme Dubois were standing looking down at a gravestone. Being out of earshot, they were no longer speaking French.

"He's done it, then," Alex murmured. "I confess I didna think he would."

Beth reached down and pulled away a strand of ivy, revealing the lettering beneath:

Erected in Loving Memory of
Anna Clarissa
widow of Sir John Anthony Peters
who departed this life on 7th February 1740
in the 45th year of her life.
Also in memory of their three daughters
Anna Mary
3rd June 1715 – 10th February 1740
Caroline Anne
12th December 1716 – 6th February 1740
Beatrice Elizabeth
25th March 1719 – 25th February 1740
May they rest in the eternal peace of our Lord Jesus Christ.
Also
their dearly beloved son
Anthony John Peters
12th February 1713 – 23rd September 1720
"Suffer little children to come unto me, for of such is the
Kingdom of Heaven"

"You mean Highbury?" Beth said, looking at the lettering. The last lines looked new, and must have been carved very recently.

"Aye. I tellt him that one day, if I could, I'd add Anthony's name to the stone, to let the world know that this wee bairn and his family were in no way connected to the Jacobite spy. He said that if I couldna for any reason, that he would if a way could be found."

"He believes you to be dead, then," Beth said.

"Aye. It's maybe better that way. He's a good man, and there's a bond of trust between us. He took a risk to do this only for a whim of mine."

"No," Beth said. "It was more than a whim, I think. It was a pledge of honour, and Highbury is an honourable man, as are you."

Alex smiled, and kneeling down placed the small bouquet of flowers they'd brought with them on the grave. He ran his fingers lightly over the lettering, then looked up at his wife.

"I'm sorry," he said. "I brought you all this way for nothing."

"Not for nothing," she replied. "You wouldn't have known

otherwise. And it's been nice to see a little of France without having to wear uncomfortable gowns and make small talk with dull people while thinking about every word I said. But I'm ready to go home now. I miss our house, and the loch, and the mountains. I'm even missing Angus! And I owe him a debt for throwing me in the loch," she added, referring to her brother-in-law's successful attempt to sober her up after the joint celebration party for her and Simon, which had taken place shortly after her return. Since Angus had learned that he no longer had to accept the burden of chieftainship, at least not on a permanent basis, he had regained much of his former humour and boyishness, although the carefree recklessness had gone forever.

"Ye'll no' be duelling wi' my brother for a good few months yet," Alex said warningly.

He turned, still kneeling, clasped his wife about the waist and placed a kiss on the soft swell of her stomach, a roundness still small enough to be concealed beneath the folds of her skirts, but which was nevertheless on the minds of the two lovers constantly.

Beth placed a hand on his head, and they remained this way for a moment, during which the postilion looked up the slope, and seeing the gesture, recognised the significance and smiled to himself. They were a lovely couple; kind, generous and devoted to each other. Their child would have a good start in life with such loving parents, he thought.

Alex stood, and turning, they started to make their way back down the slope, holding hands.

"I was thinking about names for the bairn, if it's a boy," he said.

"You want to call him William?" she asked. "After Highbury?"

"Would you like that?" He answered her question with another.

"No," she answered candidly. "Although I wouldn't object if he didn't have the same first name as Cumberland. I don't want our son to be named after that bastard, or for anyone to think it."

"Good," Alex said. "I wasna thinking of William. I ken it's customary to name the first child after his grandfather, but Angus has done that already and I'd like to name ours Duncan, if ye dinna mind."

"Mind? No, I think that's a wonderful idea!" Beth said. "And if he grows up to be like Duncan, I'd be very happy. I miss him."

"Aye, so do I, every day."

"I wish Sarah had told me about Màiri," Beth said. "I'd love to have met her." They had talked about Sarah and Duncan's ill-fated love and the result, as they'd talked about many things in the past months.

"Maybe we can find a way to do that, one day. But no' for a good while, I'm thinking."

"No," Beth said. "It's too risky. Thank you for allowing me to write, though, and tell her I'm alive. Or rather that her cousin Adam has discovered his sweetheart hadn't died of the fever after all, and that she's to be an auntie in February."

"Ye'd have done it anyway, an I'd allowed it or no'," Alex replied drily.

Wisely, she didn't answer this, not least because it was true. She, or rather Adam, had asked Sarah to pass on the good news to Sir Edwin and Lady Caroline, and to thank them for their kindness.

"If the baby's a girl, could we call her Margaret, then?" she asked instead.

Surprised, Alex stopped, bringing her to a halt too.

"Margaret? I thought ye wanted to name her after your mother, ye being so close and all."

"I did. But talking about Duncan and how we miss him made me think of Maggie. I'd like to name a daughter after her, and I'd like Iain to be the godfather too. I think it would please him, maybe make him smile again."

Alex smiled. And then he embraced his wife, lifting her off her feet and swinging her round until she giggled.

"That's a wonderful idea. And ye're right. I've wondered for a long time how to bring Iain back to us. That might do it, having a stake in our bairn."

He set her down carefully on her feet.

"Only if it's a girl though," she said. "I don't think calling a boy Maggie would have the same result."

"Well, if it's a boy, we'll just have to keep on trying till we have a wee Maggie to make Iain smile again," he observed.

"Only to make Iain smile? The sacrifices you make for your clan," Beth said, smiling.

"Aye. I take my responsibilities as chieftain verra seriously."

"We'd best be getting home straight away, in that case," she said. They carried on down the hill to the smiling postilion.

Above them the late summer breeze coming down from the mountain moved through the churchyard, ruffling the brightly coloured petals of the little bouquet of flowers on the grave, and rustling the leaves of the tree which grew by the cemetery wall.

Then it continued down the mountain to gently lift the chestnut hair of the tall handsome man currently handing his wife up into the carriage, leaving the tree, the graveyard and its occupants in tranquil silence once more.

HISTORICAL NOTE

The historical notes I've included in the back of previous books in this series have proved very popular with readers, so I thought I'd keep the custom going for those who are interested in knowing a little more about the historical aspect of the Chronicles. Please be aware, this note is to be read after the book, as it contains a good few spoilers!

The prologue deals with Prince Charles accepting a dinner invitation from his brother Henry, only for him to fail to appear, leaving an annoyed Charles sitting in the library pondering events of the recent past. Although it was a useful 'catch-up' scene, it actually did happen.

Prince Henry was a very different person from his impetuous, courageous and charismatic older brother. He was extremely pious, devoted to the Catholic Church, academic, somewhat reclusive and had an absolute terror of women and of being forced to marry. Following Charles' disastrous mission to Spain, (even the promised shipment of goods to the Highlands was never delivered) he refused to marry anyone less than a reigning monarch or daughter of a monarch, which possibility was highly unlikely. Therefore all eyes turned to Henry to make a dynastic marriage and continue the Stuart line.

In desperation Henry contacted his father stating his aversion to the worldly life and to marriage. James replied with a light-hearted comment that perhaps he should become a cardinal, which Henry seized on. James agreed to make representations to the Pope on Henry's behalf, and asked him to come to Rome. Knowing what Charles' reaction would be if he heard of this possibility, James and Henry hatched an elaborate plan behind his back, making all the preparations in the utmost secrecy.

On 30th April 1747 Henry invited Charles to dinner, instructed that a meal be prepared and then, even as Charles waited for him in ever-growing worry and frustration, Henry was already on his way to Rome. Three days later Charles received an apologetic letter from his brother in which he stated that he was upset by the attitude of the French and wanted to spend some time with his father. Charles accepted this, as relations between the French court and the Stuarts were no longer amicable, and he knew that Henry was very sensitive.

Henry reached Rome on 25th May to find that James had already made all the arrangements with the Pope for him to become a cardinal in July, which was then done.

Charles had absolutely no inkling of this until he received the devastating letter from his father when it was too late for him to do anything to prevent it, and his reaction was, understandably extreme. He saw it, rightly, as an utter betrayal of him by his father, who he had devoted his life to trying to restore to the throne of Great Britain.

It's difficult for a twenty-first century mind to appreciate just what a huge blow this was to the Stuart cause in Britain; in our relatively secular society, Roman Catholics are seen as no threat to the stability of the country, or to the Anglican Church.

Charles' grandfather had been removed from the throne in the main because it was believed he was trying to impose Roman Catholicism on his British subjects, and a huge part of the Hanoverian propaganda against a restoration of the Stuarts was that they would enforce the Catholic faith on the whole population and bring back the horrors of Mary Tudor's reign.

Although untrue, and in view of the tiny proportion of the country that was of the Roman faith, highly unlikely ever to happen in any case, it was widely believed. Fear of popery was endemic in Britain and in becoming a cardinal, Henry handed the Hanoverians a huge victory.

James' Jacobite supporters were as horrified as Charles by this decision, and made their views clear on the matter, and, to James' surprise, even the Catholic clergy were deeply critical of the move. It was the bishop of Soissons who baldly stated to the exiled king that in making Henry a cardinal, James had effectively resigned the Stuart claim to the throne of Great Britain.

Charles sank into a deep depression, and only started to come out of it on becoming infatuated with his married cousin, which relationship is just starting at Chapter Thirteen, when Alex visits the prince at St Ouen. This visit is fictional, but some of the things talked about are not. Alex notes that there was a desperation to Charles' drinking that had not been there before. This had been remarked on by a number of the princes' associates, and presaged his later descent into alcoholism and depression.

There were rumours that Henry had homosexual leanings at the time, although nobody would voice this openly. In later years the cardinal did have a number of very close relationships with other men. Having said that, in fairness to him, to the best of my knowledge no evidence has ever been found proving any sexual relationships, and as Henry had an abhorrence of debauchery in all its forms, it is possible that his fear of women was due to asexual or deeply moral tendencies rather than homosexual ones.

In Chapter Thirteen Alex also pays a visit to the Cameron chief, Lochiel, who was living with his wife and children in apartments at Fontainebleau. Charles, recognising the extraordinary devotion and sacrifice of Donald Cameron of Lochiel, had petitioned King Louis unceasingly, trying to get him to raise a regiment for his most loyal devoted supporter, and finally succeeded in doing so. Lochiel was made the Colonel of the newly formed Régiment d'Albanie. The position also carried a handsome salary. Unfortunately, Lochiel did not survive long enough to enjoy the fruits of Charles' labour, tragically dying on 26th October 1748 of what was probably meningitis.

On to Beth's adventures! You might be interested to know that the *Veteran* was a real ship, and was indeed captained by John Ricky. Every prisoner I name on the voyage was a real person too, and they were all transported to Antigua as indentured servants. A list survives of all one hundred and forty-nine prisoners, which includes their names, regiments, occupations, ages and physical description, which I make use of in the book.

One day away from their destination, the *Veteran* was captured by the sloop *Le Diamant*, captained by one Paul Marsal, a privateer, and was taken to Martinique, where the prisoners were all freed by the Marquis de Caylus, Governor of Martinique. The agent who had arranged for the transportation of the prisoners at a charge of £5 per head, Samuel Smith, now petitioned the government for the money.

The Duke of Newcastle instructed the Governor of the Leeward Islands to write to the Marquis de Caylus. So there followed an exchange of beautifully worded letters between the two governors, in which the British demanded the return of the prisoners, and the marquis refused.

What happened to the Jacobites after their release isn't known. Some of them may have stayed in Martinique, or gone to France, as the marquis suggested in one of his letters, or may even have returned to Britain.

The whole episode is a historical author's dream, but I have to admit to taking some minor liberties with history. In reality the *Veteran* sailed out of Liverpool on 8th May 1747, and was captured by Marsal on 28th June. For the sake of the plot, I've changed the departure date to April and telescoped the sailing time to four weeks (the minimum it could take for such a voyage) rather than the actual six it took in reality.

Similarly, in fairness to Captain Ricky, in the records it states that he surrendered after a 'short engagement', which may well have been more than merely a shot fired across the bows. I have no wish for people to believe him a coward when there is no evidence for it!

Elizabeth Clavering's history before transportation is partly real. She was taken 'in actual rebellion', so could have been part of the garrison at Carlisle Castle, or more likely captured after the battle of Clifton Moor on 18th December 1745. It is possible that she was following her husband, and that he was killed in the battle.

As for her marriage to Edmund Clavering in prison, this is true. Edmund and Elizabeth married on 9th June 1746 in prison in York Castle. She stated at the time that she was a widow. Edmund Clavering was hung on 1st November, and gave a defiant speech, blessing King James III.

Elizabeth was indeed on board the *Veteran* when she wrote her petition for mercy, in which she stated the facts and gave no apologies.

Her life after that is a mystery, but she was clearly a spirited woman. She was listed as a 'lady' and as very few 'ladies' were transported, she must have been pretty feisty to have merited such treatment. With that in mind, and being unable to find any more details about Captain Paul Marsal than that he was a privateer, I have invented their future relationship and adventures in their entirety.

The Marquis de Caylus was also real, and the story of the naval battle that he entertains Beth with over dinner really happened. He seems to have been quite a character.

I feel I have to comment about the chapters in which I deal with plantation life on Martinique. I did a considerable amount of research before writing these, and although the Delisles, Raymond and Rosalie, and everyone else on the plantation are fictional, the conditions under which the slaves lived, and the method of sugar production are all taken directly from factual accounts of life in the West Indies.

In Britain, we tend to think of black slavery as a primarily American issue – I certainly was never taught in school about the huge trade in slavery which brought enormous wealth to Britain as well as other countries in Europe, at such a terrible human cost. But although slavery in Britain itself was illegal, the British had no moral compunction when it came to using slaves in their overseas territories, including the American Colonies and the British West Indies.

Life on sugar plantations was particularly brutal, partly due to the climate and partly due to the intense labour needed to cultivate and produce sugar. If any of you are shocked by the descriptions of life at Soleil plantation in *Tides of Fortune*, I have to tell you that the events portrayed in my book, although all based on actual occurrences, are mild compared to the unspeakable brutalities of the punishments and living conditions the slaves endured in reality. Some of the things I read in my research will stay with me forever – and I am far from sensitive and squeamish.

I felt I had to write about this here, in case readers thought that slavery was a French institution only, as my story is set on a

French island. It is not; such appalling treatment of fellow human beings was common to all the islands, French, Spanish, Dutch and British. The history of sugar is one of brutality and greed, and as it was decisive in shaping the British Empire, I feel it should be part of the history curriculum, at least for older students.

To continue on a somewhat lighter note: anyone who has visited Martinique as a tourist might struggle to identify with my description of the island – but I am writing primarily from the point of view of the eighteenth century, and of Beth, a reluctant visitor. Not only was the climate dangerous, with hurricanes and earthquakes a relatively common occurrence, but the heat and humidity were ideal conditions for mosquitoes to breed in, and malaria and yellow fever wiped out an enormous number of people. The whites were particularly vulnerable, having no acquired immunity to the diseases, and approximately a third of all settlers died within three years of arriving in the islands. Infant mortality was very high, and few families survived for more than a few generations.

Nevertheless, in spite of the heat, many of the whites still insisted on wearing the highly unsuitable European fashions which are the bane of Beth's life. The French regulations on mourning at this time were six weeks in wool wearing badges of mourning, a further six weeks in wool, and then another six in silk. In the book I dispensed with the first six weeks, as I did not wish Beth to spend three months at Pierre's after the death of his wife, but thought it unlikely that she would be capable of throwing knives and diving into the undergrowth to retrieve them dressed in heavy black wool!

Finally, the general amnesty, or Act of Grace, which is mentioned by Caroline in Chapter Six and Simon in Chapter Sixteen. In June 1747 George II granted a 'general and free pardon, in a free and bountiful manner'.

Very generous of him, until you read the list of exclusions to 'His Most Excellent Majesty's' Act. This included, among many others; anyone who had already been convicted of high treason, anyone already transported for any reason, anyone who had been concerned in the rising and who had been 'beyond the seas' at any time between 20th July 1745 and 15th June 1747 – which included Lochiel and all the other Jacobites in France or Italy at the time. Also exempted was a long list of individuals, including Alexander MacDonald of Glencoe, and, of course, the whole of Clan Gregor.

I hope you've found these notes interesting! As for the future life of Prince Charles, I intend, now this book is finished, to write blogs, not only about him, but about other historical characters that feature in my books, and also about other aspects of the period that readers might find interesting. These will appear on my website at irregular intervals (in other words, when I'm not frantically researching for the next series, or writing my next book!)

ABOUT THE AUTHOR

Julia has been a voracious reader since childhood, using books to escape the miseries of a turbulent adolescence. After leaving university with a degree in English Language and Literature, she spent her twenties trying to be a sensible and responsible person, even going so far as to work for the Civil Service for six years.

Then she gave up trying to conform, resigned her well-paid but boring job and resolved to spend the rest of her life living as she wanted to, not as others would like her to. She has since had a variety of jobs, including, telesales, Post Office clerk, primary school teacher, and painter and gilder.

In her spare time and between jobs, she is still a voracious reader, and enjoys keeping fit, exploring the beautiful Welsh countryside around her home, and travelling the world. Life hasn't always been good, but it has rarely been boring.

A few years ago she decided that rather than just escape into other people's books, she would quite like to create some of her own and so combined her passion for history and literature to write the Jacobite Chronicles.

People seem to enjoy reading them as much as she enjoys writing them, so now, apart from a tiny amount of transcribing and editing work, she is a full-time writer. She has recently plunged into the contemporary genre too, but her first love will always be historical fiction.

Follow her on:

Website:
www.juliabrannan.com

Facebook:
www.facebook.com/pages/Julia-Brannan/727743920650760

Twitter:
https://twitter.com/BrannanJulia

Pinterest:
http://www.pinterest.com/juliabrannan

Sign up for my newsletter
(no spam, just book releases and important information)
http://eepurl.com/bSNLHD

Made in the USA
Monee, IL
03 November 2024